A NOVEL

REBECCA BALLARD

Tiny Alice

First Edition: 2019

ISBN 13: 978-1-7956-9737-8
ISBN 10: 1-7956-9737-7

Editor: Sidney Brammer
Cover: Karen Phillips, Phillips Covers
Formatting: Streetlight Graphics

Acknowledgements

My thanks to my editor, Sidney Brammer, who did much to help shape this story, and to save me from my literary shortcomings. I also thank my author friends and tireless supporters, Tam Francis, Wayne Walther, Gretchen Rix, Todd Blomerth, and Philip McBride. Thanks to readers and cheerleaders. Loving gratitude goes to supportive family members, and to my love, my heart.

Chapter One

BERT

MY PHONE RINGS. I'M INSTANTLY on guard. When I answer in a drowsy voice, I learn it's the proverbial middle-of-the-night phone call interrupting a weird dream, and bearing the worst possible news. The dream, I'm familiar with. The news?

"Yeah?"

"Roberta? It's Rick. I need you to wake up and listen."

I don't think Rick Loughlin has ever called me Roberta rather than Bert, so I grow even more uncomfortable. Rick, a local cop and my friend, is a man quick to laugh and equally quick to comfort or croon—whatever is required. My best friend, Kris, and I both love and trust him like no other man in our lives.

"Talk to me," I croak, trying to rouse myself. I turn on the bedside lamp.

"I'd like to drive out there," he says. "Can you make us a pot of coffee? I've got some bad news."

"Geez, why do you want coffee at 3 o'clock in the morning? This must be bad if you want to tell me in person. Wait. Is it Chick? Pirate?"

"No, it's not your folks."

"Tell me now, Rick, and then you can come out and we'll have coffee."

"There was a wreck on Interstate-35. It's Kris. I'm so sorry, Bert. She didn't make it."

This I do not expect. Kris has been my constant companion since she moved here to Bomar thirteen years ago. She is my *sister*, my best friend, an amazing mother to a difficult child, and like a daughter to my parents. *Kris is gone? This is worse than bad news. This is life changing.*

"Come on out," I tell him.

He agrees. I hang up and sit for a while, staring at a granny square on my afghan. My eyes travel without seeing across the pine plank floor and over to the window sash with its vintage lace curtain. I stare out at a star-filled sky, a sky as dark as the sky in my recurring dream.

I've dreamed this same theme a couple of times. I'm in some dark heaven, and Michelangelo's big, macho Sistine chapel god hands me a baby. And I drop it. It just slips away into the darkness. I feel tremendous guilt. Since I work with pregnant women, the dream is concerning. I can't work out yet just what it means.

The curtains blurring in my peripheral vision, I stare because I don't know what else to do. I'm confused. I don't know how to feel. I have no frame of reference. Maybe there are tears somewhere, but they don't come. This is too big. Too bad.

I pull on a sweatpants and a t-shirt, slip on my flip-flops, and flap into the kitchen. My tabby, Velva Jane, pads along behind me. Bad news, he said. *Kris is dead? No. I refuse to believe this.*

Focus on the familiar. I set about making a pot of coffee in my dad's old camp pot, left over from family camp-outs in the woods around our home. I was always the first one up back then, and was expected to make the coffee. I'd remove the blackened grate from the campfire, place kindling twigs on the coals from the night before. Measure the grinds into the metal pot, and add water out of the water cooler. Making sure the clear glass ball on the top was settled firmly in place, I'd replace the grate, and set the pot on it. Then I'd retrieve my dog-eared copy of the latest Victoria Holt novel, slide back into my forest green sleeping bag, and wait for my parents to wake up.

Now, I pour in my favorite heady Italian roast without measuring. I don't need to. I add water and place the pot on the gas flame. Waiting for it to boil, I check the sugar in the bowl, get the milk jug from the fridge, and sit down briefly by the kitchen window. From this side of the house I see a thin moon behind a cloud of moisture. The day will be humid as well as hot. Though it's early September, the punishing heat of summer remains. Against the moon's soft silver light, I see the silhouette of my rose garden.

The coffee boils. I pour myself a cup, add milk and sugar, pick up the cat and stumble outside, across the yard. I take a seat in a rusting metal chair in the garden. I hate waiting for anything, especially this—waiting for my world to implode. I snuggle my face on the cat's ears. She sits still on my lap, like a bronze statue with a steady purr. Velva Jane is unmoved. I envy her detachment.

Years ago, Kris and I planted this rose garden, when her daughter Kelly was just a toddler. We worked it together over the past years, placing Kelly in a play pen to keep her away from dirt and thorns, and then later teaching her how to help. After working, exhausted and slick with sweat, we'd sit here sipping wine and watch incandescent sunsets. Our favorite rose, an Angel Face floribunda, a cross between a Lavender Pinocchio and the Sterling Silver, shows one impeccable glowing lavender bloom in the soft moonlight. I sip the strong coffee and try to relax. I wait, and soon I hear Rick's cruiser pulling up my long driveway in the early morning darkness.

I live a few miles outside of Bomar in an old farmhouse,

which I much prefer to the newer, more cheaply built, houses in town. My place, on the northern outskirts of Austin, is a vintage farm cottage that Kristin helped me refurbish and furnish with cast-offs and antiques. We shopped thrift stores and roadside junk places for months to put it together. It's warm, and was filled with the history and mellow energy of tenants gone before me.

Rick parks his patrol car next to my RAV 4 and walks over. I set Velva Jane down and stand up. He wraps me into a hug and squeezes me tight, rocking us back and forth. He is a burly man with thick curly brown hair on his head and all over his body. We tried to be an item once, but our friendship was so strong that we decided not to try to fix something that wasn't broken. Of course, then he became besotted with Kristin, which had happened to me before. She was much more the besotting kind. I let it go.

"I'm so sorry, Bert. So, so sorry. I pray the Lord can comfort you. No other way I see to deal with this." Rick attends Kristin's church—a community fellowship is what they call themselves—and he shares her faith, which I do not. Early on Kris and I agreed to disagree on spiritual matters.

"Spare me your prayers, Rick." I wipe my face with both hands. My voice wavers. "Were you there? Did you work the accident?"

"No," he says. "Austin PD called me in. She was dead at the scene, Bert. There was nothing any of us could do."

Bert. Nobody calls me Roberta unless I'm in trouble.

Interstate 35 runs north from Austin to Georgetown and to points east and beyond, a conduit to ranch and farm roads leading to towns like Leander, Hutto, Taylor, and Bomar. The highway is a nightmare, a double-decked monster that eats up traffic and spits out broken drivers, passengers, and pedestrians. The roadway is so narrow in places and the shoulders so nonexistent that no one stands a chance once an accident is set in motion.

That doesn't matter now, does it? Nothing to be done. There is never anything that anyone can do in a situation like this. I shake myself and duck into the house to get Rick a cup of coffee. Back outside, he kisses the top of my head and we each take a chair.

"She got caught," he continues, "between a concrete wall and an 18-wheeler."

I start to respond and instead I lean over the arm of my chair and vomit. Rick looks the other way and I fiddle in the pocket of my sweats and find a trashed tissue. I wipe my mouth. I take a large gulp of coffee.

"She didn't have a chance. I am so damn sorry, Bert." Rick's voice sounds muffled, like his head is wrapped in cotton, or mine is. I am stunned. I am horrified. I am angry.

Kristin worked with me as an ob-gyn nurse at the Lorimar Women's Clinic. She was loved by her patients, the members of her church, my parents, and just about anyone who knew her. Smart and pretty, she had warmth and a natural beauty that drew people in. We liked the same movies and movie stars—especially the good-looking actors. We read the same books and shared everything, including all of our secrets.

"Look," Rick says. "I identified the body at the scene, but someone has to tell Kelly. I'm asking you to do that. Can you? Will you?"

My mouth suddenly tastes like dirty chrome. I laugh, or try to, at the suggestion that I break the news to Kris' sullen thirteen-year-old daughter. The only thing Kris and I never shared was the care of Kelly, who knows her own mind and doesn't like me one bit. Tell Kelly her mother is dead? Though she has been as much a part of my life as Kris has, we've never been close.

"Rick, you know that Kelly is less than fond of me. She's difficult. Kris seemed to have infinite patience with her, but frankly, I don't. And she likes you better than me."

"There is no other next of kin," he runs a hand through

his hair. "Just Kris's mother out at Brent Gardens Lodge, and she's just barely there anymore. Please, Bert?"

Kris's mom, Helen, has suffered from Alzheimer's for years and is no longer able to recognize Kris or Kelly when they visit.

I stand up and pace, drinking my coffee. "You're right." I bend over to snap a deadhead off my Mr. Lincoln. "There is no one else." *Damn me! This sucks so bad!* "I guess I have to do it."

Kris and I were floor nurses on the night shift at Mayfield Hospital when we met at the hospital Christmas party. There was instant chemistry between us. We commiserated with each other over work hassles, and we really loved our jobs. We drank a little too much red and green party punch and we were soon dear friends.

Soon after that party, I moved to the Miramar Women's Clinic to work as an OB nurse.

I helped deliver Kelly. She was one of my first babies. Kris arrived in Bomar heavily pregnant, and, as our friendship grew, she confided to me that her child was the product of incest. Kristin's older brother, Soto Ames, had raped her and then disappeared shortly thereafter. She'd left her hometown and come to Bomar, put her mother in Brent Gardens, and set about building a new life. Kelly was never told the truth about her father. She always has lots of questions about her daddy, but Kris has only told Kelly that her dad left before she was born.

I sit back down. "Kelly flies off the handle, sometimes gets out of control. She back-sasses her mom and me, plays on her phone during church, and rarely does as she's told. She seems to have no sense of humor and an inflated sense of entitlement."

Rick looks back at me with a sad expression on his face and shrugs. He's determined that I be the bearer of the worst news. "I think Kristin has done an amazing job of single parenting," I say, "but I've never asked Kelly how she feels about it. I know how she feels about me." I sigh and stand. "I guess I'll go talk to her. Wake her up to tell her. Jesus, the poor kid. Poor me."

I kiss Rick's cheek and thank him for coming. He leaves and I go inside.

I don't remember dressing, washing my face, pouring coffee into a travel cup, or walking out the front door. I have no memory of driving down the driveway or of the ten-minute drive to town. I park at the curb on Bailey Street in front of Kris' little fourplex condo. It's now almost four a.m. I imagine Kelly sound asleep, dreaming the sweaty dreams of adolescence, completely unaware that her mother is not busy on her usual eleven-to-seven shift at the hospital.

I drag myself across the neglected lawn and ring the doorbell. The morning smells like dog poo in wet grass. Kris worked double shifts for over a year to make the down payment for the crummy place, which is nothing more than a cheaply erected three-bedroom apartment, but she has a deed with her name on it—a homeowner and damned proud of it. She was so determined to move Kelly out of their old mobile home. I ring the bell again.

"Come on, Kelly," I mutter. "Wake up. Let's get this over with."

Footsteps sound on the stairs, then stop. A dead bolt turns. A chain slides against its brass groove and hits the metal door. The door cracks open just wide enough for me to see her face hardware—a silver ring in her right eyebrow.

Kelly is tall and skinny—so thin that she looks frail. She resembles her mother in some ways, but her eyes are smaller and her hair is muddy blonde. She went behind Kris's back to get the eyebrow ring and I've seen her a couple of times hanging at the DQ after school when she should have been in study hall or detention. She's a piece of work.

"Mom?" She yawns. "You forget your key?"

"No, it's Bert. Not your mom."

She eyes me through the crack in the door, and then

slams it shut. Her voice is full of sleep as she grumbles about the time and then reopens the door and fixes me with a vicious glare.

"Mom's not home. You know her schedule!"

She starts to close the door, but I cram a foot in to stop it. "Let me in, Kelly."

She reluctantly does so and then starts back up the stairs.

"Kelly, wait!"

She stops on the landing, turns, a hand on her hip. Her face burns with resentment.

"She's on deep nights. Jeez, don't you know that?"

"I know." I feel helpless and tongue-tied. "I...I need to talk to you, okay?"

She rolls her eyes. Gives me a look. I close the door softly and extend my hand.

"Come down here, please? Come sit down."

"What do you want, Bert?"

She squints at me, suspicious now, and takes two steps down the stairs. Of course, she's wary. We rarely have anything to say to one another.

"Is something wrong?"

So, so wrong. Studying her face, I am surprised all over again at how different she is from her mom. Kris was a pretty woman, fair and blonde, but Kelly is so pale she looks ill, and her mouth is pouty, angry. The beginning of acne mottles one cheek.

"Come in here." I turn on a lamp in the small living room. "I need to talk to you."

"What's the matter?" She eyes me with poorly masked fear. Her pale eyes widen. "Wait... Something *is* wrong. Is Mom okay?" Her voice rises and now she sounds like a scared little kid. "Why are you here?"

I take her wrist, so thin I fear it might snap in my hand. I lead her to the couch, seat her, and then, sitting beside her, I tell her the truth without any particular kindness or finesse. I don't know how else to say it.

"Kelly, your mom is dead. She had an accident. She's dead, Kelly. I'm so sorry."

Her eyes grow larger than I think possible, then her mouth yaws open and she gasps. I think she will cry and I'll be forced to hold her and comfort her—something I know I don't do well. Instead of tears, she takes a swing at me. Her fist catches the side of my nose as tears spring to my eyes.

"She's not dead! You liar! She's no such thing!"

I take a couple of more hits to the head and feel the warmth of blood on my upper lip. I grip her hands and wrestle her down on the couch where we both cry for a good long time, our bodies tangled together.

This is the best I can do. Or so I tell myself. It isn't good enough. Kelly sits up and retches with dry-heaves and I wonder if I should take her into the bathroom. Instead, I go into the teeny kitchen and get her a glass of juice. That's what Chick, my mother, does at times like these; she gets juice. We cry some more. I hate every lousy moment, and never in my life, never for as long as I live, do I want to do this again.

Chapter Two

BERT

WHEN FIRST LIGHT REGISTERS, I get up and tackle the drip coffeemaker. With a steaming cup in my hand, I pace and make mental lists. Call Kelly's school. I will miss work today. I will stay with Kelly. Don't know what I'll say to her or do with her, but I'll stay. There is no one else. I nudge Kelly to go up to her room and rest. Her face is tear stained and her eyes dark and startled.

I wander through the tiny condo, fingering framed photos of Kris with Kelly, Kris with me, Kris with her pastor, Tim Axtell and his family. My bond with Kris has often been tested by her faith and commitment to the Bomar Community Fellowship Church and her pastor, Tim, and his perfect wife Patti. Kris attended Tim's Bible classes and participated in the singles activities there. I went with her once and met a guy there. He was a dolt.

I visited the church a few times with Kris and was unimpressed, but most everything about religion fails to impress me. Yet, I was instantly caught by Rev. Tim's good looks and dazzling, used car dealer smile. After we left church that morning, I had trouble keeping him from my thoughts.

In Kris's little office—she's turned the third bedroom into a combination sewing area and office—I rifle through a dented metal desk looking for any official papers that might give some clue as to what lies ahead for Kelly—a will maybe, or a letter, any kind of legal document. In a dusty accordion folder, I find what looks like insurance policies, two of them, and rather than try to decipher them myself, I stow them in my bag for later examination by a qualified legal-type person. I guess I'll have to hire a lawyer. I don't know if Kris ever used one.

I pace through the quiet, chanting a mantra to myself: *This is real. Kris is gone. I will not see her again. This is real. Kris is gone.* It is such a hard truth to grasp, that I wonder how Kelly will do it.

And, speaking of the handsome Reverend Tim Axtell, he calls at nine.

"Oh, Roberta," he says when I answer. "I knew you'd be there with Kelly. I'm so glad she's not alone. Poor thing. She'll need you now, Roberta, more than ever."

"Kelly's upstairs asleep in her mom's bed," I whisper. "I'm walking wounded. And don't call me Roberta."

He clears his throat. "Patti and I would like to bring over some food and maybe sit with you a while."

Perfect. I am numb. I can't think of anything I want less at the moment than a visit from the Axtells, but can't think how to say so. Could Tim be a comfort to Kelly? He was so close to Kris.

"Yeah, sure." I roll my eyes. "Come ahead."

Tim and Patti are not my kind of people, but we've been thrown together because of Kris. Patti's smiling warmth seems genuine and they were important in Kris's life, and Tim has those eyes... Right now, though, having lost Kris and with her orphaned child sleeping upstairs with absolutely no one to comfort or care for her but me, I am not in the mood for people—God's or not.

They arrive in about twenty minutes. When I open the door, Patti gasps and the Reverend says, "Oh my, what's happened to you?"

I stand, holding the door open, and narrow my eyes toward each face.

"It's happened to Kelly, don't you think?"

Patti points a Tupperware at me. "Your face!"

Ah. I've forgotten to clean the blood off. "I'm sorry. Come in, please." As they enter, I tell them, "Kelly clobbered me and I forgot to clean up."

I snatch a paper towel from the kitchen, wet it, and begin to clean my face while they stand watching me.

Patti, who is many months pregnant, is dressed in crisp unwrinkled linen that matches her quiet green eyes. She grasps some kind of casserole and a clear plastic container of something green and white that makes me almost gag (but I control myself). The casserole is dressed up in its own ruffled calico costume. Tim wears a pained and sorrowful expression and an off-the-rack suit.

Patti bustles into the kitchen to divest herself of her burdens. "I'll make us some coffee, if you don't mind? Oh. You already made some. Whatever we can do, Bert." Her voice is quiet, calming. "Just let us know. Okay?"

"Yeah." I stumble back into the living room and take a seat.

"I'm so damned tired." I look up at the Reverend and shake my head. "Kelly's sleeping, like I said, but she's, of course, reeling from the news. She's had a good cry and wrestled with me, so I think she'll sleep a while. Of course, she's angry that I'm here when her mother is not. This would be so much easier on us, if we liked each other even a little."

"Do you know anything of Kris's end-of-life plans?" asks Tim, sounding very officious, like a pastor.

"Nothing." I bite my bottom lip. "I don't know if there's a

will or, if there is one, where it might be. Damn! We never talked about end-of-life crap, last wishes and all." Almost in tears, I follow Kelly's lead and get mad instead. "I don't want to talk about it now, damn it."

"But we must, Roberta." Tim takes hold of my shoulders. Turns me to face him. "There is a will. Kristin talked to me about it a year or so ago. Perhaps there is a copy here? If not, I think her attorney was Carter Welles. We must be sure that Kelly is properly cared for, and I know that was always Kristin's primary concern. You know about Kelly's, uh, uncle? Her father? He cannot be allowed back into Kelly's life."

"No possible way, but I have no idea what Kris would want, for a funeral, for Kelly. I know nothing, which makes me really sad. She was my best friend. I should know these things."

Tim follows me into the office as Patti calls to me. "Shall I heat up some chicken casserole for you, Bert? It's yummy."

It is too goddamn early for chicken anything! Ignoring Patti, I go through the desk drawers again, but still find nothing. Tim flips through the files in a metal filing cabinet. We both sigh a couple of times. I look up to find Tim watching me with soft moist eyes. I look quickly away. Then, at last, I find a letter from the Bomar attorney Tim mentioned, G. Carter Welles—a little weasel of a man whom I personally loathe. The letter confirms that Kris met with Welles. I show it to Tim.

"Carter and I were at high school together," I tell him. "I was homeschooled for my elementary years, and then my parents forced me into public school to be *socialized,* like I was a pet iguana that needed to learn to pee on the newspaper." I'd felt offended, but I never had the heart to tell them I had no plans to socialize with any of my so-called peers at Bertrand Toomey High School.

"Carter was a problem?" Tim sifts through papers on top of a metal filing cabinet.

"I truly disliked him—one of those skinny guys with oily hair, smudged glasses and high-water jeans. He was slick and vicious as a cobra. I hated him. Please tell me why she would have used Carter as her attorney?"

Tim shrugs.

"Okay. There doesn't seem to be anything else here," I remark.

He nods his head and says, "Welles is the man we need to talk to."

Patti appears at the door with food piled on a paper plate and speaks the familiar words—that I must eat something to keep up my strength.

"No, thanks, Patti."

Tim asks as we return to the living room, "Kelly has no more family. Right? Besides her father?"

I shake my head. "Only her grandmother. Helen has been at Brent Gardens since Kris moved here, has advanced Alzheimer's and no longer recognizes anyone. She's the only other relative."

Tim sighs and says that it is left to us—I know he means me—to look out for Kelly. I call my parents and tell them we need to talk and I'll be out there in a while, then I call the offices of G. Carter Welles, speak to his snotty assistant, Wanda Pickens, and she puts me down for ten o'clock.

Patti gives me instructions on reheating the casserole and urges me to get Kelly to eat something—*like I can get Kelly to do any damn thing*—and then we say our goodbyes, hugs all around. They're big on hugging. Everyone hugs, which means you get to smell each person who hugs you. Sometimes you hold your breath. Right this moment I must be pretty ripe, having hopped up in the middle of the night to race over here. Patti wears too much White Diamonds, though I silently wish I smelled like her. Tim, however, smells divine, something citrusy like lime that makes my knees wobble.

Patti turns to me. "This is hardly the time, and you

probably won't even go into work today, but I want to let you know that Operation Ransom will be picketing the clinic this week. It will be a peaceful protest, of course.

"Please, Patti. Don't talk to me about the right-to-lifers and their constant protests at my clinic. Not what I need to hear just now; gives me one more thing to wrestle with at this point."

I pretty much push them out the front door, then drop onto the couch and hang my head between my knees. The room spins with too much bad news. I wonder if eating something will make me feel stronger after all, but then decide I'd only vomit again.

The doorbell rings. It's Tim. He's left his sunglasses. We find them on the marble-top table in the entry. He towers over me in the narrow hallway and I stare at the tiny silver cross tie tack on his navy-blue tie. *What am I thinking?* He places his big hands on my shoulders and looks into my eyes with the intense, earnest look he gives his congregation before he starts his sermon. He says my name softly: "Roberta."

"Roberta," he says again, jerking me back to reality. "Are you going to be all right?

I stammer like an idiot, feeling foolish for reasons I am unable to pin down. "Of course, I am," I snap more harshly than I intend. *I am not a lightweight. I can handle this.* "I think so." I despise myself for the tears sliding down my cheeks, my trembling voice. "Kelly and I...I guess...oh, I don't know."

"You know that Patti and I will do anything for you?" He slips a finger under my chin and lifts my face like movie actors do when a kiss is imminent. I hold my breath. "You know that, don't you?" I breathe a little. His hand presses lightly on my shoulder, stealing my breath again. I'm having a hard time with the breathing thing.

Oh, yes. I see, Tim, my boy. I see just how far you'll go. Never mind Patti, so please let go of me and get out of here before I lose every vestige of decorum and haul off and grab your exquisite ass.

"Roberta, I know how much you meant to Kristin. We talked about you many times."

And then I think how many times Kris and I talked about him, and his cologne strips my remaining composure. Against my will, my arms slip around his waist and my throbbing head nests against that dear silver cross on his tie. I feel the rise and fall of *his* breath, which I imagine has just quickened at my touch. He hugs me and one hand presses my head. Damn, is he kissing my hair? I should slug him! Perfect wife Patti is waiting in the car. I struggle to maintain consciousness. I don't feel like myself. Where the hell is Patti when I need her? *Why didn't she come back for the goddamn sunglasses?*

After nearly thirty years of lime-scented bliss, he pulls away, holds me at arm's length and says, "If you need anything, anything at all, just call. You know we want to be here for you."

"We?"

"Patti and I." And that glorious pulpit smile lights up the room.

"Oh, yeah," I say, like a complete moron. "Patti."

Then he is gone and I stand in the hallway, staring at the front door, breathing. I am breathing. This has been one of the longest, weirdest few hours of my life, and now I am going to complicate it further and make myself even wonkier by visiting my parents, because I must now tell them about Kristin, who was like a second daughter to them.

Kelly is closed in her room where I'm happy for her to remain since I still don't know how to talk to her or what to do. I have just finished a bowl of lime Jello and cream cheese yuck when Carter Welles calls.

"Hello, Roberta. Long time no see."

"Look, Carter, let's make this short. I have no interest

in talking to you, but apparently you were Kristin Ames' attorney?"

"I still am, last time I checked. Why?"

"She died last night." I swallow hard.

"I see," he says with all the emotional content of a marble plinth. "Ms. Ames and I met over a year ago to draw up some personal papers."

"Her will, damn it!" I am losing patience. "You have her will?"

"I do indeed and I think it will be quite a surprise for you, Roberta. But it would be more appropriate if we met in person. Ms. Ames appointed you as executor of her estate."

"I guess that makes sense. So, let's have a very brief meeting to discuss this and let that be that."

"Do you have a copy of Miss Ames' will?" he asks.

"No."

"Then I'll have a courier bring a copy. You're at Ms. Ames' place?"

"Hmm."

"Well, you need to read it. I think you'll find it interesting."

Smarmy voice. I hate him.

"What's interesting?" I shout into the phone.

"She has made you her daughter Kelly's guardian."

That pulls me up short. I am at a loss. I rub my forehead. I tap the phone receiver on my thigh. Did he say what I think he did? Is he shining me on?"

"Why would Kris do that, Carter?" *And why on earth would she hire you to do it?*

"I'll have the document to you right away. And, uh, do you have an attorney?"

"No, I do not have a frigging attorney! I have never needed one."

"Do you intend to accept guardianship of the child, Kelly Ames?"

"No, I do not! Kris must have been tripping on acid when she made this decision. The last thing on earth I want is a child to care for. Kelly and I don't even like each other. Kris simply wouldn't do this to us."

"Well, then," he drones on, "if you intend to have yourself removed as guardian, you will need to file a Declination to Serve and the Court will appoint someone else. And if you wish to accept the appointment, then there will be a proceeding in which Kelly can be placed under your care until the Court appoints a guardian *ad litem*, who will represent the child's interests. There will need to be a home visit and interviews to establish your appropriateness as guardian and of course there are forms to fill out and . . ." *Blah, blah, blah . . . shades of his finesse in Debate Club.* "You are going to most certainly need an attorney and a good one. I can recommend a few of my colleagues who might handle this for you." I can hear him smiling.

"You will not," I snap. "The last lawyer on earth I would hire would be one you recommend. My dad has attorney friends. I'll get one through him. And I want a copy of all of those papers you've got. Every goddamned one. I want to read them with my own eyes."

I hang up. I curse, get another cup of coffee. Cursing usually makes me feel better. I curse some more. Then I sink into the couch and cry. I will miss Kris so much. I miss her already. I feel like a bomb has gone off inside of me.

When I've recovered from my latest tear burst, I get my cell and make a few calls. Funeral home. Connie Barrientos, Kris' next door neighbor, about maybe watching Kelly for a few hours. Chick and Pirate, to say I'll be out a little later. Drained, I fall asleep.

Chapter Three

BERT

I DRIVE OUT OF BOMAR TO my parent's place, *Cielo.* Fifteen acres of rolling Texas pasture studded with live oak, mesquite, juniper, and pecan trees. Their redwood dome, *a la* Buckminster Fuller, is an elegant sort of earthy structure trying to blend in with the rugged landscape. I pull down the long gravel drive, shaded by great oaks, and park beside red crepe myrtle and a redbud. I walk across the bricked patio which is protected from the sun by an awning made from an old silk parachute. Along the steps to the front door sit vivid orange hibiscus in pots.

I grew up here and loved my little loft bedroom, now Chick's studio. I would lie on my stomach in my own space and, through the triangle window, I'd watch our horses run and frolic with each other.

The front yard slopes down to the east, to a large stock tank where we swim. There are small perch in it and whenever someone brings children to visit, Pirate produces from somewhere short bamboo poles for fishing.

Just beyond the parachute edge I see a familiar sight—my father languishing on his worn plastic chaise, sunning himself, naked and snoring, his scrotum lopped to one side like two withered plums. For as long as I can remember, he's baked himself this way. Daily, he tosses aside his worn *kaftan,* slathers himself with baby oil mixed with iodine, fills a quart *Ball* jar with *Corona* and splays himself across his ancient, half-rotted lounger.

He refers to his daily roast in the high Texas sun as *bacon.* "I gotta go bacon the sun," he'll say. Exactly those words with the same inflection, and each time he finds himself just as hilarious as the first time he said it. If I show up while he's braising, he cackles deep in his chest and says, "Hear the fat poppin' in the skillet, Miso? Hear your fry-daddy?"

I'm not in love with the nickname "Miso," hence my change to Roberta, which was the least Aquarian-sounding name I could come up with. Miso is some kind of Japanese soup, but that's what my parents call me; I was christened *Mystic Soul,* which devolved into *Miso.*

My father, Ralph Aaron Landau, legally changed his name to Pirate in homage to the Age of Aquarius (though he's a Leo, and Chick, my mom, is a Scorpio).

I kiss his bronze, sweaty brow. "Hey, Pirate. Is Chick here?"

"Hey, Miso," he yawns. "She's inside. You wanna join me?" He slaps his little round belly. "C'mon and get some sun with me, baby!"

Pirate is enthusiastic about every aspect of life. Somehow, I missed that gene. And, where Pirate is enthusiastic, Chick is adamant, dramatic, and a know-it-all.

"No, thanks, Dad. I, uh, need to talk to both of you."

"She's working upstairs. Just holler." With an oily hand, he picks up a copy of the *New York Times.* He stands, slips the *kaftan* off over his head, and lies back down.

I pause at the front door for one last breath of fresh air before plunging into their patchouli-scented world. The dusky redwood scents have long ago blended with those of marijuana, incense, and Chick's West Coast cooking—sort of Mr. Clean meets Betty Crocker meets Abby Hoffman.

Rarely do I seek my parents' opinions. I prefer that our relationship be more social. I enjoy their company most of the time, but we disagree elementally on many issues, so that I seldom want them to weigh in on anything of importance. Besides, my life is one of those too-full plates I have trouble juggling, which they disapprove of. They believe I should chill more and relax and go with the flow.

Yet, today, I want their input on what's happened. They'll be heartbroken about Kris, but thrilled that I've sought their counsel and happy to hold forth on their many deeply held beliefs, all of which I've heard many times before. So, I brace myself to talk to them, knowing what Chick will say. She'll want to welcome Kelly into the family and not bother about how I may feel about it. I have no idea how my father will respond. I'm flying blind on this one and I need a little grounding.

Slipping off my sandals on the Saltillo tile, I call upstairs. "Chick!"

My mother's name evolved from the flower-power era when she and Pirate lived in San Francisco. One morning, on her eighteenth birthday, she entered a courthouse as—well, I don't know what her birth name was because she refuses to impart that bit of information—and became Pearl of the Sea. Yes, she chose that name. My dad and friends called her Pearl for a while. Then Pirate began to affectionately call her *my lovely chick, my chickadee.* That stuck.

Mom liked the overt femininity of it. She said that in analysis that year, she'd come into her own and, at last, understood that she was a goddess, a diva. So, Chick it would be.

"Miso!" I hear her call from the loft. "Oh, my darling! *Quelle surprise!* Down in just a second, dear!"

I go to the kitchen and pour myself some cold, unfiltered apple juice and drink it all, standing in a steep shaft of crimson light that streams through one of Chick's many stained-glass windows. For years, she created windows and stained-glass panels as a business, and it was her primary passion (next to my father and me) until the cruelty of arthritis twisted her swollen, once-expressive hands. She kept at it as long as she could, but when the pain couldn't be controlled with Oxycodone, she finally surrendered. Now she relies on cannabis.

"You're working?" I call up. "I didn't think you were cutting glass any longer."

"I'm doing something simple and small, dear. Nothing too ambitious."

She begins working her way down the steep, half-sawn log stairs, huffing and puffing. Everything about my mother is large, fleshy, and flowing. With effort, she reaches the bottom step.

"Oomph!" She mops her forehead with one of her vintage, lace hankies, her red curls flying about her wide face. Her twisted right hand holds a watering can.

"Hello, my darling Miso! Just giving a drink to the spider plants in the upstairs windows. Those stairs are going to kill me. I want Pirate to put in one of those little lifts that you sit on, but he says the angle is too steep and my ass is too wide, but that is precisely my point, isn't it? That the angle is too steep?" She kisses my cheek. "I see you found some cool refreshment. Good. I need to water the wandering Jew down here." She sees my busted mouth. "Miso! Whatever happened to you?"

"I'll tell you and Pirate together. Give me the watering can."

I place the watering can at the farmer's sink in their country kitchen.

"I thought it was rather unkind of your father," she goes on, "to make that slur about my rump, and he is so rarely unkind. I know I've gained weight and I'm no longer the svelte young thing he married that idyllic day in Golden

Gate Park, but I'm still that idealistic girl inside, and my hair is as beautiful as ever. Don't you think so, Miso? Ooh, that lip, darling!"

Chick is heavy yet elegant, her coloring vivid and rich, but she grows slower and stiffer each year that passes. She is abundant. In size, in intelligence, in the certainty of her convictions—which she is eager to impose on any unsuspecting soul within range of her Tallulah Bankhead voice. Chick believes in hands-on parenting and, in that vein, has impressed herself, her views, her dogmas and what she calls her *free-thinking* permanently into my psyche (only it's not f*ree*, because there is a cost), and she continues to impress, much to my chagrin.

Watching her, I picture in my mind how beautiful and vital she must have been as a young girl in the time of Flower Power. I've seen pictures of her wearing a crown of daisies and a long granny dress. She now has beauty of a different kind.

"Chick, I need to talk to you and Pirate about something important. Come outside and sit."

Chick's jaw drops and she hurries to the front door to bellow, "Oh, Pirate! Pirate, our Miso wants to talk! Isn't that simply delicious?"

We walk out of the dome onto the broad patio where my father pretends to doze.

I am closer to my father than to Chick. Pirate is a soft talking, gentle and principled man, a sincere and concerned activist in various causes. He continues to make the gold and gem jewelry he designed in the sixties when he and my mom had their shop in Berkeley.

"Miso, babe, what's happenin'? What's up?" he says in a drowsy voice.

I rely on Pirate's calm and thoughtful approach to challenges, the tender and patient way he deals with me and my mother. I know that he and Chick are one of life's great love stories and, however eccentric, are a great gift in my life. I don't think I've grown into the kind of daughter they expected, but they love me as I am. Pirate doesn't try to change me. Chick is another story.

My father doesn't move from his chaise. He has forsworn the *Times* and now rests beneath the sun with his eyes closed. I know he's not asleep, but is probably counting breaths. I know that when he, who much prefers to live nude, stands up, his bare ass will wear the imprint of woven nylon. Of course, he has an awesome tan, but the skin all over his body is the texture of one of Chick's vintage reptile handbags, now stowed away in mothballs. Once retro chic, now she wouldn't be caught dead carrying one, as they offend her animal rights sensitivities.

Chick goes to him and jostles his oily shoulder. "Get up! Get up this instant, my darling. Our Mystic Soul needs us! Oh, I should fix some veggies and hummus. Won't take a minute."

"No." My voice is sharper than I intend. "We don't need food. Sit." Then I add, "Please."

I take a seat at the wobbly wooden table where we've eaten meals for twenty or so years, weather permitting. Chick tugs the edge of the frayed, tie-dyed parachute that serves as a barrier to the autumn sun. She pulls up a ratty wicker chair and sits.

"What can your father and I do for you? And whatever happened to your lip, darling?"

"Are you awake, Pirate? I want you in on this." He opens his eyes and gives me a keen look. I begin.

"I have bad news. Such sad news. I'm sorry." I take a breath. "Kristin is dead." I bite back tears. I hate to cry in front of anyone, especially Chick who cries over anything.

Chick gasps and Pirate sits up, alert.

"Car accident last night." I shake my head. Her death is still unreal to me. "Kristin is gone. Just like that. Gone."

Chick's face shows surprise and then sorrow. She fumbles

in the large pocket of her long dress for a tissue, and cries into it. I go to her, and place my hands on her shoulders.

"Whoa." Pirate shakes his head.

There are tears in my own eyes, but I blink them away. After the initial shock, they both make those comforting, clucking sounds parents do, trying to show you they're with you at some meaningful level and understand the hell you are going through.

"Precious, lovely Kris," my mother wails. "How can this be true?"

"I'm so sorry, chickadee." Pirate rises to comfort Chick. Forget about me.

Kristin was like another daughter to my parents—to me, the sister I never had. Chick loved fussing over her, and Kris and Pirate had many a late-night talk by the swimming hole, passing a joint between them.

Chick asks suddenly, through tears, "Whatever will happen to Kelly?"

"I broke the news to Kelly. I didn't want to, but there was no one else. The accident was early this morning and Kelly was home sleeping when Rick Loughlin called me."

"Oh, that nice policeman friend of yours? Never thought I would like a pig, but I like him."

"Mother, please? I just can't understand why she was on I-35 before dawn. Kelly thought Kris was working a night shift at Brackenridge, but she always takes the back roads to avoid the freeway when she's coming home from Austin." I wonder why Kris braved that death trap to get home, and shouldn't she have been at work? I just don't get it.

"I don't think," Chick shakes her head, "that she should have left a child at home alone. Especially not at night."

"Chick, please listen. Anyway, I had to wake Kelly up and tell her that her mom was gone. *That's* what happened to my lip. She screamed and cried and then clobbered me, busted my lip and gave me a nose bleed."

"Well, darling, under the circumstances..."

"She's never liked me. Now she seems to blame me that her mom is gone. I just brought the news and she wanted to kill the messenger. Instead she landed a couple of hard rights."

"Poor Kelly." Chick flicks back her hair. "Poor Miso."

I give her a look. "I stayed the rest of the night there because, of course, she couldn't be alone. This is all so confusing. Then, as if there wasn't enough stress, Reverend Axtell called early, and they brought over food and we talked about insurance and wills and such."

"Is that the Reverend Axtell that Kris brought to our solstice party?"

"Yes, that's the one. Chick, try to stay on track here."

Chick rises and starts back into the dome. "We need *kombucha*. We need *kombucha* for this kind of talk."

I turn to my father. "Pirate, I can't feel my arms and legs—they're numb. My head is buzzing and my heart..."

He rolls a joint. "Babe, I know your heart is broken." He licks the papers. "Kris was a groovy gal and I know how special she was to you, but your mom is right. What happens to Kelly is the big question. Does she have any other family?"

I feel I should wait until Chick returns for the big bomb. I get up from the table and begin to pace, get my circulation going and my legs awake. "I need to talk about Kelly, too. She's a sullen teen who is already angry at life. She's had a great mom. I don't know why she's so sour. She's never smiled at me and walks away bored from any conversation I try to initiate."

I pick an orange hibiscus from the profusion of flowers along the patio ledge, and tuck it behind my ear.

"I'm sorry." I shake my head. "I shouldn't talk ugly about her."

"Ah, remember not to *should* on yourself, *padowan*," says Pirate.

"Right. Kelly and I don't care much for each other. She

was always around, like an appendage to Kris, so we put up with each other."

Chick returns with a tray that holds three sweating glasses of home brewed *kombucha* tea. I hate the stuff, but Texas etiquette requires that there must be food and drink at every family gathering, especially when someone has died.

"Now, here we go. Miso darling, continue please." She sits in her round wicker chair.

"I knew nothing about her will, but Carter Welles, Kris' attorney, has it. I spoke to the little creep this morning. I can't stand Carter, but apparently Kris hired him for this. This is why I'm here: Kris stipulated in her will that Kelly should live with me and I'm to be appointed her permanent guardian."

Silence. Several moments pass. Then Chick flies to her feet, takes two nervous steps backward for balance, and begins to hyperventilate. Pirate sits up straight on his chaise lounge and takes a long draw on his joint. I cease pacing and collapse into a cracked plastic chair. Chick calms a bit, hurries to me and takes my hand. She starts to croon to me, *Sweetest Little Feller*, a favorite lullaby of mine, and then she cracks up crying, and we hold each other and cry some more.

"Which means what?" Pirate finishes the joint, tosses the roach into the hand-painted spittoon next to his chaise. "What does the will stipulate?" He starts another joint.

"Full custody." Panic in my voice. "Permanent guardian. I mean, Dad, do I have any say in this? How locked in am I to this will she left?" We fall silent again.

Chick chews a carrot stick. The crisp sound splits the quiet. We stare at each other, the only sound the cicada's raucous singing in the pasture and the ice rattling in Chick's glass.

Then– "Fuck!" Pirate levitates from the chaise to pad bare-assed into the dome. I continue to cry. Neither of us speaks until my dad returns wearing a different *kaftan*, one

Chick made from an Indian cotton bedspread. "Fuckin' A!" he cries, and then rolls another joint.

"Pirate," Chick says. "Watch your language!"

"My dearly beloved, I choose the language that properly expresses my feelings."

"But you'll set a poor example for our overly perturbed female issue." She clasps me to her ample bosom. I find it hard to breathe.

"Ahh, this doobie is out." He taps the joint to lose the ash, and picks a leaf off his tongue. "Where's my lighter?"

"Well, what?" I ask. "What do you think? What should I do? Can I get out of this? Do you know a good lawyer?"

I extricate myself from Chick before I suffocate.

She takes a seat and brays, "This is perfect!" Her pretty face dances, she flushes, her eyes fill with tears again. "This is answered prayer. This is karma. Dharma!" She stands again and trembles over to me. "This, Mystic Soul Lando, is exactly what you need in your life right at this very moment! The Universe knows. Gaia knows, in all of her wisdom and sagacity."

"Seriously?" I want to throttle her.

Pirate puts a restraining hand on my arm. "Hear your mother out. She brought you into this world. She gave you life."

"She gave me ulcers." Pirate smiles. I sit down again.

"Don't speak in unkindness, Miso," Chick says. "It is beneath you. You must remember that your words, spoken or written, have power to suggest a false truth where real truth should be. Smiles are true, darling. Tears, mourning, hilarity—these are true. A child's love, Miso, is true, true, true. Your words can support these truths or they can be sharp-edged and dangerous, disguising contempt. I know that you do not hold me, or Kelly for that matter, in contempt, so please temper your words in this situation.

"Now," she goes on. "Ram Dass says that everything in the universe, at any given moment, is exactly as it should be.

Well, I think it was Ram Dass. It could've been Tim Leary, or that cute little Vietnamese monk. What's his name, Pirate? Anyway, everything that happens is meant to happen. Or maybe it was that awful born-again woman on TV with the messy mascara. No, it couldn't have been her. Well, someone said it. What is—*is*! And it's all exactly and perfectly right."

This kind of talk infuriates me. "Mom, please . . ."

But she's on a roll. She sweeps her arm across the burnt vista of the surrounding fields, and waxes poetic.

"The cicada's song in the trees, the pond lapping its sticky clay banks, Hot Tuna playing on the hi-fi—every single thing about this one moment in time is pure perfection."

"Chick, stop it! Stop talking!"

"Don't you see, Miso? The Goddess wants you to be Mother, to know that ultimate completion of your Feminine. This is the gift of the Universe. This, my darling, is your Fate!"

I spring back to my feet. "I am not going to raise this child! And my Feminine is not incomplete. I am a nurse. I help other women birth their babies. *That* is my fate, my work, my passion." I pace again. "I'm not the mothering type. I work all the time, get home late when I take call and I'm thinking of going back to school. I am a person who makes plans and sees them through to the finish, and Kelly Ames is not a part of my plan!"

Chick chuckles. "Apparently she is part of the Goddess' plan. And remember, too, that even Jesus told us never to send the children away, to honor them, attend them and give them a sense of importance, to validate their little egos. He was a great sage, and entrusted their care to us, darling."

I count to twenty-three before I can finally appeal to my far-more-rational father who is taking a huge hit off his Thai stick. He has been smoking dope for so long that he's just as sharp and smart when he's stoned as when he's straight.

"Dad, listen to me. I don't want to be a guardian. I don't know how! I don't want to learn how. I mean—seriously."

"Why, you have wonderful parents," says Chick. "Haven't we taught you everything about love and listening and . . ."

Pirate stands and pulls his *kaftan* off (he never stays dressed for any length of time). He looks at me with those electric blue eyes, his long thin hair wisping in the air. "Let's take a dip," he says and takes my hand to lead me across the lawn and through the little juniper grove to the stock tank.

We walk in silence. On our way, I turn back to glare at Chick over my shoulder. *See! I want to shriek. My father understands the import of all this. See! He realizes the burden this child represents for me, how frightened I am, and how this could totally sabotage my career and my sanity.*

At the edge of the stock tank, I peel off my t-shirt, step out of my cut-offs, and trot onto the small deck Pirate built many summers ago. I'm slick and sweaty from the heat and stress and I know the water is going to feel so fine. I dive in, and the buoyancy and freedom of the water immediately calms me though I am still tense and—if I have to admit it—scared. Pirate swims laps, so I join him. He does this regularly, so I tire before he does and pull myself onto the silvered pine deck to stretch in the sun.

"You know, Miso," he says, treading water to my left. "Your mother is sometimes right. I know you hate it when she is, but she's right about this. This happened for a reason. You may not understand why until you're eighty years old, maybe not even then, but being given a child—and at the same time losing your soul mate—that's some major kind of karma and not something one should easily dismiss. You must give this careful consideration before decisions are made."

"I agree about making the decision carefully, in spite of the guilt Chick puts on me, but I still want out of the guardianship, if possible."

With my chin in my hands, I lie on my stomach on top of my t-shirt so I don't get splinters in my belly. I tell him about the baby-dropping dream, the meaning of which is growing clearer. As I speak, I can see Chick out of the corner of my eye, plodding down the path toward us. I only wanted to share the dream with Dad. *How can I tell it to her?* But I give her a chance to reach us and help her lower herself onto the deck.

"I have a recurring dream, a spooky dream."

"Oh, do tell! I'm excellent at interpretation."

"I'm floating in the sky or out in space somewhere sort of dancing through the dark, and then God, who looks a lot like Heidi's grandfather—that God—hands me this newborn! I'm terrified. I'm afraid I'll drop her. My hands are unsteady, slippery with sweat and placenta and yuck. And then she tumbles, tumbles out of my hands down through the dark. And I am helpless. I watch her disappear. It's a painful dream and leaves me in a crappy mood the whole day."

"Themes of inadequacy. Failure. Fear. Lack of preparedness," says Chick.

"Heavy," adds Pirate.

"How often does the dream occur?" asks Chick.

"Oh, I don't know. It started about a month ago and I guess I've had it four or five times. I had it last night. Creepy, huh? I don't want any of this—the dream, Kris dead, and I don't want Kelly."

"Maybe the dream's talking to you about your situation," says Pirate.

"Darling, let's work on this dream of yours." Chick's a proponent of Carl Jung's method for dream work. "What is the strongest image you remember?"

"Chick, no. I don't want to work the dream now. Maybe another time."

"No time like the Now, darling! So, your strongest image?"

"The baby falling. Losing my hold on the baby."

"Good, good. And your feelings attached to that image?"

"Fear. Despair. Shame. A sense that I've done something wrong. It's horrible."

"Okay. Now, can you see Kelly as the baby and dropping or losing her as something that will bruise your tender heart and diminish your life?"

"Damn it, I knew you'd use this against me. I knew it."

"Not against, but for you, darling. This is a powerful message. You mustn't lose the baby. And more importantly, in the dream you don't *want* to lose the baby. Look at the horror you feel. I pray you think of it in this symbolic context."

"We never know what the Universe will send us, kiddo," says Pirate, leaning his head back against the muddy bank. "But we are allowed to choose whether or not to receive it. Sometimes we simply acquiesce."

"Can a lawyer get me out of this?"

"Oh, not so soon, Miso," Chick holds up a hand to silence me. "Give it some thought first."

"Sure," says Pirate. "Vic Johnson could help you, if that's the way you decide to go. He's in Austin. An old friend."

"Will you call him for me?"

"Sure!" He points his skinny finger at me. "But do think about this dream. It's a heavy message, like your mother says. And you need to be absolutely certain that you want to fight this and be clear about the possible repercussions either way."

He does a deep dive and disappears. Seconds later his long, knobby feet break the water and wiggle at me. I laugh in spite of myself. Chick still sits beside me, but senses that she should keep quiet and not burst into another lecture. Instead she pulls my head onto her pillowy lap and massages my scalp. I count my breaths. This has been her way of soothing me, calming my overreactions, healing my tummy aches since I was a child. Not long after, Pirate joins us on the deck. He wraps a towel around his skinny hips and sits behind Chick to wrap his long arms around her substantial middle.

I hear the mockingbird singing from the nearest live oak,

the low of a cow from the neighboring property, and the distant barking of dogs. The air smells of sun burnt grasses in the pasture. The smell of cedar and Chick's patchouli soothe me. Chick hums "One Toke Over the Line" and we sit in the quiet, the Lando family, facing a tectonic shift in our lives, watching a massive sun of golden orange disappear below the flat horizon.

Chapter Four

CHARLENE

RED'S DOGHOUSE SAT IN HIGH sun in an unshaded corner of the yard, soakin' up the heat, away from the cool shade of our big pecan trees. I straddled the doghouse roof, sweating in the sun, pretendin' I was a cowgirl on a big old fat bull in the chute at the rodeo. I pulled my hat down over my eyes, wrapped pretend leather straps around one arm, raised my fist into the air and shouted, "Open the chute!" and I rode that bull for eight solid seconds before he knocked me face-first into the dust. I was a champion! The first girl to be a champion bull rider! Yee-haw! The crowd was screamin'. I slapped the dirt from my hat, crushed it onto my head and sashayed back through the gates of the arena.

Pretend was one of my favorite ways to play. Sometimes, on that old doghouse, I would be a princess from India, like I seen on television, riding on a giant elephant, swaying back and forth, fanning myself. I'd stroll through the jungle to my ancient hidden temple. Huge carved stones covered in vines as thick as my arms and monkeys screaming from some kinda flower tree. So many smells in the jungle. I made it all up in my head.

This is how I spent my days—in a world inside my mind. I was good at playlike. I could decide who I wanted to be, where, and how. I'd be different people just to see how it felt to be someone else besides me. I could choose the color of the sky, the smell of the grass and other green things, the faces of my imaginary friends. I could write the story in my head and change the beginning or ending if I liked. I'd much rather be out here, by myself, at least when Daddy was working. In the empty afternoons after school, I'd rather be in this world than inside our house.

The scrub of our yard was gold by then, pale from burning in the late summer sun, and the ground was hard and dusty. For folks in other places, I imagined, September was the beginning of fall. Here it was almost the end of summer. There was no clouds in the blue sky and the air was thick and hot and every bit as miserable as July and August. Somewhere else there was cool green all around, but here there was just heat, and ole Red's rickety doghouse in the sun in the far corner of the yard.

I didn't let the heat slow me down. I just played right through it. I perched on top of the doghouse and wisht I could rise up and lift into that sky and breathe the clean air and feel the soft air that held the hawks up high. How I wanted to fly! The wantin' was a hurt in my heart. To lift my arms like a angel, like I did in the church Easter pageant, spread my arms out as far as they could go and lift up and away. . I could try, couldn't I? I almost believed that I could

I stood up and balanced carefully along the peak of the tin roof, the bottoms of my feet so tough from a summer of playing barefoot, the hot tin didn't even burn. Then I began to walk one foot in front of the other, eyes front, looking straight ahead, like Miss Delaney at church taught us to walk like little ladies with books on our heads. I stole a quick glance at the ground and it seemed a long way down. One step. Two. Three. At the edge was the pay-off. At the roof's rim, I would lift my freckled arms and catch the hot afternoon breeze and be swept into the air. If I believed hard enough, I'd be as light as the first morning cloud and soar high above the house. Then, at the very edge of the roof, just before take-off, my front foot slipped, my ankle turned and I fell with a twist onto the jagged tin spine of the roof. The stiff hot metal tore into my thigh.

I didn't cry or scream. I was not a cry-baby. I pressed my dirty hand on the cut and blood welled up through my fingers. Dang, there was so much blood! It ran through my fingers and dribbled down my leg. What if I did nothing? What if I didn't run for help, would I bleed to death? Was it that kind of hurt? And if I screamed for help would Mother run to hold me and carry me into the house, whispering sweet things into my ear? Probably not.

I unbuttoned my shirt, slipped it off and pressed it against the cut and then, bare-chested and brushing dirt from my shorts, I limped toward the house. I stood at the screen door and called out, "Mama, I'm hurt!"

My blood ran down onto the clean white porch that Mr. Bursen, the handy man, had painted a few weeks before. Dark blood hit the white boards and it made me glad, one plop after another. Plop on the white boards. Plop, red on the white boards. But that was all that I could hear.

"Mother!" I called again, right through the screen. "Come out! I'm hurt."

I waited and counted to thirty—one, one thousand, two, one thousand—but there was no answer. I pressed my face against the screen that smelled like musty paper and then I opened the door and limped into the front room. I let the door slam shut behind me. Mama hated that.

"Mama! I'm hurt. Come see!" No answer. "Mother, I'm going to bleed to death." I feared I might just, since wherever I walked I made a pretty big puddle. I called again in my best little girl voice. Nothing.

I knew she could hear me. I stomped into the kitchen and grabbed a cup towel to replace my gory shirt over the wound.

The shirt was pretty much soaked. I jake-walked back into the living room and wondered whether or not to call out again. I knew where she was— where she always was—in my brother's room. My stupid brother who was permanent sick.

I moved slow through the living room, bitin' back tears, hopin' my blood would stain the blue braided rug. I didn't want to cry, but the cut was aching now and I was frightened by the blood, and then I was standing, hands on hips, in the doorway to his room. Mother sat on the side of his twin bed, gently straightening and then bending one bony leg after the other.

I rolled my eyes and said again, "Mama, I cut my leg."

"Charlene, I'm busy right now." She didn't look up. "Can you get some Mercurochrome and put a Band-Aid on it? I imagine it'll be all right." She called us "darlin'" now. She read too many of them movie magazines.

She thought I'd be all right. What was I, unbreakable or something? She thought Brother was the only one who needed her. I held up the cup towel, soaked and dripping with blood. "I think I need more than a Band-Aid." I felt light headed.

She glanced at me, looking irritated. "Oh! My. You *have* hurt yourself. What have you done?"

"I fell on toppa the doghouse. Cut it on some tin."

I hated that I was just on the verge of tears. I mustn't cry. She was the crier, not me. She cried over every little thing. To her, life was one big sadness. I think she liked it like that.

"That could get infected," she said. "Let me . . . well, I will have to come back and finish these leg exercises later."

She took my hand, her mouth in a tight line, not gently but as if my being hurt had upset her schedule, which it had. She led me downstairs. I was still trying not to cry. Seven years old. Too old to cry. Mother picked me up and sat me on the kitchen table and looked at the wound. Shook her head.

"I swear, there is blood all over everthin'. What have you done?"

"I was walking on the doghouse, see. First, I was a bull rider and then I rode a giant elephant, a wild elephant that ran away with me. Then I suddenly knew if I jumped off the roof I could fly. I just knew it. Could I do that? Could I actually fly, if I jumped off a really high place, like the tool shed or the house?"

"Don't be silly," she pressed firmly against my leg. "People cain't fly."

She washed the deep cut with hydrogen peroxide and it sure burned like hell, then she mopped it with Mercurochrome. I blew at the sting of the bright orange stuff, telling myself if it doesn't hurt then it's not doing its job. Stupid medicine. I sang the Ipana commercial song. "Brusha, brusha, brusha." Mother rifled through a drawer, pulling stuff up on the counter, masking tape, laundry clips, rubber bands, jar lids, and finally a pair of scissors and adhesive tape. She began cutting bandages from a clean dish cloth.

"Press this cloth against it firmly. I think, if we can stop the bleeding, we won't have to go into the hospital. I cannot leave Benji alone for that long and we sure don't have the money for a trip to the hospital." She mussed my bangs and tried to smile. She was always so serious. Her eyes showed how tired she was and I wondered if she hurt because I hurt and her heart was moved, or if she hurt because she didn't care and thought she should have.

I knew she had to stay with my brother, Benji, most of the time. We couldn't leave him alone for too long. His lungs could fill. He could get a bad fever. He might have nightmares and cry out or fall out of bed with no one there. All sorta things could happen. I loved my big brother, but he was sure one of the worries of my young life. He took up all of Mama's time and lovin'. I didn't understand it. I didn't understand, but I learned early on to put up with it.

Thank God for my daddy. I don't know what I would have done without my daddy. He was so good. He'd take my hand in his big rough ones and squeeze them tight. "Don't you fret now, my little princess. You're my special girl and you're well loved."

And Mother was damn right. That bandage did help close up the slice in my leg and we didn't have to drive to Burnet to the hospital or spend Mother's grocery money. It wasn't like we were poor, but Mother and Daddy were careful about money. I heard them talk about how Benji's polio had put a strain on the family's finances, not to mention the upset it caused in our household.

He got sick with the polio when he was eight years old and I was only two. Mama and Daddy had been terrified they would lose him. Mother's friend, Cora, told me how they fussed and fretted and prayed, and drove for hours back and forth to Austin for treatments. Daddy worked extra hours for the Sheriff's department to help pay the doctors. It wasn't until I was older that I understood why Mother had to spend all of her time with Benji. She was so wrapped up in him, so far away from me.

I heard stories all the time about the troubles during the Depression. I think my parents had almost got their money back before Benji got sick, but the medicine and treatments and doctor visits set them back again. Sometimes, I resented those long-ago hardships that still had so much to do with our everyday life. I just wanted to play in my play clothes and have Mama wash my hair with Breck and put it in pin curls for the night. I wanted to lie around in my bedroom with my friends and read *Mad* magazine.

I'll never forget that day that I cut my leg trying to fly. Second fiddle to my brother. I remember wearing inflatable petticoats and dancing to Bill Haley and The Comets. I remember "duck and cover," people building bomb shelters in their back yards, the blistering heat of summer and my brother's whining voice. I have fond memories of sitting in my daddy's lap, talking to him, trying to understand so much of what I found baffling. My strongest memory, though, is of the cool absence of my mother.

Chapter Five

BERT

I AM AWASH IN FEELINGS. LOSING Kris has stirred up so much. More than ever before I long for my family, to know about my own. How I wish there was an auntie or a grandma in the wings to help me absorb this loss. Kris and I talked many times about my yearning for a bigger family. She also had no one to cling to but me. I've accepted, though—at least I think I have—that I just need to move on. With the Kelly thing, I mean.

Years ago, before nursing school, I began a bachelor's degree at the University of Texas. I did one year with a major in anthropology and a minor in sociology. Even then I was interested in family systems. I enjoyed the work and learning the different study approaches and the basic theories. But I had friends like Connie Barrientos and Marla McDonough who'd gone into nursing and had very lucrative jobs at Mayfield Hospital. They talked about the fulfillment of knowing they were making a difference, helping and healing.

Listening to them, already into their careers, I wondered how long it would take me to make a living wage in anthropology. I found I wanted to do something for others, too. A degree in anthropology meant more years of academia and I didn't think I had the temperament for the politics. I guess I do have that part of Chick in me—her love for her fellow humans and desire to always be welcoming and listening and counseling, etc.

So, I left UT and went to nursing school, and then on to work in Bomar. Recently, though, I'd thought about adding a little something more to my work. To learn more about people through academic study, maybe do some writing. So, back to school I will go. No time for raising Kelly.

I must tell Teri at work about school and my temporary responsibility for Kelly, both of which will cut into my work hours. I hope she'll be as understanding and supportive as I expect her to be.

My boss and friend, Teri Slade, an only child like me, was raised by parents who were stinking rich. She became a committed specialist in women's health, attending Cornell then graduating from Stanford Medical School, where she met Jack Slade, who was one of her instructors. Several years older than Teri, Jack brought her to Texas when he took a position at the University of Texas Southwestern Medical School in Dallas. Four years into their marriage, Jack died of a coronary embolism. Teri came south to rebalance her life and ended up here in Bomar, where she bought an old chiropractic clinic and turned it into the Lorimar Women's Clinic. She has money from her family and from Jack's life insurance, and lives in a small but well-appointed home on a quiet *cul de sac* on the north edge of town. We've been working together for ten years.

A petite brunette who wears her hair in a tight braid, she runs the clinic like a field marshal and her staff members all like her. I have tremendous respect for her abilities as a physician, and am impressed with the way she handles the damned Operation Ransom demonstrations. She stares out the window at today's protesters as I enter her office. When she sees me, she sets her mug down and gives me a hug.

"I'm so sorry about Kris. We're all in shock. How're you, Bert?"

I shake my head in an attempt to clear it. "I don't really know yet. Still sort of numb." I don't mention Kelly. I don't want to go into it right now. "Teri, I need to talk to you about something else."

"Sure. What's up?"

"I'm going back to school. To UT. My B.S. was in chemistry, but I want to finish the B.A. I started before nursing school. You know that I dropped out to go to switch to nursing. Now I want to work in anthropology. So, if you'll allow, I'd like to cut back my hours."

"You could probably use some time for yourself right now, too. But good for you, Bert! That's exciting, and yes, I think I can get Marla or Jenny to take some of your shifts. But you'll come back to us fulltime when you're done. Right?"

"Of course, I will." *Sure, if I can get this Kelly thing handled.*

She hugs me again. "I'm off to see patients. I may need your help with the Irene Salazar conflict. Irene was a patient we lost to Toxic Shock Syndrome. No fault of ours. Her family is making threats of legal action.

"You've got it, of course. Anything I can do."

I find I'm hurt. A little. I expected Teri to hesitate to bless my return to school because I'm so indispensable at the clinic, but she doesn't bat an eye and moves right on. So much for my inflated sense of importance. Ouch.

I park in one of the UT Austin parking lots, so far away from the Anthropology Department that I must hike in with my pack on my back. I pass through the Fine Arts area, past several fountains. The landscaping is immaculate and the flowers in front of old Calloway Dorm are brilliant. I pass a copse of pecan trees where we used to meet for study and discussion during my first year here. Good memories.

Though it has changed a lot, the campus is lovely, in spite of the heat and the hordes of students strolling, chatting, searching, and laughing.

Originally, I'd planned to major in anthropology or sociology, though now I'm not sure. I'm wondering if school is even a good choice right now. Kelly. My sweet Kris. Thoughts of instant motherhood and mortality discourage me. Maybe school and study will be a good balance to all the weight I'm carrying. Maybe this is just the thing to pull me out of the morass. Yes, I need this.

I'm interested in the Kinship branch of anthropology. I regularly fight with Chick about keeping her family of origin secret. She refuses to tell me anything about her family background. Hell, she won't even tell me her real name before she married my dad. I have begun to dabble in genealogical research through the several online platforms now available. Kinship Anthropology studies family and tribal systems and because of my lifelong curiosity and frustration with Chick's secrecy, I asked at the Anthropology Department for a referral to an academic advisor.

Don't we all want to know where we've come from? Many children grow up with grandparents who adore them and don't enforce the disciplines of parents, who buy them rich, gooey things to eat and cool toys and new pajamas, and, as the child grows, those grandparents act as buffers and sounding boards for secret thoughts, hopes, or wishes, and complaints about Mom and Dad. I've never had this. I've missed it.

I certainly have often found my parents confounding, puzzling and frustrating, and wished there was someone I could turn to and complain to about their obtuseness and intractable beliefs in the idioms and mores of their generation. I am sometimes embarrassed by Pirate's profanity and nudity and often mortified by Chick's airy-fairy spirituality. It's true that Pirate is forthcoming about my Landau grandparents, Joseph and Lada Landau. Joseph had a small jewelry and watch repair business in Brooklyn and they lived above the store. Pirate grew up playing on the cold tile floor of the store and then sitting on a stiff stool at his father's side, learning the craft. By age ten he was myopic and a competent assistant and Grandpa Joseph let him experiment on his own with small pieces of gold. This marked the advent of Pirate's ideas for the beautiful custom gold jewelry that has supported us well. I even have an Aunt Lily and Uncle David, though they both still live on the east coast and exchanging cards at Christmas is the extent of our contact.

I have these stories that tell me something about my father's life and give me some slight awareness of my Jewishness, and all the ethnic *accoutrements* implied therein, but I know absolutely nothing about Chick's family. She has told not one story, nor shared a single memory. No comments or hints about where she grew up, whether she was an orphan or had a horrifying childhood she can't bear to talk about, no fond remembrances of accomplishments or first love or getting kicked out of school. Nothing. And, though I've begged since early childhood for her to reveal something, she always replies, "Not important" or "I don't want to discuss that now" or, most often, just changes the subject or walks away. Ergo, my interest in family studies and relational systems.

The Department of Anthropology people assign Dr. Grady Powell as my advisor and give me the phone number of his office, so I call and make an appointment. I'm familiar with Purvis Hall, so I show up early and wait to be called into this guy's office. I wait for twenty minutes. He's late. I can't abide lateness. I'm pissed off. I ask the girl at the front counter if he's actually in there behind the closed door or if this is just a tease, but she assures me he is there and will be out in a moment. Finally, the scuffed wooden door opens and out walks a tall, lanky, sandy haired fellow reading a newspaper, humming a tune that sounds like the UT fight song. Imagine. He waves me into his office, but doesn't raise his eyes from the paper he's reading. He sits at his desk and points to a chair.

The first thing I notice are his particularly long fingers. Why is that the first thing I notice? I cannot say. I take a seat and wait, run my hand nervously through my short hair, and try to read the spines of the huge collection of books that fill the wall behind him. Some are stacked vertically and some horizontally, the asymmetry of which increases my discomfort. Classes begin this Monday and the mall is bustling outside his dirty office window. Why don't they have the janitors clean the windows in these old buildings? There is a dead philodendron on the window sill.

At last he finishes reading and looks up. Surprise shows clearly on his face, as if he's forgotten I was there.

"Miss Lando? Yes. How do you do?" He stands now and extends his hand, his long arm stretching over the desk to meet mine. "Grady Powell." We shake and then he sits down again and I hand him my intake file. "So, you're interested in an Anthropology major? Right." He checks my papers. "Shall I call you Roberta?"

"Please call me Bert. Everyone does. Ms. Lando would be my mother and I am most definitely not her."

"Bert? Short for Roberta. You don't like Roberta?"

"I like it just fine, but for some reason few actually call me that, so it's Bert."

"You're Ralph Lando's daughter?" I nod. *Oh, God he knows my father.*

"I know your father slightly," he says. "He's called Pirate, isn't he? Cool nickname. We have a few mutual friends, play handball at the same club." He smiles with one side of his mouth, a charming smile that looks cagey, so I wonder if he knows something I don't.

"Okay, then Bert. You know, of course, that I'll be your academic advisor. You are..." He rifles through the papers. "...a freshman then?"

"I did one year here, but I left for a nursing career, so technically I guess I'm a sophomore.

He nods. "Hmm. And why did you change your mind about Anthropology?"

"When I first came to UT, I just felt a need to do more for others. And I enjoyed that year. I have friends that went into nursing, a close friend who was a nurse and I missed working with her. I decided to go back to being a nurse, felt the work would give me more self-satisfaction. I'd be doing more for others. Anthropology seemed like a closed system that doesn't benefit the greater good."

He smiles. "I don't think I agree with you there, but we can talk it over some other time?"

I nod.

"Good," he continues. "Then we'd better get to work setting some goals and mapping out your degree plan. You can begin with my 101 class which meets MWF at 8 a.m." He glances at the clock. "Uh, this could take a while."

"No problem. I've the afternoon free," I say and blush for some reason.

He grins again, a grin that seems almost too large in his narrow face, and, I may be imagining it, but I think he's examining me and likes what he sees. *God, am I that conceited?* Dr. Powell isn't exactly handsome but is definitely what Chick calls a "tall drink of water," with just a touch of the "aw, shucks" charm that native Texans find so endearing. Dressed in jeans and a starched, pressed white shirt, he shows no condescension, and I can tell he's eager to get to work. His enthusiasm is contagious and I find I'm thoroughly engaged.

"Okay, Bert, can you please bring your chair back behind the desk? It's easier to look at the syllabus if we're side by side."

I am happy to. Once seated beside him I can feel his heat and smell the clean scent of him. We go through the catalogue discussing which courses would come next for my degree plan. When we are done and I have safely returned my chair to the front of his desk, we are both obviously uncomfortable and desperately trying to hide it. So, does he feel this energy that I do? How weird would that be? I truly have never felt this before. Not that I have dated a lot. Rick Loughlin and I had that thing and I once dated a musician for about a year. I don't know if one ever "dates" a musician or not, but we hung out and had sex a few times. But this giddiness, this is brand new.

Finally, he says, "So that's set now and I will, uh, see you in class on Monday. I have some good assignments planned to get us off to a solid start, so don't miss class." Again, he rises and shakes my hand. I sort of stumble to the door, mumbling, "See you."

With Kelly in school, I meet with lawyer Welles to discuss some of the details of Kris' will. He had told me earlier that she'd left money to go toward my care of Kelly.

He shows me into his office. I'm impressed. His space is decorated like that of a small Central American dictator—gigantic glossy desk flanked by Texas and U.S. flags, floor to ceiling mahogany book shelves, a huge window with a broad vista of Town Park.

Welles takes a seat behind his desk, dwarfed by his massive leather chair. "Ms. Lando, this should only take a moment."

"Of course. It better. So, what do I need to know?"

"You and Kelly Ames will be comfortable on the bequest of Kris Ames. She has provided the proceeds of one of her life insurance policies for Kelly's care. $70,000 after fees and expenses"

"Okay, that sounds generous," I stutter.

"The money is held at Parson's Bank here in Bomar and will be available for your needs as soon as you sign some papers. I have those papers here."

I sign the damn papers and leave Welles behind. I don't want that money. But I'll probably need it.

Dr. Powell strides into Samson Hall on long legs, takes a moment to settle himself at the podium, clears his throat and flashes a big grin, then proceeds to charm every student in the amphitheater for the next fifty minutes. We all fall in love with Kinship Anthropology. Powell is sharp, funny, and makes his presentation entertaining. At the end of the period, after taking us through the syllabus, he gives us our first assignment: to prepare a personal family tree for the next class meeting. Great, mine will have two twigs.

As the bell rings, a bevy of sorority girls, all years younger than I, hustle to the front to get his attention, fawning, and giggling. I am thoroughly grossed out. I'm what they call a non-traditional student, which means old. Well, I'm sort of non-traditional everything. Then I remember that Dr. Powell and I are closer in age and that soothes my rattled composure. I need to talk to him about the lack of fruit on my family tree, so I hang back until he extricates himself from the darlings and then I follow him back to his office.

I knock on his open door. He mumbles, "Yes, yes," dumps his books and materials on the scarred oak desk and stows his battered leather briefcase beside the lovely old barrister's bookcase I admired at our first meeting. How old is he, I wonder? I am in my middle thirties. I decide he must be in his late forties, but could be a little younger. Damn, he's nice looking.

"Ah, Ms. Lando." The sound of his voice makes me lightheaded.

"Remember, call me, Bert, please. May I come in? Do you have a minute?"

He smiles and I think he might be glad to see me. "Please." He gestures to the chair. "Yes, come on in."

"I need to talk to you a minute about our assignment."

"Family trees." He grins. "Great fun. Have you ever done one or done any rooting into your family's history?"

"I've only just begun the rooting and, see, that's my problem. I know next to nothing of my family. All my life, it's just been me and my parents. I know my dad's parents were from Brooklyn, New York and were Jewish. That's what I know about them, and my dad has shared a few stories about his childhood and his brother and sister. It's my mother's side of the family that I haven't a clue about."

"She just doesn't know?" he asks.

"She knows. She won't tell. I've plagued her for years with questions about her origins, relatives. She insists she sprang from Zeus' head."

"Hmmm, do you suppose there is some mystery, or some big secret? This could get interesting."

"I have genuinely tried to talk to her about this, but I meet with silence every time. She simply will not give me any information. I've wondered if she's protecting me from something, but I don't know. Just how could this get interesting? I mean, how can we find out anything, if she won't tell us?"

"You know her maiden name, don't you?"

I shake my head. "She won't even give me that. I know that she and Pirate changed their names in their hippie years and I know that Pirate's former name was Ralph Aaron Landau but I've no clue about Chick, and Pirate refuses to go against her wishes and wants to respect her privacy.

"There has to be a marriage certificate. Do you know when and where they were married?"

"In San Francisco in the late sixties."

He looks at me. "I'm a few years younger than your parents," he says, "and was a couple of years too young to make the San Francisco scene. I chose a more traditional path and went for academia."

"So," he continues, "There will be a marriage certificate, that is if they filed one. If you'll write down your father's information and the approximate date they were married, I can do a little research and see what I can find."

I'm pleased that he is willing to spend some time on this. I'm sure he's a busy man, so it says good things about him that he'd take the time to help a student personally.

I scribble Pirate's birth name on the index card he gives me. "I was born in April of '68, just two days before the Reverend Martin Luther King Jr. was gunned down, the event which Chick likes to say precipitated her going into labor. LBJ was president and the war in Viet Nam had my parents' generation up in arms. So, count back nine months from then and go from there for their marriage date. I've at least learned that my folks met at a gathering in Golden Gate Park during the Summer of Love and I was born nine months later. Go figure. I think that would mean they met in June of '67 and Pirate told me once that my mom had just arrived in San Francisco then. If he knows from where, he won't say. He was one of the first people she met."

He makes quick notes on the card and says, "Okay. I'll see what I can do."

"Thanks for doing that. I'm sure you must be busy."

"No problem." He grins again. "But you go ahead and put what you know on a family tree, at least what you know about your father's line, and—would you mind if we discuss this with the class?"

I'm captivated by the way he looks me directly in the eye as he speaks. I like that in a man. I didn't know that before today, but I decide now that I like that in a man.

"I'm sure there are others," he continues, "who know little or nothing about their own families and your situation might open a discussion. Also, I'm working on a project that might interest you, taking oral histories from older Texans who live in small rural towns around the state. It's really fascinating to hear what they have to say. They've seen so much, lived through so much history. I'm planning to choose a team of students to work with me on this and you would certainly benefit from the experience."

"It sounds intriguing. Count me in."

It's difficult, but I stand, heft my books and hold them to my chest, suddenly feeling about six years old, and not wanting to leave. I say rather doltishly, "Well, uh, thanks for all of this. I guess I'll see you in class."

"That you will, and I look forward to it."

Chapter Six

BERT

I'VE HEATED UP SOME HOT chocolate and sliced some zucchini bread that Connie Barrientos made for us. I want Kelly to be comfortable, if possible. I want me to be comfortable.

She sits silently on the couch, arms crossed, bottom lip trembling, staring at the steam rising from the hot drink.

"Kelly, would you like to talk about your mom?" She stares. "I would. I'm not sure what I'm going to do without her. She was so important to me."

She shoots me a look of what must be contempt. What right have I to talk about my loss? And she's right. That was a dumb way to try to draw her out.

"I'm sorry. That was thoughtless of me. I know your loss is even greater than mine." The look of hatred again. She's barely tolerating my babbling.

"I want to help. I do. I thought maybe, if we could share some memories, tell some stories, it might help us both."

She kicks the coffee table. "Ew, zucchini bread is gross." She speaks!

"Well, yes, I kind of agree, but then Connie made it special so I think we ought to choke some down, don't you?" A tiny upturn at one corner of her fractious mouth.

Then, more silence. I rise and let out a sigh. "I'm going to go sit in the garden and cling to some memories. You do whatever you need to do."

I sit contemplating my roses for less than five minutes before I hear the screen door hinges squeal. She takes a seat across from me, roses at her back. She holds her hot chocolate. Takes a sip.

I smile. I want to reach out to her, touch her, but I'm pretty sure that isn't the right thing to do. "I'm glad you joined me. I remember..."

"Don't," she warns. Then the tears come. And we both cry.

We wind our way down FM 2292, en route to *Cielo* for a cook-out, so Kelly can meet Chick and Pirate. I think, after our good cry, in which she wouldn't let me touch her, a visit to my parents might lift her spirits. She doesn't want to go, of course, but I talk her into it—against her better judgment. Kris came out to *Cielo* with me a few times, but Kelly was never with us.

"So," Kelly pipes up, "why do you hate your parents so much?"

"I don't hate them," I say, swerving to miss an armadillo. I call out the window, "Live another day little one!" and turn in at the white rabbit mailbox. "I just haven't fully forgiven them yet."

"For what?"

"For...a lot. I don't hate my parents. I don't. True, for about ten years I interpreted my ambiguous feelings toward them as hatred, at least toward my mother. From age fourteen to twenty-four I held my mom, Chick, personally responsible for every psychic glitch in my makeup. I did the whole therapy thing (my mother is big on therapy), placed an imaginary Chick in a chair and beat hell out of her with padded clubs and whined tearfully to a fat stuffed bear in a tutu, then traded places with the bear to express what I thought Chick's feelings towards me might be, which turned out to resemble, to my horror, my own feelings about her. That was enlightening."

"God! You did all that? How stupid."

"I did it all and, in the end, had to face the fact that my childhood under their tutelage, however vulnerable or impressionable I might have been, was after all not so beastly."

"Your childhood sounds like it sucked. I don't feel that way."

"I think you had a competent mother, Kelly. That makes a world of difference. So, you want an example? Every year for Halloween when all the other Bomar girls were dressing as Barbie or Strawberry Shortcake, I would be dressed as a CPA or a hairdresser, characters Chick considered ghoulish enough to scare the other kids. That sort of thing."

"I don't get it."

"Neither did I. I have an early memory of sitting on a crowded floor, lights swirling all around. I realize now it was probably the Fillmore, a concert hall in San Francisco where we lived. I'm five or six I think, breathing marijuana haze, watching the bodies move rhythmically around me, the bright moving colors projected on the walls, black lights causing smiles to glow, the glitter from the mirrored ball in the ceiling, the day-glo paint on the giant black amps, as The Grateful Dead blared and pulsed at too many decibels, and wondering where my parents had gone. Finally, a roadie—

"What's a roadie?"

"—guys who carry equipment—a roadie picked me up and carried me on stage, held me up by my ankles like a fish he'd caught on a Mazatlan vacation, and yelled into the microphone, 'Hey, man, did somebody lose this?'"

"Pirate then appeared from the mob, as Chick danced

undisturbed, and I was handed down a highway of smelly hands into his arms. He carried me back to the corner where the roadie found me, plopped me down, ordered me not to move a muscle and then disappeared again into the writhing throng. That was then, and... . My goal now is to learn to relate to them as fellow adults in an adult world, a goal I've been pursuing with true tentativeness for over a decade."

I park next to my parents' old Volkswagen bus and smile at Chick's bumper stickers— "Make Love, Not War," "Eschew Obfuscation," and "Beam Me Up, Scotty." We find Pirate beneath the parachute, wearing only a pair of boxers with red lip imprints all over, sweating like a stockbroker on the trading floor, poking at the coals in his hibachi with an implement of his own devising—a long cooking fork attached with duct tape to the end of what used to be a broom (so he doesn't have to leave his comfy chaise) to turn the meat. A tray heaped with chopped fresh veggies sits on the table beside him.

"Hey, Miso! What's shakin'?" Then to Kelly, "Welcome! *Nuestra casa es su casa!* Groovy!"

Enormous hug. I peck his grizzled cheek. He turns to Kelly and grabs her stick arms in his broad brown hands.

"And here's the Golden Child! Kelly, I'm Bert's daddy-o. It's so groovy to meet you."

"Cool," says Kelly, as if she's not sure how cool it is. He wraps her in a hug. "So sorry about your troubles, babe." He tweaks her nose and she makes a face and rolls her eyes.

Chick's contralto precedes her from the dome's back door. "Here you are, my darlings! My girls!"

Chick has never needed instruction in projection or elocution. She speaks in the tone and manner of a female Sir John Gielgud. Today she wears purple palazzo pants and a taxi yellow silk top, with her mass of hair tucked into a disintegrating straw garden hat. She carries a Howdy Doody pitcher in one hand and straightened coat hangers for veggie-kabobs in the other.

"Allow me to divest myself of my burdens," she croons, incapable of a simple statement like, "Let me put this down." She deposits the tray and coat hangers on the table, then in one swift embrace, buries me in the canyon of her great bosom.

"Oh, my darling Miso, how I love you," she intones. It occurs to me that skinny little Kelly might not survive such a greeting, but I cannot act quickly enough. Chick envelopes the kid. I see Kelly snatch a quick breath just before her wan face disappears into Chick's bosom.

I murmur, "Chick, Kelly. Kelly, Chick, my mother."

"Welcome to *Cielo*, little one." Chick says. "*Cielo* is Spanish for heaven, which is certainly this oasis in which we live, though it's hot as Hades today. Do you care for lemonade? Miso, are you parched?'

Chick begins pouring drinks and I pull up a chair. Kelly squats on the bricks at Pirate's feet. "Miso?" Her face wrinkles up in a question.

I explain quickly about my name and as I do the sudden burst of energy that greeted us quietly recedes into the thick heat, as we sip lemonade and stare at tiny red ants marching through the sand between the patio bricks.

"So, did you talk to Vic Johnson?" I ask my dad, and Chick, like a fat flustered hen, begins making faces, waving her hands and shaking her head as if in warning, worried I suppose for Kelly's sensitivities (if she has any).

"It's okay, Mom. Kelly knows I want out of this. She wants out of it to. Huh, Kelly?"

She shrugs, chooses a piece of bell pepper from Pirate's tray and pops it in her mouth.

"Yeah, I talked to him," says Pirate. "He'll take the case and charge you on a sliding scale, since you're my kid. But, Miso, he gave the same warnings as we gave you, and that is for you to be 100% sure this is the action you want to take."

"Okay. So, what has to happen?"

I see that Kelly, chewing her sweet pepper, has fixed me with her resentful stare.

"Oh, you know," Dad goes on. "He'll argue all the reasons you're not a suitable choice for guardian, that your relationship with Kelly is strained, and he'll make recommendations about who might be appointed in your place, though I don't know who that would be."

"How about my dad?" Kelly says flatly.

"What?" I glare at her. I hear Chick's quick intake of breath.

"My dad. Duh! Why can't we try to find my dad? I could live with him."

"Kelly." I take a carrot and gesticulate with it. "Your dad hasn't been around since before you were born. What makes you think we could find him now? Besides, he's not a nice man. I'd never let you go with him and I don't think the courts would either. Right, Pirate?"

"How do you know he's not nice?" Her eyes flash with anger. "Have you ever met him?"

"No, but he deserted you years ago. Your mother never wanted anything to do with him. So just drop it." I toss the baby carrot into my mouth.

"I won't go to that county home! I can sure as shit tell you that!"

Chick and Pirate, charmed by precocious profanity, share a good laugh.

"Now, don't worry, child," says Chick. "We'll see you are well taken care of."

"We think you'd do just fine with our daughter," says Pirate.

"Who asked you?" I say, and grab a cherry tomato.

Pirate smiles, rattles the ice in his glass. "Chick, *leibchen*, can you hit my rum with a splash of lemonade?"

"Can I have rum in mine?" Kelly chimes in, and Chick and Pirate laugh again.

"Look . . .," I feel the need to explain myself (yet again). "I make a comfortable living for myself, but can't afford . . ."

"You don't have to!" Kelly cries. "Mom left money for that. For me."

I concede this is true and point out that, also, I would be unable to attend school functions, teacher conferences and such. I'm confused that Kelly now sounds as though she wants to stay with me and I wonder at her change of heart.

"Sheesh, lots of parents miss those things. Big frickin' deal."

I argue that there are no kids where I live. "I'm on the outskirts of town and the closest neighbor is a mile away. It's too isolated. You'd hate it."

"I don't care," she returns. "I like to be alone. I don't have any damn friends anyway."

"You'll sure as hell be alone plenty, if you live with me." (No one laughs at *my* profanity.) "The truth is I'm just not mother material, Kelly. I take care of mothers, but I don't know the first thing about being one."

"You don't have to be my mother," she says, helping herself to more lemonade. "Just like a roommate. You know, like we're equals or something. Just like being my mom's best friend."

There is quiet between us and I think I see tears in her sharp blue eyes.

"But it's different now. I'm a grown woman and you're a little girl. We are not remotely equal and . . ."

"I am not going to the fucking county home! I'm a teenager, not a little girl." She crunches a carrot stick.

"My," says Chick, returning with Pirate's rum, "the girl has a respectable scatological vocabulary!"

"Okay, that's enough, young lady." I am sounding very much like Miss Irma Patterson, my freshman English teacher who never shaved her legs and wore nylons that smashed the dark hairs down against her white skin. The thought worries me because I detested Miss Patterson. "That kind of language is unacceptable, so just cut it out right now."

"See, Miso?" says Pirate. "You sound just like a mother now, don't you? You've mastered the vernacular already."

"Hey, I like this parachute cover thingy. It's awesome," Kelly says. "Totally awesome." Then she asks to see inside the dome. Chick grabs her hand and leads her inside for the tour, leaving me with Pirate.

"Dad, help me out here. You know I don't want to do this."

Pirate faces me, elongated fork in hand, like a spear chucker in a Shakespeare production. He gives me one of his soul-searching looks where his pupils narrow and he tries to see beyond my ego into my Third Eye. I've been getting this look all my life and what pisses me off is that he often sees some fledgling truth blazing in the middle of my forehead.

"The universe is perfect," he says in that gentle and mellow voice I love. I've heard this all my life too, and I hate it when he quotes my mother! "This moment is perfect, Miso. All is as it should be. Why must you struggle?"

"People plan to have children, Dad. They fall in love, marry and commit to one another and then they have babies because they want to. I haven't done any of those things."

"Not everyone plans. You were not planned, Daughter, but we were ecstatic to have you join us on our road of life, and even when plans are made, they can change."

"Didn't you hear me say I don't even like this kid?"

And I begin to cry, much to my dismay. Pirate pats my back and whispers, "It's not true that you don't like Kelly. I can tell by the way you've cared for her so far that you like her just fine, or you're trying to find a way to. You have your mother's vast heart, Miso. It is good to feel deeply and to have convictions, even when you deny your feelings."

This makes me even madder and I am tired of the bullshit, so I stop crying and say much louder than I intend to, "You know what? I'd like some goddamn rum in *my* lemonade!"

I storm inside where the dome is looking its homiest, with the afternoon sun shooting through the stained-glass porthole in the west wall, colored fingers of light splayed like the hands of celestial creatures across the floor—a wordless, late afternoon blessing. The warmth of hand-hewn furniture, crocheted afghans, macramé plant hangers, the decoupage tabletop—the coziness of it all enrages me even more. I slam the refrigerator door as Chick blusters down from the loft with Kelly. She catches her toe on the bottom step and shoots forward.

"Mother, for Christ's sake . . ."

She is able to right herself before she hits the floor. "Those damn stairs'll be the death of me, darlings."

"This is the coolest place," Kelly gushes, her eyes unusually bright and clear. "I love it here. I want to live here. How about it? I can live with Chick and Pirate."

For a brief second, I note the look of terror in Chick's expression before she, accomplished actress that she is, breaks into a broad smile and shakes her copper curls. "Oh, that could never be, love, as much as we'd adore having you. Why, there's barely room for Pirate and me and we're far too ancient and addled to look after you properly. Oh, my, far too old."

"Stop it, Chick. You're not old at all. Fifty is the new thirty, right?"

I follow them back onto the patio, Kelly beside me, and I lean to whisper into her ear, "They were never able to properly care for me either." Chick hears and gives me a look, not unlike Kelly's now familiar glare.

"Dinner is served," announces Pirate, cup towel folded over his arm. In his right hand, a tray overflows with chicken and tempeh and grilled sweet peppers, carrots, zucchini, potato wedges and small, perfectly round ivory onions.

"Ooh, Pirate, love, it looks fabulous," brays Chick, "and smells heavenly! A true gastronomic display."

To my surprise, we are comfortable for the next twenty minutes, passing trays and heaping food on our plates. Chick refills everyone's drink, though mine is near full already with my daddy's dark rum. We sit in what passes for silence, amid the distant roar of trucks on the farm-to-market road, the chorale of insects soughing through hackberry, mesquite, and chinaberry trees. Pirate eats noisily and with great relish, and his slurps and smacks add to the homey sounds that lull us.

Rarely do I feel peaceful in the presence of my mother, but I try to relax (the rum helps) and enjoy the sense of camaraderie that descends on us. There is a sense of family here, however unorthodox. The sun sits low on the empty horizon, a hot glowing eye in the dust of twilight. Maybe it's the rum trickling into my bloodstream that sends a fond smile toward my father, a grimace in Chick's direction. I bestow what I hope is a gentle grin on Kelly, who breaks our self-imposed quiet.

"I want to live here," she says, her wiry body suddenly tense. "I want to stay with Chick and Pirate and live at *Cielo*."

Three Landos stare at her for several seconds and then, and for entirely different reasons, say in unison, "I don't think so." Everyone, except Kelly, laughs.

Chick graciously changes the subject. "Oh, Miso, I wanted to let you know that the Operation Ransom protests are heating up. I don't dare miss a day in the trenches now. I seem to have a gift for disarming the crowd, soothing their self-righteous ire. Sometimes I even persuade them to go home."

Operation Ransom, a local right-to-life group, was founded and led by Reverend Tim and his perfect wife Patti. Since the Lorimar Women's Clinic performs medically necessary D&Cs (dilation and curettage), we are their favorite place to picket. Lately they're particularly worked up about a case we handled some time ago.

"Whatever are they up in arms about now, darling?"

"Salazar. Still."

Poor Irene, raped by a family member, had wanted the

abortion desperately and gone through all sorts of cloak-and-dagger measures to keep her family from finding out. Now the ones who abused her, the ones she feared most, are turning her death into a cause for their own agenda and greed.

"It's the toxic shock case, Chick. A patient named Irene Salazar came to us pregnant. A victim of familial rape. We helped her, against the responsible family's wishes. Afterward she developed an infection but never returned to us for treatment. She died from toxic shock. The family, of course, blames us."

"Absurd," says Pirate and takes a draft of his rum.

"Tragic," I agree, "but we had nothing to do with her death. If she had come in, we could have treated her. Her family says she was coerced into an "abortion" by the counseling team at Planned Parenthood, and would never have agreed to it otherwise. They're suing Teri and me."

"Well, I'll work up some verbal weaponry for our skirmish today. I'd think you've had enough on your mind with Kris, Kelly and school without dealing with a possible malpractice suit."

Kelly wipes her nose on her arm. "Bert the Baby Killer."

Partially digested rum backs up my throat like saline in an IV tube. "This is me ignoring you."

I swallow, stand and walk around for a few minutes, then realize that much of this has happened before. G. Carter Welles represents Operation Ransom and he has never put together a decent case in his life. All he does well is injunctions. I choose not to worry about it.

"I'm not afraid of G. Carter Welles," I assert. "He's the worst lawyer in Lorimar County. And they have no case. We did nothing wrong."

"Just a lot of ugly publicity," says Pirate.

"Whew!" I drop into my chair. "This has been one helluva week!"

We are quiet and by the time dark is fully upon us, Kelly

climbs into Pirate's lap. Chick reaches for my hand and I let her take it. We listen to night song and Pirate tries not to fall asleep. For a while, we sit in this peaceful tableau out here in our little corner of scrub. No one talks. We just sit in comfort together.

Though considerably mellowed by the rum, I decide it is time for Kelly and me to leave. I direct her to help me clear the table and we carry the soiled plates, trays and silver into the dome's tiny kitchen. Chick refuses to own a dishwasher, though I've offered several times to buy one. She says washing dishes by hand is a meditation. Kelly and I make quick work of the washing-dishes-meditation, say our goodnights, and start the drive home.

At a brief after-class conference with Dr. Powell, I see a few other students lined up in the hall waiting for their turn, so I know I won't have long. He's checking in with those of us who will work the field for his reminiscence project.

"Bert, come in and have a seat."

He's again dressed in jeans and a starched white dress shirt. *How many of those does he own?* He straightens a stack of file folders and places them on the corner of his desk.

"Bert, I just want to confirm that I've assigned you to interview Alice Slezak in Fallon Springs. That's my hometown, you know. Mrs. Slezak is known as "Tiny Alice" and I'm sure she'll give you permission to call her that. She's a sharp woman, in her early nineties, but very with it. She's lived on a farm all her life."

"Sounds interesting. I'm sure her life has been different from my parents' or my own."

He smiles. "Indeed." I like the dimple in his left cheek. "I knew her growing up. She was actually quite a significant friend of mine for a while. She's a natural storyteller. That's why I assigned you to her. You'll like her."

He gives me a clip board and a small tape recorder, as well as a list of questions. I feel armed for battle.

"Don't worry," he assures me. "You'll do fine. She's very warm and open, and wise. She'll probably take charge of the interview and you won't even have to refer to the prepared questions."

"Okay," I say. "I've never done anything like this before, but it sounds like it might be a cool thing to do."

He takes a sip from a coffee mug that has left a ring on his desk, and clears his throat. "I've got other students waiting." He glances at the door. But I'd like to talk to you quickly on a personal note. I, um, I'm not in the habit of . . . really, I've never done anything like this before...do you think . . . that we could . . ."

Come on, big guy. Spit it out. Then, I decide to ease his pain. Is he going to ask me out? Really? So soon? I mean, I love the idea.

"Are you asking me . . .?"

"Coffee," he stammers. "For coffee." He runs a shaky hand through his thick hair. "I'd like to meet somewhere for coffee. Am I ahead of myself? Am I out of line here? I know we've only just met. And I'm your professor. You're my student. But I'd like to get to know you better. I think."

He's asking me out. I can't believe it. I like it. I've hoped that he might. I decide to summon all the poise and *chutzpah* I've inherited from Chick and ease his pain. "Dr. Powell, you're asking me out? For coffee?"

"Yes." He sighs. "I am. Am I being presumptuous?"

"I'm a big fan of coffee. I'd like to have coffee with you. You know, we can maybe go over my first interview with Mrs. Whatzit."

"Tiny Alice Slezak. You'll like her, I promise. Really, Bert, I don't usually do this—I mean ask a student to coffee. It's really totally inappropriate, I know."

His discomfort is making me uncomfortable. Now it's my

turn to clear my throat. “Look, uh, can I call you by your first name?”

“What?”

“Your name. I don’t particularly want to have coffee with ‘Dr. Powell’.”

“Oh, yes, of course. Grady. My name is Grady.”

“Grady, I do think this is a bit weird; however, I would like to have coffee with you, but on my turf. There’s a diner in Bomar where I live. Do you know Bomar out north? There’s a place there, the Buttered Biscuit. They make terrific coffee. Shall we meet there? And when?”

“Tomorrow?” He smiles that amazing lopsided smile. “Is that too soon?”

“Done.” I really must go now. “What time?” He says 8:30. Then I say, a stupid grin on my face. “Now tend to your other students, Grady.”

A wrinkle between his brows. “What? Oh yes. I’ll do that. Yes.”

I make my exit, trying not to look like the one sitting in the catbird seat.

Chapter Seven

BERT AND ALICE

I DRIVE WEST ON HIGHWAY 71 and turn north on FM 652; a sign indicates Fallon Springs is twenty miles away. Today is my first appointment for Dr. Powell's Elder Reminiscence Project. I drive out to his hometown of Fallon Springs to meet my first subject. I don't know what to expect, exactly, but I've got my folder of suggested questions and my cassette recorder. The day is sultry, the sky heavy with autumn moisture, the air warm and yet crisp. A dark cloud builds on the horizon and a flash of lightning heralds a coming storm.

A narrow creek runs beside the road, lined with cottonwoods. I drive through cedar and mesquite, giant old live oaks with branches gnarled and bent like I imagine this woman will be. She's an old farm wife and I'm sure is work worn. The land is rocky in places, little more than gravel, *caliche*, and oak scrub, but, in the distance, I see tall grasses sway in every shade of gold, ochre, and some faint greens. A small dust devil spins and the road seems to dance in the spiral of it.

I'm nervous and a little excited. I feel good that I'm helping with Dr. Powell's—I mean Grady's—proposed journal article.

I want to nail this assignment, not only because I'm a hound for good grades, but because I'm growing to like this man. *Enough. Pay attention to the road.*

The farm-to-market road becomes Main Street in Fallon Springs, and feeds me right into the heart of town. The square has seen better days: graffiti-tagged plywood in windows, dogs asleep on the courthouse sidewalk, no one stirring. It's kind of spooky, a sort of *Twilight Zone* in the hill country. There's still a functional Farmers Bank, a Rexall Drug store, and the empty hull of a boot and tack store. A ragged, faded awning waves the name of Goodman's Department Store. On the southeast corner of the square sits one busy enterprise—Cawthorne's Bakery. There is a Chamber of Commerce in a small space on Main Street and the Lometa Café on another corner.

I pass through the town proper and then I'm back into the country where the land begins to undulate and grow more fertile. I hope I'm not lost, but I find Pitcher Road, per the directions I've been given, and pass a small subdivision called Pastoral Meadows. Chick calls these "ticky-tackies"—homes that appear to have sprung like magic mushrooms from the manure in the fields. There's not a tree in sight until I drive past a couple of small farms and come to a mailbox that reads, "Slezak."

A white clapboard house, not unlike my own, is lovingly maintained. There is a broad front porch shaded by old oaks and pecans. Fall flowers thrive around the old porch and potted evergreens sit on either side of the wide steps. An old yellow lab greets me with wagging tail and copious slobbers as I park in the gravel driveway that arcs across the front of the house. I give him a scratch, and then wipe my smelly hand on my jeans. I climb the steps and ring the bell at the gingerbread screen door. I take a couple of deep breaths as the door opens.

She is tiny, not even as tall as I, with broad cheekbones and a sharp chin, wide brows above deep green eyes. And wrinkles. Lots of wrinkles in her tanned skin. She's dressed in a simple blue jumper, a pink blouse and sensible brown shoes.

"Come in. Come in, dear."

Her voice is raspy and tough, like I imagine her life has been. Her gray hair is wavy and styled in a fifties bob, teased a little at the top and sprayed. Arthritis has curled her hands, yet there is elegance there in the strong wrists, broad fingers and shiny nails. A rugged looking ring encircles her ring finger and she wears an old man's wristwatch.

"Come in this house!" she says, and takes my two hands in her own. "Come in, come in and have a sit-down. Don't you look official there with your book bag and notebook?"

I take a seat on the weary couch she indicates and take out my recorder. She eyes the recorder and then asks if I want coffee. I tell her yes, with cream and sugar, please.

"Yep. That's how I take mine. Can't stand the taste of black coffee."

While she's in the kitchen I shake out my hands, turn the recorder on and off, trying to release some of my nervousness. I hope it won't be hard to draw out her stories. I wonder what tales she might have to tell.

I look around the small living room. Antimacassars drape the chair and sofa and an antique wooden sewing machine, now a table, occupies one wall. Alone in the center of another wall is a large framed photo of a tall, good looking man in farm attire and two curly haired children. Above the picture is a crucifix.

Alice returns with the sodas, seats herself beside me and hands me the cold drink. She straightens her jumper and says, "Okay, now, how do we get this thing started?"

"We just begin, I guess. I'm as new to this as you are."

I turn on the recorder and speak into it. "Elder Project, Dr. Grady J. Powell, Dept. of Anthropology, 'Voices of Rural Texan Elders of the Twentieth Century'. Roberta

Lando interviewing Mrs. Alice Slezak. It is the afternoon of September 25th."

I start with a question and she immediately interrupts me. Grady has told her that I go by Bert, and she wants to know about that, and then I ask about her nickname.

"I've been 'Tiny Alice' round these parts most of m'life. My papa started callin' me that when I was knee high to a grasshopper, then my Granny and friends. Lute loved to call me that too. Lute is my late husband." She indicates the framed photo. "He called me 'Tiny Alice' right away when we first met and just always called me that. That's Lute there in that picture, with our children, Charlene and Benjamin. We had a few more, but they died."

Her tone is so matter of fact, I am speechless for a moment.

"I noticed that picture," I say, "and thought it might be your family. 'Tiny Alice' certainly suits you."

"Hell, you're no bigger'n a minute yourself, young lady. So, what do you want to know? Lord knows why anyone'd want to know about me, but here we are." I set aside my list of questions. "Is there a particular story you'd like to tell me?"

She grins. "I got a million of 'em. Let me see..."

She does not stir for several minutes, and then she sighs deeply and closes her eyes.

'Alice Mary Kathleen Fitzmartin McGloin!' my mama, Siobhan, called at me. 'Have you got your pinafore on? Get Granny to tie your sash!'

Granny Fitzmartin come in. 'Here baby, Granny'll help you.'

"I turned so she could tie me up in a big fluffy bow. Papa come in strugglin' into his one good suit coat and got on his knees in front of me.

'Here Tiny Alice, you can button in my collar for me, cain't you?'

I smiled at my Papa. Buttonin' up his collar was something I could do. When I finished, I wondered if I'd done a good thing. He looked so uncomfortable. He liked his overalls and work boots better. Granny patted my bottom, kissed the top of my head and whispered, 'Yer braids are a little messy, but maybe she won't notice.'

"She and Papa left my room and I sat on my little bed and started the fight to put on my lacey socks and Mary Janes, but then I got distracted by Miss Gladys, our yellow tabby, who was fat as a pimple with a belly full of babies and curled up in a cardboard box in the corner. I was afraid she might pop while we were gone to Mass and I wanted to be there when the time came. I once watched Papa birth a colt and it was a wonder, so tender and sweet.

"Siobhan flew into my room, hat and gloves in one hand, and smacked my face with the other. 'I cain't believe that you don't have those shoes on, Alice Mary!'

"I drew back. Without a word back to her—I knew not to talk back—I forgot about the cat and began putting my shoes on.

"Granny come in again and said to mama, 'Katy Siobhan, you leave that child alone. She's just a baby and needs help to get ready, help that her mother ought to be givin' her.'

'Baby, my eye.' She stuffed her red hands into her gloves and started yanking them down on each finger. 'She's old enough to get ready for church of a Sunday, Ma.'

'You're too hard on her, darlin',' said Papa from the doorway. 'Ease up a bit,

won'tcha?'

"He placed a hand on her arm, uneasy, like he might draw back a nub. She snatched her arm away and, seeing she was being ganged up on, left the room with her mouth in a straight line. She was mad, but was holding it in. I heard her call my big brother from the hallway.

'Frankie! You ready? Get that truck started.'

Alice comes out of her reverie and turns soft eyes on me.

"Maybe Siobhan was tender and calm when I was a baby, but I knew the flame of her temper early on. I often thought maybe I'd done some terrible thing to rile her, but Granny Fitzmartin told me that, no, it was Siobhan's sin and not mine. Granny helped me not to feel so bad all the time."

I cleared my throat. "Uh, I'm sorry to stir up painful memories."

"Little girl, everbody's got painful memories. But there's good, too. Back then, worse than the smacking though, was the shaming. That was her worst weapon against me. She could shame me down to tears. I'd feel somehow disconnected, unsteady on my feet. If I broke a rule or sassed her, she would take me by the shoulders and shake me.

'Look here to me, young lady. Don't you look at the floor, Alice Mary, you look me right here in my eyes.'

Alice turned her eyes back to the window, and seemed to go inside herself again.

"She took me by both shoulders. 'My how you disappoint me, Alice. I'm sure let down by you sassin' me and stompin' yer foot. I don't even know you, you bad little girl! Where is *my* Alice? Where is my good little Alice? What have you done with her?' She shook me hard.

'I don't know.' I tried not to cry. 'I'm standing right here in front of you, Mama. I didn't go away anywheres.'

"I felt like my joints had come unhinged. How could I not be there, when I was? She turned me around and swatted my bottom hard. 'You go on outta here, bad little girl. You go and find my good Tiny Alice and bring her back in here to obey her mama.'

"I went to my room, anywhere to get away from her, from her spoiled expectations, from her shame at having a little girl who wouldn't obey, from the mystery of being not there when I was. I went to my room and sat on the bed and wondered whatever I had done that made me not me. And, if I wasn't me, then who was I? Good or bad? I didn't know. I cried a good long time until I heard her call from the kitchen.

'Alice, you come down here like a good little girl and take your medicine. I'll teach you not to sass me.'

"I didn't think I'd sassed her, but down to the kitchen I went where she waited with a willow switch that she'd cut from the trees that grew along the banks of the creek. I knew what that meant, 'cause that day neither Papa nor Granny was there to stop her. I pulled down my panties and bent over a kitchen chair and she whipped me good. Then she handed me a towel and told me to wipe my nose and said how she was surely glad that ugly bad girl had gone away.

"Then she patted me on the shoulder. At the stove she said, 'You set that table, little girl.' So, I did.

I cried. I tried not to, but it was no use. She didn't like to hear me cry. Maybe my tears lived too close to the surface. I reached the utensils into just the right place—fork and napkin on the left, spoon and knife to the right, just as Granny taught me. I placed a cup towel for a napkin at each setting. I set out the glasses to be filled with milk. I still didn't know which little Alice I was."

Alice smiled to herself, shook her head. "The ways of parents are always a mystery to their children. But I have good memories too, like I said.

"Later that same night, I sat in Granny's lap on the night-dark front porch. She brushed back the hair that'd escaped my braids and crooned to me, humming in her chest the tunes of old hymns I'd heard at Mary Jon Raintree's church when I visited, the First Primitive Baptist Church—hymns I didn't know because we were Catholics and belonged at St. Ignatius. I wondered how Granny, a life-long Catholic, knew those tunes. I leaned back against her and felt the rumble in her chest as she hummed.

"The air smelled of the moist soil around the roses and the dry *caliche* blowing off the road, of fresh greens and pale nightstar jasmine. I could just see a sparklin' of moonlight on a curve in the creek and hundreds of fireflies winkin' around the yard.

"My big brother, Frankie, would try to act older and be serious so he wouldn't chase the fireflies anymore, and I never wanted to give up my place in Granny's lap. Jamie and Bobby, though, would run around wildly and little Ginny would toddle after 'em. They each carried a jar with a hole poked through the metal lid. Granny kept the jars on the porch for just that purpose. We caught the little bugs in their jars, and watched their bodies blink on and off, like magic lanterns in the spring night. Granny never let us keep 'em for long because she wouldn't suffer 'em to die. She made us let the bugs go and after a while the boys and Ginny would come back up on the porch and sit.

"When the lightning bugs went to bed and there was only a sliver of a moon, the night moved in thick and black around us. I could hardly see the faces of my brothers seated at Granny's feet. Ginny climbed up in Granny's lap with me and curled onto her other shoulder.

"Ginny was a sweet tender little girl. Even Siobhan was kind to her. I loved being the older sister, having her look up to me and need my attentions.

"Granny told us stories. She was a good storyteller. Our favorite was "The Little Boy That Went Fishin'," one that changed every time she told it. The little boy would take his cane pole to the creek and catch a few fish and play and have adventures and make discoveries and make mistakes and sometimes get hurt in the process. But he always returned home safely, shamed if he'd done wrong or alive with pride if he'd caught fish, and he usually learned a lesson in the bargain. We loved that little boy like he was one of our own and never tired of hearing about him, and my brothers would often go down to act out the stories at the creek.

"After a story or two, we sat swathed in the dark, wrapped in the songs of crickets and katydids, and we'd cherish the safe, dark night.

Chapter Eight

BERT

On my way back to Bomar, I think about all the things Alice talked about: her abusive mother, corporal punishment, a grandmother whose love soothed the lack of a mother's care. Alice, in spite of a hard life, has a sweetness about her.

My mother has never been physically abusive and I've always known she loved me—well, maybe not when I was a teen—so why do I think she did such a poor job of raising me? *Why am I unforgiving? Why do I still blame? And why am I so terrified of caring for Kelly?*

I'm not a bad person. I'm not all that selfish. My work is caring for others. I care for excited mothers-to-be who, new mothers, those who are tired, and pregnant teenagers who are scared or pissed off.

I fear I might be an angry mother like Alice's, but I don't think I could ever raise a hand to a child or use guilt to manipulate. I'd like to think that I wouldn't, but I don't know, do I?

I suppose I could say that my life so far has been self-centered in that I enjoy being single, living on my own, and building my career. I've never had much interest in the idea of sharing my life with another. I've never met an "other" who qualified as someone I'd wish to share my life with. *Hey, it's my life. You can't have it.*

I like being single and plan to remain so. I don't want a family because my family was almost too much, without moral checks and balances, and my parents raised me within the philosophical limitations of *Be Here Now* and a committed conviction of cultural and personal peace-and-love. Hence, I don't want to bring a child into this world, much less inherit someone else's.

Children must be like small clay figures—malleable, impressionable, innocent blank slates for parents to shape according to their own desires. And once so stamped, the kid carries that mark forever and ever. Not even as a savvy adult will she be able to shake off the life paradigm of the parents' egos.

I don't want to be a mother. If that makes me selfish, then so be it. I don't want to honor my best friend's wishes and take on her difficult daughter. If Kris had discussed this with me and given me time to adjust to the idea so I could rearrange my life a little and work on my attitude—maybe. But I have no guidelines, no instruction booklet, no *Mothering for Dummies*, no model of responsible parenthood to fall back on, no grandparents to take up the slack.

I own my little clapboard cottage in a cow field off the interstate. I have my own rose garden. But now that Kris is gone, I don't want to work the garden with Kelly. I don't want Kelly moving into my house. I don't want to go to Kelly's teacher conferences or talk to her when she starts her period or help her with some geeky science project, or watch her consort with one inappropriate boy after another. And, Kelly wouldn't have a father to take up the slack like Alice did. I don't want to mother Kelly. I don't know how. And that does not make me a bad person.

I love myself and my life. I love my parents both in spite of and because of their eccentricities. Now I wonder if I am some kind of cold-hearted bitch, because Kris's request seems so repugnant to me. I don't think so. I'm just me. I nurse. I ride my stationary bike. I garden. I bite my nails. I record Maury Povich and watch him at night with a bag of Doritos and a Dr. Pepper, and, when I have time, I enjoy a good historical novel or an essay by Susan Sontag. I watch crime shows, listen to Patti Smith and Bette Midler. I water ski with Rick Loughlin, and often I visit my parents to ride my horse Belly Up and swim in their stock pond. So far, my life has been fine, thank you. Now I am suddenly expected to be someone else? But I know, even if no one else knows, that I am not anyone's mom.

I wish we could turn back the clock to before Kristin died, back before we found and read the will, before I knew how thoroughly screwed I am; I wish I could take my reality from before, start over and leave out the Kris's being dead part, let her finish parenting Kelly and then we could grow old together growing roses and sharing our mutual lust for Pastor Tim, and getting letters from a grown-up and straightened-out Kelly who lives hundreds of miles away. *Can we do that please? I don't want to be the bad guy.*

I meet Grady Powell at the Buttered Biscuit. I am as nervous as a ninnie. I insisted on the diner close to home, so I can make a fast exit if the whole encounter goes south. I feel more at ease this way, though not very. We seem to make each other nervous.

He orders not just coffee but a big country breakfast to go with it—*huevos rancheros*, *frijoles,* corn tortillas and butter, bacon and grits and—oh my god—biscuits and gravy. I wonder how he stays so trim. I'm far too nervous to eat, so I hug my coffee mug. The Biscuit makes terrific coffee. I jump in and start the conversation.

"Grady, I've been wondering about something. The girls at school say that you're married. I'm sitting here with you hoping that isn't true. That you would have mentioned that. Care to elaborate?"

"Part of it's sort of true." He blushes a little. I like him for it. "I, uh, got so flustered with you yesterday that I totally forgot to say something. I'm not married. I was, but my marriage dissolved over a year ago." He sighs. "My wife decided she wanted to sleep with other men. She split."

"Ouch. That must have hurt."

"I'm pretty traditional in many ways and the sanctity of marriage meant something to me. At least it used to. I'm not so sure now."

"You should know that I'm pretty nontraditional." It seems fair to warn him.

He smiles. "After some time, I asked for a temporary separation so we could each think about it, and hopefully decide to get back together and work things out."

"And did that help?" I swallow. I very much want to hear that it didn't and that he's now divorced.

"We separated." He looks down into his black coffee. " I found a nice apartment for her and I stayed in our house in Hyde Park. That's what she wanted. What she did, though, was move in with her latest guy, and then over the next several months she bounced from relationship to relationship."

"The bitch. Oops, sorry." His smile was warm. "I guess I'm on your side."

"I'm happy to have you on my side, Bert. Thanks."

"Go on, please."

"A while ago she hired an attorney and filed for divorce. So, you see, I've been on my own for almost a year and the divorce will be final in two months."

"That's a pretty sad story, but you seem to be holding up well." I give him a wicked grin.

"Does all that make you less likely to date me? Are you disturbed?" There is amusement in his golden-brown eyes.

"I'm disturbed, yes, but I've been that way for years." I grin. "Is that what we're talking about here? Dating? I thought we were just meeting for coffee, in regard to my class work. I haven't dated in a while."

"I find that hard to believe. You're so attract . . ."

"No flattery, please. I don't buy it. Knowing that you're divorced—well, almost, makes me more inclined to, as they say, keep company with you. I thought today was just about having coffee, but I have to think about dating. What does that mean for you—dating?"

"I told you I was kind of old fashioned and I guess for me it just means spending time together, getting to know one another, and then maybe growing close and then . . . see what happens. But—not seeing other people. Bert," he leans across the table, "when you first came to my office, I was drawn to you at once. Did you feel the chemistry?" He is blushing again!

"I don't know about chemistry. I did feel strange, but I thought it was just nervousness about coming back to school and shock over the number of reading assignments on the damn syllabus. But, yes, I did feel something. I don't think I felt the same thing you did—chemistry."

As he talks, I watch the pink edges of his lips move as he says, "How about now? Are you more comfortable now? Don't you feel there's a connection between us?"

"You mean, beside the fact that you're my teacher and I'm your student? Maybe." I enjoy teasing him. I guess I'm flirting. "I may be more comfortable meeting here in a public place rather than in your claustrophobic office."

"My office is claustrophobic? Are you claustrophobic?"

"No. I mean yes. No. Your office is so small that when I sit my knees bump your desk and my back is against the door. I'm not claustrophobic, but, if I were, your office would freak me out."

Just then, from the corner of my eye, I catch sight of my mother's flowing, frenetic bulk plowing through the Biscuit's front door. Grady catches the change in my expression and asks what the matter is.

"Oh, God, my mother. Oh, Jesus, not right now..."

Of course, I don't want Chick to see us together. We're not even officially what Kris called "an item" yet and meeting Chick will just ruin it from the get-go.

"Your mother? I'd love to meet her."

"No. You would not." I raise my napkin in front of my face and peek over it to catch a flash of purple gauze floating past the hostess station. She has seen me and is definitely moving our way and, dammit, she is between me and the exit. There is no escape.

"Can I meet her?"

"I guess you will now," I concede, just as the reek of patchouli collides with the thick smell of fried eggs and cream gravy. Then she is upon us, her waist length hair flying behind her like red-orange streamers in a parade. She's a little out of breath from the strenuous walk across the room.

"Miso! Darling." She blares in her trumpet voice and extends a big-knuckled hand to Grady. I reflect that, if he still wants me after this, it says a lot for his character.

"Chick Lando," Mother booms. "I must say I never expected to see my Miso dining in this death trap, but I saw your car in the parking lot as I was passing, darling."

I hide my face in my napkin, but Grady smiles and rises to his feet to shake her hand. He has had no preparation for the phenomenon that is Chick. "Grady Powell, Mrs. Lando. Pleased to meet you."

"Not Dr. Grady Powell who is Miso's academic advisor at UT? The same?"

"I am Bert's advisor, yes. Uh...Miso?"

"Oh, she is not Bert to me and her father; she is our Mystic Soul—Miso. Aren't you, darling?"

Grady looks confused and amused and curious. Chick turns her attention to me.

"Darling, here is Vic Johnson's phone number in Austin." She waves a neon orange sticky note. "He's the attorney your father recommends assisting you in rejecting the guardianship stipulated by your poor dead best friend, and shame on you. I hope you'll reconsider engaging Vic, though he is so fine at his job. I admit it is difficult to imagine yourself in the role of parent. The mantel of authority rests more comfortably on some than others. Still, I think Kelly Ames would be fortunate to have us, and I do hope..."

I snatch the note from her and thank her. "No, I've not reconsidered. I am still hiring Mr. Johnson. And now, if you'll excuse us, Grady and I are having breakfast."

"Yes, I can see that," she intones. Then to Grady, "Young man," she eyes his eggs and gravy. "You shouldn't put all of that animal protein in your body. It clogs up the colon, raises your cholesterol and increases the incidence of testicular cancer—".

"Mother!" I am shrieking and other patrons in the cafe are turning to stare. I start again, calmer and quieter, noting Grady's puzzled embarrassment. "Chick, please, may we finish our meal?"

"Yes, of course. Certainly, dear. Don't let me stop you."

"We're having breakfast, Chick."

"I can see that, darling. I'm not blind. I'm en route to the clinic. Operation Ransom is demonstrating over the Salazar mess again today. But they can't scare me off. If they are there to picket, I will be there to picket their pickets!"

"My mother. The committed queen of guilt."

"*J'adore*," she says, "engaging in battle with those narrow-minded, tight-assed."

"Chick, some of those people are my friends, and they enjoy a constitutional right to speak."

"Friends. Yes, well, pity for you. I just stopped by to bring you that number and save you the trouble of driving out to *Cielo* again." She nods to Grady. "*Cielo* is our home, Dr. Powell. Miso doesn't often let us know what is going on in her life, but perhaps she might bring you round some day. We have a lovely place."

Grady lifts his eyebrows at me. To Chick he says, "I'd be honored."

"Young man, it is so nice to meet you. I know an excellent colon therapist in Austin who specializes in coffee enemas, an extraordinary detoxification method, if you'd like her number. Have Miso bring you round to the dome sometime to swim with us. That's about all one can do in this lingering heat. Will it ever subside?"

She extends her hand, and a fresh cloud of patchouli scuds across our table. She busses the top of my head, and I flush as she sweeps away, moving liquidly through the room, regal, like a noble brigantine cutting through calm waters.

I let out a breath I didn't know I'd been holding and look at Grady. I mouth the words, "I'm sorry."

"No. She's refreshing. Odd thing, though, I think I know your mother from somewhere. She looks familiar."

"No, you don't know her. Not possible. We try as hard as we can to keep her confined to the hospital grounds."

He laughs. "Miso?" he asks, eyebrows raised. "*Cielo*? Enema therapist? And who is Kelly and what is she to you?"

"Miso is a derivative of my birth name, Mystic Soul. Yes, that's what they named me."

"Isn't it also a Japanese soup or something?"

"Yes, yes, it is. Well, we're just beginning our dating relationship I suppose and you've told me about your lame marriage. I guess it's time to tell a little about me. And I must warn you, it's complicated."

I tell him, as briefly as I can, without going into much detail, about my parents and my ridiculous name. I tell him about their beautiful place and that I will take him out there someday. I am hesitant to say anything about Kelly. I don't want him to think that I'm a bad person for not wanting her. I'm growing afraid that I might be a bad person.

"So, I'd prefer that we hold off on the story of Kelly until another time. Is that all right with you?"

He says it is and we continue getting better acquainted over animal protein.

Chapter Nine

BERT

I DRIVE TO THE CLINIC, WHERE a crowd of about twenty women and children have gathered. The Operation Ransom-ites mill around on the front sidewalks, some already claiming the spotty shade of a row of red crepe myrtle along the southwest side of the front lawn. Some carry placards and most look to be mothers with children of every age. Infants swing pendulously from their mother's chests, bonneted toddlers sit in double and triple strollers, and a few six-to-eight-year-olds range about helping to corral the youngsters. A small red-headed, freckled boy runs back and forth across the curbside with a kite that never leaves the ground. It's like a church carnival, for chrissakes!

Why aren't these kids in school? Don't these people have jobs? Don't these women have committees or boards to sit on? The mothers dispense boxes of juice and bottles of water to their politically active progeny. A reporter from KFAX, that cute blonde from the six o'clock news, passes her microphone around, and, in the midst of it all, I see my mother flitting through the crowd like a large, vivid, multicolored butterfly that stops here, takes a hand there, ruffles the hair of a small child, her head high, chest forward. She gesticulates, haranguing the demonstrators one at a time, up close and personal, pointing out that they are simply wrong, totally mistaken, and, if they'll just listen to her, she will explain why.

"Your precious children need you engaged with *them*," she tells them.

She berates a young mother with babe in arms, two in a twin stroller and one about five or six clinging to her skirts. The lady wears a stunned expression on her face.

"They need to connect with *you*, dear, and not with some outdated, arcane, narrow-minded quasi-political/social belief system. Don't you agree, darling?"

The question is asked so sweetly and, seriously—how could the woman respond to that? Chick knows how to appeal to their self-doubt. Sometimes she simply shames them into going home.

To avoid the front entrance, I pull into the parking area in back and go inside. Our receptionist, Sharon Hilgers, a sassy, outspoken woman who helped Dr. Teri Slade open the clinic, looks up from her computer screen.

"You're wise to come in the back way, Bert. They're already out in full force."

"So I saw. Is there an issue for the gathering today or are they just out there to socialize?"

"Salazar. I think."

"How are your boys, Sharon?"

Sharon is a single mother, raising two boys who attend the consolidated high school in Bomar. She could undoubtedly teach me a few things about mothering.

"Oh, they're great. I'm so dang proud of those boys. Blaine is first string quarterback this year, and Thomas—well, Thomas is determined he's going to MIT so he spends his time in equations, proofs and theorems on his white board and designing military shoot-em-up games on his computer."

"They're good boys. You did something right."

"Cracking the whip, that's what did it." She laughs.

"Where's Teri?" I ask.

"Here I am," she calls as she comes into the office from the back entrance.

She places her briefcase and purse on the counter, gives me a long deep look, and holds out her arms. I step into them and lay my head on her shoulder.

"Bert." She pats my back gently.

I'm a little embarrassed that I need this propping up, but I do and I relish it. She holds me away from her then and says, "Work will be good for you. Let's roll up our sleeves and get started."

"Exam Rooms three, six, and eight are already full." Sharon hands us each a day sheet of our appointments. "How are you, Bert?" Sharon's voice is filled with concern.

"I'm okay, I guess. Sad. I'm...so sad. And slightly panicked. There's a feeling that it's all unreal. That Kris is actually still with us and I just haven't seen her for a few days, you know?"

Teri nods, and then turns her attention to the melee in front of the clinic. "I'm tempted to call the police to come and escort each one of our patients into the clinic this morning. No one's going to want to walk through all that condemnation. People are just going to turn around and go back home."

Teri and I start back toward the coffee room.

"Will the police do that?" I glance at the list of appointments. "That's what the demonstrators are hoping, I guess. It's better press."

"I don't know," she says, taking her mug from the upper cabinet, "but I'm going to call and find out.

I don't mention Kelly. The whole thing still has me reeling. Teri must sense how uptight I am and hugs me again, then is off to see patients. I peer through the window and watch as my mother listens to a red-faced woman who is obviously spitting vitriol into Chick's face. She stands strong and patient, a beatific smile on her face. So easily ruffled at times, she manages to remain calm and peaceful at these rallies. It frustrates the hell out of the protestors.

Sometimes I'm proud of my mom. I know very well that, when the woman pauses for breath, Chick will share gently and softly that maddening logic of hers and have the woman doubting her convictions in a matter of minutes and feeling ashamed of her outburst. That's another one of Chick's gifts—undermining one's confidence.

I survey the crowd, and see Reverend Tim making his way toward the front door *sans* perfect wife Patti. Great. They're usually present for these things and he'll of course want to give me his talk about responsibility and morality. I'm not in the mood.

I don't want to see him anyway. He makes me nervous. He makes me examine my motives for being his friend. *Am I his friend?* I don't know what to think of him, only the lust I feel for him, and sort of half-way how he feels toward me . . . and *that* might make me a bad person.

Sharon buzzes me on the intercom. "Rev. Axtell's here for you, Bert. Big surprise." I love Sharon's irreverence.

I go out front, armed with coffee and crankiness. "Tim."

He comes toward me to take my hands in his, sees that my hands are full. "Roberta. I've been wondering how you're doing."

"I'm fine. I'll get by."

"And Kelly?"

"We're both feeling our way. What's up?"

He looks at the floor. "Just the usual." He smiles. "Trying to convince you to cease putting your patients' immortal souls at risk."

"Look, Tim. We help our patients stay healthy and deliver healthy babies. We did nothing wrong with Irene Salazar and you and I and Patti have discussed this already. I wish you'd take these people away. They're here for the wrong damn reasons."

He gives me a patient look, like he's indulging a recalcitrant child. I want to throw coffee on his slick suit.

"This isn't the time or place," he says, "to finish this conversation. I just came in to say hello. You know Patti and I care for you deeply." He fiddles with that little cross on his tie. Damn him.

"Yeah, yeah. Hello." And I turn my back and walk away.

After work, I start for the grocery store and then decide to run home first and give myself some alone time before Kelly gets home from Connie's. I park the RAV and before going inside I take a seat in the rose garden. I know my way around roses. I know nothing of how to care for Kelly, but I know how to care for my roses. I know to dust them with sulfur when the spiders come in July. I know to keep the topsoil loose and aerated at the root ball, and sprinkle Epsom's salts around them in the spring. I know when they're not getting enough nitrogen from the soil, when one has thrips or has contracted black spot. The care and feeding of roses I know. I savor the sight of my Angel Face and the Charlotte Armstrong poised majestically, and wonder if *Sunset* magazine or *Reader's Digest* has put out a how-to book on teenagers. *Teenagers for Dummies*?

I've made a lot of decisions out here, spent a lot of time sipping wine with Kris and friends, pondering fate and questioning the sanity of elected officials. Damn!

I cry a little. By Chick's rules, all I get is a five-minute pity party. I wonder again why Kris was driving on I-35 at the crack of dawn. All I can come up with is that she must've been seeing someone in Austin. Maybe she had a date with him after she got off work. But why would she keep that from me? We shared everything. I thought. Well, except the thing about Kelly if Kris died. Big thing not to share. Maybe Kris withheld more than I know.

I kick the metal chair a couple of times, which hurts my toe. I go to the RAV and get my briefcase, some files, and a half-gone Diet Dr. Pepper and go inside. I'm confused to find the front door unlocked, and then I hear the television. Kelly shouldn't be home yet, so who the hell is in my house? I set down my burdens, step back over to the garden and grab a hoe I've left leaning against the big pecan tree. I burst through the door with my weapon raised.

From the couch, Kelly throws back her head laughing. She is not at Connie's. She is on my couch, laughing at me, her skinny legs thrown over one end. She cannot stop laughing. I'm embarrassed and furious enough to sputter, "What the?" And pretty soon I'm laughing, too. Sort of.

There she is looking so like her mother it makes my heart hurt—blonde hair hanging off the couch like this, she reminds me of the Mrs. Beasley doll I had when I was ten. The coffee table is littered with an empty Doritos bag, a bowl that must have held salsa, two apple cores, and a Big Gulp cup of some bright red liquid. When at last she stops laughing, she doesn't greet me, but trains her eyes back on the too-loud TV.

"What are you doing here?" My voice is higher and thinner than I'd prefer. I lean the hoe edge-down against the front door, march over, turn off the TV, and repeat my question.

"Hey, I was watching that!"

"You're not watching it anymore," I yell back.

"Connie dropped me off. She had to go on shift at five."

I start toward the kitchen to put water on for tea.

"So, jeez, I can't even watch TV around here? This is so unfair."

I return from the kitchen. "Yes, it is unfair, to both of us, but it is what is and we have to find some way to come to terms with it. We have to achieve . . . détente. Kelly, can't we have detente? At least for this evening?"

"I don't even know what that means."

"It means sort of agreeing to get along together."

She gives me a look of total disgust, snatches a magazine from the table and pretends to read. I think for a moment about how best to handle the situation, and then I move to the chair beside the couch.

"Please put the magazine down and look at me." She does not move. "Kelly, I will knock you down and sit on your chest and force you to listen to me. I can do that. Wouldn't you rather participate of your own accord?"

At last she lowers the magazine and glares at me. "The way you talk! Damn. What? What do you want?"

I am certain at this point that there is some age-old tradition or maybe a manual about these kinds of talks and challenges. *Conflict Resolution for Dummies?* I'm unsure where to start. I wonder what Kris would do, which is an utterly pointless thing to wonder. *Why didn't I pay more attention when she was here? Why didn't I participate in raising Kelly after I helped her into this world? Wouldn't that be something a best friend would do?* I sigh a couple of times while I work this out in my mind.

Then, finally: "Kelly, look, I don't know how to do this. I've been a fighter most of my life, but I don't know how to fight with you. Can't you cut me a little slack, if I'll do the same for you?"

"I hate you!" she screams, throws the magazine and stomps off to the room that is to be hers. I swallow tears as I watch her go. I'm not used to feeling helpless, but I surely do now.

The room falls silent and the house rests for a while. I move to the kitchen, the weight of my ridiculous world on my shoulders. I rinse out the Royal Doulton teapot I bought on a trip with Kris to Fredericksburg last year, and unwrap three bags of Good Earth Original tea, a tea that Kristin introduced me to, and drop them into the pot. Everything I see, everything I do—is about Kris. She was such a huge part of my life and her absence presses in on me. *How can I not do what she has asked me? How can I not learn to love Kelly as a part of Kris?* Then I shake it off and go into my bedroom, change into a large t-shirt and boxers and wash my face and hands.

The tea kettle whistles. I pour boiling water and drape a cup towel over the pot as a cozy. I turn and see Kelly watching from the door, her face pinched and white, dark smudges beneath both eyes. Her jaw is set, lips pressed firmly together.

"Are you all right?" I ask, praying that she is because, if she isn't, I don't know what to do about that either.

She shakes her head. No, she is not all right. The tight mask begins to crumple. Her lips separate and her mouth opens wide and a sound comes out—sort of a cry. Not a scream. Almost a feral howl. There are no tears on her face.

"No, don't do that," I say. I step forward, reaching toward her, waving my hands like Chick does when something is too intense for her. "No, seriously. Kelly? Don't do this. Okay?"

Should I touch her? Will that invade her physical space? Does she need to just yell? Does she need to be held, or should I back off and let her roar? I have no idea.

"It's okay, Kelly," I try. "It's gonna be okay. I swear."

I don't know how anything is ever going to be okay again, but I sure as hell can't tell the kid that. She slams her back against the door jam. Her knees buckle and she slides to a sitting position on the floor, her mouth still open, her eyes wide. The horrible pained sound seems to enlarge the room, raise the ceiling, stretch the walls.

Before I know it, I'm on the floor next to her, pulling her onto my lap. We are clumsy together. She is so long and skinny and lightweight. I think of oyster shell—her skin is that same iridescent white, and she weighs no more than a big doll. I feel solid and heavy as she leans into me and I imagine that we are sinking deeper into the floor. My ears ring from her cries that are now sobs, and somehow it feels as if I am sending down roots, pushing through the floor into the moist darkness, deep beneath the house into the earth below. I feel grounded, as if something is rising inside me, some kind of potential maybe. I wonder if Chick's prognostications are coming true, if she is correct in her belief in me. *Can I be a decent mother? Can I learn? Is that what's happening this very moment?*

In time, Kelly calms. I hold her in my arms and she quiets, her head on my shoulder. Yes, maybe I can mother this child. At that moment, I feel anchored and strong, and I hold her and we rock side to side, like a loose halyard in an easy wind. We sit and rock until she cries herself out. I grab a cup towel and wipe her nose. She makes a toddler's face.

"You want a cheese sandwich?" My voice is croaky and I'm embarrassed at what I've just said, yet I think that offering food is definitely a motherly thing to do. It's what Chick does.

She shakes her head. "I'm not hungry," her voice is listless.

"Do you like your new room? I moved my Nordic Track out onto the screened in porch. My computer is still in there, but I can put it in my room. I just haven't gotten around to it."

"Don't bother. I don't care."

She stands and leaves the kitchen. So much for newly established connections. I hear the click of the door closing, the lock turning. I wonder if it was a good idea to put that lock on the door. I stand for a while, staring at her door across the hall, thinking that she has somehow missed the significance, the numinosity of the moment we've just shared. I pour my tea and add honey, and then bang out the screen door to sit in the nightshade of the garden.

"Holy shit, Kris," I say to the Angel Face rose. "How do I do this?"

And, I cry.

Chapter Ten

BERT AND ALICE

FOR MY NEXT MEETING WITH Tiny Alice, I stop at the bakery in Fallon Springs and pick up a pound cake. According to Alice, Delta and Billy Cawthorne opened the bakery in 1938. Delta was known around town for the heavenly pies she took to shut-ins, to new mothers, and to church socials. Her pecan was her best and her crusts were perfect. They married in '36, and he could bake such good bread: salt-rising, sourdough, pumpernickel, and started the bakery in their own home on San Jacinto Street. Then they got the place in town just down the street from First Baptist. *More than I really wanted to know about the Cawthornes.*

I turn the corner onto Pitcher Road and see Alice's old yellow dog, just a speck in the near distance. As I come closer, he raises his head at the sound of my car. I give him a scratch and knock on the door.

Alice greets me with warmth. I like this woman. I like that at one moment she's care worn and country, and then she says things that are poetic and wise.

"Ready to get started?" I call towards the kitchen. *Wanna bet she's gone for Dr. Peppers?*

She comes out with two drinks on a tray. “Yes, ma’am. I’m sure ‘nuff startin’ to enjoy this.”

“What shall we talk about today?”

This time she slides even more easily into the distant place where I am not present and her thoughts carry her back in time. She fixes her eyes out the window on something in the yard. Maybe the daisies and asters in the side bed. Maybe the ancient tree swing in the live oak. Or maybe she gazes even further out at the cottonwoods that line the creek.

“I crept to Frankie’s room. The door was ajar. I could hear someone talking soft, but I couldn’t tell if it was Siobhan or Granny.

‘Alice Mary, you can come in,’ said Siobhan. ‘I hear you lurkin’ out there. I reckon these flu germs are just about everwhere anyhow. You might as well come on in.’

“The door squeaked as I stepped in. Granny was there, too. I’d been in Frankie’s room a hunnert times, but it’d never smelled like this—like fever and camphor, like mustard plaster and sweat, like fear.

‘Would you like to sit with him, darlin’? Your mama could use a break. Siobhan, why don’t you go on out and git some fresh air.’ Granny threw her a look that shouldn’t be argued with and Siobhan stood, weary. She put a hand to her mouth and took in a big breath, shook her head, and left.

“I took her seat and reached for Frankie’s hand that was hot and dry from fever. He grunted at my touch. His face was dark with the flush of the heat. The days were still hot, and it was already October.

‘H’lo, little girl,’ he whispered through dry, white lips. ‘You come in here to catch my flu? You always did want to have whatever I have.’

‘Don’t talk at me, Frank. Save your breath.’

“He closed his eyes and lay still. I looked at Granny and

she said in her singsong voice, 'It's all right. He needs the rest. Lots and lots of rest.'

"It was the Spanish flu they told me. Our school shut down 'cause everone had it. Effy Smith died of it. Vern Perkins was in bed now, like Frankie. Day before we'd gone to a funeral for Artie Simkis, the butcher's boy. Seemed mostly the children was dyin'.

"When I thought he was sleepin' I swallowed hard. 'Is he gonna die, Granny?'

'Shhh.' Granny shook her head. I didn't know if she meant 'no, he wouldn't die' or 'no, shhh, let's not talk about it.'

"A lump grew in my throat. What would I do if Frankie died? At first, he just had a headache that grew worse and worse and, before we knew it, he had high fever and complained his legs and arms ached and his throat was sore. Since two days ago, he'd been stuck in bed. Siobhan had spent hours in here with him.

"Granny showed me how to put a fresh cool cloth on his forehead to draw out the fever. She lifted the cloth from his sweaty forehead, rinsed it in the water sitting in a small pan on a chair they'd pulled up to the bedside. I rang it out 'til it didn't drip anymore and touched it gently to his face. His headaches were so bad he cried out in pain. Tears come out of his eyes and mixed with the sweat 'til I couldn't tell which was which.

"Next day, Siobhan left me and Granny to it. We bathed him all over with cool water. Granny made a tea of briar rose and turmeric that we forced him to drink. He didn't want it. He didn't want anything, but we made him drink, just the same. Siobhan made a plaster of dry mustard and flour to ease his chest, and give him hot black coffee to clear the mucus that clogged his throat and liked to choke him. Granny and I made a tent of a wet bed sheet and Siobhan would bring in the tea kettle full of boiling water. The steam sometimes eased his breathing and quieted his wracking cough. We did everything we knew to do. I could see clear that he wasn't getting any better. It grieved me deep.

"I sat by his bed and gazed out the window at the blankness of late fall. A few fall leaves laid on the wheat colored grass, like they were tired of blazing with color. Chinaberry branches reached out their bony arms pointing to the dead, slate gray sky. The fields lay dark and hollow, a landscape like a ghost town, without a hint of life.

"I sat and watched Frankie, sorrowed for his suffering. and a fear I couldn't recognize gripped my guts. He was my protector against the bullies in town who teased me for being small and shy. He was my playmate, Tarzan to my Jane on the mustang grapevines in the woods, Wyatt Earp to my Doc Holliday with wooden pistols Papa had carved. He was the clown who made me laugh after Siobhan switched me. I was furious that none of us could do any good for him.

"Next day, Granny fixed biscuits and gravy for breakfast 'cause Siobhan hadn't come in yet from her room. When she did, she walked into the room with a face like death.

'Your Papa's sick, Alice. Why don't you go up and see him?' Tears glistened in her eyes, but she never cried about nothing. 'Mother...ah, you put up the coffee,' she said to Granny. 'I thank you.'

"I ran into their room and Papa waved his arm at me, motioning for me to pull a chair up to the bedside.

'Now, Tiny Alice, don't you fear any.' I sat quietly in the hard, wooden chair. His voice was kind and soothing. 'Papa's gonna fight this off. Y'all need to care for Frankie. He's my firstborn and my son. We got to figure how to save him. Don't let 'im die, Tiny.'

"In the morning, I had the sore throat, too, and the headache. By the end of the day I was coughing and spitting up. Siobhan and Granny had to care for me, too. The doctor come one day and then a nurse, but they just brought more camphor and told us to do things we was already doin' and we had to pay 'em or barter, if they helped or not.

"I felt like I was gonna die, but, in several days, I sweated it out and so did Papa, and our sick was nothing like Frankie's. Toward the end he stopped talking, his eyes big and dark in his thin face, and his skin seemed see-through.

"Siobhan and I were in his room, once again bathing his body. He hadn't said a word in days. Wouldn't eat. Barely drank.

'Oh, Francis, don't leave me. Don't leave us,' Siobhan began to cry great, loud, ugly sobs. She'd always doted on Frankie. I reckon we all did. Granny come in from tending the kitchen and stood lookin' out the window. Papa was out doing chores even though Siobhan and Granny both had scolded him not to.

"Frankie made the most pitiful moans as he lay unable to move or talk. So, we watched him and listened to his breathing get slower and slower. Siobhan stood up and joined Granny at the window. I took her seat.

"I held his hand in mine. 'I love you, Frankie. You're my best friend. You'll be all well in a few days.' Tears and snot ran down my face. 'And we'll git up a game of kick the can with the Osterman boys.'

And then, a couple hours later, he give a deep sigh and his chest didn't rise any more. Siobhan couldn't stop crying, so she left the room to go get Papa. Granny put pennies on his eyes and her and I washed him and dressed him in his Sunday clothes. Henry Bursen and Juan Gonzalez put the coffin together, using scrap wood from behind our barn. Father Socha read a Mass for his soul and Frankie was buried in our family ground."

Alice roused herself and gave me a long look. The lines between her eyebrows deepened.

"I don't think Siobhan ever got over it. They say losing a child is even worse than losing your husband or wife. Maybe it was true of Siobhan. She still had Papa, Bobby and me and baby Ginny. Though she never seemed that close with Papa, and after Frankie died she closed in on herself even more and her anger grew even fiercer. Sometimes I felt she was mad at me for being alive with Frankie gone. No, I don't think she ever recovered.

"Well," Alice rises with some difficulty. She stands from a sitting position with her back bent at the waist, her hands on her knees, and then she straightens up. The movement looks painful. "I guess that's enough for today, hmm? I'm feelin' like I could use a nap."

We make a date for my return. And it's no surprise that she's tired, talking about the difficult times in her life. But she seems happy to explore the past and share it with our project. She thanks me for the pound cake and tells me once again, "The Cawthorne's started baking at home and then opened that place in '38."

"Tiny Alice," I extend my hand. "Thanks for sharing the hard memories. I think we're headed down a solid path, don't you?"

"I do indeed, young lady. Thank you so much for comin'. I look forward to our next meeting."

"You get some rest."

We say our goodbyes, and I let myself out the front door.

Chapter Eleven

CHARLENE

I WAS SICK OF LIVING WITH a mother I couldn't talk to, sick of heart and soul that my sweet Daddy had passed and even sicker that I had to watch him dwindle away and help take care of him while Mom cried in the parlor. I couldn't get out of town fast enough. Most of all, I was sick of living in a narrow-minded backwater full of people totally different from me. And, to make matters worse, I was pregnant.

A couple of months back, I'd been sitting by the railroad tracks back behind the football field with my sort of boyfriend, Micah and his friend, Ben. They were my regular hanging out buddies. Tim Sullivan and Billy Brent were there that day, too. We shared a pack of Marlboros. We came here often to smoke cigarettes and sip on whiskey or wine. That day was practice before the big Friday night game. There was a rule that team members could not "consort" with their female friends on the day of the game. But in spite of that, all of a sudden, standing in front of me with one hip cocked and a football under his arm was Treece Harmon, captain of the football team, along with a few of his cronies.

"What do we have here, boys?" he sneered. "Pretty

Charlene hanging with the sissies. Can't you keep better company, girl?"

I was thrilled that he spoke to me, thrilled to be singled out, something I never thought would happen. All of a sudden, I was aware of how ratty my long, unbound hair must be, wondered if I had put on too much Cover Girl foundation, wondered if I had B.O. All things I'd never cared about before.

I got up the courage to say back, "These are my friends, Treece. Be nice."

He laughed and so did his buddies. Micah just sat there, his eyes large. Tim and Billy got up and walked away.

"Oh, thanks, guys!" I call after them. "I knew I could count on you!" Then to Treece, "What do you want?" I began to work on a cuticle with my teeth.

"Well, you sure know how to pick 'em, don't you," he went on, grinning. "Listen, I was wondering if you'd like to go somewhere after the game tonight. You know, go hang out with me and my friends?"

There was a very long pause as I tried to figure out what to say—so long that Treece finally said, "Well, if you don't want to, it's no skin off my nose."

"No! It's not that I don't... I just never thought...I mean, I'm not..."

"Just yes or no will do, darlin'," he said, kinda disgusted.

"Yes!" I hated myself for jumping at the chance and I was aware of how my eagerness must've hurt Micah. "I'd like to go."

Micah puffed air in a disgusted way. Shook his head. But he didn't leave me alone.

"You got a problem, Herndon?" Treece jerked his chin up toward Micah.

"I got no problem with you, Treece." He looked pointedly at me.

"Cool. We'll just hook up after the game, okay? Come to the gym and wait outside the locker room."

His friends were kind of chuckling while they watched all this. He smiled and said, “I’ll see ya’,” and they walked away, leaving me and Micah and Ben with our mouths half open.

That night I spent a long time deciding what to wear. I didn’t want Treece to think I dressed up for him, so I stayed pretty close to what I usually wore—jeans, one of my daddy’s white button-down shirts, Keds, and tiny studs in my pierced ears. I put some Tabu behind my ears and laughed to myself at the perfume name. That was me, baby. Tabu—by choice.

I let my hair hang down and teased up the crown a little bit. My long hair was the one thing I liked about myself back then—the one thing that made me feel pretty like the other girls in school.

After the game, I stood outside the boy’s locker room at the gym and watched the players come out one by one. Some had girls waiting and they’d hug ‘em or kiss ‘em. I could tell some were French kissing. When I’d asked Mom about that kind of kissing, she’d said that it was almost like sex and just wrong.

A lot of the kids who were kissing were steadies. I’d secretly always wanted to go steady with some cute boy. Micah had never asked me, just assuming I was his girl. I wouldn’t let myself believe it could happen with Trcccc, but having a date with him might make some other kids like me. At last, he came out with his bag slung over his shoulder. His hair was wet from the shower and when he came close, I could smell the clean on him.

“Evenin’, Charlene,” he said, grinning. “You ready to go?”

“Sure.” Now, I tried to sound bored or distant like I usually did, an attitude I’d taught myself when I wanted to keep things to myself, but I was a little breathless and sounded anything but bored.

He put a muscled arm around me and we walked to his big pick up—his daddy’s, I knew, but he drove it to school and all around town. He looked good in it, too, with his tanned arm on the window sill and a package of Kools rolled up in the sleeve of his t-shirt. He helped me into the passenger seat, tweaked my butt cheek as I climbed in. I said nothing, ‘cause I didn’t want him to think I was a prude.

“What are we gonna do?” I asked.

“Uh, I thought we’d drive around first. You know, make the circuit, drive the square, and then head out for the Dairy Queen. You like a Coke float? Or a Dilly Bar?”

“I surely do,” I responded, sounding as eager as a kid and prim as my mother.

We drove the square and then out to the Dairy Queen. The place was full of kids who fell quiet when we walked in. I stuck out my chest and buffed my fingernails on my jeans. Candy Cartwright, sitting with the Johnson twins, sneered at me. Treece found a booth next to Milton Sager and his steady.

Hardy Williams, who’d been there when Treece asked me out, joined us in our booth and teased me. “Damn, Charlene. Most of us thought you just didn’t date. We thought all you wanted to do was hang out at the tracks and smoke. Now here you are with my buddy Treece and lookin’ mighty fine.”

I smiled and nodded. I didn’t want to come off as too proud, too eager, but I was still dumbstruck enough that I couldn’t think what to say.

Treece squeezed my thigh. “You don’t have to be so shy, Charlene. Hardy’s not going to bite you.” He laughed softly. “I might, though.”

I smiled and nodded. He was so good looking with his hair slicked up and back, his tanned skin, his straight white teeth. He looked nothing like the farm boy he was.

Hardy said, “Hey, Treece, a bunch of us are going up to Miller’s Farm to hang out. Y’all want to come?”

I tensed. I knew that Miller’s Farm was where all the kids went to smooch. I couldn’t believe that Treece would want to make out on our first date. But I wasn’t about to say no and have the date end when it was just getting started.

"Sure, I'd like that. Would you like that, Charlene?"

"I guess so," I stammered.

We drove up to Millers and Treece pulled in under a big sycamore tree. Hardy pulled up behind us. He'd picked up Suzanne Carter at the DQ, and Denny Baldwin and Sherry Carr came with them. I could see in the rearview the tiny red dots of cigarettes inside the other car. Just then, Treece pulled out his pack of Cools and offered me one.

He lit my smoke and I scooted my butt up against the passenger door, tilted my head up slightly and blew the smoke up slow. He grinned at me, like a fool I'd say, if it'd been any other boy. From under his seat he pulled out a brown paper bag. "You like whiskey? I know you drink it with your boyfriends down at the tracks."

"Yeah, sometimes. It's okay. I never drink much."

"Well, you can drink as much as you want tonight."

We sat and sipped and finished our cigs. We didn't have much to say. I knew nothing about football and the only books he'd ever opened were textbooks. So, we kinda sat without talking for a while. Then he put the cap on the bottle and stowed it. He leaned over and pulled me close and kissed me, forcing his big fat tongue halfway down my throat. I was not ready for that! I pulled away.

"Damn, Treece, you liked to choke me!"

"You don't like the way I kiss?" he said in a rough voice. Then he pulled me to him again, this time gentler. This kiss was slower and easier, but still with the tongue in my mouth. I didn't like it, so I jerked away again.

Then with a grunt he slammed me back against the seat and I hit my head on the door handle. He dropped his full weight on me, knocking my breath out.

"Now, you know why we come out to Miller's Farm, don't you, Charlene? We come out here to get some. Don't you want to do it with the team captain? Hmm?"

I felt completely pinned to the seat by his weight and

when I tried to push him off by lifting my pelvis or kicking my legs I realized how strong he was. I couldn't get free.

"Dammit, Treece, get off me! I'm not one of your idiot girlfriends. I'm not all that impressed. Now, get off."

He forced a kiss on me, then raised himself up and looked me in the eyes. "Oh, you'll be impressed. Don't you worry, little girl."

He began to fiddle with the zipper on my jeans and, angry, jerked until it ripped out. I bucked and twisted and made it as hard for him as I could, but his big, heavy body made it near impossible to move. Then he ripped the buttons off my dad's shirt and he fell on my boobs, kissing and biting. I smashed my fist against the side of his head and he looked at me with rage in his eyes and slapped me across my face. It near knocked me out.

Cold fear filled me up and I bit my lip not to cry. I tasted blood. I screamed for help but no one came. I knew the others were just a few yards away, but they weren't gonna interfere with Treece's little party.

"Ow! Treece, that hurts," I said through clenched teeth. I didn't want to cry. I didn't want to give him the satisfaction. I finally went limp. He was stronger than I was. It was his game. I surrendered rather than take another blow to my face.

"That's not the only thing that's gonna hurt."

How he got my jeans down in those close quarters I will never know, but down they went. It was over fast—fast and rough and ugly... and I hurt. I hurt in every way. In a matter of minutes, I wasn't a virgin anymore. He roughly shoved me away and told me, "Straighten yourself up." My hands hurt, my head hurt, and down there. A whimper leaked out of me—my soul rising up in protest. He grabbed me by the jaw and spoke close in my face, his breath all cigarettes and booze.

"Listen, bitch. This never happened. Not a word about this to anyone. If you tell, I'll say it never happened and that you're just some poor country girl with a stupid crush on me. My folks'll back me up. Their word against you and your pitiful mother. And Hardy will say that I left the Dairy Queen with him. You know everyone will believe him." He stepped out of the truck to tuck his shirt in his jeans.

I ached something awful and thought I was bleeding. My insides hurt all the way up to my belly button. I closed up my shirt, pulled on my torn panties and my jeans. The zipper was broken, but I straightened myself as best I could.

"I mean it," he went on, climbing back into the truck. "If this gets out, I'll come after you. Got that?"

I nodded. I was furious, but I was also hurt and somehow numb at the same time. I knew his threats were real. I could tell my daddy's deputy friends, but they'd believe Treece before me. And I knew, if word got around, my mama would feel such shame. I felt ashamed at having been so gullible. "You bastard. You planned this whole thing, didn't you?"

He grinned. "And I won me a good bet. A bottle of Hiram T. Walker and a carton of Kools from the boys. Pretty good win, I'd say."

So that's what my virginity was worth—smokes and whiskey. How perfect. I hated myself for being taken in, for not seeing what he was up to. I felt ashamed that I couldn't push him off me, but he was so heavy, so dang strong.

He drove me home and dropped me at the end of our driveway. I snuck in and went straight to my room. I was sick for a couple of days, sick with shame for getting myself in such a situation, sick from the hurt inside me, and sick with anger at Treece and all boys like him.

Several weeks later I missed my period. I waited and it never started. Then I missed another one. And I knew. Boom! Pregnant. I was horrified with myself for being so stupid. When I told Treece, I got just what I'd expect from a Texas boy with a football scholarship in his future; he couldn't have cared less and told me it was my problem and then, with menace in his voice, warned me not to tell anyone—or else. I understood what he meant. His high and mighty parents would run me down. I'd already fallen from grace mighty fast. I was simultaneously riddled with guilt, and angry as hell.

First, I ran to Micah's mom. I was painfully embarrassed by how I'd treated him, but Patsy was always there when I couldn't talk to Mama. I didn't know where else to turn and I knew, if I swore her to secrecy, she'd keep it quiet. For the two years I had gone with Micah, I'd thought I wanted to go all the way with him, and I'd talked to Patsy then.

"Baby girl—let me get you some iced tea." She'd sashayed over to the refrigerator. "You have to listen to your heart and then let your head have a couple of words to say. I don't believe in making too much of a thing, but gettin' your cherry popped is also givin' away your heart, ya' know? Or it should be, and that is a big decision. You end up giving away much more than that. You have to decide what you'll do to keep from getting pregnant. I'll buy Micah some rubbers if I need to."

"I can't do that. Talking to Micah would be so embarrassing."

She smiled. "Oh, I'll give him a good talkin' to. But the two of ya' might just be too young to start up this shit. You gotta trust each other. I'm tellin' you. if you cain't talk to 'im about this, then it isn't time yet."

Now, here I was turnin' to Patsy again with a worse problem. She made some iced tea and handed me a glass, scratched her head with a long fingernail, and lit a cigarette. "I got a doc over in Austin, a lady's doc. I'll take you in to him and we'll find out for sure, and then see what you need to do."

My head swam. I was barely in touch with what was happening at the examination, which confirmed that I was pregnant. Then Patsy's doctor explained to me that I had two options. I could carry the child "to term" and put it up for adoption (he said "it" and not "her" or "him"; it made my stomach turn). Or I could do what I knew I wanted—end the pregnancy.

"Ending a pregnancy is against the law," he said with a clear look of distaste, "not only here in Texas, but across the country. I cannot recommend terminating your pregnancy, nor refer you to any physician who will help you terminate."

I watched with fascination as he simultaneously wrote on a notepad, which he then slid across the desk.

"...But call this number and never ever say that you got it from me. You will be safe and well looked after. Are we clear?"

I looked at the slip of paper. It read: *Esteban,* followed by a phone number. Now I was even more frightened than when this had all begun. The doctor rose and said, "Good luck."

I was ushered out of the office; no follow-up appointment was scheduled. I stood on the sidewalk in front of the building, dazed and uncertain, a sharp spring sun slicing through me. Patsy took my arm and led me to the car.

"Did you get what you needed?" she asked.

"Uh, yes, I think so." I handed her the note and she looked at it. She touched my face. "You have to tell Micah. You know that, don't you?"

I nodded, knowing that would be one of the hardest things I'd ever have to do.

"Good, then I guess we'll make all the arrangements with this Esteban fellow and no one else but the two of us need ever know anything about this, right? Since you have the doctor's recommendation, in spite of him being all cloak and dagger and all, we'll assume these people will be safe and we'll call and let them guide us from here on, okay?" I nodded agreement. What else could I do? I let myself be directed. I had no thoughts of my own except that I wanted the nightmare to end. Having Treece's baby inside me just reminded me of the ugly violence of that night and my own stupidity. Do I truly wish to go through with this? Could I choose the other option? Live at home in shame for nine months, and then give up the baby when the time came? Or would I love her instantly when I saw her and not want to give her up? At the doctor's office, I'd thought I knew my own mind, but now I felt uncertain. I had to do this, I decided. I couldn't imagine a life as an unwed mother in Fallon Springs. That was simply not something I could do.

I went home and hid in my room. I didn't think I could look Mother in the eyes without bursting into tears. I knew I was doing the right thing, but not her Christian thing. She'd think I'd be condemned to a hell I didn't believe in. Could I live with years of guilt about letting her down, or would she ever be able to forgive or love me for myself? Was I making the smart choice in favor of the life I'd imagined for myself, away from this town and away from her control? I curled up under my chenille bedspread, rubbed the soft nubs of the fabric on my face, inhaled the clean scent of Ivory Snow laundry soap, and fell asleep.

Patsy and I made the call together the next day. The phone number the doctor had given me was a number in Mexico City. We asked for "Esteban" and as we waited, I wondered, "Would I be going to Mexico? How would I get there? How would I pay for this?" I'd squirreled away a few hundred dollars toward college, but not what I imagined an abortion would cost.

We received instructions from Esteban. I bought a plane ticket with money Patsy gave me. She kissed me, told me to be brave, and put me on a plane to Mexico City.

Chapter Twelve

BERT

AFTER OUR TIMID BREAKFAST AT the Buttered Biscuit and Chick's splashy intrusion, Grady calls a few days later and catches me in the garage washing clothes. I don't know why I'm surprised that living with a teenager triples the amount of laundry I must do. She must go through three outfits a day—ratty t-shirts, cut off jeans, sweat pants and tank tops. Adding those to my usual loads of scrubs, jeans, and shirts creates a mountain of wash every two or three days.

I tuck the phone beneath my chin and ask Grady, "So what's up?"

"I just wanted to call and tell you how much I enjoyed our meeting at the cafe. I was also pleased to meet your mother. She's a character."

I roll my eyes. "She is that. I wish you could have met her in a different setting. Not so impromptu, so I could have prepared you for her...uniqueness."

"No problem." He falls silent and the quiet stretches out until I'm uncomfortable and am compelled to speak.

"So, you just called to tell me...?"

"Oh, just to, sort of, well, I guess to hear your voice. I don't know. Listen, Bert, there's something I want to say to you. If any of this—me being older than you, being your professor, being divorced—if any of it makes you uncomfortable or raises questions about my..." He trails off again.

I bend into the washing machine and scoop up a double armful of jeans. "Uncomfortable? I'm not uncomfortable. Jeez, Grady, I'm not some eighteen year old you're leering at or taking advantage of. We're both adults and I like you and would like to get to know you better. All we've done so far is meet for coffee."

I pull the hot clothes out of the dryer and drop them into a wicker basket. "Does this mean *you're* uncomfortable or you want to drop this ball before we run with it?"

I stop what I'm doing and take the phone in one hand, other hand on my hip. I don't want him to say "let's drop it". I like the guy. I loved our coffee date and I'm excited to see him every other day in class.

"I'm not handling this very well." His voice is low and easy. "I just want to give you a chance, I guess, to put the brakes on if you want to."

I shake my head and watch a wolf spider make his slow way across the dirt floor of the garage. My first inclination is to stomp him, but I remember to be kind and live and let live, so the spider gets a reprieve.

"I don't want to put on any brakes," I state. "I'm looking forward to the next time we get together." He says nothing. "Okay?"

"Great." He sounds relieved. "Then, I'll call you again soon. I've got to go to class now. But soon?"

"Sure. Call me any time, and if you don't get me, leave a message. I'll get back to you."

We hang up. I turn on the dryer, put another load in the washer, and take a seat in the garden. The thought occurs to me that it has been a long time since I've been interested in a man. Not since Rick Loughlin, and that seems like ages ago.

In my twenties he and Kris and I had great times together. We went out on his boat and water skied on Lake Travis, sprawled in the sun at The Pier and drank ice cold Tecate with lime. A few times Rick and I went out without Kris, when she worked a different shift than I. I felt a strong pull toward him, which I shared with Kris. She told me to go for it, that her interest in Rick was strictly platonic. So I pursued something more. We went out a few times and spent a couple of nights in bed together. I thought it was great, but then when we were all three back together, I quickly realized that it was Kris he really wanted and not me. They eventually paired off and dated for a couple of years. The whole experience left a bad taste in my mouth and I hadn't really met anyone since.

Oh, there was that cop friend of Rick's, Sam Hershell, a cute redhead and a bad kisser. That didn't work out. And Malcolm Days, a guy from Kris' church. He was sweet and smart, but only ever wanted to talk about the Bible. I've been on my own since. By choice. I think. My life is plenty full—with work, and my parents, and school. And now Kelly. I guess it's about time for someone like Grady to come along. It doesn't have to be an all consuming passion, but it just might be a delicious surprise! I certainly want to explore it and see. I hope he calls me back very soon.

Kelly bangs out of the house, screen door slamming, and yells, "Who was that on the phone?"

"None of your business." I pull my arms up high for a stretch. "What are you up to?"

She shrugs. "Watchin' TV."

I take in her thin frame, taller than most girls her age. She wears knee length workout pants and a midriff-revealing top with lace around the bottom.

I sit up straighter in my chair. "Is that what you wore to school today?"

She looks at me like I am the newest admission to the psych floor. "Duh. Don't you pay any attention to me?"

"I suppose I should pay more. It was my professor from school. Who called."

"The one you met for coffee?" She makes it sound sordid.

"Yeah. That one. He called me." I grin. "He likes me."

"Oh, gag. You're so old."

I stand up and push the chair back with the backs of my legs. "Old people like each other too, Kelly. Besides, I'm not that old."

Her eyes narrow. "How old are you, then?"

"I'm in my thirties. Want to help me fold clothes?"

"Not particularly. That seems really old."

"Why don't you turn off the television and start on your homework? I'll come in when this is done and see if I can help you."

"I doubt it."

She flounces off and I return to the garage.

The phone rings. "Hello?"

"Bert, it's me, Grady."

"Hi!"

"I said I'd call soon."

We laugh. We talk about his work, the elder project I'm working on, and the journal article he hopes to publish based on the material his students gather. He talks more of Tiny Alice Slezak, and how she was a source of guidance to him in his teens. He doesn't mention the kindnesses he's shown her that she's told me about. I like that about him.

When we're done talking and I carry the wash inside, Kelly is still staring at the TV. I turn it off and she stomps dramatically out of the room toward her bedroom. I smile, not at her theatrical exit, but at how Grady's voice makes me feel.

Chapter Thirteen

BERT AND ALICE

I arrive at Alice's house a few minutes early and she takes me out to her rose garden. I marvel at the varieties. She has many of the old-fashioned roses and wild roses. My garden is more hybrids.

"Now, this one here, this is the Cherokee Rose," she tells me. "And back along the fence is the Smooth Rose. You can see, almost no thorns. And this little, sweet, pink one is Rosa Carolina. Aren't they so pretty?"

"I grow roses, too," I tell her. "Do you have a favorite?"

"Oh, I'm partial to the Mr. Lincoln and the Mardi Gras, but my very favorite is called Angel Face. It's lavender."

"Oh, my God, that's my favorite too!"

"Well, it's one of the prettiest. It surely and purely is. I made us some cinnamon rolls to have with our coffee. Let's go back inside. I have some special memories to share with you today."

We get settled at the kitchen table with coffee and the most delicious rolls I've ever put in my mouth. I have to lick my fingers carefully before I touch the tape recorder.

She leans on her elbows. "Today, Bert, I'd like to tell you

about Lute, my husband. He was the center of my universe, and I'm who I am today 'cause of him and the years we spent lovin' each other."

A sense of wonder in her voice is palpable. This is a story I can't wait to hear.

She reaches over and takes both of my hands in hers, looks me in the eye. "It was a hot Saturday night in June. Siobhan was yelling at me and Papa and anyone else close enough to hear. I slipped into my room to escape. I decided I was going out that night and have some of the fun like my girlfriends talked about. Never mind that Siobhan was always worrying about ever little thing making people talk. Never mind that Papa told me all the time that I was his good little girl, clearly frightened that I was no such thing. I'd been good and I was done with it."

Alice pats my hands and then releases them. "Can we move into the other room?"

"Of course," I say, "wherever you're most comfortable."

"See, I like to look out that window when I remember. It helps me let go of you here and just be with my thoughts. S'that okay?"

"Of course."

She settles in her usual chair, holding her coffee cup on her lap. "I'd heard so many stories from the girls—Cora Lee, Mary Jon, and Letitia—about the fun they had kicking up their heels with the boys. They always talked 'bout a place over on the county line called Mona's Crossing."

She smiles and shakes her head. "I was seventeen and didn't care for any man or boy I had ever met and couldn't see a future husband in any of the Fallon Springs boys, but I knew it was time I started lookin'. I was good and ready to get married and start a family. That's what women did in my day. But I also wanted to get out from under Siobhan's roof. Lord, did I!"

I chuckle. "It sounds like you were right on the edge of taking off on your own. What did you do?"

"I was mighty shy with people I didn't know and especially with boys, but I knew I had to get my own life. Cora told me she'd take me to Mona's. She was my same age and we, neither of us, were old enough to be in a place that sold beer. But Cora passed for older and I don't think the place was picky about who showed up there.

"I put on my one nice dress, a blue gingham with an eyelet lace collar that Granny'd sewed a few Easters past, and my church shoes without the ruffled socks. I was of a mind to see this Mona's Crossing and what it was like on a summer Saturday. My little sister, Ginny, was in my room and I took her by the shoulders.

'Now lil' sister, you listen to me. You gotta keep your sweet mouth shut 'bout this. I'm goin' with Cora and I won't be back 'til late, so you just git yourself to bed and, if anyone calls me out, you just say I'm already in bed asleep. Got it?'

"She nodded, her eyes wide. So, when Cora tossed pebbles against the window, I crept out of the house and we sneaked off down the road. Cora said Mona's was about four miles. All the small towns around Fallon Springs were dry, you see, and Mona's was the closest that served beer."

I choked on my Dr. Pepper. "Four miles? That seems like a long, long walk!"

"We walked everwhere. No choice. So, it didn't seem that far to us. My feet was hard as rocks from running all over our the farm. In fact, that evenin' I carried my Mary Janes and socks in my hand so they wouldn't get dirty." I took off my nice shoes and socks to walk barefoot. I didn't want to get there with them all scuffed and dusty.

'Oh, Tiny Alice,' Cora said, 'Look at you, dressed like yer going to a church social.'

"She wore a tight red crepe de chine dress and high heels. She bought her clothes in Austin or down to San Antonio.

The Brisbanes were the richest family in those parts. No homemade clothes for Cora, and she did look a lot older'n me.

"She says, 'It hurts like hell to walk in these heels but, I'll be damned if I'll walk all that way barefoot.'

"Are you meeting someone special?"

"She shrugged. 'Not particularly. Juan Gonzalez will be there and I suppose I can get him to buy me a beer or dance with me, if I need to. Daddy hates me mixin' with the Mexicans, but he'll never know, will he?'

"I asked her if she drank beer. She turned to me and started walkin' backward. The wind caught the hem of her dress and it floated about her calves.

'Sure,' she said. 'It doesn't taste like much but it makes you feel warm inside.'

"I interrupted. 'You ever taste your daddy's shine?'

'Once't I did. He let me have a taste, so I'd see why he didn't ever want me to drink it. It was the nastiest stuff I ever put in my mouth. Burned all the way down and made me cough, made my throat close over. I don't even like the taste of beer. I'd rather a sweet cold Dr. Pepper.'

"When we got there Cora asked me if I was scared. I was scared, but I was ready. I put on my shoes and then walked up to the old building.

"We started up the worn wooden steps and that group of boys outside parted like the Red Sea and we walked right through 'em, me holdin' my breath, my eyes on my Sunday shoes. Not one of those boys said a word as we passed. No wolf whistles, no smart remarks. They just moved aside and let us pass. I guess they knew Cora 'cause a couple of 'em tipped their hats. Maybe it was because I was so tiny or so young, they sensed somehow that I was off limits. My heart was thumpin' and I was breathin' kinda shallow. I was surely lightheaded. We stepped through the door and the noise slapped me in the face. The air was thick and blue with cigarette smoke.

"Cora waved. 'I see Juan and Jimmy. You go on over and git a Coke and before you know it someone'll step up and pay for it. Remember that I'm close, if you need me. Just holler.'

"The full moon sent in shafts of light that turned the smoke into a thin curtain. I could hardly see at first, so I waited for my eyes to adjust. Then through the smoke, I saw him. Standing at the pinball machine, one hip cocked up against it like he was about to mount a fence rail. He told me later that was how he controlled where the little ball went on the machine, with a gentle bump of his hip. He held a cigarette in his big hands and a pack of Lucky Strikes peaked over the top of his pocket. His straw hat sat back on his head. He peered at me and I held my breath. He was tall, so tall. His eyes were hard to see in the dim, so I couldn't see the color, but his hair was auburn-brown. His chin and jaw were sharp, his mouth large. He was the most handsome man I'd ever seen in my life. He saw me and stopped his game, walked over.

"'Well, now, what have we here?' he says in the smoothest voice I'd ever heard.

"I took a step toward him and everythin' around me stopped—all sound, the din of voices, ever movement. It seemed as if it was only him and me there in that shabby shadowed room, lookin' crost our lives at each other and both of us knowin' that, somehow, we'd be together. Someday. No matter what.

"I wondered to myself, does it happen like this for others? You meet your first and only love and know it in that first moment? You see a future before you like a moving picture. You know somewhere deep that your story is about to be made. Does it happen to others?

"I swallowed big, took a deep breath and took the cigarette from his mouth. I surely did not know what I was doing. I had never smoked until that minute. Didn't even know how, but, from reading my movie magazines, it seemed to me what Carole Lombard or Joan Crawford might do. I took it and took a puff, held the smoke in my mouth. Ooh, I was praying to God Almighty that I didn't choke. Of course, I didn't suck the smoke down inside my chest the way real smokers do. I exhaled and the smoke traveled high up toward the tin ceiling. I gotta tell you, I felt so full and alive I thought I might die. I must have looked a sight—so young and small—tryin' to act grown up.

"'And what're you doin' outta school, little lady?'

"No one had ever called me a lady before. He spoke through a wide grin, his voice refined like the preacher who'd come down out of Dallas for last year's revival, a voice so smooth that it did not seem to go with his rough good looks.

"I looked up through my lashes. Lord he was so tall! He towered over me when I whispered with barely a breath, 'Maybe I need me a new teacher.'

"He leaned down so close that I could smell him, a sharp clean smell like the outdoors and mint on his breath. I tell you, I thought I would faint.

"'Child,' he sez to me, 'You are gonna get me in big trouble. Yessir. I can see that right now. And what is your name, angel?'

"'My friends call me Tiny Alice.'

"He chuckled. 'Fits you. I think I'd like to be one of your friends.' He extended his hand. His hands were so big. He took mine and said in that low, slow voice, 'Lutheran Humble Slezak, Alice. My friends call me Lute.'

"I tell you right now that was the biggest and finest name I'd ever heard. I saw his buddies 'round the pinball machine laughin', and one guy shook his head and took over his game. Nelson Eddy singin' *I'm Falling in Love with Someone* came on the radio, and Lutheran led me to the center of the room.

"We danced most of the night. I knew nice girls didn't dance, at least that was what the Baptists said, but, all of a sudden, I wasn't interested in being a nice girl. Nice didn't seem important. I just wanted to be in his arms and for him to feel the same about me.

"Between dances he taught me to play pinball, bought me Dr. Peppers, and all of it—the playin' and the dancin', the laughter and looks, the closeness of our bodies—why, I knew nothin' of lovemakin' then, but that is what it was like for us, all slow and sweet, and it changed our lives. And later when we were married and did lie down with each other, there were no surprises. We had already come to know each other on that trembling night at Mona's."

She falls silent and I allow her some space. I don't want her to stop, though. I reach and put a hand on her knee. "So, did Lute ask permission to court you? What was the courtship like?"

"After that night at Mona's, I didn't see Lute again for two years."

"Two years!"

"He whispered in my ear that he wanted me for his own, but that I was still a baby—his Tiny Alice—he said, and he needed to improve his circumstances so my papa would accept him and give him my hand. Cora and I walked away from Mona's. I was in a dream, my mind clutchin' ever word he'd said, ever dance, ever breath, wondering if I'd done or said anything dumb and feelin' certain that I must have. Why, I'd never flirted before or danced much, and so I know I wasn't polished or sure of m'self. Lute told me later on that I was sweet and innocent and he never missed any so-called polish. I carried home with me his promise and fed on it for two whole years."

"That would never happen today," I say. "People are in so much of a hurry, especially young people."

"I told Siobhan and Papa that I'd met the man I wanted to marry and, of course, that told the tale that I'd been at Mona's, and they accused me of all manner of sin and degradation. I explained that we were only guilty of talkin' and dancin' and that he had asked me to wait for him. I told Papa that Lute wanted to work and save money, so he'd think it was a good match and that Lute could care for me.

"He asked me what Lute did for a livin' and I told him he wrangled for Mr. Brisbane, and when Lute was younger he rode with the Texas Rangers like his daddy before him. That sure enough impressed my papa.

"Then Siobhan spoke up. 'Them rangers are nothin' but thugs on horseback, and wranglin' ain't even dependable work. Goodness, Alice Mary, what was you thinkin'? Did anyone we know see you down there? Your reputation could already be ruined in this here town and no other man will want you.'

"They kept up with the questions. Had he finished school? Who were his people? What church did he go to? Did he even go to church? What sort of man was he? And what in the hell kind of name was Lutheran Humble Slezak anyway? A damn Polack!

"Why, I couldn't answer any of those questions. Papa asked around town about Lute and most folks said he was a good man, though he never attended church. So, Papa gradually settled into the idea, but Siobhan stayed wary. So, I waited. But I certainly never thought it would be two long years."

"Tell me how the two of you finally got together."

She places her drink on the small table beside her chair and walks to stand in front of Lute's picture.

"Our lives returned to normal, but not a day went by that I didn't think of Lute and wonder when he'd come to ask for my hand. I went to daily mass and confession. I finished high school and went to the senior party with Petey Hemphill. Granny made me a sweet batiste dress with a gingham apron and Petey brought me an iris corsage. I spent a lot of time with Petey, and Papa seemed to git what kind of different Petey was, so they felt that I was safe with him squiring me around.

“One day Papa said to me, ‘Tiny, I cain’t believe that, after all this time, this Slezak fellow is going to return to claim you. Hasn’t all of that just been a dream and should have faded by now?’

“He’ll come for me. You watch and see.”

“I assured him that I did not dream up Lutheran Slezak, that we’d sworn to each other and that swear would stick. Lute loved me at first sight and wanted me for a wife and would work his way back to me, whether or not Papa and Siobhan approved or believed. Nothing they could say or do could convince me otherwise.

“I think they were shocked at me, ‘cause I usually didn’t have opinions of my own. My belief in Lute was absolute, and my folks found that unsettling.

“Then one day Siobhan and me went into Shelty’s Feed and Grain for some seed and worm medicine for the goats, and there was Lutheran Slezak heaving feed in heavy bags up onto the high shelves. I gasped and stood in the door and watched him for a few minutes before he felt my eyes on him and turned. He smiled big as he stepped down and brushed his hands on his overalls.

“Siobhan was in the store chatting with Evie McMillen, so I walked up to meet him.”

‘Hello, Tiny,’ he said in that radio announcer’s voice and I felt my knees go soft. ‘I see that while I wasn’t watching, you became even more of a looker. Did you think you’d never see me again?’

“I knew you’d come when you was ready.”

‘At’s my girl.’ He lit two Lucky Strikes and offered one to me. That was the second time I ever smoked and I said not a word, but just looked at him and he at me. We gazed at each other until Siobhan came out on the landing and bellowed at me. I quickly put out the cigarette.

‘Alice Mary, what on earth?’

“She yelled like a hog caller. I was so embarrassed that I wished one of those bags of feed would slip off the shelf and crush her right then and there. Lute mashed out his smoke in the wood shavings on the floor, grabbed his hat off a peg on the wall, held it to his chest, and stepped right up to her.”

‘Lutheran Humble Slezak, ma’am. So glad to make your acquaintance. I see where Alice gets her looks.’

“Siobhan glared at him through narrow eyes, her jaw set, determined not to like him one bit. Her purchases—seeds, a trowel, some chammies—held tightly to her chest, she looked from one of us to the other and shook her head. No doubt, he was the smoothest man she’d ever come acrost, but that meant nothin’ to her. In her mind, he’d ruined her daughter’s reputation and kept her mooning after him for years and she wasn’t going to forgive him that.

‘Ma’am, if I can be so bold, I’d like to ask permission to court Miss Tiny Alice.’ His smile was guileless and his tones sincere. “Siobhan sniffed. ‘Since you ast nice and proper, Mr. Slezak, even though this is hardly the proper place, I’ll talk to Mr. McGloin and he will let you know. Let Alice know your whereabouts.’

“She snatched my hand and led me away. I looked back over my shoulder. Lute had his hands in his overalls, rocking back ‘n forth on his big feet.”

Chapter Fourteen

CHARLENE

I WAS SEVENTEEN YEARS OLD AND I flew to Mexico City alone with those few hundred dollar bills I'd saved tucked in my denim hobo bag. My very first time on an airplane. I didn't know what lay ahead. Images of coat hangers and memories of slumber party horror stories roiled inside me. I was more afraid than I had ever been in my life and was nauseated throughout the entire trip, which seemed to last forever.

When, at last, the plane landed, I walked through the airport, clutching my bag to my chest, looking all around, scanning the area for Esteban. We had been told that Esteban would meet me and he would hold a sign with my name on it. At last I saw him at the back of the crowd near the door, waving his sign that read "Charlene" above all the other heads. My name! I was horrified. Not that anyone in the Mexico City airport would know me, but still... I approached him.

"I'm Charlene," I croaked.

"*Hola.* I am Esteban. *Bienvenida.* We will go outside to the van."

I'd been told to bring only night clothes and clothing for the next day. I would be here for only 24 hours, if all went according to plan. Oh, dear Lord, let it all go right, I said to myself. And now here was this stranger I knew nothing about and I was supposed to get in a van with him and be whisked off to God knows where to be placed in the hands of...who? It all felt wrong.

Esteban stuffed the sign bearing my name into the nearest trash can, gently took my elbow and steered me through sliding glass doors. We stepped outside into the hot wet noise of Mexico City's airport. Taxis from every direction lined up along a driveway that ran the full length of the airport building—more taxis that I'd ever seen in my life. Exhaust hurt my nose and brought tears to my eyes. So much noise! Policemen pacing the street with rifles. I had never seen such a thing. I was familiar with my daddy's hunting rifles, but I'd never seen the rifles these soldiers were carrying on any public street. Unarmed, uniformed men directed traffic, blowing shrill whistles, stopping pedestrians from crossing into the slow-moving traffic, stopping cars for mothers with children and older folks. Horns honked all around us. Then Esteban opened the side door of a green van—a nice van, not new, but clean—and inside were three other girls about my age.

No one spoke or smiled. I took my seat in the back with the girls and Esteban climbed into the driver's seat and pulled into traffic. I wondered if these girls were in the same predicament as me. They must be, right? Being in Esteban's van sort of branded them as being like me—irresponsible, selfish teenagers with no respect for human life. That is what we were. That is how I felt and I wondered if they felt the same.

We drove for what seemed like an hour, winding through the poorest of neighborhoods, with dogs in the streets, children in nothing but underwear. What had I done? How did I find myself here? Should I call a stop to what seemed like insanity and return home and live out my *mea culpa* in the suffocating little house with my stunned mother? Should I repent of my sins and hate myself for the rest of my life? That surely was what St. Ignatius Church would have me do. Finally, we reached an elegant neighborhood filled with large stucco mansions with orange tiled roofs set behind fancy walls covered with the lush vegetation of bougainvillea, hibiscus, and wild grape vine.

Esteban pulled into a driveway of a three-story palace and drove to the back where there was a small parking area filled by a Cadillac and two Mercedes. He hustled us from the van like a tour director. We were escorted into a room at the bottom of the house, a meeting room with chairs lined up like an audience. Esteban invited us to be seated and then he disappeared.

Seated in our chairs, we all stared forward. One girl gave me a brief half smile. Another smiled and gave me a wink. What was that about? The silence was excruciating and I wanted to jump up and scream obscenities just to make some noise.

Then the girl who'd winked at me, a tall, big-boned brunette spoke up. "My name is Jana. Who are y'all?"

Silence. I was not about to say my name. Who wants to get acquainted at an abortion clinic in Mcxico City? It is not as if we would ever see each other again. God, I simply wished to bring this nightmare to an end as quickly as possible, park it deeply behind other more pleasant memories, and never think of it again. Apparently, I was not alone in such thoughts.

"Oh, come on," said Jana, turning a bit pink in the face. "Don't be embarrassed. This isn't anything to be ashamed of. We are doing what we think is best for our own lives and to hell with those who think otherwise."

Under different circumstances I might have agreed with Jana's statement. It made sense to me. I knew it was impossible that I live as an unmarried mother in Fallon

Springs and never do any more with my life than raise a kid, settle for a boring marriage, and maybe work at the five-and-dime on a part time basis. I could not imagine such a life, especially having to absorb the disapproval and dislike of the townspeople, church members, and, of course, my mother.

"What's right for us maybe," said a stocky blonde with thick glasses and a ponytail tied with a scarf. "But we're committing murder." Then she added in a small voice, "I'm Lynne." She looked like a high school cheerleader, except for the glasses.

"We are not!" argued Jana. "There are no babies in our bellies. Just blood and stuff and it all depends on your cycles whether that lump gets passed or takes a firm hold. That is what one of the nurses told me last time."

Last time? Every head in the room snapped up and we stared wide-eyed at this bold and, I thought, probably amoral girl. She must be close to my age, but had actually been through this before, and obviously carried no guilt and hadn't learned her lesson. I was flabbergasted. If I'd not been scared out of my proverbial wits, I would have asked to hear Jana's story.

"Yes, I've been here before and don't y'all go judging me. I'm just unlucky, I guess or maybe," (and here she giggled) "maybe I'm just too boy crazy. Maybe I'm just too hot."

"Too hot?" asked another brunette, a petite girl with a Barbie doll nose. "So, isn't there, like, a limit on how many times you can do this?"

Jana shrugged. "I don't think so. But I can swear to you that this my last time. I'm on the pill now." There was another gasp and then, apparently bored with us, Jana shook her head and pulled out a book called *The Female Eunuch* and began to read. Now, I knew what a eunuch was, but a female eunuch?

About this time, a tall woman with frizzy hair, wearing a nurse's uniform and sensible shoes, swept into the room.

She was very confident and stood up in front of us, speaking English.

"Hello, girls. I am Nurse Debbie. I am going to orient you and talk a little about what you can expect to happen here today and tomorrow. I believe you were all instructed to bring notepad and pen so, if you've done so, please get them out and, if not, you will have to get the information from one of the other girls who came prepared."

I was ashamed I'd forgotten my notebook and pen. I would ask to see Jana's notes later. We sat immobile and speechless; even Jana was quiet. The entire experience felt like a dream, like when I lay on my back in a dewy pasture back home, counting falling stars with my friend Doris. Like in church when I was bored stiff and I'd start thinking about making out with Micah and I'd sort of float out of my body and up out of the church and forget where I was and what was going on around me.

"I hope you've all had time to get acquainted, hmmm?" No response. "What, Jana? You haven't got everyone's name, rank and serial number yet? Now, pay attention because here is your schedule. When we've finished here, you will each be shown to a room where you can settle down and rest for a while before you're taken in to supper."

They want us to eat? Why would we have an appetite? My only appetite was for escaping as soon as I could. Could I run away at this point? Did I dare? But then I would get hopelessly lost and I had the feeling that being lost in Mexico City, even in a fancy area like this one, would not be much safer than being in this place.

Someone named Leona, who wore a crisp white uniform and spoke no English, led us down a narrow hallway, each to her own room. She smiled a lot and called us all Miss (pronounced *Meece)*. She said to each of us as she showed us our rooms, "Welcome, *Meece. Aqui esta' su cuarto.*" I'd grown up around Spanish at home and kids who spoke a cross between Mexican and Texan, so I understood this simple statement. Leona kept bobbing her pretty head and, when we came to my room, I closed the door on her, set my bag on a chair, stretched out on the twin bed and cried myself to sleep.

Later, someone knocked on the door and woke me and an unfamiliar voice called, "*Meece, Meece.* Come please. *La comida.*" Dinner. Great. Who could eat? I still had frogs creeping around in my sour tummy with my knees still trembling, still barely holding back tears. I followed this girl (who said her name was Teresa-like-the-saint), down the hall as we gathered all of the other girls. We followed like little ducklings down the hall, up three stairs and into a big dining room, a room full of heavy wood and leather furniture, beautiful, if I'd been in the mood to care. Smells that made me feel sicker floated above the long table set with heavy pottery and lit by heavy carved candleholders.

We sat and some of the girls ate and then eventually talked a little. Preventing Texas girls from talking for any length of time and for any reason is difficult. I didn't eat or talk and neither did a little redhead named Sally. Jana talked a blue streak at the far end of the table. Nurse Debbie walked around the room touching a shoulder here, ruffling a few curls there, fussing at us to eat. "Remember, nothing after midnight," she cooed.

After dinner, we each met with a doctor. I don't know how many of them there were, but they were obviously American. I sat down in front of Dr. McKay, who introduced himself as "board certified in obstetrics and gynecology."

"Where are you from?" I asked, my voice breaking.

He hesitated a moment. "I'm from Newport, Rhode Island."

"But you work here? In Mexico?"

He seemed rattled by my question. "I work here in Mexico on a voluntary basis for two weeks every six months," he answered. "Terminating pregnancies in the U.S. is illegal and consequently it's difficult for girls like you to get the help you need. We want safe professional procedures made available to young girls, so a donor set up this clinic, and doctors and nurses volunteer. We're AMA sanctioned." *Whatever that means.* "Now, let's talk about you."

He asked me several questions about my health and how I wound up there (as if he didn't know) and then explained that after leaving his office, I would go with a nurse into the clinic for some blood tests, a urine test and a pelvic. Though he didn't say so, I assumed a "pelvic" was the same kind of humiliating examination I'd had in Austin. That pain had been uncomfortable, but the embarrassment was much worse. I mean, the doctor's face right down there. Shit!

After meeting our doctors, we met again in the meeting room and Nurse Debbie told us that we should turn in early tonight with nothing else to eat or drink, and we would be wakened early by one of the nurses. We'd be taken to a procedure room, given medicine to make us sleep, and the doctors would do their work. When we regained consciousness, she said, there would be a nurse to care for each of us.

I couldn't fall asleep. Mexico City was full of sound. Traffic, horns, and the noise of large loud trucks, vendors selling goods in the street, music and the laughter and shouts of a nearby party. I was afraid, afraid of being so far from home, so completely alone in a foreign country. I was afraid of what would happen to me in the morning. I'd heard the most horrible stories and I'd forgotten to ask the doctor if any of them were true. I'd had a large number of fearful questions that I'd not had the nerve to ask. What exactly would be done to me? What would happen to the baby? Was it a baby? Was it alive in me and would they kill it and take it out? How much would it hurt? And where would I stand with God afterwards? I knew too well where I would stand with Mother, my hometown, and most of the State of Texas.

God never had been important to me. I ignored most of my mother's shaming threats of damnation, and talk of mortal and venal sins. I liked how church looked--the priests in their colorful robes, the cute guy who carried the cross at ten o'clock mass, and the altar boys in their crisp white surplices, the incense. It was almost like going to the movies. It entertained. I never felt very holy or that I needed to "look inside myself" to find Jesus. What a creepy idea. When I took the host and the blood, though I know others believed like crazy that the wafer and the wine actually became the body and blood of Christ. To me it was like some kind of white magic, though most of my fellow churchgoers would be horrified at the very mention of magic of any kind. Magic wasn't just about kid's birthdays; there was magic that came from Satan, I was told. Still, enough of all that talk hit home, so that I was afraid of the decision I'd made and I wondered if, like the girl said the day before, I was guilty of murder. I couldn't bear that, so I buried it along with other dark thoughts in the back of my mind, and finally fell asleep.

I barely remember that morning. Even in this nice neighborhood I heard the cock crow and chickens squawking. I was led to my appointment by little Teresa-like-the-saint into a room full of large bright lights with a table that looked like the torture thingy at the other doctor's office. I remember getting into a cloth gown that tied in the back and climbing onto the table, my bare back and butt on crisp paper. There were other people stirring around and I think someone placed my feet in the stirrups and after that I have no memory.

When I came to I first saw light, bright enough to make me wince, and then I saw windows. Then, I became aware of the pain, a cramping flame in my belly. I didn't understand where I was or what caused the pain, but I understood that it was crippling and might rip my guts out, if I wasn't careful. It was the worst pain I'd ever known. I felt like I'd been emptied out.

"Ees okay, Meece," said a voice, over and over. "Ees okay." And someone was patting my hand, which I snatched away to cradle my burning insides. I moaned even though the sound filled me with sorrow and seemed to come from a distance, separate from me. Then I realized there were other moans and someone was crying. I turned my head to see a long row of hospital beds, each with a nurse at the bedside and I assumed a girl in each bed.

I groaned, “It hurts. It hurts so much”

I cried for myself and for the little baby who was no more. Or was it not a baby at all, like Jana said? I wept from the pain and the guilt that twisted inside me. I was seventeen, and felt like I had lost who I was, that I would have to find another Charlene, that I could not turn back and had to keep going forward to make sense of it all. I had to stop feeling sorry for myself and hating my life. I needed to find a new person to be and leave this ugliness behind me.

“Ees okay, *Meece*. Will be better soon.”

I cried like a little girl. I felt all alone and there was no one to comfort me but the little *senorita* by my bed.

Chapter Fifteen

BERT AND ALICE

We settle with our Dr. Peppers on Alice's porch. The temperature is cooler at about seventy-five degrees. A welcome change. Alice takes a long drink and then jumps right into a story.

"Did I tell you that Papa became a moonshiner?"

"You did not." I reply.

"Granny and Siobhan were staunch teetotalers, so they had fits when they found out."

"Go on," I urge. "I want to hear!"

"Siobhan was outspoken and had no fear of anything or anybody, and she had no use for drunks. She and Dinah Malvern, Polly Brisbane, Cora's mama, and Erma Gonzalez—they marched in town carryin' placards and scoldin' the men who passed on the street. Granny went with them much of the time and dragged me along, if I was anywhere nearby. I tried to be off down to the creek when they were fixin' to go downtown. There was a mighty stir at the time.

"My papa, like any Irishman, loved his whiskey. He didn't drink too much like some men did, but he loved what he called his libations. Times were hard 'cause of the drought.

It wasn't as bad as the Dust Bowl, but it was bad—bad enough that we all lost crops and struggled to make ends meet. Everythin' just burned up. The sun had no mercy.

"That fall Papa come up from the chinnery one day and called us all together out on the porch. I sat with Bobby and Jamie on the bottom step. Granny took a chair and held Ginny on her lap while Siobhan leaned against the screen door with her arms crossed on her chest and give Papa the stink eye."

'I gotta tell y'all somethin',' he started to say. He kicked the dry dirt with his beat-up boot and the dust settled on me and m'brothers' feet. 'And Siobhan you just hold yer tongue 'til I finish. Right now, I cain't keep the farm going. I reckon things'll get better when some rain comes, but I don't know what else to do right now, 'cept what a lot of our friends are doin'. There's good money in corn likker. Folk's need it, want it, and even though there's a law aginst it, now, they're gonna get it.

'I've built a still with the help of some of my friends. It's well hid in a deep place of woods and scrub. You kids, now don't you talk to anyone about this. Though I'll wager some of your pals' daddies are doing the same.'

"Siobhan couldn't keep quiet any longer. 'Michael McGloin, you are sure enough going to burn in hell for this and no doubt about it.'

'He is not gonna burn in hell!' I cried, just plain scared.

'You keep quiet and I'll deal with you later,' he growled at Siobhan.

Her eyes held Papa's. 'I'm ashamed of you. Can't you keep on with the farm like decent folk are doing and let the low-lives handle the moonshinin'?'

'Calm yourself, woman. This is what is best for the family and I'm the one who decides that. You will go along with what I decide.'

"Papa started for the door and Siobhan acted like she'd bar his way, but he set his mouth and made his jaw even more square than usual and she stepped aside. We ran in after him. He marched to the sink and began to wash up.

"Siobhan tossed her apron at me. 'Don't stand there with your mouth open, Alice Mary. This is none of your affair. All of y'all git to your rooms. And you too, Ma."

"Granny took my hand and led us out of the kitchen. She shook her head, but I knew she agreed with Siobhan that moonshining was devil's work. We went to our room, but could still hear my folks yelling."

'Cooking up that liquor, Mr. McGloin, is no work for a good Christian man and you know it. What will people say?'

'If they find out—and I 'spect they'll look the other way—they'll say I was smart enough to find a way to feed my family in this god-awful drought, that's what. You'd be surprised who else has taken up a still.'

"I could hear Siobhan pacing 'round the kitchen and then I could hear the plates clanking together and the spoons and forks rattling as she washed the dishes.

'And what about my mother and me? Folks'll look down on us and put us on the prayer list as backsliders and drunks.'

"Papa groaned. 'Don't carry on so, woman. You know I don't give a good goddamn what other people think. I'm gonna do what I think is best.'

"I told the kids to stay back and I crept back in and squatted behind the butter churn, so I could peek around. It sure made me happy to hear Papa stand up to Siobhan.

"He stood in the middle of the room, the sun shining through the small window over the sink, makin' dust fairies in his hair. He looked like a god, his big rough hands on his hips and smilin' at Siobhan's narrow back.

'You cain't change my mind and the still is already built down in the old gulley that runs through our east fields. No one can find it but me and them that helped me build it. They won't turn on me. I won't get caught, anyway, because Sheriff Devine knows me and he also knows that some of us have turned this way to keep up our families. He's happy to look the other way.'

"Siobhan shook her head, but kept her back to him. 'And what about the children? How do you think they feel about it? That their daddy's a scoundrel and a law breaker?'

'Not if half their friends' daddies are doing the same. Now I want my dinner and no more words about this. You and your mother will just have to live with it.'

"Siobhan mumbled to herself. 'I won't be able to hold my head up.' Papa went off to the bedroom to change his shirt for dinner.

"I didn't mind Papa making liquor if it put food on the table. I might coulda been embarrassed or shamed I guess, but I wasn't."

Chapter Sixteen

BERT

Home from work, I push open the door with my foot, a grocery bag in each hand, diet soda cans dangling from my little finger. Kelly doesn't budge from the couch.

"Don't get up," I say. "I can do this myself."

"That's how you usually do it, right?" she snaps.

If I had a free hand, I would bean her with a can of stewed tomatoes. I stagger into the kitchen and drop my load. Back beside the couch, I am about to read her the riot act and dictate chores, when I notice something round and shiny protruding from the skin on the side of her nose.

"What is that?"

"What's what?"

"In your nose. Tell me you didn't pierce your nose."

"I pierced my nose."

She never takes her eyes off *That's So Raven,* which has mesmerized her.

"You what?"

Body piercing is, of course, a personal choice and I have no deeply set prejudice against it, but Kelly is only thirteen and she is under my care, and I feel responsible. I am pissed.

"What? To go with your eyebrow? How? Where? When? Didn't you go to school today?"

"It's *my* nose, Bert! Mine."

"Was it even sanitary? Who did it? Do I need to worry about infection? I have hydrogen peroxide. I have antibiotic ointment."

"It's cool. Just chill out. I'm hungry. What's for dinner?"

She's hungry. Never mind the stainless-steel stud above her left nostril and the bacteria lurking there that could, by morning, bloom into full-blown septicemia. Just get the kid some dinner. I am exhausted and confused about how I should react to this blatant act of rebellion. I don't know how to respond, so I decide to cook.

I heat a can of green beans and add a tablespoon of bacon fat, like Kristin taught me. Chick would lecture me, but Kris said good Texas cooks put bacon fat in everything. Unfortunately for me, "bacon" brings to mind the roll of tanned fat bulging over the top of Pirate's boxers, but I add it anyway. I make grilled-cheese sandwiches in my tiny non-stick skillet, while Kelly rummages through the refrigerator. Ladies and gentlemen, she's off the couch! Guess I'll have to buy a bigger skillet.

"Geoff Farmer's mom did my nose."

"Rita Farmer did your nose?"

"Rita's a nurse."

"I know Rita. Well, at least you didn't have a friend stick a sharpened pencil through it or something equally moronic."

"I'm not a moron, and it's *my* nose."

"Right. And I respect your right to have your own nose."

"Oh, Jesus!" She plops down at the table.

I realize I am burning the sandwich and flip it. That one can be hers.

"I've got milk or orange juice. You want some?"

"Yeah, I suppose," she sighs. "If that's all we've got."

"Which?"

"Which what?"

"Milk or orange juice!"

"Jesus! Milk. Please."

I lift an eyebrow at the "please" and pour up the milk in one of my Howdy Doody tumblers. We sit at the table and eat our meal in silence, avoiding polite conversation. Then she starts in.

"Do you date Rick Loughlin now?"

"Why do you ask that? And no, he's just a friend."

"I know about you and Mom," she says, as if she knows something so scandalous that just the act of speaking it out loud could ruin me forever, as if her mother's death and this custody arrangement hadn't already ruined enough.

"What do you know?" I spread orange marmalade on the crust of my sandwich.

"I know you were a couple of dykes."

I inhale the crust, the tart marmalade, and begin to cough and sputter. I race to the sink, draw a glass of water, drink it down, and gasp for breath. At last I manage to take a sip of air and realize Kelly has risen from the table and is pounding my back. When I am able to get my breath, I turn and blurt, "What are you talking about?"

She returns with complete nonchalance to her green beans, saying with marked boredom, "I know you and my mom were, you know, lovers."

I pull my chair up and lean in close to her. "You know no such thing, Kelly Ames. I loved your mother, that is true, but we were never lovers. Ours wasn't that kind of love."

"You slept together," she says in a sullen tone.

"Because you didn't have a goddamned guest room!"

I try to remember when Kristin and I last slept together. I spent the night at their condo many times, but usually made my bed on the couch downstairs.

"And you had your arms around each other," she continues. "You were cuddling in bed together. I saw you!"

I look into her rage and cannot imagine what she thinks she is remembering.

"When?" I plead. "Tell me when you saw us like that?"

"New Year's!" she shouts, like a sportscaster yelling "touchdown!" "You slept over on New Year's and I saw you!"

Then I remember. We'd had several screwdrivers at Kris' before we went to her church's New Year's Eve party. Tim's church, of course, wouldn't serve liquor, so we put on our buzz before the party. Then after lusting madly after Tim for a few hours, we left the celebration around one-thirty, both of us hang-dog jealous that perfect Patti Axtell would get to go home and ring in the new year with her sexy husband.

Back at the condo, we made Sapphire martinis. Kelly had stayed up with the sitter to watch the ball drop in Times Square, but we sent her to bed, and then took the Sapphire gin and our glasses up to Kris's room, stripped to our panties, put on sleep shirts, and crawled into her king-sized bed with each other and our mutual lust for Tim.

This is what Kelly saw —Kris and me sloppy drunk, hugging each other and laughing, drooling over her minister. Shameful? Yes. Lovers? Uh-uh. Not that I have a problem with that. Kris was the best kind of friend, one who allows you to humiliate yourself, but never uses it against you. Now I am inclined to laugh, but I don't want Kelly to think I am laughing at her, so I smile and shake my head, hoping to look wise and tolerant.

"Kelly, your mother and I were pretty drunk that night. We were celebrating, talking and laughing, sharing secrets the way girlfriends do. It wasn't sexual. Don't you do that kind of thing with your friends at sleepovers?"

"I've never been to a sleepover. I only have one friend."

I am immediately sympathetic. I was not a popular child. Of course, I thought it was my goofy parents that kept me off the Bomar social register.

"Who's that?" I ask.

"Had. I *had* one friend—my mom."

Her resentment sits between us, looking much like mine

at her age. At length, I say, "You haven't cried much, about your mother."

Aside from the kitchen meltdown, which I naively interpreted as a coming together of our female selves, she seems so controlled, so untouched by the giant loss that leaves me feeling gutless and empty. She seems to be handling Kristin's death with more maturity and restraint than I.

"I'm not a crier," she says with a shrug. "But I miss her."

"I miss her too, Kelly. She was the top-notch nurse in a respected hospital. She worked thirteen-hour days, occasional double shifts, and spent her free time at home with you, or with Rick Loughlin and me. Occasionally she dated some doofus, but she was a special woman. You can be proud to have had such a mother."

I serve Kelly the last of the green beans, feeling satisfied that I've provided a fairly nutritious evening meal for us and then I take the dirty dishes to the sink.

"Hey, get over here and help me load the dishwasher."

As we straighten the kitchen, the lack of further conversation bears down on us like a Texas thunderhead. I feel bad that I can't think of anything else to say. Truth is, and I'm ashamed to admit this, the only thought in my head is that *Natural Born Killers* is coming on Showtime at 9:00 and I won't get to watch it, if Kelly is still up.

"What's your bedtime? Usually, I mean."

"I don't have a bedtime."

"Sorry, but I don't buy that. How about nine?"

I feel guilty, trying to get rid of her, but I've been waiting to watch this movie and it's just the kind of mindless violence I need right now.

"Ten," she tries. "Mom let me stay up till ten on school nights and midnight on weekends."

"Nope," I interrupt. "I'm not as dumb as I look. Why don't you run yourself a hot bath? Is that something you can do? I mean, should I run one for you?"

The truth is I have no idea what a thirteen-year-old can do for herself, what to expect, what is asking too much. I am so in the dark I think any minute I might walk nose-first into a wall.

We argue for twenty minutes about the bath, but I finally win by bribing her, reassuring myself that bribery was an effective motivational strategy of Chick and Pirate's gonzo parenting. It is something all parents resort to, a time-proven, accepted, if not respected, practice. Why can't it work for me? I tell her she can watch the first thirty minutes of the movie with me. I can think of nothing else with which to negotiate.

I fill the tub for her, sprinkle in sandalwood bath crystals, and pour in three capfuls of bubbling bath oil. I never allow myself more than two, but I am feeling expansive. I put Enya on the portable CD player, but she whines that it is old people music.

Why do kids whine? Do they think it's more persuasive? Jesus. I bring in a transistor radio Pirate gave me when I graduated from middle school, tune it to the most obnoxious rap station I can find, and leave the girl sinking in mountains of fragrant bubbles.

The first thirty minutes of the movie upset her. She covers her face with her hands and peers through her fingers. We watch the entire film. At the end, she says she can't sleep alone in that room. She says "that room" as if referring to the execution room at the state penitentiary.

All of a sudden, she lays her head in my lap and I start to rub her scalp the way Chick rubs mine, her way to soothe me. I have no fingernails, where Chick has these long, thick, perfectly shaped scratching tools, but the rub works. Kelly begins snoring softly in my lap.

I ease out from under her, cover her with an afghan, leave on the tiny light above the stove in the kitchen. If she wakes, she'll be able to find her way to her room, the bathroom, or to me. I don't want her to feel afraid.

I wander out into my garden, checking each rose bush in the moonlight. This garden is my chapel. I can't do church, but I am never more aware of God's presence and my own value as a created being than I am among these roses. I sit and peer into the dark, thinking maybe Kristin might appear and perhaps tell me why she did what she did, shaking up my life so totally, or maybe she will explain to me the finer points of tending to Kelly. All I see of Kristin is the light of the evening star, winking softly on the Angel Face rose.

Chapter Seventeen

CHARLENE

Jana Hughes sat with me on the flight back to Austin, and by the time we landed I knew her life story. She could talk to anybody about anything. From Dallas she'd flown out of Love Field. On the return trip, she had a layover in Austin

She had an hour before her connection to Dallas, so we found our way out of the terminal to a small spot of grass and sat cross-legged, talking, smoking Marlboros, jets roaring above us. When a plane flew over and drowned our conversation, Jana would throw back her head and scream at the top of her lungs. I joined her. It was so freeing. Then when the roaring behemoths were past we'd resume talking.

The more I listened to her—no fear, completely sure of herself, no question about what to do or where to go, the more I admired her. Undaunted by expectations, she seemed immune to criticism.

"What right do parents have?" she asked. "They've paid me no never-mind most of my life and now that I'm almost grown they want to rag on me about how I live my life? Bull shit. Hell, my parents have more money than they know what to do with and they spend it on travel and building vacation homes, and hiring winsome young governesses to watch after me. I don't really miss Mom and Daddy, and I can get those caretakers to do whatever I want.

"Two months ago, at Eeyore's birthday party (that's a jam at an Austin park), I met up with some kids. We smoked weed and I rolled in the sack with a couple of really hot guys (probably why I flew down there again--a defective rubber or something). I've caroused in Houston, Galveston. Yeah, I've been all over Texas and now I want to travel some more, maybe out to California to try the scene there.

"Austin, though," she went one, "is one of my faves—skinny dipping at Hippie Hollow, shopping for roach clips at Underground City Hall, patchouli, and those long, imported skirts that feel so erotic, if you don't wear panties underneath, concerts in the park. So much going on here." She turned to me. "Are you going home to that sad little town you came from?"

I shook my head. "I don't see how I can. I don't know. I got nowhere else to go. I got no money for travel or food. I don't know what I'll do with myself. I don't know anyone outside my hometown that I could stay with who wouldn't contact my mother. Well, except for the friend who got me to Mexico City, but I can't ask any more of her."

"Hmm, do you know anything about San Francisco—what's going down out there?"

"I know a little," I replied. "I read *The Rag* when I can get one and I watch the local news. I know something about the kids heading to San Francisco. I know that they preach "love and peace," though I'm not sure what that means, and they make no truck with the establishment. And I know that the war has taken a lot of the good guys from my home town and some of them will never return. I know that much."

I couldn't stop talking, and as I talked I began to think that San Francisco might be as good a place as any to leave behind my small town beginnings.

"Before I found myself in the family way," I continued, "I was way ahead of everybody I knew and completely bored with high school. From age five, I read everything I could get my hands on. I guess I consider myself an intellectual. Never thought much about becoming a hippie."

"San Francisco is positively swimming with hippies!" said Jana. "I'm a hippie, you're a hippie. It means we've chosen a different way of living our lives—that what worked for our parents simply will not work for us. They want us to look pretty, act delicate, find a husband and procreate. Maybe attend college for a couple of years and pledge a sorority. That's it. Nothing more; nothing less. Is that who you want to be?"

"Hell, no," I said. "I don't want anything to do with all that. That is what my mother expects of me and I feel I'm choking on her plans and expectations. I'd like to take a stand for something—something I feel strongly about, and maybe the peace and love movement can be that for me."

"But you can become a member of the movement here in Austin." She pulled a Chinese yo-yo from her bag and fixed it to the end of her pointer fingers and began to stretch it out and release it, stretch and release, stretch and release. "You don't need to leave. San Francisco could be a major head trip for someone like you. Could you move into Austin, maybe with that friend you mentioned? People are coming to Austin from everywhere and the scene here is really groovy. It seems like a good plan for you. I can hook you up with some cool people."

"No, I think I want to get farther away than Austin. What about San Francisco? Think I could do it?"

"If Austin doesn't fit your fancy," she said, "I know someone who's about to drive out to San Francisco and I bet he'd let you hitch along. Willie's cool, laid back. Cute little piece of ass, too. He'll get you there."

"Are you going?"

"No, I've got to get back and be at home for a few weeks,

acknowledge the parents while they're between international trips, and mollify the governess before I venture out again. But I may come out later. If I do, I'll try to find you."

"Who's this Willie?"

"Willie Barger. He has this terrific Volkswagen bus that he's painted with flowers and sunsets, and he and a couple of friends are leaving in the next few days. If you want, I'll call him and see if he has room for one more."

"But I don't even know this guy. Is he all right?"

She laughed. "Everyone is groovy, darlin'. Copacetic. You just have to be willing to trust. Besides, I'm recommending him, so isn't that enough?"

"I don't know you all that well," I pointed out.

"Jesus H. Christ, girl! Open yourself to the possibilities. They're endless! Willie's adorable. No judgment, no fear, just a big heart full of love, and a healthy lust."

Before her flight left for Big D, she called Willie to meet us at Mueller Airport and pick me up for his jaunt to San Francisco. I didn't ask any more questions, just tried to open myself and trust that I would be safe driving across the country with this guy I'd never seen before.

We met at the airport and I placed myself in Willie Barger's hands. I would strike out to find a new home and make a new me. I knew I couldn't return home after all of this or face Mama.

Willie drove me home to pick up a few things for the trip. I made him park down the road and I climbed into my room through the window. I threw some jeans and jean shorts and two t-shirts into my hobo bag, a hair brush, and some female pads.

I didn't know where Mama was, but I quietly called my close friend, Doris. She was the closest girlfriend I knew and, even though she was a Negro and our friendship was frowned upon, we hung out together. I told her I had to see her. She said she'd meet me at the A&P. Willie agreed to wait in the van. I told him Doris was the only person I wanted to say goodbye to. I knew I should talk to Micah, but I just couldn't bring myself to face him, no matter what I told his mom. I left without saying anything to him.

Doris ran into the store and got a Coke for her and a Big Red for me. We sat on the bench in front. She swung her legs back and forth. I was nervous as hell.

"Let me just talk and don't say anything until I'm finished. Okay?"

She nodded. So, I told her about Treece and Mexico and San Francisco. She put a hand on my arm. We were quiet together for some time. Then she said, "I'm sorry for your trouble. This makes me real sad."

I hugged her and kissed her cheek. "I don't know if I'll come back, but if I do I'll call you. You've been the best friend a girl could ..." My throat closed up. "Good bye, Doris."

"Take care of yourself, hear?"

I nodded and then joined Willie in the van and we started back to Austin. I didn't tell Mama goodbye.

I liked Willie. He was small and skinny, had a boyish face and a young voice. His jean shorts were ragged against his tanned thighs and he wore a tie-dyed t-shirt, like someone washed it with the wrong colors on the hot cycle. He wore a necklace of some kind of shells on a string and an aftershave I didn't recognize. At home, all the boys wore Old Spice, but this was something earthy and sharp. I liked it.

Traveling with us were Sunshine, a dainty blonde with a dark tan, Glory, whose long brown hair fell to her butt, and Ava, a shapely Negro girl with an Afro.

Faded calico curtains shaded the inside of Willie's bus. The seats in the back had been removed and a mattress covered with a colorful cotton spread and large bright pillows filled the space. I guess Willie, like Jana, came from a well-to-do family because the back of the van was filled with drinks in coolers—beer for Willie, white wine for Ava,

Sunshine and me, and Big Red for Glory. He never asked for me to pitch in with the cost. There were chips, pretzels, brownies, and apples and oranges. There were also several soft blankets, afghans and other bedding.

Ava and I rode in the back of the van, laying back all mellow. “Ava, can I tell you something honest?”

She raised up on one elbow. “Are you for real? Talk to me, girl.”

“You know I come from a tiny town. It’s real prejudiced there. And because of growing up around all that...I’m not proud of it or anything...” I pulled at the hem of my dress and felt the stubble of my unshaved legs, running my hand up and down my calf. “...but I’m afraid of Negro men. I’m afraid they all want to rape me. Does that make me a horrible person? Does it make you mad for me to say so?”

She smiled and stretched her neck side to side, took out a pik and fluffed her afro, then took my hand. “Girl, a lot of white women think that. I don’t know where that started. It isn’t true. Black men—we don’t say Negro anymore—are interested in Black women. I think very few of ‘em want to cross over. You need to let that shit go. I’ll bet, if you made friends with a black man or were around more of ‘em, you’d relax and leave that hinky thinkin’ behind.”

“Have you ever been hassled by a white man?”

She let out a big laugh. “I’d say so! White men got no pride. They’d do anything female, Mexican, Black, white. I grew up in the black part of town, but I had cause often to go over to the other side to the drug store or the post office. When I did and walked by a few men, maybe standing around at the front of the grocery store, they’d call out rude shit. They liked the sway of my black ass. And let me tell you that put the fear of God and white men into this little girl. Hell, we all know that God is white. So, you girls are not alone.”

“But you trust Willie?”

"I'd trust Willie with my life. He's a little wacky like rich boys are, but he's the gentlest and truest friend I know."

"What is your family like? Honestly, I just don't like mine very much."

"I come from a big family. Eight of us kids. Six boys and two girls and I'm the youngest. We had a lot of fun growing up and I was babied by all my brothers and sister. I just didn't want that life. Not one of 'em went to school past high school. I wanted something bigger, better. Lord, I imagine my Mama is down at the church right now screaming and praying over me. It's okay. She's got lots more kids to pour her shame into. I got no regrets about coming with Willie."

She took a deep breath and I marveled at her mocha beauty, the width of her nose, the broad forehead, her sensual mouth, so different from anything I'd known. Then she spoke again and her voice was soft and low.

"I was raped. By an uncle. When I was eight. It was bad and my mama ran him out of the neighborhood. But after that, she always thought of me as stained, bruised like a bad plum. I still dream about it sometimes, but we gotta move on. We move on."

"I hope we'll be good friends." I straightened my long skirt.

She put an arm around my shoulder and pulled me close. "I think we already are."

Willie and Ava and I took turns driving. I only had my learner's permit, but no one seemed to care. We drove about six hours from Austin to Lubbock and the next day we'd head for Albuquerque, New Mexico.

The girls decided to give me a new name to celebrate the new me. I'd always hated my name, so I agreed. At first, they suggested Filigree, which I thought was just weird and then Feather, but after a lot of talk and laughter we all agreed on Phoenix. "Because your hair," said Ava, "is like new fire all around your pretty face. You're rising from your own ashes."

This helped put me more at ease with her. Later when I'd

eaten a brownie laced with pot, I got sleepy and withdrawn, and my companions said they should change my nickname to Stony.

That first night we slept on the side of the road just outside of Lubbock. Willie and Glory paired off into a two-person bedroll. Glory grabbed two sleeping bags sewn together. I claimed a quilt and a pillow from the back of the van and joined them outside to count stars. The sky was wide and black. Stars leapt out of the dark to greet us, somehow brighter than those back home.

"Did you know," Willie asked, "that there are ten billion galaxies in the sky and—get this—one hundred billion stars? Look, there's Cassiopeia, and the Ram and Ursa Major over there."

I knew nothing about the stars. He knew a lot. I was impressed. Then I got quiet as Willie and Glory talked about Carlos Castaneda and Hermann Hesse. I didn't even recognize their names, but the talk sounded heavy and I couldn't join in the discussion. What a drag. I felt like a little kid who didn't know what to say or how to act. And that's exactly what I was. I was hungry to learn all I could from these cool people.

Ava came out and sat down beside me. She asked softly, "Phoenix, what was it like in Mexico? That is, if you don't mind talking about it."

I thought about that for a long time and finally said, "I didn't see much of Mexico. "I felt sad to remember it. "The way we went to the clinic took us through some poor sections—poor like nothing I've ever seen, and then into a pretty neighborhood. I wasn't much aware of my surroundings. My thoughts were on what I was about to do.

"You don't have to say anymore, if you don't want to," She took my hand and began to rub it with her thumb.

"It was the hardest decision I have ever made and I think that I will carry it with me forever."

"Heavy," said Willie, drawing on a joint.

"Bummer," said Glory.

Yes. Bummer. We fell quiet then and after a while Ava went back to the van and I decided Willie and Glory might like some privacy so I moved a distance away, slipped from my jeans and halter top, and rolled up in my blanket.

So many thoughts flitted through my mind. The first joint we'd smoked zonked me, so I passed on the good night smoke. I didn't need or want to be any higher. I'd smoked my first joint, and been included in intelligent conversation. Something I'd longed for back home. Tonight, I'd studied the skies and listened to enlightened talk on philosophical subjects. I felt I was in heaven. This was what I'd wanted for so long. This was who I hoped to be, someone who was widely read. I'd read a lot of novels and I'd read one book by Sartre, but there was still so much I had to learn, and my new friends made me aware of that.

I wondered about these kids from the big city. Ava, Glory, and Willie were from Dallas, which seemed to me to be as big and as hip as New York City. Sunshine came from Houston, another big city I knew nothing about except that it was full of oil money. At twenty, Willie was the oldest.

How were they different from me? Had they left all of their parent's values behind? Was their confidence such that they felt no guilt or uncertainty over their choices? Did they fear the future as I did? What did Sunshine and Ava hope to find in California?

Moans coming from the bedroll under the stars broke into my thoughts. I imagined I could see Willie's and Glory's shadowy movements in the moonlight.

I was certainly drawn to Ava, partly because she had such a confident and serene air about her, and also because I felt she had much to teach me. She reminded me of my friend, Doris, who'd been my compatriot growing up. Yet still I wondered if any of them felt as unprepared or as insecure as I did about this improvised life. Certainly, Ava didn't seem to. She seemed to be completely content.

I didn't miss my mother and felt ashamed of that. I didn't miss school or the few friends I'd left behind, except for Doris. It felt good being on my own. I felt I'd handled the abortion as well as I could. I'd done what I needed to survive and to prove to myself that I could make decisions about my future, without the so-called guidance of adults.

No, I didn't miss my mama. I felt love for her, but I'd never understood her and I never got from her what I needed. And shame was something I longed to leave behind in my past.

Suddenly someone stood over me and I started. I looked up to find Willie naked with a blanket over his shoulders. "Shhh," he said softly. "Glory's asleep. Can I hang out with you a while?"

"Sure." I pulled my blanket tighter around me.

"So, Phoenix, what do you think of our merry party and journey? Are you groovy with it?"

"Groovy?" I smiled. I knew the phrase but had never actually heard it used.

"Yeah. Copacetic, you know, okay with the whole thing. Happy."

"I feel a little out of place, since you all seem to know each other."

"Nah, don't feel that way. Glory and I came from Dallas to go to school at UT. So did Ava. We just met Sunshine for the trip. Ava got kicked out of her dorm for smoking pot and just said 'fuck this shit.' She's an awesome lady. I'd posted a notice in the Student Union about our trip, fishing for riders, and she contacted me. She seemed cool, so I invited her to come along. We found Sunshine the same way."

I kept wondering if they liked me, which embarrassed me. It seemed so immature. Was *Fallon Springs, Texas* written on my forehead? Could they sense how nervous I felt? Could they tell I was still in some pain and bleeding? Still...bleeding...I'd bought some pads at our first stop and hid them in my pack. I hoped we'd stop again soon enough for me to change. Geez, my insides still felt raw.

Willie moved closer and tugged at my blanket. “You want to fool around?” he buried his face in my hair.

I put an elbow in his gut. “Hell, no, I don’t want to mess around. Jesus! With what I’ve just been through? Besides, didn’t you just fool around with Glory, your girlfriend?”

He grinned and ran long fingers through his chin-length hair. “We’re not together. We just dig each other.”

I tightened my grip on the blanket. “Leave me alone, Willie. I just had an abortion two damn days ago. I’m supposed to be resting in bed.”

I was mortified to say it, but I wanted to put him off. I wasn’t willing to deal with this on my first night out. “I’m sorry,” I said. *Why the hell was I apologizing? Be confident, Charlene.*

He reached again for the covers and said, “We could just cuddle and touch. That would be sweet, wouldn’t it? No pressure.”

I looked at his earnest face and hopeful grin in the starlight and thought only briefly before I decided that I might enjoy something sweet like that. Treece Harmon sure didn’t touch tenderly in our wrestling match. Though I felt shy and awkward, I nodded yes.

We spread the blanket and stretched out next to each other. The night was cool and peaceful. He wrapped his arms around my shoulders and began to stroke my back. I relaxed and let him pull me closer. To my surprise, I started to cry softly. He ran his fingers across my neck, my shoulders. I had never felt such a touch—soft, caring, easy, and yet exciting in a way I didn’t understand. There was no tension between us, even when I felt him hard against me. My tears went away.

“Is this all right?” he whispered. “I want it to be all good. No worries, no regrets. You were meant to feel like this. You’re a beautiful girl, Phoenix.” It took me a second or two to remember the nickname they’d given me. “We are all meant for this. Love. You know, 'love is all you need.' It's all about love."

I was thinking it must be a bit about getting turned on, too, because I knew no other way to describe what I was feeling, the warm wetness between my legs, the way my breath hitched whenever he touched me. Micah and I never got that far. I don't remember feeling anything like that with Micah, certainly not Treece who'd been interested only in winning his bet and not at all in what he might give to me. Willie wanted to give. His kisses were tender and not demanding, a gift I was hungry to receive. No dang tongue pushing into my dry mouth. He handled me like a fresh born baby, like treasure, like a wonder. We fell asleep that way in the cool night of the desert, and woke the next morning still wrapped around each other.

The next day we made it to Albuquerque, then through Gallup and a few hours more to Flagstaff, stopping for a picnic after fifteen hours of driving in three shifts. We found a roadside park with a concrete shelter from the high desert sun and pulled the cooler from the bus. Later we restocked in Bakersfield with hard salami, cheese spread, and bread—whatever looked good. And everything looked good because we all had the munchies. Ava opened a new bottle of Annie Green Springs wine and Sunshine poured cups full of organic apple juice. After we ate, everyone seemed exhausted, so we stretched out under the tree and fell quiet.

"Are you excited?" Ava spoke softly, as always, "To see a big city? Austin is small change compared to San Francisco. It'll blow our minds, girl."

I shrugged my shoulders. "I don't even know what to expect. I can't imagine what it must be like. I feel like such a greenhorn, as my daddy used to say."

"You are a greenhorn." Her laugh was musical. "A sugarfoot. You seem so young, yet you're only two years under me. How are you so innocent, after all you've been through?"

I thought for a few minutes. "Growing up in a small town, I guess. Austin is the only place I'd been out of my home town. We went there for UIL competitions, regional basketball finals, and my church youth group went in to a big conference at St. Mary's Cathedral. Man, I've never been to Dallas or Houston, not even Corpus Christi.

"What happened with Treece—I feel soiled, yet I suppose I seem untouched, since my experience with sex..." I paused and looked at Willie. "until now has been brief and impersonal. Downright ugly."

"I'm sorry that happened to you," said Sunshine. "You know, though, Phoenix, you can move on. You don't have to carry those bad feelings around. Chill about it. You know? Let it go, baby."

Rested, we began the next leg of our trip up I-5 to San Francisco. We smoked more dope and sang songs. Sunshine strummed Willie's guitar and we sang *If I Had a Hammer* and *Blowin' in the Wind.*

We took our time. No hurrying these folks. We were having a good time that we didn't want to end. Even though San Francisco was our destination, we were wrapped up in the experience of the trip and our sense of togetherness, shared laughter, the new love we felt for each other.

After Indio, we drove to Los Angeles. Willie parked the bus, illegally, and we decided to check out the scene on the Sunset Strip. We met some cool kids panhandling on the Strip who said we could crash at their place in north Hollywood for the night. Willie and I were given the bedroom and he explored more ways to excite me. What an education! Next morning, we started up the Pacific Coast Highway to San Bernardino and then took most of the next day to reach the City.

Chapter Eighteen

BERT

Lying in bed, as a steely moon peeks into my window, I think of Grady and replay the scene in The Buttered Biscuit. I must admit to myself that, aside from the disturbing appearance of my mother, our coffee together was a success. After Chick left, we talked so long that the breakfast crowd thinned and the lunch crowd began to show up.

The moon and I decide that we like this man; he's intelligent, kind, soft spoken, and a little unsure of himself. He listens well, and his crooked smile makes me lightheaded.

"I wonder, Mr. Moon, is this—this thing I'm doing—is this what folks call "falling in love?" I squeeze my pillow to my chest.

Is this what it's like for most people? This exhilaration over some timid understanding of a shared desire? This delight in discovering that the other's sense of humor syncs smoothly with your own? This longing to press my lips to his to stop him talking?

"I think I maybe I have it bad for this man, Mr. Moon. I think we have achieved *chemistry.*"

I didn't expect this to happen to me, but it has, and I

decide that rather than resist, I'll go with it and see if I can enjoy the journey.

The next morning, after Kelly's caught the school bus and I'm about to leave for work, the phone rings. It could be him. I panic and pace around the room shaking my hands like I'm flinging off drops of water. Finally, I take a giant gulp of air and answer.

Grady. He has tickets to a production of *The Trojan Women* by the UT Drama Department for Saturday's performance.

"Some of their productions," he sounds almost as breathless as I do, "are very high quality, some of the best we have here in Austin."

"Sure, I'd love to go." I would go to a tractor pull, if he asked me. "What does one wear? I don't have too many fancy clothes."

"Just wear your normal clothes. This is Austin, remember? Dress-up is pressed jeans and shined boots."

Add a blazer, and that's my wardrobe. I drive to *Cielo* to drop off Kelly and hurry quickly home to wait nervously for the sound of his 4x4 coming up the drive. He arrives at sunset. Such a gentleman, he opens my car door. He smiles and the dusk casts angular shadows across his face. We're both quiet on the way into Austin.

That night sitting in the theater next to him, I don't hear one word from the stage. The whole cast is up there doing choral speaking and all I can hear is blood thrumming in my ears. His scent on his corduroy jacket tightens my chest—pipe smoke and Chap Stick. That aroma. Pirate wears Chap Stick 24/7 and, when he's not smoking dope, he smokes a pipe. So, the fragrance of either one makes me feel all warm inside, and I devour the pleasure of being so close to Grady.

About halfway through the second act, Grady reaches for my hand. I let him take it and continue to smile and drift off above the stage, out of the reach of the chorus and the dancing and the wailing and gnashing of a tragedy. I have an out-of-body experience looking down at this handsome and happy couple in the thirteenth row, seats 197 and 198. I will keep my ticket stub for years. And as quickly as that, my heart is lost. I trust this man. I feel safe being myself with him; don't feel I need to pretend. Not judged, but appreciated. Totally accepted.

He drives me home and I invite him to sit in the garden. I pop inside and pour us each a glass of Cabernet. We sit in the metal chairs amidst the roses and he comments on their beauty and I tell him about Kris and me, our friendship, and how we worked the roses together.

"I'd like to meet her," he says. "Your friend, Kris."

Then I realize he knows nothing of Kelly, who is sleeping at Chick and Pirate's, or that Kris is dead. I decide this is a good time to tell him. So, I begin.

"Kris died a couple of weeks ago."

"That's hard. I'm sorry, Bert. That's terrible."

"Yes, it is terrible. It's the first time anyone close to me has died. But...and I'm going to unload on you here because this is about me and my life, and I think you should know—that is, if you want to have a relationship with me. As my mother would say, I'm in a bit of a pickle."

"I do. I do want to be with you, so please tell me."

So, I tell him about Kris' will, about Kelly's attitudes, and my feeling of being stuck, and G. Carter Welles, and Chick thinking I should take care of Kelly. And before I know it, I've told him about Tim and Patti, Operation Ransom, and the demonstrations at the clinic. The poor man gets a crash course in the life of Bert Lando.

"Which brings me to us," I say. "She's spending the night at my parents' place, but Kelly is living with me here. I don't think I want to be her guardian. That's not a role I've ever imagined I would play. In the meantime, having Kelly with me certainly stretches me as a person. A teenager—defying me, piercing her nose, and generally being a pain in the ass. So that is the circus you've walked in on, Dr. Grady Powell. Would you like to run now?"

He laughs. "That's a lot to take in on a first date, but I can listen. In the field study I've assigned you to, the interviewees are so eager to tell their stories that they get going and won't stop. I usually have to call a halt to the session. I'm truly sorry you've just lost your best friend."

He reaches across the arms of our chairs and clasps my wrist. "Whatever I can do to help. I've never had children, but my parents set me a pretty good example. And I learned some from Tiny Alice of how a grown-up handles a teenager. Will you let me help?"

I shake my head. "Help how?"

"I don't know." He shrugs. "Maybe I can help run her around to appointments and stuff. Or we can occasionally take her with us on outings. I don't know. I just want to help."

"Thanks."

I wonder if I shut up, whether he might lean over and kiss me. I wonder if I should shut up and kiss *him*. Then he stands and I jump up, wipe my sweaty hands on the butt of my jeans. He wraps his arms around me and pulls me close. "I think I want to be with you just about all the time, now. Is it too soon for me to say that, Miz Lando?"

I shake my head and he gives me the longest, sweetest kiss I've ever known. As he drives away, I watch his car tail lights glow into the darkness until I see his car turn onto the main road. I wonder what being together all the time means to him. I can't stop shaking—the good kind of shaking.

In the morning, I'm back at the clinic ready to start the day. Once again, I park in back to avoid the protesters. Will they always be here—a part of our everyday lives? I'm sure Chick is out there; she rises earlier than I. But I have work to do, so I don't go out front to see her.

"Good morning, Sharon. How's it going?"

"Hmph," she says.

"That good? Glad to hear it."

"Forgive me. I'm only on my first cup of coffee," she says with a grimace.

I hold up my go-cup. "I think I'm ready for a second. You want to pull up the schedule for me?"

"Sure," she sighs, pushes some buttons, and turns the computer terminal toward me.

I've got two new-mother wellness checks, one pregnant teen, and two post-partum checks—a full day. I look especially forward to the teen. Maybe because of Kris, I have a soft spot for the young girls who get pregnant by a boy who then disappears. I think the boys should be forced to take care of the girl and their baby. They can't deny their involvement. I guess they can blame it on someone else. They ought to be locked up.

I have such a desire to help in any way I can. The girl that's coming in is Billie Borenton, from one of the wealthier families in Bomar, and I'm pretty sure her parents don't know about the pregnancy yet. I wonder if she'll tell them.

I finish the first post-partum and rest in the break room for a bit, sipping yet another cup of coffee. At ten o'clock, Billie comes in. I peek into the front and see that she's not showing yet and seems horribly embarrassed to be seated in our waiting room. I think she must have come in from the back, because I'm sure amid the protestors are women she knows. She's holding what I guess to be a urine sample, covered by a brown bag. It looks like she's packing whiskey to a frat party.

My medical assistant, Wilma Thompson, steps into the waiting room and calls, "Billie Borenton? Would you like to come back?"

I've told Rory to place her in the Education Room. I want to talk to her before I examine her. I imagine she's scared to death and doesn't know what she wants to do.

"Hi, there, Billie. I'm Bert Lando. I'm one of Dr. Slade's nurses and I'd like to talk with you before we go into the exam room. Your urine test confirms that you are pregnant. From what you've told me about your last menses, I'd say you're about nine weeks along. I'll have you go to our lab to get some blood drawn to confirm the urine test and tell us other things—mainly that you're healthy overall."

She stares at me through angry eyes, and says nothing. She's putting up a front but I can tell she's fearful, and maybe a little suspicious of me. My experience has taught me that girls in her position fear being judged by anyone who knows their predicament. I want to give her a hug, but I don't think she wants to be touched. She's wound too tight.

"So, have you thought about having this baby, Billie?"

"Oh, shit!" she says and shrugs her shoulders and rolls her eyes, reminding me of Kelly. The thought hits me that she's only a few years older than Kelly, and my stomach flip-flops.

I try again. "How do you feel about having this baby?"

"I hate it. I just want it out of me!" She bites back tears.

I sit beside her and try to take her hand. She draws it away. Quickly the tears are gone and she has put on a solemn front.

"I don't want to have this baby. Can you help me?

She pulls out a phone from somewhere and starts texting, like I'm not even here. And now I want to smack her for her snotty indifference. Then I remind myself that I don't know her circumstances and my attitude softens. I'm pro-choice but I hate to see such hardness and anger in one so young.

"Yes, well, you may have answered my next question. You're seeking to terminate the pregnancy? Are you sure? That's a very serious decision. Would you like to see a counselor before you move forward? I can arrange that, if you need."

She looks up from her phone. "I don't want the baby. I hate the guy now and he'll never admit that he...or help me with money, the jerk."

"Well, then, here we only perform what are termed

medically necessary D&Cs, but I can put you in touch with someone who can help you. You need to hurry, though, because in Texas there are restrictive laws on when it's legal to abort.

"I assume you're on your parents' insurance." She nods. "But you don't want them to know?" She nods again. "Well, should you decide against an abortion, the hospital offers free labor and child care to those who need it. We have a social worker who has information on other resources or needs not met by the hospital or our office, and she can see that you get whatever you need. That's who I would send you to next. Her name is Gail Carson and she's a kind and knowledgeable woman. I think you'll like her."

"I'll go and see her," says Billie Borenton, and begins texting again.

"Is there anything else you'd like to know—anything more you need from me?"

She shakes her head, eyes on her phone, thumbs working furiously. I stick my head out the door and call Rory, who meets me in the hall.

"Get Billie in touch with Gail Carson. I think she wants to abort and Gail can refer her to the right practitioner." Rory nods. "I'm going to let you wrap up the visit. This one doesn't want our help. You'll see."

I usually feel close to the young girls and they trust me to be sensitive to their situation, but Billie Borenton is different. Most of my teen mothers check in with me even after they've had their babies. I sigh. I hope Billie gets what she wants and stays safe and healthy... and doesn't get pregnant again.

I go to the break room to eat my PBJ for lunch and down a quick cup of coffee. Then I go to see Pam Strater, a lovely mother of three, and her newborn boy. I'm anticipating this visit will put the earlier exchange out of mind. I do love this work.

Chapter Nineteen

BERT AND ALICE

ALICE AND I SIT IN the glider on her front porch. It's a blistering day for autumn, but that's how it is sometimes, with the cruel sun pale in a white sky. The shade from the awning on the swing helps a little. We sit for a while, enjoying our Dr. Peppers and the comfy silence. Alice's low voice breaks the quiet. "You wanna talk about anything special today?"

"Let me see. I was wondering last time on the drive home how you entertained yourselves, uh, back then. Small town out in the scrub. How did you blow off steam? How'd you relax?"

She chuckles, takes a piece of gum from her apron pocket and chews for a bit. "I can still chew my Juicy Fruit. Got most of my own teeth, still." She shrugs. "We got together. That's all. Just gittin' together, everybody bringin' somethin'. Never fancy, but most of us enjoyed it." She grins.

"Yeah?" I bat at a mosquito. "Births, weddings, that sort of thing?"

She slapped at her arm. "These skeeters are as big as the blue jays this year. They should be gone by now, it being so late. Um-hmm, we celebrated most any old thing and it never cost us much money. Papa and the men often gathered in someone's barn for some of his corn liquor to liven things up and the women got together to quilt and sew, and talk about child-rearin' or puttin' up vegetables, pickles, fruits. And then there was the Fourth of July. We surely enjoyed markin' our nation's birthday. It was an all-out celebration in these parts."

"Can you remember any Fourth of July celebrations?"

She took a long draw on her soda and scratched at the bite on her arm.

"Oh, my, now which one can I remember best? One year, Bull Osterman had a heart attack and that was a big dust-up. They got him to the Burnet hospital in record time and he pulled out of it. But it sorta put a damper on the picnic. We went ahead without him, but everbody was real worried."

"And did he make it?"

"Yes. He was big and strong like most of the men. Oh, now I remember! The year I turned fifteen. We had a mighty party that year. Everbody was strugglin', but it was before the really bad time. I figured I'd become a lady by then. I thought I was so grown up. I started wearin' lipstick when I was away from home and Cora Lea showed me how to smooth my wavy hair with a touch of Papa's Wild Root Hair Tonic. I put it up with the tortoise shell combs she give me for my birthday the year before.

"She was ever an education to me, Cora Lea was. Knew things I knew nothin' about. Had her own ideas and plans for the future. I think maybe we grew up faster back then than they do now. Most of my schoolmates got married and settled down at fifteen. Fern Jackson married Jimmy Albert from over in Marble Falls and they settled across the tracks here in Fallon Springs. Jimmy was a pipe fitter and a good one at that. And he could always find work. Mary Jon Raintree and Jeter Osterman, Bull's oldest, had just got married that past spring. So, by fifteen years of age I felt a woman, even though I didn't yet have a young man in my life. Yes, I remember that year.

"We were coming back from the drought and things had picked up for a lot of us. I'm not saying we were getting rich, mind you, but things were much better and so everyone had a lot to give for the celebration. All our neighbors and church members brought food and drink. We held the party on the grounds at St. Ignatius. It was mostly us Catholics because the Baptists and Assembly of Gods didn't much go for parties and wouldn't be caught dead at a Catholic church. They were altogether too serious—that's what Granny Fitzmartin said.

"Father Socha managed to find some used bunting, so one outside wall of the church was draped in red, white, and blue. Flags—the Texas Lone Star and the Stars 'n Stripes—were flying on either side of the big table that the boys made out of old doors on sawhorses. Father Socha led us in prayer to begin with, and then we fell to eating. Two big tin washtubs were filled with iced-down Lone Star beer. The womenfolk made coffee and fresh lemonade and there must have been gallons of iced tea. Siobhan fixed her famous baked beans with salt pork, molasses and onions, and Erma Gonzales and her mother brought a whole tub of *tamales*. There was coleslaw, and every kind of pie – strawberry-rhubarb, blackberry, apple, buttermilk, shoo fly. Polly Brisbane made peach ice cream. It was a feast to be sure!"

I drained my DP. "So that was the primary entertainment—eating?"

"There was plenty to do besides eating. Us older children played Red Rover and Kick the Can, and the little ones played tag and hide and seek. Some of the older boys and girls went off behind the church to play Spin the Bottle and other kissing games. Though I didn't go, Cora did. But Mrs. Malvern soon found them and put a quick end to that. Ebb Daugherty brought his fiddle and Milt Burns his guitar, so there was dancin' and foot stompin'."

"You were outside? What was the heat like?"

"The grown-ups stayed in the shade. It was god-awful hot and the dogs laid around pantin' in the steamy dirt. Horses blew and pawed the ground where they were hitched to trees. We were all sweatin' and laughing'. The men'd brag and swear. The women told quiet stories they didn't want their men to hear. I've always found it odd that when women get together they love so much to tell the story of birthin' their babies, each tryin' to be the one who'd hurt the worst, who'd labored the longest.

"In that terrible heat, Siobhan sweated through the back of her summer dress and had Papa run her home to change. She had to come back in her house dress, because that was the only other dress she had except her Sunday one, but folks understood. The sad thing was the heat never let up and soon her dress was soaked again.

"And there were other excitements. Late in the afternoon, I noticed Opal Lometa and Josie Mendoza squatting and poking with a stick into a hole on the side wall of the church. I wondered what could have caught their attention. I watched as they grabbed thin branches from a pecan sapling and then shoved them into the hole and then quickly backed away. Then I remembered that there used to be a big old bumblebee nest down there that scared us so's we never went 'round there. It seemed there were always bees buzzing lazily around that hole, but that day there were none. Maybe it was too hot outside for them.

'Opal Lometa!' I called out. 'You better get away from there. There's bees in there.'

'I don't see any,' Opal called back. 'Do you see any bees, Josie?'

"Just then, Josie backed away and turned toward me. Her eyes were round with fright and her mouth formed a perfect O. 'There is!' she cried. 'And they're comin' out!'

"Before Opal understood what was happenin' and before Josie could get her feet movin' to run away, out they come in a snarlin' black and yeller swarm and fell upon the stupid girls.

"Now, a sting from a bumble bee hurts like hell, but Mrs. McMillen had brought some baking soda, just in case, so she made a paste with vinegar and doctored 'em."

'I tried to warn 'em,' I said to whoever cared to listen. 'I tried, but it was too late. The darn fools.' I felt pretty smug.

'Tiny Alice McGloin,' said Evie McMillen. 'Watch your tongue and don't be cruel.'

"Oh, there was much screaming and crying, but the mothers calmed them down and sent them to lie down in the Cawthorne's wagon under a big willow. Then Pettus Goodman came running around from the side of the church calling, 'He fell right out! He fell right out of that big live oak and I think his arm is broke!'

"The men turned from their beer drinkin' and a few of 'em took off after Pettus. Next thing I knew, Warren Brisbane—that was Cora Lea's daddy—came back around with Petey Hemphill in his arms. Petey was crying something awful.

'McGloin,' Brisbane said to Papa. 'Get my Cadillac and we'll lay him in the back and get him to the hospital.'

"Papa raced to get the car and the two of them drove off to Burnet. Pettus and some of the other boys called after them that Petey was such a baby because he cried. I wanted to tell them a thing or two, but didn't because I knew they didn't care what I thought.

"I guess you can't get a big group that large together without a couple of injuries or someone falling sick. One or two of the men drank too much Lone Star, and two of the Goodman boys, all pale with red hair and freckles, got sunburned something terrible. I was fair and freckled, too, so I wore a sun hat all day long.

"We stayed 'til the sky was full dark. Henry Bursen had made sparklers out of steel wool on wire, and there were noise makers and fireworks, beautiful against the night sky, and only a couple of children burned their fingers. All in all, it was a glorious celebration of our freedom. A memorable night."

"Sounds like it." I'm chuckling. "I'm glad you thought of that story. It's fun to share these remembrances. You're a gifted storyteller."

She sighs and straightens the lap of her skirt with slow hands.

"Well, I think that's about all my old brain can take for the moment. You wanna freshen your drink?"

"I do, but Alice, I don't want to exhaust you. Shall we move inside where it's cooler?"

"I 'spose I am just a wee bit tired, though this doesn't seem right just me talking about me. There's nothing people like better than doing just that, you know. I read in the *Reader's Digest* that the best way to put people at their ease and to get to know them is to ask them questions about themselves. You're a wily young thing, Bert. You're going to know everythin' about me. But I'd like to know more about you. Why don't you tell me somethin' about you?"

I shake my head. "No, no. I'm here for your stories, not mine. Have you got one more? A short one maybe so you don't tire too much?"

"Yep. I'll tell you about when old Buddy Boy met his end. You ever seen a hog slaughtered?"

I swallowed. "No. I can't say that I have. Do I really want to hear about this?"

"It's a big part of farm life and somethin' I had to learn about as a child. It gave us food and all kinds of other things. We had this big old boar. I mean he was huge! I'd named him Buddy Boy. Don't know why. It just seemed to fit. Papa always said we oughta not name the animals 'cause we'd get attached and get upset when they had to go. But I'd made friends with Buddy. One, because I liked him and two, because I wanted to prove I wasn't scared of a huge old hog.

"Well, one fall afternoon I heard Buddy Boy squealing, makin' an awful racket. I could tell somethin' was wrong and I reckoned I knew what it was. I ran around to the back yard to see Papa and Milt Burns, Angie's daddy, wrestling Buddy to the ground, which was no mean feat. Papa held him while Milt stuck that pig with a big hunting knife right into his backbone just behind his head. That stunned him but didn't kill him.

"They dragged Buddy by his hind legs over to the block and tackle. Race Minton was there, too, with his usual big chaw of tobacco in his jaw.

"'Papa, no! Please no!' I threw my arms around his legs. My eyes were full of tears. 'Not Buddy, please don't kill him.'

"He took my arms from around him and knelt down to look me in the eye. 'Too late, Tiny Alice. We need this hog for food this comin' winter. No way around it. Now, you see why I ask you not to make friends with the stock? This is what we raised the hog for. He's servin' his purpose.'

'But he's my friend.' I started to cry in earnest and couldn't stop myself.

"Using our block and tackle, Minton raised Buddy up by his hind legs and before I knew what had happened, Milt set a basin below him and sliced his throat acrost. I screamed.

"Papa raised his hands toward heaven and said all angry, 'Girl, get inside with your mother and you don't have to see nothin'. But I won't stand for these interruptions. I got work to do.'"

I clear my throat. "Shall I freshen our drinks, Alice? Do I want to hear the rest of this? It's pretty grim so far."

"You do, if you wanna know about our life on the farm. This was a big part of it. We killed our chickens, goats, turkeys. We needed the meat, like Papa said. There'd usually be babies comin' up to replace them that we kilt, or we'd sell some of the meat and buy more stock. It was what we did."

She thought for a moment, worrying her forehead with a bent finger. "I walked aways off, over to the cistern, and stood sobbin'. I didn't want to watch, but then my curiosity got the better of me. That black blood had gushed from

Buddy's neck, splatterin' Papa's work boots. I cried even harder, but couldn't turn away. The sick sweet smell that only got worse burned my nose.

"Once the blood had drained, they slid the basin out of the way. Papa took the knife and slit the hog all the way down the body and the guts fell out. They splatted on the ground and steamed and made the smell even worse. I gagged, which stopped me crying. I watched the rest of the butchering in silence. Soon, the hog quit lookin' like my Buddy and began to look like the hams and hocks hanging in the smoke house. By the time the meat was all cut up, the sun was setting and the men had started drinkin' beer. They laughed and talked like they were at a Sunday social and never mind the mess they'd made of Buddy."

Tiny Alice pauses here to catch her breath. "Now I think I've had enough, Bert, but I'll look forward to you comin' back again. I'll try to think up somethin' interestin' to tell you, and a mite milder than the Buddy story."

I press her hand with mine. "I'll take whatever you've got to offer. I appreciate you being a part of this study. I'm sure benefiting from it."

She walks me to the door and we say our goodbyes. For now.

Chapter Twenty

BERT

PATTI AND I HAVE A noon lunch date. We've met a couple of times for lunch or at the park with her kids. She's not the bow-head I thought she was, and I'm genuinely interested in knowing more about her.

She has Mother's Day Out two days a week where she drops off her two perfect kids at the church nursery so she can lunch and shop. She's about to pop with a third. I'm surprised that she has called and I wonder what prompted this lunch invitation. I meet her at *Antonia's*, Bomar's best Mexican food joint, run by the Esquibels, a brown, wizened couple in their seventies, and their eleven children and numerous grandchildren. The whole family works—Antonia and Pedro, Consuelo, Faustino and more. They serve buffet style and make the best salsa I've ever tasted.

I place my order with Javier at the counter, and then help myself to iced tea. I'm glad we came early because I find a table in the corner by a window. Patti's entrance turns several heads. She wears slim jeans with high heeled sandals and a tunic of muted rose over her bulging belly, and a gold and pink enameled necklace that is too big on her tiny body. As graceful as she is, she's begun to waddle slightly. Her lovely hair is artfully mussed. She is the epitome of Texas womanhood—perfectly made-up and coifed, nails immaculate, clothes color coordinated with her shoes and earrings and eye shadow. She has naturally blonde hair, creamy smooth skin and a pert nose—smashing.

I seldom see her upset, which is one of the qualities I find so amazing about both Patti and Tim, their equilibrium, so convinced that their God steers the ship of their lives with only kindness and their best interests in mind. They are serene. I wish I knew a God like that. More often than not, I feel that God is playing some darkly funny joke on me. The Axtells are both so damn even-tempered that I feel like a neurotic bundle of out-of-control nerves in their presence.

She adds two packets of sweetener to her tea.

I'm envious of her beauty and jealous that she is married to Pastor Tim. Whenever we're together, I feel invisible with my short hair and my medical scrubs and nurse shoes, or jeans and boots.

I tilt my head toward the counter as she rises from her chair and waddles up to order. As she approaches the table with tea and silverware, I note her flushed face, her teeth working the lipstick on her bottom lip. At our table, she sets down her purse and phone, takes her seat and, blinking back tears, attempts a smile. Something is wrong.

"Patti, what is it? What's the matter?"

"Oh, Bert, I don't know what to do. I'm not sure I can talk." She seems bewildered. "Without crying, I mean. I don't want to cry in front of all these people. She glances at the café crowd around us, disgusted by her show of emotion. "This is so embarrassing."

I take her hand. "Do you want to leave? We can take our food to the park where we'd have more privacy, or over to the clinic, even out to my place, if you'd feel more comfortable."

"No. I'll get a grip on myself. Just give me a minute." She smiles and digs into her petite Louis Vuitton handbag, pulls out a hankie—not a tissue, but a lace hankie. She blows her nose quietly, in an amazingly lady-like manner, smiles at me and says, "There. I'll be calm now. I promise." And she is once again the most poised person I know.

Rudi Esquibel calls my number. I retrieve my burrito plate and grab a bowl of salsa and some fresh jalapenos from the buffet. When I return, tears are streaming down Patti's perfect face again, and I know it's not from jalapenos. How I wish I could do that—cry without yowling. Patti has it down. I think lots of women here pattern themselves after Jacqueline Kennedy in Dallas, 1963: poise and grace in the face of the most horrid realities. Patti would make Jackie proud.

I set down my lunch and again take her hand. "What's going on? Talk to me."

"Bert, have you ever been insanely in love?"

The passion in her voice embarrasses me. "Uh, no, I don't believe I have. That is—maybe not until recently."

"You know that next to the Lord, Tim and the kids, of course, are the center of my life. Loving and caring for them is what gives my life meaning, next to serving the Lord, of course."

"Lose the disclaimers, Patti. I know how strong your faith is. Okay, so you love Tim madly and the kids insanely and that's making you cry?"

"Tim is the dearest, kindest, wisest, most devout man I've ever met."

"Yes, and he's also a hunk."

She sobs loudly, not daintily this time, into her napkin. A couple at the table next to us turns to stare.

"Aw, Patti, come on. I'm sorry. What's going on? Talk to me."

From somewhere deep inside, she lashes her crippled soul to some anchor, wipes her eyes without disturbing one iota of mascara, sits up straight and resumes complete control of herself. Very Jackie-esque. All that is missing is the pink pill-box hat.

"I'm sorry," she says with great dignity. "Forgive me."

"We should've gone over to the park." I can't think of anything else to say.

Patti's number is called, and I go for her food, nod to Frosty and say hi to Isabela. When I return, Patti has regained some composure and we dig into our greasy, cheesy meals (Chick would be appalled) and I wait for her to enlighten me. She stabs at her *chile relleno.*

"Tim's having an affair. I just know it."

I drop my fork in my frijoles. "You can't be serious! What on earth gives you that idea?"

"I'm sure of it, Bert. I just don't know who it is, yet, or if—if it's even only one woman." She grips her fork and shoves it repeatedly into her chili, making sort of a brown, green, and red mush. The tears begin again.

"Tell me why you think your husband, possibly the holiest man either of us know, is screwing around."

"Can I speak candidly?"

I nod.

"We have, um, such great sex, so sweet and romantic. He's a wonderful lover."

I add more salsa to my beans. I don't want to hear about their sex life.

"Of course, I don't have anyone else to compare him to, you know, but..."

"So, he's a wonderful lover," I prompt her. "Yes, yes. Go ahead."

"He's just not interested anymore. Hasn't been for months. So many nights working late, the head of so many committees. He visits shut-ins. What if it's one of his shut-ins? Oh, Lord, help me."

"Aren't they terribly old or sick, the people he visits?"

Her voice takes on an edge. "I don't know who he visits, do I? I mean, he's rarely home before ten. I go to bed alone every night. I bathe the children and read them stories. I tuck them in and have them say their prayers, calm their fears, soothe them when they have an upset or a bad dream. He's never there! I'm raising our children alone, and then when he does get home and climbs in beside me, it's too late or he's too tired. He doesn't want to have relations and he definitely doesn't want to talk. I'm sure he's seeing someone."

"Why don't you just ask him?" I smear butter on a corn tortilla. "The two of you seem to communicate well. My God, Patti, he's a marriage counselor! Wouldn't that be the best way to straighten this out? Talk to him."

"No. I can't do that." She dabs her moist nose with her paper napkin. "I've thought about it, but it's not right. See, if he's innocent, what would he think of me for suspecting? He'd never trust me after that. It would ruin our relationship."

"Sounds like it's pretty ruined already. How could it be worse? Look how upset you are. Even if he's guilty as charged he wouldn't want you to feel miserable like this."

She takes a noisy gulp of air and tosses her fork onto her uneaten lunch. "I can't sleep. Can't eat. I'm losing weight, Bert, and I can't afford to. It's not good for the baby and I feel so small, it's like I'm not here anymore. He doesn't see me when he looks at me and he never touches me anymore." She begins to boohoo again.

I'm at a loss. I don't know what to say. I don't know how to reassure her. It is beyond my imagination that Tim would ever have sex with anyone but his perfect wife, never mind my fantasies to the contrary. I believe him to be a paragon of virtue, a truly moral man. I think maybe Patti has slipped a cog somewhere and is imagining all this.

"Patti, have you considered seeing a counselor?"

"Whom could I see?" she pleads. "I'm the minister's wife! Everyone in town admires Tim and many have counseled with him. He knows their secrets and comforts them in all sorts of trials, but maybe he's got some secrets of his own. Still, I can't disillusion anyone. If I went to a counselor, it would get out and spread all over town in a matter of minutes. I can't humiliate Tim like that."

"See someone in Austin. Austin's crawling with shrinks."

"Yes, I know, but..." She falls silent.

"So, what are you going to do?"

I don't hear her answer because I'm wondering why she chose to confide in me. On the one hand, it feels good to think I am a close confidant. On the other, I am certain there is little I can do to help, and she knows I never say the right things at the right times. I don't share her faith, so any response I might make would not be from what she considers a Christian point of view.

Apparently, she reads my mind then, because she says, "I just need to unload on someone, Bert. I don't expect you to fix anything. I probably won't do anything at all but wait and see what happens. I just had to talk to someone, to say it out loud, and I can't do that with anyone from church."

I nod my head as if I understand. I don't. If Kris were alive, damn it, I would call her immediately and drop this little bomb on her. We had such ecstasy over Tim in our collective minds, and I'm feeling somewhat betrayed that he's chosen neither of us for his clandestine affair.

"Patti, who on earth could it be?"

"Anyone from church. Anyone! He counsels members of the congregation so that he's closed up in his office for hours a day. No one would dream of interrupting him during a session. I have suspicions about a couple of women who seem to hang around too much. It's as if they invent reasons to talk to him and they constantly offer to volunteer in the office."

"And who would that be?"

"There's Minette Deauville. She's like his volunteer extraordinaire, at the office all the time, answering the phones, helping fold programs. She could go into his office and close the door and no one would be the wiser."

Minette is the wife of Dennis the dentist and definitely a looker and more worldly than Patti.

"Then there is Karen Larsen."

I know Karen as a divorcee with an eye out for another husband, but is she the type to get involved with a married man?

"Patti, I'm sorry, but I think this is madness. I don't believe Tim is unfaithful to you, but I respect your right to suspect him, and I'm touched that you chose to confide in me. I will do some snooping and see what, if anything, I can find out."

As we finish our meals. I tell her to call me any time she needs to talk. She and Tim have helped me through some difficult times, like when Chick visited their church and began a debate with Tim during the sermon, or when Rick Loughlin and Kristin got together. I owe her.

I strap on my fanny pack. She picks up her Louis Vuitton, and we walk to our cars. In the parking lot. More hugs. She looks just as burdened as she did when she arrived and I feel terrible for her. I am not the most empathetic person and I have no answers for anyone. Hell, I've no answers to my own questions. I think that I must talk to Tim about this. If Patti won't confront him, then I will. I just need to get a grip on my own feelings. Shit.

Back at the clinic I make my way through the sea of now familiar women who protest, several that I know, feeding their children dried fruits and juice from boxes, some with babies at their breasts. Chick isn't present yet, but I see Tim talking to some of his flock. My stomach burns at the sight of him, but for now I ignore him and go in the front of the clinic. Sharon is at her work station.

"Hey, Sharon. How're things?"

"Things are." She wipes down the counter with a disinfectant wipe.

"I see our friendly neighborhood cretins are back. At least there aren't too many of them."

"Yeah, they started gathering at noon. That Reverend Axtell brought 'em over."

"Of course."

"How can you stay friends with Axtell and his wife? Y'all are pretty close, aren't you? They're such rabid right-to-lifers."

"Got to know them through Kris. They're just fighting for what they believe in. Last time I checked, that right is still protected in this country and even in our fair state. We disagree philosophically, agree on some things spiritual, but we try not to let our differences tarnish our friendship. They're good people." *I think.*

I head to the break room where I can smell old coffee burning. I rinse out the old and fill a clean pot with water and put in the filter and grounds, push the button to start the drip. I get my mug from the dishwasher. Sharon comes in. "Bert, there's a call for you. A Miss Emily Justice? You know who she is?"

"No idea whatsoever."

"Well, she sounds like she's got a cob up her butt. You want to take it?"

"Just tell it like it is, Sharon," I say, using one of Chick's favorite expressions. "I'll take it." I enjoy Sharon's bluntness. She keeps things sarcastic and funny around the office.

Sharon returns to the front and puts the call through. A receptionist on the other end informs me that this is the Marilyn Beckwith Middle School and I'm to hold for Principal Emily Justice. It must be about Kelly. What is going on?

Emily Justice indeed sounds tense and cranky as she informs me that Kelly has had an "episode." When I press for a definition of the term, I'm told she has argued with her Combined Mathematics teacher, refused to leave the classroom when she was ordered to the principal's office, and had to be carried bodily down the halls, kicking and screaming obscenities. She now waits in the school nurse's office.

I am not happy. What am I expected to do about this? I have patients to see. I tell the principal I will be there in thirty minutes, trying not to yell at her. Then I hang up, clench my teeth, count to ten and then..." Oh what the hell." I heave the telephone across the coffee room and scream, "I don't want to do this!"

I calm myself, wash my hands, and go in to see Sylvia Sanchez. Sylvia's a new mother, her baby girl born two days before, in for her first post-partum check. The exam tells me that her bleeding is under control, no swelling or tears. This is her fifth baby, so she knows how to do it. I check her nipples for crustiness or hardening.

"How's the breast feeding going?"

"Fine as always." She smiles. "I always have lots of milk."

"That's what we want to hear." I pat her on the shoulder. "Your blood test shows that you're pretty anemic this time. I think we'll schedule you for an iron infusion. Okay?"

She nods. "Is that why I feel so damned tired? I don't remember this with any of my other kids."

I place my hand on hers. "Could be. We'll take care of it and have you feeling great soon. What did you name your daughter?"

"Farrah. You know the others all have 'F' names: Frankie, Fred, and Faith. Frankie and Fred were named by their father. I picked Felicia, Frances, Faith."

"That's great." We shake hands. "Rory will come get you and walk you out and Sharon will set your next appointment."

I leave the exam room, thinking of Kelly and Miz Justice. What am I walking into, I wonder. At the front I tell Sharon, "Please order some iron supplements for Sylvia Sanchez."

What is this thing with Kelly? I remember a couple of times when she just went off on Kris and had to miss school a couple of days, but Kris didn't go into detail when she mentioned it. My stomach clenches, and I think again of my conversation with Principal Justice. And then I'm off to Kelly's school to handle God only knows what.

Chapter Twenty-One

BERT

I TURN INTO THE SCHOOL PARKING lot, skid into a slot, turn off the ignition, soothe myself with ten deep breaths, and walk inside.

Ms. Emily Justice is almost six feet tall. She wears an orange and green knit jacket over an olive knit skirt *a la* 1970s, and I get the impression she thinks she's chic. Her perky, Doris Day hair is all wrong for her face, and I dislike her before she ever utters a word. She moves with great confidence to shake my hand, towering over me, and offers me a seat in a hard, straight-backed wooden chair in front of her huge, government-issue metal desk.

"Where's Kelly?" The words fly out like an accusation, and I realize to my surprise that I am on Kelly's side in this, though I still don't want to deal with it.

"Kelly is lying down in the nurse's office, but I wish to have a few words with you before I take you to see her." Ms. Justice sits stiff and straight in her chair, hands clasped together in the exact center of her exceptionally tidy desk. "Are you aware, Ms. Lando, of the emotional problems Kelly's experienced over the last year or so?"

I shake my head. "Kelly was sort of left on my doorstep. No note, no instructions. I didn't even get a basket or blanket out of the deal. What kind of problems are we talking about?"

She arches a thick eyebrow. "She was in our Personal Expression Group last year, at her mother's request, a group under our school counselor, Evelyn Blaylock." Justice clears her throat. "Kelly has failed to make friends at school, keeps to herself. Her grades have fallen severely this year and she is barely passing in some subjects. She has had a few of these episodes, tantrums really, where she becomes impossible to deal with, dangerous even. Our recommendation is that she be seen by a professional for a psychiatric evaluation."

As she drones, I wonder several things. How dangerous can a skinny thirteen-year-old be? My busted lip not withstanding. *Why am I unaware of the problems my best friend had with her only child?* Kristin never mentioned any of this. *Why do I have no personal knowledge of this alleged behavior?* I mean, Kelly is frequently angry and often rude, but I've never seen her throw a tantrum, if that's what this is. There was the meltdown at my place the other day, but I've never seen Kris carry her anywhere kicking and screaming. *And what the hell do they expect from a kid whose mother just died? They expect maybe Marcia Brady?* I swallow hard.

"Kelly's mother just died." I state the obvious. "Suddenly. As I am sure you know. Don't you think that could at least partially account for some negative behavior? Ms. Justice, I'm not going to have Kelly with me much longer. I'm refusing permanent guardianship. I think."

Her lips pucker like she's sucked a lemon, but she says nothing.

"It's possible," I go on, "that she'll end up in foster care. I don't know, really. I'd hate that, but we don't have many options. One way to handle the situaion would be to let Child Protective Services take over."

Now she spoke up. "Kelly Ames is a troubled child, Ms. Lando. Her mother worked closely with our school counselor, Miss Blaylock. We were under the impression that Kelly is living with you and you are responsible for her. Perhaps you should talk with Miss Blaylock, who believes that Kelly has a conduct disorder. Miss Blaylock and I agree she should see a psychiatrist for an evaluation." She digs in her desk drawer. "Here is Evelyn's card. You can call and make an appointment. Now, if you'll follow me, we'll get Kelly. I'd like you to take her home now. She may return to classes tomorrow, if she feels like it. For now, we'll take no disciplinary action."

I take the card. "Ms. Justice, I think I'll just keep Kelly home from school for a while. She needs time to accept her mother's death, and I think I may have let her return to school too soon. I'll take her off your hands for a time."

I follow her ramrod-straight back down a staircase and three narrow hallways to a small windowless cinder block room on the lower level. I wonder how the kids ever find their way through this maze of stairs and hallways.

Kelly is curled up like a cat at one end of a vinyl cot, a UT Longhorns stadium blanket wrapped around her legs. She hugs herself tightly, rocking her body like autistic children I've seen in made-for-TV movies. Her gaze skitters from one corner of the room to the other, lights on me for an instant without recognition, and then scurries away. My heart lurches at the sight of her.

I sit beside her and say her name. She looks at me and, as recognition slowly dawns, she throws her arms around me, buries her head in my chest, trembling violently. "Get me outta here," she says in a small voice. "Please."

Ms. Emily Justice turns and leaves us. "She probably needs some sleep," says the nurse.

I disagree. I think Kelly looks like she could use some valium or a shot of Southern Comfort, thoughts I will not act upon.

I wrap the blanket around her shaking shoulders, assuring the nurse I'll return it sometime, though I have no intention of actually doing so, and lead the silent child through the halls and out to the car. As I drive home, her teeth chatter audibly. I decide maybe I'll see about a psychiatrist after all. I'll also talk to Chick and Pirate, and maybe Grady—get their ideas on the subject.

Once home, Kelly goes straight to bed in the spare room (I still cannot refer to it as *her* room), and falls soundly asleep. I decide to give Grady a call. Maybe I'll check with Reverend Tim and his perfect wife Patti as well.

Egads, what has my life become—death, parenthood, and legal shit? I'm a new mother to a neurotic teenager and I may be in love for the first time. What's next? Wait, I'm in love? Am I calling Grady to discuss Kelly or so that I can see him again? Who said anything about love? We're just dating—right?

When I call, he picks up on the first ring. "Bert? Is that you? It's you. Of course. I have Caller ID. What's up?"

He sounds thrilled that I've called. Maybe he's been wondering about love, too? Maybe. Probably?

"I want to bounce something off you." I tell him about the uproar with Kelly at school and ask if we can get together to talk about it. I want his opinion. He says of course and we make a date.

I do some weeding in the garden, then shower and climb into bed without supper. I'm bone tired and I doze off. The baby-dropping dream begins again. I've had the dream several times since Kris died. I don't know how long I've been asleep, but I wake in the dark to find Kelly standing over me. "Can I get in with you?" she whispers.

She sounds, again, like a small child, she with the silver charms on her face. I rub my eyes, toss back the old quilt and fluff a pillow for her. She climbs in, shaking, careful to stay on her half of the bed. No touchy-feely stuff with this kid, at least not when she's lucid. But, when is she lucid? A three-quarter moon floats beyond the window behind her, soft light but distant, and without connection. A cool silver glow illuminates my side of the room, but shadows Kelly's face.

"How're you doing, kiddo?"

"I'm okay. And don't call me kiddo." She pulls her knees up under her chin.

"Want to talk about what happened today?"

"Why don't you tell me? I don't remember much." She picks at a loose thread on the quilt, and I ask what she means. "I remember talking back to Miss Lobato, who totally pisses me off. I don't remember much after that, until you were there. Did I do anything stupid?"

"I think you just got real mad." Nervousness buzzes in my right ear and I scratch it absentmindedly.

I describe her escalating rage, her being wrestled to the nurse's office, the call to me, my bringing her home. I tell myself to refrain from judgment, at the same time wondering how she can forget such behavior. "And you've slept since we got here this afternoon."

"Did you stay here with me?"

"Sure. We came home and I worked in the garden while you slept. Are you hungry?"

She shakes her head, turns and gazes up at the moon. I can see her face now and the deep circles that ring her young eyes. Sleep has not been all that restorative.

"Do you like herbal tea?" I try to sound bright, perky. "I have several different kinds."

"Like what kinds?" She still won't look at me.

"I've got one that's real spicy and sweet with cinnamon. Would you like that?"

She shrugs, her gaze still out in the heavens somewhere. I get up and put the kettle on, put a bag of Cinnamon Spirit in each of two porcelain cups and then crawl back in beside her.

"Kelly, what do you need? Like, from me? I honestly don't know. Can you tell me in words what I can do to make things better for you?"

She looks at me with the saddest expression, one entirely too full of despair for such a youngster. Maybe I'm wrong about her keeping her distance. Maybe she isn't so stoic. Maybe she feels things much more deeply than even I do, God help her.

I remember Chick oncc trying to describe to me her own quixotic temperament. I was Kelly's age when Chick spent six weeks in a psychiatric hospital for depression. She says the worst part of depression is that you feel it will never go away—you'll feel that desperate until you die—like a long narrow tunnel with nothing but darkness at the end. Life is a crushing weight. She describes a sorrow, an emotional suffering, darker and larger than anything I'd ever imagined. She said she considered her vast heart and emotions both a gift and a curse.

On one hand, Chick is a talented artist, a deeply compassionate person. On the other, she forever teeters on some razor edge that most of us never even approach. A mixed blessing, that kind of heart, in which life may be experienced as sweeter, richer, but wounds are deeper, nerves more raw, and everything enhanced to a giddy extreme.

Kris was steady and stoic. Maybe Kelly is put together more like Chick, even more so than I.

"Do you think I'm going crazy?" Resignation oozes from her question.

"No, of course not. But, hell, you're a teenager, which means you're naturally a bit more intense than the rest of us. You've had a rough time. The death of a parent is not an easy thing to accept or understand."

"You still have both your parents."

An accusation. I feel instantly guilty. I change the subject. "The, uh, principal at your school said your mom had you working with some counselor?"

She nods again. The kid doesn't have many words, or simply isn't inclined to use them. No wonder she looks so tired and strung out.

"What was it like working with the counselor?"

A sigh. "Stupid."

The kettle whistles from the kitchen and I make tea and bring it into the bedroom on a bamboo tray. When I am settled back in bed, she stares into the liquid red-brown tea.

"You didn't like Ms. Blaylock?" I try again.

"Stupid." She shrugs again. We're getting nowhere.

How can I help her, if she can't articulate her needs? If she hates Ms. Blaylock, wouldn't she be likely to hate a psychiatrist too? I decide not to pussy-foot around. "Do you want me to take you to a psychiatrist?"

"See!" Her eyes gleam, two laser points in the moonlit room. "You do think I'm crazy."

"Not crazy, Kelly, but hurt. Wounded a little. Bruised? Banged up, in a way? That's what psychiatrists do—heal the wounds. They help you put the pieces back together after something like this happens."

The shrug again. The gesture annoys me, since it seems to imply either utter boredom or total indifference. At last, the tea seems to soothe her and she falls asleep. I sip my tea and watch her sleep and let my mind run through the events of the day. I wonder if her emotional issues could come from her father, since Kris seemed so stable. Perhaps so. I finish my tea and fall asleep only to dream the baby-dropping dream again. This time I catch the baby and have no idea what to do with it. I look up for the big father-god and he's not even there anymore. I'm on my own.

Chapter Twenty-Two

BERT AND ALICE

I'VE ASKED CHICK OVER TO stay with Kelly, who is still exhausted and withdrawn after her episode at school. I'm shaken as well, but am eager to meet with Alice again.

Driving out to Alice's, thinking of the remarkable stories she's told, I realize how little tragedy has touched my life. I grew up with loving parents. We make certain allowances for each other's differences. I'm sometimes crosswise with Chick, but I've never doubted her love. I've enjoyed a few close friends, been relatively healthy, and I'm a success in my chosen field. Until now, I've been very fortunate. I whisper a quiet "thank you"—to God? And then I turn my thoughts to today's visit with Alice. What tales will she tell today?

We decide to picnic under the flowering plum, though it's too late for it to flower. Alice slips on a light sweater. I'm fine in my scrubs. We carry a thermos of hot sweet tea, a large plastic butter tub of chocolate chip cookies and a handmade quilt to spread on the ground. Alice slowly lowers her tiny frame onto an old camp chair. I take a seat on the quilt.

"Alice, can I make a request?"

"Sure, anything. I hope you know that."

"I loved the story of you and Lute. It was rich and told me so much about you. I wonder if the two of you had a wedding and what it was like."

She unscrews the top of the old plaid thermos, nodding her head, and pours tea into the china cups she's carefully packed in linen napkins in the old basket. She hands a cup to me and lifts her own cup to her lips.

"Eventually Papa give permission for us to marry, and Lute and I courted only a few weeks. Papa decided he liked Lute, and they'd sometimes sit on the front porch at dusk and share a smoke or a beer. Siobhan was still sour, as always, and Lute worked at winnin' her approval, and to coax a smile from her.

"When Papa died some years later, he left the house and the whole farm to Lute and me. My brothers Bobby and Jamie had gone off to live their own lives and sister Ginny had married Curt Wood. We worked the farm through the Depression and brought it back round. We never produced as much as Papa did when the farm was at its best, but we cared for it until the small farmers were pushed out, and then we sold all but these five acres I live on now.

"You know, Fallon Springs folks pull together when things get tough and that was doubly true after the banks failed and slowly, one by one, we saw the local farms go. We were no different. We had acres lying fallow, some burnt by the sun and just plain blowing away. But we kept our farm. We had to slaughter our best hog and a calf to get through the winter and we wanted to share that meat, since so many of our neighbors were hungry. The men who didn't farm lost their jobs, but Lute kept wrangling for Mr. Brisbane as if nothing had changed, and, shortly after we married, he started filling in part time at the Sheriff's Department.

"We were married right here in this little house. Outside actually."

She peered through the willow branches to a place on the horizon and lost herself in the memory.

Crocuses were up and the redbuds glowed bright pink. Every tree the elm, oak, thc willow—shone a different shade of green. Granny Fitzpatrick stepped outside onto the porch and called out.

'Tiny Alice! Come on in now and wash up. I want to work on your weddin' dress.'

"I slid out of the tree swing in the side yard where I'd sat since breakfast, my thoughts on Lute and all that marriage could mean. The bible said we'd become one flesh, and face the world together for the rest of our lives. This was my belief and I clung to it, cherished it.

"I hurried into the house. In the kitchen, I washed my hands and face, and dried quickly with a cup towel. Granny helped me pull the white lacy dress over my head. She had me stand on a chair so she wouldn't have to go down on her knees much to pin up the hem.

'My achy old knees won't do much crouchin' these days, Tiny Alice. Now you need ta' hold mighty still while I do this, hon. Straight back, and let your arms hang relaxed at your sides.'

"She placed several straight pins between her lips and talked through them as she began to turn up the hem, measuring against where the delicate cloth fell against my ankles.

'We're awful lucky the friends we have. Nobody has much these days but everbody pitched in for this dress. Miz Brisbane organized all the mothers and grandmothers to pull ribbon and lace trim off of old dresses and linens. Miz McMillen donated the heirloom tablecloth that's most of this dress. Miz Mendoza had left-over lace from Letitia's first communion outfit and her *quinceañera* dress.'

"I shook one leg. 'My foots goin' to sleep. Can I move a little?' Granny stood back and nodded. 'My dress is just plain pretty, Granny. I love these old lace hankies you sewed at the neck and the velvet and lace trim. Has Siobhan done anything to help?'

'Be still now," demanded Granny. "She's been bakin'—sweetbreads and pies. I guess that's her contribution.'

"The morning of the weddin' dawned cool and a breeze whispered across the front yard. But by nine o'clock, when folks began to decorate outside, the pleasant temperature was replaced by humid heat. Sadie Winnot, Ebb Daughtery's lady friend, oversaw the drapin' of gingham and net bunting around the front porch and down the rail by the steps.

"Granny and Evie McMillen set a door on wooden saw horses to make a table, and covered it with one of Miz McMillen's lace tablecloths. Fern Jackson brought a milk pitcher full of fresh wildflowers.

"The service was planned for early in the day, before the heavy heat was full on, but most of the helpers were already sweating.

"Cora Lea arrived, lookin' elegant in a fashionable suit from Scarbrough's in Austin. She and I ducked into the house to do up my hair. Cora swept up my long auburn hair and pinned it in place on top of my head. She fixed a spray of Queen Anne's lace into one of them fat curls. I was tickled with how it looked.

"Standing at the mirror I examined myself. 'I look right nice, don't I, Cora Lea?'

'Why, Alice, you look gorgeous! Lute's gonna swoon when he sees you.'

"Arm-in-arm we left the bedroom, by we were told to stay inside until the ceremony so Lute wouldn't see me before. I was a nervous nelly, but we didn't have to wait much longer.

"Father Socha called through the screened door. 'Alice, you can come on out now.'

"The priest took his place beneath the weeping willow in the side yard. Lute stood before him with his brother Pietr as a witness. Granny sat on the porch, zither on her lap, and played the old hymn, *I'll Abide*. Cora Lea, came through the door and down the porch steps to take her place, and I followed with a posy of daisies in my hands.

"Lute sucked in a gasp when he saw me, and fixed his blue eyes on me. I hoped he was thinking what a lucky man he was.

"Me and Lute knelt on a low bench Papa had fashioned, covered with a colorful afghan. Father Socha read the rites as sweet Granny played another hymn. Papa gave me away as Siobhan stood watching. And when all the seriousness was over, me and Lute, both with tears in our eyes, moved off to the small crowd of friends who'd come to celebrate.

"Granny switched tempo from hymns to dance tunes, playing *Don't Sit Under the Apple Tree,* and *T for Texas.* Fern fixed a plate for her husband, Jimmy Albert, and Juan Gonzalez stood at the back of the crowd, with Beau Stinson and Petey Hemphill, smokin' cigarettes and lookin' tough. Well, Petey couldn'ta looked tough no matter how he tried. He just kept grinnin' his big old toothy smile the whole time. Mary-Jon served iced tea to Pettus Goodman. Leticia Mendoza moved into the shade of the weepin' willow to nurse her newest baby, Gloria, and Blackie O'Connor stepped around the corner to the back of the house to sample some of Papa's liquor. I was deeply gratified to be surrounded by all my friends and those I loved the most. And I was at last with my Lutheran. It was a grand day.

Alice shakes her head to return across time to look at me with a wistful smile. "My, I do love my memories. When you live alone, memories become some of your best friends."

I squeeze her hand. "I'm so glad your wedding was such

a lovely, happy occasion. And your marriage was a strong one. I just don't see people staying together much anymore. Though, my parents have been married forever it seems."

"I'll tell you, Bert, no matter that I felt good about my looks and that I had all my loved ones around me, I still shook. My knees felt weak and knocked together. Truly! And when we took the Holy Eucharist, my hands shook something awful. I went to put Lute's wedding band on him and almost couldn't do it, I was shaking so bad. He finally took my hand in his big, steady one and guided me to slip the ring on his finger. We had no money for the rings, so Lute made ours by curling horseshoe nails to fit our fingers! Not fine or precious metal, but one of a kind, like my Lute. He didn't shake one bit. That man was forever steady. He stood so tall and grand and rock solid that I could hide in his tall shadow and feel safe.

"So, we had a "make-do" wedding, eating greens and cornbread and molasses cookies. Petey Hemphill's mother made lemonade and Mrs. Rainwater made iced tea. Siobhan made hot coffee and set out some bread 'n butter pickles she'd made the summer before.

"Papa walked me up to Lute and give me away. Siobhan sat with the guests, her jaw set. She gave me a brief hug afterwards and whispered, "You be a good wife to your man, ya' hear?" and shook Lute's hand. Lute glanced over at me and shook his head. He and everyone else knew what Siobhan was like. They accepted her ways and ignored her when she got mean.

"Granny had to talk to me about the birds and the bees, and she was so old she could hardly remember. Oh, that was a frightful embarrassment to us both, but it had to be done so I knew how to be a right and good wife to my Lute.

"We didn't have a shivaree or honeymoon. Granny moved into the house with my folks, and Lute 'n me took the little cabin out back. It was a good home to us for many years, until our family at last began to grow. When Papa and Granny died, we took over the big house and Siobhan took the cabin.

I have real fond memories of that wedding. It mighta been poor, but it was grand."

Chapter Twenty-Three

BERT

At home after my visit with Alice, I straighten the kitchen and fret over what to prepare for dinner, and then I want to talk to Grady. There is something so quietly strong about him. Though he's bashful, he seems serene, wise. I sit at the table, calm my nervous stomach, take a deep breath, and call him. When he answers, his voice sends a shiver down my back.

"Hello? Bert?"

"Yes, it's me. Do you have time to talk?"

"Always have time for you, ma'am."

I love that old Texas charm. I share more concerns about Kelly. He's sympathetic and suggests we talk over dinner in Austin. I agree, but then I ask if he will take me earlier to meet with Vic Johnson, my dad's attorney friend who will represent me in the guardianship situation. Since I sound upset, he offers to drive out to pick me up.

"Are you thinking breakfast instead of dinner or both?" he teases. "Are you prepared to spend an entire day with me?"

I say that I am, so he braves the traffic on I-35 to drive

out and pick me up. We're still shy with each other. He greets me with a kiss on the cheek. In silence, we take the back roads to Austin through flat fields of varied greens, the checkerboard of cotton and corn fields that remind me of the pink and black tiles of the bathroom we had in Berkeley when I was a child. I fill him in on what I've learned from Kelly, surviving to the end of my narrative without shedding a tear, though I do pause a few times to breathe. He's patient and says nothing until I'm done.

"You're really all wound up about this, aren't you? I'm sorry this is so difficult, Bert."

"Lately, it hurts just to wake up in the morning." I scratch my head. "I need a sabbatical, a year in Timbuktu, or maybe a weekend in Galveston would do. Isn't it amazing how life can just disintegrate? Some other person, maybe even a person totally unknown to you, makes a decision that sends your life into a free fall and you're stuck. You're left to clean up the after-party detritus and you weren't even invited. There's no one else who's quite as impacted as you, because the party was held in your home, at your expense."

We stop at Denny's just south of Georgetown for a breakfast of what Chick calls fried fatty solids, and then Grady drops me at the attorney's office near the campus, saying he'll be back to retrieve me in about an hour.

I like Vic Johnson immediately. He's a wiry black sprite of a man with small, pointed ears—an elf, like the ones who make cookies. You can tell by the springy way he moves that he is in top physical shape, quick and responsive, the kind of fighter you'd put money on. I learn that he and Pirate met years ago doing Tai Chi in Pease Park, went for coffee afterward, and have been friends since. That was back when Pirate left *Cielo* occasionally. These days he stays pretty close to home.

Vic's office reeks of cigars and is decorated with trout and elk remains that would cause Chick to spike a fever.

"So, you are Pirate's Miso! How about that daddy of yours,

huh? Is he a character or what? One of my favorite people. He's told me a great deal about you, young lady, about how smart you are and all of your accomplishments. He's very proud of you, and I'm glad to get to meet you at last."

I nod, not in the frame of mind, particularly, to appreciate my father for praising me to someone I don't even know. I am here to dismiss myself from a complicated dilemma.

"Please call me Bert, Mr. Johnson."

"Bert?"

"Yes, Bert. Short for Roberta. I'm not Miso anymore."

"Okay, whatever you say, Bert. Vic. Call me Vic. Coffee?"

"No, thank you, I'd rather get down to business." He watches me intently for a few seconds.

"Your dad said you were like this, direct and to the point. He admires that in you. Funny, with Pirate for a dad I wouldn't expect you to be such a serious soul."

I try to sound chummy. "I'm sorry, Vic. I don't mean to be antisocial. I have a long day ahead of me."

I explain, I think concisely, all the crucial facts and my reasoning for not wanting guardianship of Kelly. Vic listens carefully, occasionally jotting a brief note on his yellow legal pad. When I finish my monologue, he picks up the phone.

"So, you don't want the guardianship?"

"Correct."

"You're sure about this?"

"I'm sure. Kris' attorney said I could file something to get me out of this."

"Sure. Decline to serve. The Court will probably meet in a couple of weeks and we can file then. They'll appoint a different guardian and you'll be off the hook. There is no relative who can take her?

"Just a depraved father who is also her uncle."

"I see. And does he want the child?"

"He's been gone all her life. It's not a possibility."

"Okie dokie. The child is staying with you now?"

"That's right. Temporarily."

"Good." He buzzes a clerk. "Katrina? Find out when Lorimar Court At Law will meet and let me know." He turns back to me. "So, Miso, we're all set."

"I prefer Bert, thank you. Will I have to go to court?"

"No. I'll file the Declination and attend the hearing, but you can come, if you want. The judge will confirm with me that you are declining and are aware of the finality of your declination."

For a moment, I look out his massive window at the dark green snake of the Colorado River winding its lazy way through the heart of the Capitol City. *Am I doing the right thing?*

"Is that the bat bridge down there?" I ask.

"Yep, that's the one," says Vic. "Have you ever seen them?

"No, just heard about it. Read about it."

"Quite a spectacle. Fargo's is a good place to have a drink and watch them. Usually packed like a rush hour bus, but the bats are worth it. And Fargo's bartender makes a mean margarita."

When I'm done, Grady picks me up as planned and we have lunch at Shady Grove, each enjoying a mammoth Shady Thing, the house cocktail. Huge live oaks shade us, cooling the sun-parched air. Then, heads spinning and hearts full of good food and conversation, we head to the new Blanton Museum which is still under construction. We walk through the few exhibits, and then later we check out the Umlauf Sculpture Garden. Truth be told—we're much more enthralled with each other than with the magnificent art surrounding us. Nevertheless, we saunter through the dark green, lavish foliage, surrounded by brilliant sculptures in bronze and marble—angels, saints and nudes, even a rhino. One piece strikes me to the heart, that of a mother and babe in marble, the mother with her face in her hand as if despairing of being able to care for her child. Later, we see another marble bust of a mother holding her child and her head is tossed back. She wears a serene expression, or maybe it's ecstasy, and I think I want to feel like *that* about Kelly. But how?

After the Umlauf, we do the State Capitol building and then wander down Congress Avenue. We stop in at the Elephant Room for perfect martinis and then we drive out to The Oasis for dinner.

As we're shown to our table, I look around at the high limestone cliff where we're perched. "God, we're so high," I say, ignoring the double *entendre*. "I could use a cup of coffee, if you don't mind. I've had more liquor today than in the last six months."

He laughs. "You're a lightweight." We ask the waitress for time to peruse the menu. We decide on burgers and iced tea. I explain about the special counseling group Kelly was in and how Kris had never mentioned any of this.

"The school's requested I find a psychiatrist for Kelly."

"I know an excellent psychologist," Grady says. "She's a prescribing clinical psychologist so she could recommend the proper medication, if it's needed at all. Dr. Angela Frederick with Falls Creek Psychological Associates. I saw her, actually, after my wife left. I'll give you her number."

"Yes, do. I'm starting to feel sorry for the kid, you know? Man, she doesn't have anyone at all in her life but me and her rotten father."

"But her father hasn't been in the picture for a long time. Right?" He reaches across the table and takes my hand, sending tiny electric sparks up my arm.

"He hasn't been around for her entire life, but as far as I know he's alive and could show up at any time and make claims. Though I don't know why he would. Poor kid. That would be the worst possible scenario."

"Didn't you say she wanted you to find her father?"

"She mentioned him as a preference over me, but we all basically ignored her. I mean . . . well, I guess I can tell you, Grady. Kris was raped by her brother and Kelly is the child from that."

"No criminal charges were filed?"

"Kris just wanted him to disappear, and so he did. You see why Kris and I would never want him to come close to her."

Grady whistles. We fall quiet. The waitress returns and Grady orders a pitcher of sangria.

"Bert, don't get mad when I say this, but do you think you would ever change your mind about the guardianship?"

My throat starts to close up. Not Grady, too. "You mean accept it? Raise Kelly as my own? No. No way. I'm not right for Kelly. You sound like my mother. Don't be my mother, Grady. The painful truth is that I don't know how to act when I'm with Kelly."

"Calm down. In my opinion, you would make an outstanding guardian for any child."

I turn away and look out at the startling vista, the steep, white cliffs down to Lake Travis, the sun hanging ripe and heavy above the glassine surface of the lake.

"This place is so beautiful."

Grady pours me a goblet of fruit-filled sangria.

"Thanks for bringing me out here." I take a sip of the sweet punch. "I've never been."

Grady begins to chatter, but I hardly hear him. My mind, assisted by night air and wine, makes a paradigm shift and I cease listening to him. The sun has gone now and the night is close. I watch the bright shadow of the moon slide across ebony water, dusted with the reflection of thousands of stars, glistening and winking.

"Like one of those punched tin lanterns you get at Mexican import shops," I say out loud.

"Hmmm?"

"Ooh, look! A shooting star. Did you see it?"

"I did. Have you been out there with the moon or here listening to my scintillating conversation?"

"What? Oh, sorry, but I did lose track. What were you saying?"

We finish the sangria and then have dinner and Grady orders coffee. Sitting, looking at each other, holding hands, we think our own thoughts. I try to ignore the charge I feel shooting from his hand to mine, up my arm and into my gut. Damn, he is a nice-looking man.

"Would you like to go downtown and listen to some music?" he asks. "Do you like blues?"

"Truth is," I tell him. "I don't know what kind of music I like any more. I grew up on 60s rock'n'roll, then I got interested in jazz, but I don't listen much anymore, and I know next to nothing about the blues."

"Ms. Roberta Miso Lando, please allow me to introduce you to the blues."

I am unaware of the ride downtown to Antone's. I cannot tell you what the club looks like, inside or out. I'm in a heady place of feelings and aromas: the skin behind his ear when I steal a kiss, the press of his thighs in a slow dance. I sort of "come to" in Grady's arms after many dances. We are both sweating and sipping cold Coronas with lime. I feel at peace for the first time in over a week, until someone at the bar sounds last call and I panic.

"Oh, shit, what time is it? Grady, we have to drive all the way back to Bomar!"

"One more dance, Miss Roberta. One last dance, then back to the real world."

"I was supposed to call the real world at midnight."

He doesn't wait for my permission, but leads me back to the dance floor. The tall, thin crooner who's been wailing all night is cranking up *When a Man Loves a Woman*, one of my favorites. But this singer's voice is thicker, richer, and sexier than Sledge, Jim Morrison or even Elvis.

I bury my nose in a moist, sweet-scented crevice of Grady's neck, and twirl my fingers in his hair, inhale the scent of him and grow aware of his hips, firm and solid and as warm as twilight's shoulder, pressing against mine. We fit. I forget to be impressed with singer or band. I forget Kelly and Chick and Pirate. I forget Patti and Tim Axtell and Kris and becoming a goddamn mother. I lose all awareness of anyone and anything except Grady Powell's arms around me and his breath in my hair. We are alone, he and I, amid the crowded shuffling in the dark. My head is spinning with his scent and the unintelligible words he pours into my ear. His breath, as hot as *Cielo* on summer afternoons, makes my stomach muscles jump. Soon there is no music, no singing, no bumping elbows or crunching feet. Soon there is only the heat of us and a huge, startling desire.

We walk up the street to the first hotel we come to. Grady signs us in and, as soon as the bolt chain is secured, we tear at our clothes, fall on the bed, and look and touch and smile and lick and treasure each other for most of the night. In the morning, when dawn peeks through the sheer drapes, all soft peach and tangerine light, we sit propped on pillows, sipping bad coffee, our feet tangled together.

"Miso?"

"Hmmm?"

"What is Miso? Why does your mother call you that?"

"Okay, here we go. My real name is Mystic Soul and, if that wasn't bad enough, they shortened it to Miso. There are thousands of kids from my generation walking around, hiding under names like Roberta, Gail, Jenny, whose real names are Sunray, Feather, Harmonica." I put my face next to his. "Does it matter? Do you think less of me?"

He kisses me, his tongue darting across my teeth, and I reel with the taste of him.

He laughs. "I won't hold it against you. I'll tell you my middle name. You're not allowed to laugh, though."

"Tell me. Tell me. What is it?"

"It's Mervin."

"Shut up! Grady Mervin Powell?"

"Bert, I said no laughing. We're sharing truths here."

I laugh until I almost wet the bed, but make it to the john

just in time. When I can stop laughing, I call Bomar and am thrilled that Pirate, and not Chick, answers the phone.

"Daddy?" I giggle stupidly. *When did I last call him Daddy? For that matter, when did I last giggle?* "We, uh, had a little too much to drink. Spent the night." More giggles.

"I thought so, when you didn't call," says Pirate, softly. I love the sound of my father's voice, so solid and soft at the same time, like Grady's chest.

"Kelly's just fine," Pirate says. "We're enjoying her. Miso, are you all right?"

"Hmmmm."

"Everything's groovy? Headed home?"

"Soon, Daddy. Real soon."

I hang up and turn my attention back to my lover and we continue our explorations.

Later, after breakfast and lots of coffee, Grady takes me to Dr. Frederick's office to see when I can meet with her about Kelly. I spend forty-five minutes in her office, explaining my situation to the Office Manager, Ms. Rita Thurgood. I fill out her forms and questionnaires, though I don't know answers to most of the questions. I can't remember Kelly's birth date, don't know her medical history. I don't know her childhood diseases, or her family medical history, with the exception of her grandmother's Alzheimer's. Hell, I don't know my own, and I don't know a great deal about what Ms. Rita calls "the nature of her complaint," only that the school called it a conduct disorder.

The doctor isn't in, so I am forced to continue being polite to Rita, who says, with much pride, that the doctor is at that moment testifying in a murder trial. Great. Rita is dithery with the drama of it all and quite proud of her employer's respected expertise. I can tell she finds me irritating and an unscheduled intrusion on her previously well-ordered day—sort of like how I feel about Kelly. I feel the same about Rita and she can tell, but I won't let up.

"Listen, Rita, I need to leave here with what I came for.

So, can you make me an appointment for Kelly to see Dr. Frederick?" She does.

When I am at last free of Ms. Rita Thurgood, it is eleven thirty and Grady drives me home. The traffic is horrendous and we spend a good hour sitting, as if for a portrait, on I-35 with a thousand other commuters. I disengage my hand from his and pull my cell phone out of my bag. I call Chick and Pirate to let them know we're on our way. They've spent most of the day swimming in the stock pond. Pirate is going to grill some eggplant this afternoon.

"And her skin, Miso!" Chick booms through the phone, "is the color of boiled lobster! Oh, child, she is so sunburned! She's stretched out on Pirate's chaise now, under the parachute, sipping lemonade and rubbing cocoa butter everywhere. I tried to put aloe on her, but she would have none of it. She's a doll, Miso. What a precocious child, surprisingly rational for an adolescent. We adore her!"

"Yeah, she's a peach, Chick." But rational? "Look, I made an appointment for her with a shrink."

"Don't come get her just yet. We are enjoying her so."

"You want her to stay longer?"

"Yes, yes. Why don't you and your young man go have a long lunch somewhere?

"Maybe we will grab some lunch." I look at Grady and he nods. "We'll find a place to grab a quick lunch and a couple of beers. and then Grady will drive me home. Okay?"

"Sounds good, darling. Are you where you can watch the bats?"

"Oh, I forgot about the bats."

"Fascinating creatures, bats. Nocturnal. And they have radar. Did you know? I feel somewhat akin to the ugly little specimens."

"Mother..."

"The radar, you know. I am somewhat psychic. I have a strong sensation that this man will disappoint you in a major way. Expectations will be dashed. Why, you're losing your head over the man, bestowing upon him all manner of saintly qualities. You and Kris practically deified him."

"Not now, Chick."

"I slept upside down for a while, back in the early seventies. Pirate bought me one of those gravitational frames where you hook your feet in the boots and..."

"Traffic's moving. Gotta go! See you later."

Once back in Austin, we stop at El Cabron for Tex-Mex and then drive to Zilker Park to wander hand-in-hand through the botanical gardens. In the rose garden, we come across an arched arbor covered with climbing Iceberg. We stand beneath the arbor and spend far too long looking into each other's eyes. Oh, we've got it bad. I'm already thinking of finding another hotel.

Chapter Twenty-Four

BERT

After the park, Grady drives us to Fargo's to watch the bats. We order drinks and grab a table by the window, sitting close to each other. Two *grande* margaritas later, the bats take flight and we ooh and ahh over the curtain of night that slips like smoke from the bridge shadows and takes wing into the twilight, and, on tequila's back, I soar with the little buggers and am saddened when it is over all too soon. Grady suggests a stroll along Lady Bird Lake.

"The fresh air will clear your head," he says.

"I hope not. I want to feel this way forever, but you must take me home now. Took off work today, and I should get back. But maybe one more day? Maybe I can take another day off to play. I can plead mental and psychological exhaustion. What do you think?"

He grins and squeezes my hands. So, I call work and leave a message that I need another day off. I rarely miss work, and it makes me uncomfortable as hell. Sharon will get the message, and she'll tell me that things are still slow because, yes, the demonstrators are still there. She doesn't think they'll ever go away, but urges me not to worry about it. She'll bring in one of the other nurses to see my patients. I call *Cielo* and Chick reassures me that, besides her bad sunburn, Kelly is happy, and yes, they would love to have her for another night.

I look at him. "I guess you're stuck with me for one more night, Dr. Powell."

"Oh, poor, poor me." He laughs and I lay my head on his shoulder. "How about my place? Let's stop there tonight."

His tiny house is all white stucco and rough oak beams, furnished in browns and golds. Masculine but warm and welcoming. So full of each other, we make a bee line for his bedroom.

Later, after more gentle, then frenzied lovemaking, I feel expansive and suddenly want to talk to this man who is such a good listener.

"You know," I begin, "as marvelous as these two nights have been, when we pick up Kelly at Cielo, I know that I have to get out of the car and look my parents in the eye and ignore their knowing looks and try to act like everything is the same as when I left two days ago. And it's not. You have made a definite impact, Dr. Grady Powell. And I know myself. I know that the overwhelming urge to instantly justify my actions, to ward off any disapproval...but maybe they won't disapprove. Hell, no! They'll probably cheer. This will at long last provide proof that I have a healthy sex drive, something I think they've doubted over the years."

"Seriously? They worry that you..."

"Yes, well, I spent almost all my time with Kris, and I never brought home any of the young men I dated, except for Rick, of course, whom they approved of, in spite of the fact that he's a cop. But the thing with Rick kind of faded. He took an intense liking to the beautiful and poised Kristin over short, pert Bert, and our relation changed back to just friends."

"That must have hurt."

"It did, though I've never given it much thought until

now. You're not only a good listener, Grady, you're gifted at getting people to tell their tales. I never talk about myself this much."

"Perhaps you should." He gathers me in his arms and kisses the top of my head. "So, Rick was the only serious relationship you've had?"

"I don't think I even considered it a serious relationship, just a friendship that tried to be something more. You know what I mean?"

"Maybe we can both learn from Tiny Alice Slezak. She's had a unique love story."

"Yes! Her story about Lute is crazy! Love at first sight, then apart for two years? And they waited for each other. She seems tough and sweet."

He kisses my right ear. "I think you're like her in that way."

When we fall asleep we are tangled in twisted and moist bed sheets.

On the hot, bright morning-after, riding through the countryside, Grady is a golden god with his hair blowing in the wind, his tanned arm resting on the open window. On our way back to Bomar, where all the challenging reality of my life waits, I try not to feel guilty about the last two days. I am, after all, a grown woman. I will not defend or rationalize, not even to my parents, although they will no doubt have plenty to say, or to ask. *Why am I even rationalizing now?*

I like Grady. I like Grady a lot. Last night I believe we became "us," and I like the sound of that, because it means I no longer must walk through my life alone. I'd thought I wanted it like that. Now, though, I can have a companion, an ally, and I like the way that feels. So, I refuse to regret two nights of passion and elation, no matter what crass innuendoes Pirate or Chick might make.

Grady interrupts my thoughts by running his broad, tanned hand across my thigh and smiling. A shudder begins behind my left ear and moves through every bone, muscle, and joint until even my right pinkie finger quivers. *I like this man.*

I feel languid. I feel full and ripe. I feel all the evocative words one reads in romance novels. I feel beautiful, with my short hair and clean, unpainted face and simple clothes. I feel like a cat stretching after a nap in the sun. I'm already looking forward to the next time we can be together.

"Penny for your thoughts, Miso." He traces his fingers down my arm.

"You're not going to start calling me that, I hope. Because you should give that some thought. You, after all, are actually Grady Mervin, and I could—that is, I am not averse to—using that against you."

"Okay, Bert. We'll leave Miso for your parents," he laughs. "So, what are you thinking?"

His voice is a bit hoarse, but soft, like the ragged edge of frayed satin, and I know that is because we whooped and laughed through dawn and into breakfast. He sounds sexy, like a cross between George Raft and Richard Gere.

"I'm thinking what it will be like to reunite with Kelly and with Chick and Pirate."

"Uncomfortable? Because we spent two nights together?"

"My parents exalt nosiness to heights previously unknown, all under the guise of 'telling it like it is.' They'll probably ask you how I was in bed."

"You were fine. And I don't mean okay, I mean *fine.*" He squeezes my knee and his touch feels hot through my jeans. "And I imagine their so-called nosiness is just their concern for their much-loved daughter."

"And Kelly, she of the pierced pug nose, will be there so we'll not only have to dodge my parents' curiosity, but my reluctant daughter's as well."

"Daughter?"

"Only a figure of speech. I'm so confused. Conflicted. I'm not sure what I want anymore."

"And Kelly goes into the foster care system? That's kind of harsh, don't you think?"

"Ah, I can't think about that right now. It's starting to hurt—my head and, yes, my heart. I don't want to spoil this time with heavy, hard thoughts."

We ride the rest of the way in silence, as I mentally replay spectacular moments from the night before. I wonder if Grady is doing the same. *Do guys do that? Relive the intense moments, the feelings?*

We pull into *Cielo*'s long drive at ten forty-five in the hot morning, a plume of dust behind us. At the dome, Chick lumbers out in a voluminous baker's apron, her hands coated with flour.

"Dear ones! Pirate and Kelly are having a dip. How was Austin?" She pushes a whitened curl from her face, leaving a smear of flour across her wide forehead, like graffiti on an alley wall. She flashes her open palms at us. "Can't talk, darlings. Have to punch down the dough for its second rising."

She goes back inside and Grady, holding the door for me, grins. "That was relatively painless."

"Just you wait."

We stroll down the hillside to watch Pirate and Kelly frolicking in the pond, the water brown with churned-up mud.

"Wait till you see my cannonball!" Kelly screams, and grabs the edge of the pier with bony white fingers, and pulls herself from the water. I forgot to pack her swimsuit so she's swimming in a t-shirt and what looks like a pair of Pirate's boxers. Her burned skin and narrow body are slick and wet like a young otter's. She backs up, runs, launches herself into the air, wrapping arms around folded legs, and drops like a bomb into the murky pond. The splash rises a good four feet into the air, and Pirate applauds. Her wet head appears from under the water, her hair like transparent noodles glued to her little skull.

"What do you think?" she yells.

I yell, "I think that may have been one of the cleanest, most artful cannonballs I've ever witnessed!"

"Cool." She treads water beside Pirate. "We don't have to leave now?"

I nod. "Yeah, I think we do."

"Dammit, I'm not done swimming."

"You are now. Hey, Pirate," I say, feeling suddenly shy. I blush.

"Hey, Miso." He turns and calls to Grady. "Come on over here, Dr. Powell!"

"Grady. Just call him Grady."

"I know his name." Pirate winks.

Grady joins us, and I make introductions. Then he sits beside me on the pier, glancing back toward the dome, a thoughtful look on his face. Pirate invites him in, but Grady pulls off his shoes and socks, rolls up his jeans and dangles his feet in the water. Kelly swims with smooth strokes for the pier, crawls up and stretches herself to dry like a prize animal pelt, and that is when I see the glint of yet more metal embedded in her flesh.

"What the fu--?"

"So I got my belly button pierced. No big deal," she announces. "Do you like it?"

Sighing, I place my hands on my hips and shake my head. "How did this happen? Did it by any chance involve my mother?"

"Chick took me to a guy she knows. I wanted to get a tattoo but she said it's not legal on someone my age."

"Kelly! I don't want you to keep poking holes in yourself. Besides, It's tacky."

"Gee, it's just a little body art. All the kids have them now. Don't have a conniption."

"I'm going to have a serious talk with Chick. You—get dressed. Right now. Pirate, we have to go. Grady's got work to do and I've got to tend my roses. I think."

Kelly screeches that we can't leave yet. Chick is baking bread and they're going to grill veggies when the heat fades.

"Yeah," grins Pirate.

"No." I get to be the hard-ass again. "We have to go. Run up and get your things together. And put on some dry clothes, damn it. I don't want you soaking Grady's car seats."

"Do I have to?" she whines.

"Yes, you have to."

"How deep is your pond?" Grady asks my dad.

The sun in his eyes, Pirate squints as a pirate should. "Deep enough for a righteous dive or a cannonball. You should come in, I'm tellin' ya."

Grady demurs and looks off across the field. Kelly wraps a beach towel around her.

"Please can't we stay? I'm not ready to go. I'm having fun!"

"Go! Git. Go!" I shout.

Pirate chuckles. "What a fierce drill sergeant you've become, Miso."

"Structure," I announce like a pundit. "Children need structure. Too much freedom frightens them. Right? They like to know that someone older is in control."

"Is that so?"

My father grins up at me and his question is sincere. I decide not to debate him at that moment. "Well, Dad, thank you for trying to watch Kelly. You couldn't keep her out of Chick's clutches, could you? I love you anyway. See you later."

He salutes jauntily and watches us round the water's edge, then calls after us. "You two kids have fun in Austin?"

Grady and I stop, look at each other, and say in unison, "Yes, sir."

"Glad to hear it." He disappears beneath the water.

Grady shakes his head, kisses my cheek, and we follow after Kelly. I don't even want to see Chick, I'm so angry, but she trots out and forces us to take a fresh loaf of bread, and

I remember that Saturday mornings are devoted to what she calls the kneading-punching meditation. When I first moved out on my own, Chick's bread is one of the things I missed. Nothing in the stores ever measures up.

I grab her elbow and pull her aside. "Mother, how could you—encourage Kelly to get even more piercings? What were you thinking?"

"Belly rings are the cool thing now, and I thought it would nicely echo the ring in her eyebrow and the cute little stud in her nose."

"Chick! Forget it. I may not forgive you for this. I'll have to think about it."

I take the bread and Kelly's hand. We start for Grady's car.

Kelly says, "So you're Dr. Powell, huh?"

"Guilty," says Grady.

"Well, I didn't know Bert was going to stay so long in Austin. I hope it was worth it."

Grady catches my eye and winks.

Chapter Twenty-Five

BERT AND ALICE

STILL FLOATING FROM MY TWO-DAY rendezvous with Grady, I start back out Highway 71 to see Alice for more stories. On the trip, I wonder what I'm going to do with Kelly. That belly button ring is just one more example of her rebelliousness, even though Chick encouraged and arranged it. I don't know how long to expect Kelly to grieve for her mother. I still miss Kris horribly. I'm sure Kelly must feel untethered in an unkind world. *What can I do to make things easier for her?* I'm not sure taking her to a counselor is the complete answer.

Alice is ready for me and we sit at the small chrome and Formica table in the small, square kitchen. Above the sink is a window that looks over a side yard. An ancient refrigerator graces the end of one row of cabinets, and a rear door leads out back.

"I think I'm gonna make some egg salad while we talk today." One thumb massages the thumb joint of the other hand as she talks. "It'll give me somethin' to do with my hands, and I need it to carry to church tonight."

She rises with some difficulty, and I offer to help with the salad prep. She retrieves a

cold Dr. Pepper from the fridge and hands it to me.

"You just sit right down now, and drink your sody water. I been doin' this by myself for sixty or seventy years. Lord knows I don't need any help."

She makes her way slowly to the counter by the stove, takes a dozen eggs from the egg basket, and sets them to boil in a large pot. From a metal basket hanging over the sink, she takes a large onion.

"Let's see, we left off last time talkin' about Lute's and my wedding, huh?"

I nod and savor the taste of my favorite drink.

A thoughtful look comes into her eyes. "It took me two years from the wedding to get pregnant and I miscarried my first-born son, Michael Lutheran, named after my father and his." Her voice chokes a little, and she turns toward the cutting board, presenting her back to me. "If he'd been a girl, we'd chosen the name Belinda, but he was a boy, a precious, tiny little feller who never took even one breath. I was in my seventh month, so I had some labor with it. All that work to push out a dead child." She turns to me. "This is hard to talk about, but I want to tell you."

She turns back to her work and shakes her head.

"I'm sorry, Alice." My words are feeble and inadequate.

As she begins to chop the onion on a heavy wooden chopping board, the pungent odor fills the room, the rhythm of the chopping emphasizes her words.

"Labor is such work. Lord, lord. I don't remember where Siobhan was at the time, but Letitia Mendoza come to help me when the pains began, and with each cramp came fear, because I knew it was too soon. Lute knew it was too soon. We all did. Letitia sat with me, wiped my forehead, reminded me to breathe and told me it was okay to cry. I didn't know then that he was dead. I believed I was pushing him into the world a little bit early is all."

She reaches for a large crockery bowl from an overhead cabinet which she places on the counter, wipes her hands on her apron and comes to sit at the table with me. Her hands smell of onion. She fishes in her apron pocket and uses a tissue to wipe her nose. I don't know if the tears are from the onion or the story she's telling.

"Lute couldn't bear the sounds of my moaning, so he sat on the porch with Sheriff Devine and smoked til 'Titia broke the news to him. He come in and took me into his arms.

'It ain't your fault,' he said.

He choked back tears and looked at little Michael, unbelievably tiny and near perfect. We did everything possible to revive 'im, but he come too early and there was nothin' to do but bury him in the family plot in the north pasture."

She rises again, restless. From the refrigerator, she takes two jars and sets them beside the mixing bowl, then reaches again for a third jar. She spoons in sweet pickle relish, mustard, and mayonnaise. She adds the onion and mixes the ingredients together. When she's done, she slips a vinyl cap over the bowl and goes to the stove to turn down the heat under the eggs.

"I hadn't known pain in my whole life like mournin' for my baby. It's a grippin', tearin' pain, like movin' your hand into the steam of a kettle, fiery and scalding. 'Twasn't only my innards that burned, but my soul, too. The damage screamed through me. 'Course I had no idea then what else the good Lord had in store for me.

"Michael's funeral was a quiet, little gatherin' of close friends. Henry Bursen, tall and somber, built a tiny box for Michael, and Siobhan wordlessly helped me wash his little body and wrap him in the cotton towelin' we used for swaddlin'. We put him in his little box and sprinkled him with dried wildflower petals--bluebonnets, cosmos, and dried herbs. Siobhan was quiet the whole time. She had no comforting words for Lute or me, but she helped git my son ready to go into the ground, and I figured that musta been her way of showing how sorry she was. Michael was her first grandchild, and I'm sure she was thinking of losin' her Frankie the whole time.

"Father Socha said the Mass, and the Goodmans, Petey, Cora Lea and Billy Frank were there. Little Ginny was beside me. My brothers had left Fallon Springs by then to look for work in the cities, Jamie to Austin and Bobby down to San Antonio. I longed for my Granny Fitzmartin, but she had gone to Jesus the year before, another loss that would never heal. Before Lute found me, she'd been my rock and guide."

Taking the pot of hot eggs to the sink, she runs cool water over them, then turns back to me. "I apologize, Bert, for talkin' on such a sad subject, but babies dyin' was sure a part of life back then." She gets an ice tray from the freezer and empties it into the eggs.

I want to reassure her. "I understand. It must be hard for you to revisit these feelings. I appreciate your courage. These are what we need in our study." As I say this, I realize how trite it sounds.

She waves a hand. "I know the Lord is supposed to lead us and hold us up in times of trouble, but Granny was all that to me, and then she was gone. We all prayed over the grave for the repose of Michael's soul and sang a few songs, our low voices lifting acrost green pastures and into the willows 'long the creek side, sad and soft. With Lute's strong arms around me, a breeze carrying our songs, the smell of the fresh earth on the grave mound, I said goodbye to my boy.

"I grieved long and hard, and felt mighty sorry for myself. Friends visited. Father Socha checked in on us. And then, at last, it was just Lute and me at home without our son. Most men don't talk about their feelings. They take their suffering quietly with not much said. Lute was the same, but he was so good to me, right patient and kind.

"In the mornings, before he left for Brisbane's, he'd hold

me in bed and whisper to me. 'It'll get better, Tiny Alice. We'll try again. Just got to get you out of bed to have your coffee in the kitchen and...to stop cryin'.'

"And we did slowly get better, and happiness slipped up on us when we weren't lookin'. Our sorrow sat quiet inside us and, though on the outside we appeared unchanged, we'd never be the same. Never the same."

She stops again, begins to crack and peel the boiled eggs. With her back to me, she muses.

"One night, months after little Michael passed, we sat out on the porch. The air was gritty with dust. We drank coffee, grinning over the fact that we seemed to be feelin' better. Lute had a smoke, and we talked about the children we'd have in the future. I sat in Lute's lap. It was dark dusk, but we hadn't dared hope for rain, though it sure looked like a storm was on its way.

"We watched the sky grow black, and heat lightning danced acrost the flat horizon. You could smell the rain in the air. Before too long, the sky busted open and lightning shot down and thunder shook the house. Then the water come at us in heavy, hurtful drops, blowing almost sideways so that we ran inside to keep from getting soaked. Oh, it was a glorious storm. At last the drought was broken and the rains came. We had survived it and were doin' our best with the Depression and the loss of our baby, and all would be well again.

She sighs and drops her head into her hands, then looks up at me for a moment and runs her hands down her face.

"You know, years later I lost another child. A daughter. She was just a teenager when she ran off, I guess. I never knew what happened. My Charlene. And I haven't seen or heard from her since."

My brow furrows. "She just disappeared?" I'm shocked.

"Sure did. But that's a story for another day. I got to finish up this egg salad, Bert. This has been hard talkin' today. Do you mind if we stop now?"

"No, of course not. Alice, do you mind if I give you a hug?"

She grins and wipes her hands on a cup towel. "Nah. Huggin's good."

I wrap my arms around her tiny form and am surprised by the wiry strength of her. Though I don't know why that surprises me.

As I leave, I think of how much I want to hear about a disappearing daughter.

Chapter Twenty-Six

BERT

PASTOR TIM AND I SIT in the rose garden, cooling ourselves with tall iced teas. Earlier I asked Kelly to stay in the house. I want privacy for this exchange. I reflect briefly that, if I can't have Kris in the other chair, Tim might be my second choice, though probably now it would be Grady. My imagined passion for Tim seems to be decidedly less lurid lately. I drink in his good looks, noting that the lines at either side of his mouth give his youthful face a serious cast. No. Grady or no Grady—I still find Tim damned attractive.

I've fallen asleep many nights imagining Tim's hands on me. Until Grady, I lived for so long without the touch of a man. I know it's wrong to covet another woman's husband, but still the feelings are there. I'd long ago resolved to enjoy my fantasies, not to beat myself up about them, but never to act on them. Now, I'm thankful for Grady in my life, while Pastor Tim's shining armor is tarnishing quickly. Remembering Patti's fears, I realize that I will be deeply offended if Tim turns out not to be the saint I've imagined.

He crosses one long leg over the other and I try not to stare at his hands dangling over the chair arm. Those hands—

the hands of Kris's teacher, her spiritual guide, her moral example and once the object of my lust. I've transferred that lust to Grady now. Just the thought of our time in Austin flips my stomach, and I keep remembering, even now as I sit beside Tim. Then I remember my lunch with Patti. She can't be right about him. Not Tim.

He takes a sip of tea, his gaze somewhere over the small pond that sparkles down the hill from the rose garden. How can Patti suspect him? He'd never betray her.

"According to Miss Emily Justice at Marilyn Beckwith Middle School," I begin. "Kelly's had several episodes of hysteria at school over the last year. Kristin had her in some kind of counseling group or class. I don't know. The school wants me to take her for a psychiatric evaluation. I want to get your take on this. What do you think?"

He takes another sip and the tea moistens his lips—those great lips. "I think it's significant that the episodes began before Kristin died. In that case, her mother's death is not the sole reason for her behavior." He turns watering eyes on me. "I miss her, Bert. Kris was such a...a good person. I miss her."

I'm surprised by the apparent depth of his feelings. As Chick would say, he must be in touch with his *feminine*. I pat his hand, and he grasps mine. I flush at his touch, and pray he doesn't notice. In truth, I'm embarrassed that I ever had feelings for him, and I'm angry. If he really is cheating on Patti, then he is the lowest of the low. A church leader having an affair is contemptible. But then, I'm having an affair with my professor. Maybe I'm being too judgmental? Still, I'll confront Tim, just as soon as we're done talking about Kelly.

"I'm having a hard time, too, Tim." I try to steady the tremor in my voice.

"We need to stick together." He clears his throat. "Those of us who loved Kris—we must help each other through this." He lifts a hand to his forehead like he's about to bow his head, then he sees me watching and takes my hand and presses his lips against my hot skin. I withdraw a little, though part of me would like for him to go on. "You mean so much to me, Roberta. You and Kristin have been such dear friends to Patti and me."

He keeps my hand in his. I don't pull it away. I clear my throat. "I've had an appointment with a lawyer about the guardianship, and I'm still convinced I'm not the right person to take Kelly. I have no idea how to deal with her emotional issues. I can't even deal with my own."

I pull my hand from his, look away, and then fiddle with a cuticle on my thumb. "Though the guardianship isn't legal yet, there is really no one to speak for Kelly or see that she gets the help she needs. I'm it in her life...for now. That said, I've spoken with a therapist in Austin and I'll take Kelly to her for evaluation. I've thought about waiting until Social Services takes over to let them pay for it." My voice cracks. Heat rises to my face. "Is that horrible? Am I a terrible person? My thoughts are all jumbled."

"I don't think waiting is the way to go. Kelly should be seen as soon as possible, so she can get the care she needs. And I still believe you're her best hope."

"Okay. Well, maybe. But, uh, aside from Kelly, there's something else I need to ask you." My mouth goes dry and my lips stick together. I lick them and swallow. Tim turns in his chair and leans towards me, those terrific eyes intent on my face. I pull my hand from his.

"What's that?" He assumes his pastoral care persona.

"Are you screwing around on Patti?"

His head snaps back as if I've landed a right cross to his jaw. His brow furrows and something dark moves in his eyes, a quick summer storm. His entire face clouds for a moment, then his broad smile comes back like the sun after a cloudburst.

"Why on earth would you ask that?" He seems truly dumbfounded.

"Are you? I've...uh...heard rumors."

A spasm of pain contorts his face. He looks away and shakes his head. "I can't believe you'd think me capable?"

"Tim, I didn't think it could be true. I knew you wouldn't. But nevertheless, that's what I've heard. They say you keep such late hours. I *really* don't want it to be true. Patti's so delicate. She's crazy about you and if she—that is I think she's heard the rumor. She, uh...knows something's wrong. She told me. I guess she felt she couldn't talk to anyone at the church so she just told me she felt something was wrong."

"Oh, Roberta," and now he laughs and ruffles my hair with his hand. His fingers feel delicious on my scalp. "My sweet, blunt, brusque Roberta. What would we do without you?"

I pull my head away from his hand, a little alarmed at the gesture. "Yeah." I nod, dumbly. I stare at the cedar bark beneath my feet and relish his touch, the terms of endearment. Oh, Grady Powell, where are you when I need you? Tim stands and stretches his tall frame.

"I'll reassure Patti that everything is fine. Thank you for letting me know."

He pulls me out of my chair and crushes me in a hug. I squeeze back. He looks me in the eye and says, "You're a true friend."

I grin madly, like a child who got an A on her report card, and inwardly I pat myself on the back for being direct and bringing this out in the open. I knew it wasn't true. Then I realize he never said it wasn't true. He managed to side step the question. I'm such an idiot.

"Talk to her, Tim. Let her know there is no one else for you but her."

He says he will, and then, "Will you send Kelly out to talk to me? Maybe I can encourage her to get some help."

Based on Patti's confidences, I'm thinking maybe he is the one who needs the help. I go inside and send Kelly out.

I stay in so they can talk without me hovering. I don't think he makes much impact, because soon Kelly bangs through the screen door and heads to her room. When I come back out, I tell him goodbye. As he drives away Kelly appears at the door. I motion to her to come out and sit. We don't talk, but watch the sunset glisten on the pond's mirror at the edge of the field. Diamonds, Kristin used to say of the sun on the water. The only diamonds she'd ever own. I share that memory with Kelly, who seems even more agitated than earlier, maybe even a little angry. I ask her if everything is all right.

"I don't like him much, that's all."

"Tim? What's not to like?"

"I know how much you like him. I don't know." She shrugs. "Just something about him. Never mind."

After lunch, we tackle the spare room. I still don't plan for her to occupy it for long, but there is no reason it can't be straight and nice for her while she's here. We clumsily move the heavy NordicTrack into a corner of my room, and drag two bookshelves into the living room. We rescue a warped chest of drawers from the garage, and I promise to buy paint. I make up the futon with clean sheets and retrieve the light cotton blanket and floral comforter from the dryer. We're stretching the sheet over the mattress when she says it.

"He and Mom were doing it."

"Excuse me?"

"Reverend Tim. He and my mom were...you know."

"Uh-uh." I shake my head. "I don't know. What are you saying?"

"Doesn't it just make you sick? Mom and the preacher?"

She makes an ugly gesture with both hands, one I remember well from grade school. I stare, mouth agape, when somewhere between shock and vehement denial, I hear the putt-putt of Chick's old VW van coming up the drive. Kelly smiles at me, as if fully aware that her revelation has slain me. Tim! That bastard! The slime.

I stumble out onto the porch, trying to gain control of my breathing and am forced to watch the spectacle of my mother exiting her van. Then it occurs to me: I don't have to deal with any of this. I've had enough to deal with, thank you Goddess—as my mother says. I can simply be somewhere else at this moment. So, I turn and start down the hill toward the pond.

I begin Lamaze breathing, the kind I teach my patients to use through the different stages of labor. *Hee-hee, blow-blow; hee-hee, blow-blow.* My breath over the little pond is insignificant, no ripple wafts across the surface of murky brown and green. I want to be that water—not dark and muddy—but smooth and unruffled.

"Miso?" Chick bellows from the house. "Are you all right, child?"

I want to yell back for her to stay there and please not invade my safe place on the banks of equilibrium, but I cannot find my voice. My voice has been swallowed by betrayal and is holding its breath just below the surface of hysteria. *Hee-hee, blow-blow.*

I hear Chick's heavy breathing as she works her way toward me from the house, and want, more than I've ever wanted anything, for her to go away. Maybe I can follow my voice to the depths and never come up. But still she comes, breathing almost as noisily as me. Closer now. Maybe I'll just spin around and deck her. If I can knock her out with one punch, I won't have to hear her philosophize about how I must accept Tim's humanity and not make him a god on my own personal shrine. If I can flatten her before she opens her mouth, I just might be able to face Kelly's hideous pronouncement. *What horrible thoughts! I* am *a bad person!*

I stare into the pond and say to myself, "She's not here. Chick is not here. Kelly is not here. I am alone. Alone and quiet."

"Miso!" She trumpets and claps a heavy hand on my shoulder. I rock and spin like one of those Russian dolls with rounded bottoms. "Child, talk to me! What on earth? Are you ill? Have you had a vision?"

I look at her, her face flushed and sweaty from the short walk, and she must see something in my face, because she shuts up immediately, almost as if she might possess some sensitivity and has, at least partially, grasped the gravity of my mood.

"Chick, I can't talk right now. Okay? Here's what you do. Go inside and make Kelly a peanut butter sandwich, whether she wants one or not. Make her watch something inane or offensive on television. I don't care. Sit with her. Do not ask questions. Do not listen to anything she has to say. Leave me alone. Can you do that for me?"

"Well, certainly, darling." She turns, takes a deep breath and starts awkwardly back toward the house, then turns back around. "Miso, let me help you. Please. Let your mother be a comfort and strength for you."

I look at her and at my house, which now looks tiny to me and miles away from where I stand. I'm about to cry. My lips form a pout, and I nod my head.

"Oh, darling," she moans and joins me at the edge of disillusionment.

I sit on the bank, and she lowers herself to sit beside me. I shred the grass between my fingers and do some more deep breathing. My mom puts a heavy arm around my shoulders and draws my befuddled face into her bosom.

"Oh, my darling. Tell me what has happened."

Touched by her tenderness, I disentangle myself from her embrace, toss acorns onto the pond and revel at the ripples they make. "Oh, Kris," I blurt to a homely brown duck that skates through the water.

"Kris?" Mother's voice is deep and rich and warm. "What about Kris?"

"Kris!" I yell. "My life is losing its mind and I don't know what..."

I lean into my mother's soft shoulder and have a long,

shameless cry, making as much noise as I want. *Hee hee, blow blow.* My nose runs, and I wipe it with my t-shirt hem. Hee-hee, blow-blow. I bite my lip until it bleeds.

"Okay," I say to Chick, the pond, or God, or whoever the hell is listening. "Okay. Tim had an affair with Kris."

Chick makes a harrumph sound.

I go on. "I can understand that. Sort of. I mean, I was crazy about the guy, but I would never have acted on those feelings!" I look at my mother's beautiful face. "But Kris. Kris acted and said nothing to me. Patti was right, and I was wrong. Tim *has* been unfaithful. He's not a paragon of virtue." I bite my bottom lip. I won't allow tears to come. "He's horny and selfish like all the rest of us. He's flawed—ah, shit! And secretly, and with my best friend! And why wouldn't she confide in me?" I sob some more. "And Kelly knew about this, but said nothing until now. Why did she wait?"

"Miso, can you quiet yourself even a little?"

Ignoring her, I strip to my undies and dive in. I swim laps until there is no breath left in me, until my muscles burn and my legs tremble and then I lie naked on the bank, my head in Chick's lap. She runs her fingers through my hair, the way she does, and I close my eyes and see a naked Tim chasing a nude Kris across the back of my eyelids. Then the head rubbing begins to loosen the bonds that suffocate me, and I start to relax in my mother's lap. When I'm good and calm, I rise and dress.

"Come, Chick, let's to the house!" I announce like Shakespearean royalty. I help Chick up out of the grass and we march up the hill.

Chick brews tea and cuts sandwiches, PBJs, into cute little triangles with crusts removed. She only does this under special circumstances, because she insists the crust is the most nutritious part of the bread, so she never allowed me, in all the unstructured years of my childhood, to eat a crustless piece of bread in her presence. She, Kelly, and I sit around my little table, as silence takes a seat and dusk gently darkens the kitchen. Finally, Chick begins.

"Dear one, no wonder you are so discombobulated. This is a big, hairy truth to swallow. My heart hurts for you! Heavy duty!"

I turn to Kelly. "I need you to tell me, slowly and calmly, about Tim and your mother. I need you to use tact. Do you know that word? You have a tendency, like me actually, to blurt things out and I'd like you to think about what a special friend of mine your mother was, and keep that in mind while you tell me this story."

"Nicely done." Chick pats my arm and I roll my eyes at her.

"Okay," Kelly says, her mouth clogged with peanut butter. "He came over all the time, late at night. To pray or counsel—that's what Mom called it. And sometimes he'd be there for dinner." She smacks as she chews. "Then they got to where they'd make me go to bed, they'd tuck me in, like a mom and dad. It was kind of cool, but one time he wanted to talk to me in private and he said how this was our little family secret and I was not to ever mention his visits or the special friendship he and Mom had. Well, I mean, how stupid do I look? Mom's room is right next to mine and I could hear them in there breathing and moaning...

"That's enough!" I hold up a hand.

"And the bed was squeaking..."

"Let's just stop a minute and have some more tea." Chick rises to the occasion.

She pours. We all sip. Several minutes crawl by until I am ready to continue.

"Can I start again?" Kelly asks, and I nod. "So, I never told anyone 'cause I kind of liked having him around, for a while."

"You just said today you don't like him."

"I don't. Now."

"What changed your mind?"

"Well, you know. He did it with my mom and he's married. Kinda shitty don't you think?"

I can't argue there.

"I'm sorry, Bert," says Kelly.

And I can't believe my ears. A gentle tone comes into her voice. "I know this sucks, big time, but I thought someone, especially you, should know about it." Tears form in her light blue eyes. "You've been nice to me. I don't want you to feel bad."

Amazed, I tell her, "I'll live. Seriously. Why don't you get your bath?"

"Ah, you just wanna get rid of me so you can talk to your mom about 'the Rev'" boinking my mama." I shiver and say she is right and to get into the bathroom now.

"Can I use your bath crystals?" she calls back from the hall. "Yeah, use the crystals, for Christ's sake."

She smiles. She now knows me well enough to "play" fight and she knows I know that is what she's doing. I finish my tea and begin to clear the table. Chick watches, as if she understands that I want to think rather than talk. I run dishwater in the sink and wash our cups. I need to clean and straighten and organize. Chick busies herself gathering crumbs from the table. Waiting.

"You know, you're right about washing dishes being soothing," I tell her.

She picks up a tea towel and begins to dry the dishes.

"It's appalling to discover how little I knew Kris. That she could hide from me her struggles with Kelly, her relationship with Tim...What other secrets did she keep?"

"Miso, think of the child. What she's been through."

"No, Mother. Think of me! I do think of Kelly. I wish I could stop thinking of her, but I need for you to think about *me*. And don't start on me now about keeping Kelly. This is not the time."

"I think I've been a good mother to you, Miso."

"How did you learn? How did you get along with your mother? What was she like?

"Like all of us, my mother did the best she could."

"And that's it? That's her legacy, according to you? Oh, never mind. You'll never budge."

"I refuse to think that I have not been a tonic in your life, and I know you could be so good for Kelly. You could help her transcend all of this. With patience and by building trust, you could help her process..."

"*I've* got to get over it first, Chick!

"Miso, it is not all about you. It's also about that innocent child in there who's had to grow up way too fast, because of all the dysfunctional adults in her life. The choices you make now need to be as much about Kelly as about you. Listen to what I am saying. What about Kelly? Have you decided about the guardianship?"

"Vic Johnson's doing his thing, and then I can be out of this nightmare, this Clive Barnes film, this ongoing act of domestic terrorism."

Chick speaks softly. "Remember when I used to say, 'don't push the river'? A Gestalt therapist named Barry Stevens said that. It's a wise saying that's helped me pilot through the torrents of life."

I think of Tim's hands and my fantasies about them. Kris knew the touch of those hands.

"Miso, do you hear me?"

"Don't push the river. How could I forget?"

"The river washed Kelly to you. You are to retrieve her from the wayward currents and give her respite, like Miriam with Moses."

"Mom, this is the twenty-first century. We can *cross* the river now. We can dam it up, build bridges to safety. We can tunnel underneath the fucking river!"

"We are able, that is true, to do all of these things, but would that course be wise? Your father and I believe it is better to go with the flow."

“And be dashed against the rocks? No thanks.”

“That’s a possibility too, but there also exists the potential that, if you stop fighting, the current can transport you to a place you’ve never been before, possibly to a place you need to go.”

“Enough with the metaphor. I don’t want to be transported anywhere against my will.”

“Oh, but you already are, aren’t you, Miso? Aren’t you headed there right this minute, in spite of all your efforts otherwise?”

A delicate china cup, hand painted with pale lavender violets, slips from my soapy hand and crashes to the floor. I dry my hands, walk over to my mother and put my head on her shoulder. She hugs me and looks into my eyes.

“Get the broom, Miso, and clean up the mess.”

Chapter Twenty-Seven

CHARLENE

OUR VAN OF INTREPID TRAVELERS arrived in San Francisco during the Summer of Love. It was a magical time. Festivals and parties marked our first weeks there. Ava said the celebrations "heralded a major cultural shift in the communal mind of San Francisco, a new Way of Being" that would echo into future decades. Ava was always so eloquent.

We were welcomed into a home called Haven, a weathered Victorian house owned by Ben and Laurie Dawkins, two friends of Willie. We were given rooms with pallets on the floor for sleeping. Haven was full of colorfully flamboyant characters like Beanie, who had his Ph.D. in astrophysics, Evelyn who wrote poetry in the style of e. e. cummings, and Carlos who practiced yoga and sang in Swahili.

Golden Gate Park—the huge, heavily wooded urban sanctuary built on empty sand dunes a hundred years before—was always crowded. Most of us played in the "Panhandle," a part of the park located just north of where we lived, the same section where something called the *Human Be-In* had taken place months before.

Thousands of us gathered that June to celebrate life, free

love, peace and one another. I'd come here to break free from the restraints of home, never imagining that my mind and way of life would be totally changed. We'd see happy groups of jugglers, musicians, dancers, sword swallowers, tarot readers, singers, and poets. San Francisco policemen patrolled on horseback—a familiar sight that reminded me of Daddy and Sheriff Devine sometimes riding their rounds. Every single person was unique.

Some guys wore their hair long. Leather and beads were popular. Some sported square or round wire-rimmed glasses, and everyone wore flowers. The girls wore garlands with ribbons flowing down their backs or a single bloom tucked behind one ear.

The landscape offered giant eucalyptus trees that sent off their spicy fragrance. Shrubs and flowers grew wild along the trails. Ponds and waterfalls were surrounded by great pines and oaks.

Ava told me the City worried that San Francisco couldn't handle the thousands of kids arriving that summer. Thousands! Whew! The paper everyone at Haven read (I think it was the *Oracle*) told of free clinics offering birth control and counseling services, help for pregnant girls and folks with drug problems.

City programs offered help with housing and sanitation. A weekly street paper that looked just like the Fallon Springs A&P's weekly fold-out section. The paper warned about which drugs were safe, and which to stay away from. Music and art were all over the place. It all came together that summer, and I was there! Right smack dab in the middle of it.

One warm night, I danced with Glory and Ava in a clearing in the park. We swayed and sashayed, and wove in and out of each other's arms, wearing garlands of daisies and Queen Anne's lace. We wore gossamer gowns that we'd made for ourselves on a borrowed and battered sewing machine. Our dresses floated when we walked, when we twirled and leaped in ribbon wings and angel sleeves.

One warm night, the entire Haven crew walked to the Park early in the evening. The moon was up, stars were out, and the fog that had rolled in around three that afternoon was lifting. The park was crawling with people. Ava and I heard baroque, folk, and bluegrass music.

As we wandered through, rock music pounded from every direction, yet small dales and bowers still sat peacefully. A guy we passed played mandolin, accompanied by a girl with a funny shaped guitar—which Willie said was a lute—and their sound was warm and rich. There were fireworks, and there was pot to smoke, and Willie and Glory wandered off to try LSD. I was scared to try it. My mind was already expanding at jarring speed and I didn't want to explode! A small group sat in a circle. They sang *If I Had a Hammer* to guitar accompaniment. People discussed literature, politics, and drug exploration.

I swayed under the stars to lute music, my ribbons and mind flying, when I spied a young man of remarkable beauty. He wore a trimmed beard, and his hair was dark and shoulder length. He sat in the lotus position wearing a gold and white kaftan, sharing a joint with a redheaded guy next to him. His eyes, dark and deep, brimmed with poetry and passion. He watched me dancing. I thought I saw the hint of a smile.

I pretended not to notice, but continued to dance, slyly glancing his way over and over again. Sunshine jumped up to join me, and Ava began to pick an old ukelele she'd found at Haven, trying her best to make the uke's tinny sound blend with the lute. After what seemed like hours of dancing I stopped suddenly, stretched my arms wide like angels' wings and fell backward onto a carpet of soft moss and wild daisies. The night spun around me and I went with it, around and around until, through the dizziness, I saw that sweet face with the amazing eyes looking down at me.

"Hello, love. Thirsty?" He held up a *bota* of wine and extended his hand to help me up. I staggered up and, still dizzy, fell against him. I tilted my head back and he squeezed wine from the *bota* and the wine ran down my chin and stained the neckline of my dress. Oh, I wanted to drown in his wine.

"What's your name, Tiger Lily?"

"Tiger Lily? Not Tiger Lily," I laughed. "That's not my name. My friends call me Phoenix." I ruffled my long hair.

"Hello, Phoenix. I'm Ralph."

"Ralph?" I giggled. "Ralph? That is the most un-Aquarian name I've ever heard." I giggled at dreamy Ralph's expense.

"It's a venerable old name," he joked. "Been in my family for years. My middle name's Aaron. Do you like that better?"

"Ralph. No, I think you should be proud of your name and that is what I'll call you. In fact, did you know that I read somewhere that to speak a person's name is to steal that person's power, you know, their mojo. Have you ever heard that?"

He took my elbow, and said he wanted to hear all about it, and steered me through the bodies on the park lawn to the base of a eucalyptus tree. We sat in the perfumed air. My head spun. I sat down hard. I hadn't eaten since morning and the wine hit me hard.

We talked all night, of music and poets, and current politics and the new credos of people like us who followed a simpler way of peace, nonviolence, and love. Ralph believed reason should be practiced as well, reason and common sense. He was older than me, fascinating and funny. He was so much wiser, more widely read and educated than I. He'd marched in Birmingham in '63 with Dr. Martin Luther King, Jr., and even knew Alan Ginsburg and Jack Kerouac from hanging out at City Lights Books on Grant Avenue.

As we talked and the night wore on, the circus around us calmed and people wandered off in couples or groups, looking for a patch of privacy or heading home. Ralph walked me to his place—a tiny efficiency in a Victorian overlooking Buena Vista Park. He lived alone with, like, five hundred books. We left the windows open to the wet night air, and he wrapped his arms around me and we made sweet, patient, passionate love in ways I'd not known before. I awoke in the morning in a tangle of bedclothes, cool breezes blowing long white curtains across the bed. Ralph sat in the lotus position on the floor and again with his dark, passionate eyes were on me.

I stretched my arms toward the ceiling. "Are you meditating on me?"

"Good morning, beautiful. Sleep well?"

My head hurt, but I gave him my bravest smile and asked him for coffee. He prepared a cup in his tiny kitchenette. I told him cream and sugar, and he brought it to me. Who was this man and how did I end up with him this morning? Why did I feel so lucky? Why did he fix me with his intent look, with his soft fawn's eyes, with his groovy awareness? Then I realized I was naked.

"Oh, my," was all I could say and I yanked the sheet around me.

"Now, don't fret," he stood. "Already I know every glorious inch of you. We know each other—yes? I kissed you to sleep, then I lay awake drinking in your beauty. You are a remarkably lovely young woman. You know that, of course. Don't you? Like a woman painted by Titian—fire on snow. Never mind. That is for another night. I have so many things to share with you.

"What time is it?"

"It's early morn." He kissed the tip of my nose. "The sun's not up yet."

We sat in quiet comfort on the floor, our backs to the wall. I felt the deepest affection rise up, an intense connection to this gentle man. In time, we set our mugs aside and moved again into each other's arms. This time our passion was even stronger and we moved more expertly together. This time I gave away a part of myself. This time I lost all sense of separateness and merged with him. And when he came he called out my name, and I knew we were bound together for always.

At length, I said I must get home. I thought Willie and Ava might be worried about me. Ralph said he doubted it, that everyone was pretty accustomed to friends staying over with other friends, but he would take me home.

"Is that what we are? Friends?"

"We are more than friends, my lady. We are lovers. We are One. Do you wish to be my lady?"

"Oh, I do! I do! The Haight? Can we walk it? Is it far? I'd love to walk now when the city is still asleep and the ocean breezes are blowing in."

"Haven isn't far," he told me.

"You know Haven?"

"Sure. Ben's an old friend from graduate school. It's a groovy place to crash when you first get to town. Safe, and tremendously good food."

We smoked a joint, then dressed and set off, coffee mugs in hand. When we reached Haven at dawn, Ava and Ben sat at the great table laden with grapes and oranges, avocadoes, cherries, coffee, juices and thick whole wheat toast with real butter. Ava peeled an avocado and lifted her eyebrows to me and smiled. Later, I would describe to her every delicious detail I could recall of my time with Ralph. We drank cold unfiltered apple juice and ate artichokes while Ben held forth on an article from *The New York Times*.

Ralph stayed the morning, though I found myself left out of his long discussion with Ben about free clinics and the services needed in the Haight. I wanted all of Ralph's attention as I'd had the night before, and I wished Ben would go meditate or something. I wanted to take him up to the roof to see the view of the city, where Ava and I often watched the soft, warmly colored sunsets.

After that day, though, Ralph Landau and I were never

apart. I moved my few belongings into his place and began to imagine what I wanted my very own home to look like. We spent hours talking and learned everything we could about each other. He was Jewish and from Brooklyn. I knew nothing about New York. I shared little about my upbringing, which was nothing I was proud of. He loved his home and family and learned gold smithing from his father, who was a jeweler. He had earned a degree in Political Science from Columbia, and would attend grad school in the fall at UC Berkeley. I told him I'd dropped out of high school to come to San Francisco, but intended to educate myself through reading and maybe auditing some classes at San Francisco U.

"We'll find a bigger place to live," he said. "And you can enroll in school and study whatever you like."

"I can't afford anything, but auditing's almost as good."

He took my hands in his. "I have a small jewelry business that seems to be growing, and I got a little bit when my father died. Maybe in time we can find a way for you to go to school. Would you like that?"

I was stunned. "I'd love it! How thrilling!"

We did search the city for a larger place and rented an apartment on the Marina with two bedrooms, a big kitchen and dining room, and a small fenced yard in the back. It was beautiful—hardwood floors, shutters on the windows, a big bay window in the front. I wanted to make it our own.

Sadly, as miraculous and life changing as the summer was, the City had been deluged with disenchanted kids from all over the country and city services were maxed out. There weren't enough places to crash. The free clinics were swamped. Along Haight Street garbage piled up in the gutters. Young people died of drug overdoses. Hippies were done with celebrating. In October of that year, a funeral was held for the hippies. Many left, and those of us remaining didn't want to see any more kids wander glassy-eyed into our city.

Also in October, I found out I was pregnant, but happily so this time. Ralph and I were married in the park by a rabbi friend of his who wore a top hat and a clown suit and conducted a groovy ceremony. We didn't need a church, for neither of us professed any belief system except our belief in Love and the basic goodness of all living creatures. We spent our honeymoon at home, which pretty much consisted of lovemaking, painting the apartment, drinking coffee or wine, and reading poetry to each other. We shopped for used furniture, and we talked, and laughed, and talked some more. We talked about our little blooming person, wondering if we'd have a boy or girl, what names we wanted, how we wanted to parent. Our life was perfect.

One day at the park for a picnic I whined about my provincial name, which I had always hated, when one of my friends, Leo, told me I could go to court and change my name to anything I wanted. Lots of people were doing it. Ralph, Ava and Willie knew me as Phoenix, but I didn't want that for a permanent name, and I didn't want to tell Ralph my given name. To choose one's own name seemed a monumental freedom, an act to be undertaken with weight and judgment. I played around with names that might represent my personality, or a symbol of something I should aspire to. I decided on Pearl of the Sea. I figured I'd grown like a pearl, a constant irritant to my mother, but Ralph helped me realize that I was beautiful and smart, that I had something unique to offer. I'd fallen in love with the sea and the Bay and often took the bus to the beach to swim in the cold salty water, or go to Cliff House to see the sea lions. Sometimes Ralph called me his "pearlie." I thought about Pearl of Great Price, but I chose Pearl of the Sea and I would go by Pearl. As soon as I turned eighteen, I went to court and became Pearl of the Sea Landau, ridding myself of the last vestiges of my family of origin. Goodbye to Deborah Charlene Slezak and all that she represented.

Ralph and I imagined names for our baby. I believed I was having a girl and, if so, I wanted a romantic name for her, but one that was true to who we were. We considered Star, Arabella, Seraphina. We talked about Antigone, Cassiopeia, and our favorite, Mystic Soul. For a lad we thought of Gaylord, Tristan, Elliot, and Taurus.

The year following the Summer of Love, some of our friends moved across the Bay to Berkeley and Oakland. Berkeley had a more sophisticated, better educated vibe due to the University of California campus there. Other friends in the City stayed so high, we couldn't reach them after a while, so our social life suffered. I felt sad to see the Haight come to an end, but we chose to stay in the Now and roll with it. We moved to Berkeley into a small garden apartment where we had an extra room for Ralph to work on his jewelry and a tiny room (no more than a large closet) for a nursery.

Our darling girl was born at home in our bathtub. My dear Ava attended and there were no complications. Ralph and I argued about home birth versus hospital and he favored the hospital, in case anything went wrong, but, in the end, he went along with me, and the birth went off without a hitch. We named her Mystic Soul and she had spiritual green eyes, eyes that reminded me of my mother, that seemed to see far down the path of womankind, and her beatific smile hinted at mysticism and magic. We could tell immediately that hers was an old soul.

The jewelry Ralph was making had successfully metamorphosed from puka shells and macramé to the gold work he'd learned from his father. His family had owned a small jewelry shop in Brooklyn and much of his childhood had been spent working the store. The switch from hippie beads to mainstream jewelry helped us get on our feet financially.

Once we settled, I enrolled at UC Berkeley with a major

in Clay Arts and a Literature minor. I had audited a pottery class in the fall and loved the turning wheel and the soft hands required to shape the spinning clay—a sensual and expressive act. Literature gave me a handle on many of the books, treatises and articles Ralph discussed with his friends. I always felt so smart when I could contribute to the conversation. My second semester, though, I discovered stained glass. The colors and shapes and juxtaposition of patterns, the decisive yet delicate touch needed to properly cut the glass—this became *my* work, and the glass and I had a solid partnership from then on.

When Miso (the nickname that seemed to fit) was one, we had a playtime group with Ava and her daughter, Felicity, who was a year younger than Mystic Soul. Ava had taken up pottery and had become quite adept at it.

"You're almost to a level of expertise, my darling Ava, of being able to sell your wares. We could even set up a booth at a street fair together!"

She shook her head. "I don't think I'm ready. But someday, yes."

"Let's make a little enclosure in your 'mud' room for the girls. They can play while we make pots."

"That's an outstanding idea. I like to get high, though, before I start creating something."

She rolled a joint while I used two wooden baby gates to fashion a roomy play area for the children. I put quilts on the floor and tossed in some largish pillows. We toked a bit and watched the girls play.

Ava extinguished the joint and turned to her work. She threw a slab of clay on the wheel and began to pump a foot pedal to turn it. A deep bucket of water sat beside her and she reached in regularly to moisten her hands. The clay expanded and contracted sensuously, like a soft gray taffy, as she pushed and pulled all the while, with the spinning, the turning, the speeding up, the slowing down. My, the concentration! I lacked that kind of focus.

"There is something so elemental about having the clay in your hands," I reflected. "And molding something from the earth."

"What are you working on now?"

"I'm doing some vases for an art fest in Palo Alto. I'm going to share a booth with some friends from the co-op."

"Groovy. Can Miso and I go with?"

"Of course, you can!" Her eyes twinkled with delight. "Everything is more fun when I share it with you and Miso."

"Ah, Ava, you are the best of friends."

"I certainly hope so."

Eventually, after two semesters at UC, I stopped school to work full time on my stained glass art. Ralph and I then opened our little shop, The Golden Mean, in Berkeley on Bishop Street, and we began to make a comfortable living.

We placed Miso in a Montessori preschool and in two developmental play groups, one specifically designed to develop fine motor skills, and another to work on creative play. She was advanced beyond her peers. She had always been ahead, sat up at six months, stood and spoke at nine months, and walked at ten months. Even at one and two, she showed superior reasoning skills and intelligence. Her vocabulary developed so fast we were stunned and, by age three, she'd become highly opinionated.

One evening, we basked in the company of Ava and her date, Alfonso. Ava always seemed to bring a different date to our get-togethers. Never the same man twice. Ralph was by now calling me Chick, for my legal name "Pearl" had evolved. Alfonso asked if it was a nickname.

"Of sorts. I always hated my Christian name. I changed it some time back to Pearl of the Sea, and then I had a personal revelation, quit analysis, and insisted I be called Chick. Enough said."

"And so she is called," said Ralph.

Alfonso nodded. "Chick is like girl?"

"I suppose."

"And Chick calls you Pirate?"

I nodded. "That is his name now. After we settled here in Berkeley, Ralph decided his own name could be tuned up to better jive with mine and Miso's. So, now he is Pirate."

"And why Pirate?" Ava reached for a slice of cheese.

"Reasons having to do with my nicknames growing up," Pirate told him. "My parents called me Bup when I was a tot, which soon became Bucko. In my teens, Dad playfully called me Buccaneer. I chose Pirate as the only appropriate adult version of my previous nicknames."

"Makes sense," said Ava.

"And our daughter, Miso," I added, "is actually Mystic Soul. Are you now thoroughly confused?"

"Thoroughly," laughed Alfonso. "So, I should call you Chick and Pirate, yes?

We agreed that he should, though I knew he'd not see us again, poor dear. Then Ava chimed in, "Well, what should my name be?"

"Ah, I see," said Alfonso. "We play a game. How about Rosicrucia?"

We howled. Ava smiled. "Then I shall call you Vlad."

Chapter Twenty-Eight

BERT AND ALICE

WE SIT ON THE WORN couch together with Dr. Peppers over ice, and I turn on the recorder. With no prompting, Alice begins to talk.

"One evening, I was busy making pies for a baby shower at St. Ignatius for Letitia Mendoza. She had just had another baby, a girl she named Juana. Lord, she was always havin' babies.

"Everbody liked my mincemeat pie. I made a mean peach and apple too, but my best was pecan. I wouldn't share my dough recipe with anyone, though. It came out so nice and light. It was my sweet secret. I was cleanin' up, pies in the oven, and out on the window sill. Lute come tearin' into the driveway, the pick-up throwin' gravel ever which way, scatterin' chickens in ever direction. Fear lit on me like lightning on dry cedar. What could have happened to rile him up so? I raced to the door as Lute took the front steps two at a time."

I shift in my seat. "That must have been scary since Lute was so easy going. What was it?"

"What's happened?" I cried at 'im. I didn't know what to think. Had someone died? Was there a fire? What?"

'They've bombed Pearl Harbor!' He blurted. 'They've bombed us out!'

"I didn't even know that Pearl Harbor was in Hawaii. That was half a world away to me. I wasn't even sure where that was. Until that day, I hadn't paid much attention to the radio news. I didn't even read the *Fallon Springs Clarion*. All I knew about the war overseas was whatever Lute or Cora Lea told me. Cora usually kept up with things, but we hadn't talked about the war much a'tall. I never paid attention to what went on outside of Fallon Springs.

"Lute held me tight in his arms for a second and then turned on the radio. Breathin' hard, he wiped his arm acrost his mouth and bent his head closer to the speaker. The announcer on the radio talked so fast that I only picked up words and phrases here and there. President Roosevelt said he'd ask Congress for a declaration of war.

"I asked Lute what it meant. 'I thought we weren't in the war!' I said. Lute took me by the shoulders and looked me in the eyes.

'We're in the war now. We have to fight back,' he says.

"I remember there were tears in his eyes. I knew my Lute felt things deeper than most, but the thought that this had moved him to tears made me dizzy. I felt like a weather vane in a cyclone."

Alice's hands move the knitting needles faster. She doesn't even bother to count her stitches. How can she do that and keep talking?

"I told Lute I was so darn sorry. I asked him what I could do for 'im. He sat down hard on the chair next to the radio and put his face in his hands. That scared me for sure!"

I put my arm around her and give her a soft squeeze. "I don't blame you. I would be, too."

She looks at me with sad eyes. "I was thinking that this whole thing had happened so far from home that I couldn't see how it could hardly affect my husband so. He put his arms around me and pulled me down beside him, held me close, and buried his face in my hair. He breathed deep and then kissed me long. I could smell the winter air on his skin and feel the chill up his back.

"Then with his head down, he whispered. 'I have to join up, Tiny. I cain't ignore this. I couldn't stand myself if I stood by and let other men carry my load.'

"A couple of days later he enlisted. My blood run cold." He followed me into the house and I walked from one end of the front room of the other, wringing my hands. I don't know why I was surprised. When I thought about it, I knew that Lute loved his country as much as the next man, but he hated all things rough.

"So now it come to me that, whether he hated violence or not, he'd be goin' to war and would be in harm's way ever day. I'd have to bear up. I didn't see how I could get by alone. But then I realized I wouldn't be alone. Lots of my friends would say goodbye to their boyfriends and husbands, brothers, and daddies in the coming weeks. We'd have to hold each other together while our men were away."

The quick and graceful movements of her knobby hands, fluidly moving through the repetitive pattern hypnotizes me. I think of Chick's hands and her continuing insistence that she must work with glass. No matter that her hands are almost crippled. I guess they just ignore the pain.

She sees me watching her hands and smiles. "You youngsters talk all about your meditation. Well, you should take up needlework. It calms you down and when you're done for the day you feel good, like you've done somethin' worthwhile. You've made somethin' useful and pretty with your own hands."

I smile. "Maybe you'll give me some lessons some time? I don't have any skills like that."

I gently guide her back to her story. "So, once you

understood that the U.S. was in the war and Lute was going away to serve, what did you do to prepare yourself?"

"Oh, I dropped a stitch. I'll have to back out about ten of 'em." She sets her mouth in a firm line. "A while before Lute left, I sat with Mary Jon and Cora Lea in Cora's pink ruffled bedroom where I'd spent many a night as a girl. We were at the Brisbane's place because Cora had moved back home after Billy left. We sat there like teenagers on the bed and talked about our men. Cora and I knitted wool socks and scarves.

"Cora Lea's husband, Billy Frank, had joined the Navy a year ago and had shipped out soon after, and she still had no idea whether he'd been at Pearl Harbor or not. Mary Jon Raintree had married Jeter Osterman the year before. Jeter was with the Texas National Guard at Fort Bliss and was about to be sent out, but she didn't know where to."

Knitting blindly, her eyes searching out the front window, Alice unwinds her story and disappears into it.

"Cora was scared. She worked a loose loop on the chenille bedspread. 'If I could only hear that he's all right. Just how long will it be before they get word to us?'

"Same as me," I told her. "How long after Lute leaves will I have to wait to hear from 'im? Why cain't they tell us where they're going? Surely they'll do all they can to get word to us."

Mary Jon started to cry. I placed my hand over hers. "There's a lot of cryin' goin' on."

'I don't want Jeter to go at all!'

'Why, neither do any of us!' Cora teared up. 'Don't cry, Mary Jon. We have to be brave. Besides, it'd be treason for Jeter to not go.'

"I started to taking my hair down and comb it through my fingers. Just something to do with my nervous hands. 'President Roosevelt has called on ever man and woman.

Some of us girls'll have to get jobs or work from home. I want to do my part. It might make the time pass quicker if we stay busy, and I'd feel closer to Lute, like I was helpin' him out some ways.'

"Mary Jon sniffed. 'I guess I'm more selfish than you are, Tiny Alice. I just want this all to be over and life to get back to normal.'

"I began to braid my hair. 'I don't think we'll see normal 'round here for quite a while. As for us, we need to keep our homes together. Take care of our kids.'

"Then a thought come to me and *my* eyes filled with tears. 'Why, I'll be in charge of the farm and the money and payin' the bills and such. I've never done any of that. What if the truck broke down? Lute's brother Pietr doesn't have to go for some reason. Maybe he'll help me.'

I turned to Cora. 'Do you think your daddy might could help me with the money stuff?'

"Like Lute's brother Pietr, Cora's daddy had some kind of medical problem that kept him from having to go off."

'He might can,' she answered. 'If he can find the time. But I don't have a farm to keep up. What can I do to help out?'

'Well, for one thing you can help me with puttin' up come spring,' I told her. 'I'll have tomatoes and onions, cukes for pickles.'

"Mary Jon pulled a hankie from her pocket and wiped her nose. 'We can all pray for our boys and write to them, too.'

"I nodded. 'And only tell 'em good things, not say one complaint or any bad news, just 'bout how much we love and miss 'em. I can tell Lute about Benji and what he's learnin'. He's gonna start walkin' here soon and then I'll have a merry chase! And there's the Red Cross. They need helpers. There'll be plenty for us to do.'

"I thought to myself—do you really believe all that, Tiny Alice Slezak? Or are you just actin' brave to calm yourself and encourage your friends?

"It was a little bit of both. The comin' of war was terrifyin', and watchin' our men, young and old, leave for somethin' we didn't understand, goin' off to places we'd never heard of. What on earth do we know 'bout combat, battles, divisions and battalions? It's like a foreign language!

'All we know 'bout war is what a few of us have heard from uncles or fathers who come back from the Great War and were never the same. Sometimes I think I'd like to stick my head in the sand."

"Mary Jon sat up straight. 'But Texas women are tough and ornery. We can buck up and show our courage.'

"Weeks later Cora Lea and I sat in my front room. 'Of course, Lute had to go and join the Marines,' I told her. 'He said he wanted to be a part of the toughest and best outfit and that was the Marines.'

"The night before he left, we sat together in front of the fire. Our Christmas tree was all decorated, strung with popcorn garlands and paper chains we'd made together. I nursed Benji and Lute smoked and stared into the golden flames.

'Are you scared, Lutheran?' My voice was just a whisper. I felt shy asking him such a thing.

'Yeah, I'm scared.' He run his hand through his hair. 'I'm about to go to work for the government killin' people. Killin' boys and men from another country that I don't know nothin' about. They'll train us to kill. That'll ream out my soul, Tiny. But if this is what needs to be done, then I'll do it.'

Alice slips back into the present and seems surprised to see me sitting on the couch next to her. I finish my drink. "It must have been hard to hear him say those things."

"Oh, it hurt my heart. What I loved most about Lute—

he was brave and strong and he was gentle, too. I couldn't imagine him fighting a war. I just couldn't see it.

"A hush fell in on us that night by the fire, until I rose and carried Benji to bed. When I come back, we stretched out on the sofa, body to body, my head on his chest, his arms 'round me. I could feel the strength of him, the beat of his heart."

'My Tiny Alice.' He breathed into my hair. 'I talked to Bill Thompson over at the bank and he's goin' to sell our back ten acres—not for much—to Harlan Bouvier, and put the money by for you. I want you and Benji to be proper cared for.'

"I told him I'd write him ever day. He said he'd write back whenever he could. He said he was sorry he'd miss Benji's first birthday, his first steps, his first words, but, with good fortune, he'd be allowed some leave and could come home for a brief visit in a year maybe.

'If we can wipe 'em out fierce and fast, then it'll be over before you know it.'

"His duffel bag sat by the door. The coffee pot was on the stove, ready for the morning. Lute could always calm me. My breathing slowed and his matched mine. We fell asleep holding each other and wishing tomorrow would never come."

I shake my head. "That's the saddest...how difficult for both of you."

She stops her knitting and lets the afghan fall into her lap. She looks at me, tears brimming in her startling green eyes. She swallows, takes a sip of her drink, and then places it on the little maple table at the end of the couch.

"Things happen, Bert, unplanned and unwanted, that change us from the folks we've been into people we don't know, events that change everthin'—how we see each other, what we see when we catch a look in a mirror, what voice we hear when we speak or pray. Folks are changed, what they know, what they're sure of, their routines. Our idea of the world and our place in it goes crooked. But we hafta stumble forward, achin' for the old and yearnin' to find peace with the new.

Chapter Twenty-Nine

BERT

EVENING SHADOWS DAPPLE THE ROSE garden. I wait for Tim, and drink four glasses of wine. Too many. Three too many. I'm fuzzy-headed, mad as hell, and ready to do battle. I've sent Kelly to her room to study and threatened bodily harm if she so much as pokes a nose out of her door. To my surprise, she does as I say.

He parks his car and ambles toward me like the star of a hokey western TV show; he flashes his smile and sits, legs crossed, hands dangling—all the mannerisms which only yesterday seemed so endearing. Now that he's here I cannot sit, but instead I pace the cedar bark path of the garden. Finally, I plant myself in front of him and take a deep breath.

"What did you think you were doing? Did you think? Did Kris? And how the hell did you think you could get away with this? How can you allow people like me and the members of your church to look up to you, to trust you and..."

My voice wavers. He reaches for me, but I bat him away.

Lowering my voice, I glance toward the house. "And Kelly! How could you submit Kelly to this sad situation—telling her not to tell, that it was your little secret. How sick is that? I know it all, Tim! About you and Kris." I rake my hands through my hair. "Why wouldn't Kris confide in me? Jeez, we fantasized about seducing you. I'll wager half the women in your congregation have that fantasy. But we weren't supposed to act on it! And poor Patti. You bastard! You lying hypocrite!"

"Bert," he stammers. "We didn't plan to—it just happened. And once we started we couldn't stop."

Lord, then it hits me. "Wait a damn minute! Was Kris out late on that miserable highway because of you? Did you meet her in Austin? Is that why...speak up!" He remains silent. "Oh my god."

He grasps my shoulders and spins me around. His whole body shakes. "I'm sorry. I am. I'm sorry. We were...we met that night and we fought. She wanted to end it, but I couldn't let her go, so we argued and she took off crying. There was nothing I could do."

"Ah, damn you both. I understand now, how the accident happened. Not because of the dangerous traffic on I-35 at two in the morning, but because she was so upset that she couldn't see, she couldn't think. You're worthless, you know?"

"We wanted to tell you about us," he whines. "Really we did. Especially Kris. She said you could keep a secret, but I was afraid and then she wanted to stop and we fought and..."

Is that genuine torment in his voice? He seems truly regretful. I shake my head to clear it. I don't care how he feels. "Of course, you were afraid. You had a great deal more to lose, didn't you? Damn! It's not just me or Patti or even all the other people who look up to you, who depend on you. Kelly's just a child! What have you taught her? How can you live with yourself?"

He reaches for me again. "Bert, please calm down."

I spin away. "Oh, shut up! I've been hysterical for some time now. My life is in ruins and you've just joined the demolition crew. So, shut the fuck up and just stand there impotently and watch me cry."

After several minutes of tears, I calm myself. "I have more questions, Tim." My voice trembles. "I want some kind of explanation. Do you realize the damage you've caused, to Kelly, to your position as a pastor?"

He nods, shifts his weight onto the balls of his feet as if preparing for flight.

"Do you plan to deal with this? To bring it out into the open, and try to somehow redeem yourself?"

He ducks his handsome head. "I suppose I'll ask forgiveness from Kelly and Patti?"

"Is that it? Don't you need to make some kind of public confession to your church? I think they need to know about your little 'slip up'. And frankly, if you don't own up to this, I'll pay a visit to those people and tell them myself."

"I can't. I can't let them know. It would ruin everything—my career, everything. For Patti, too. Bert, please."

"You should've thought of that before you seduced a lonely single mom! What was it you used to say? 'It's okay to let lust get his foot in the door, just don't rent him a room'?"

"Are you going to tell Patti?"

"That's your job, but if you don't, I will."

"Can't you understand? It just happened. We never meant..."

"Bullshit. I'm getting sick to my stomach. My skin feels dirty. Get out of here, Tim. Just go."

He drives away, the car's tires throwing gravel into the air along the road.

I want Grady. If Grady were here, I'd feel cleaner and then I could put some distance between me and too much hurt. I'll call him. He'll come over. I look up through the trees at the smiling man in the moon. I flip him the finger. "What's there to smile about?"

I think maybe I should sleep alone tonight, but I call Grady anyway and ask him to come out. When he arrives I'll unload the whole sorry story, and he'll listen in that patient way he does. Grady cares. He'll care what this has done to Kelly, care about my utter disappointment, not to mention the trauma to Patti. To Tim, Patti seems an afterthought.

I put on a pot of coffee and then fill the old iron claw-footed tub with hot, hot water, splashing in some fragrant sandalwood oil. I soak until my fingers wrinkle and all of the knots in my neck and back are undone. I wrap up in my tattered robe, even though there isn't a breath of air and it's eighty degrees outside. I wait up for him on the couch with a quilt up to my chin. Out the open window I see the moon again, still floating happily through the darkness.

"If you were me," I whisper, "you wouldn't be smiling."

The next morning, I call Pirate. At my request, he comes to pick up Kelly so that Grady and I can have some time alone.

I'm certain that, with Grady I am safe. He's gentle and funny. He'll bring me down from my righteous ire at Tim. Strong and steady, well informed and wise, Grady makes me laugh, and I like everything about him, even his soft snoring and his creepy middle name. I hope he feels the same about me.

Though Grady and I have not known each other that long, we trust each other more and more, with secrets large and small, fears, and vulnerabilities, in the knowledge that what we have found together is not a passing enjoyment, but rather something we each want to relax and sink into. I'm pretty sure that I'm in love. This is what love is, right?

When his car pulls up, I instantly feel lighter and more in control of my feelings. Later I lie in his arms as hazy light bleeds through the shutters on an easy perfumed breeze, the scent of early autumn, the hint of cool to come, uncommon for this time of year—the opposite of yesterday's heat and trouble.

I raise up on one elbow. "Grady?"

"Hmm?" He pulls me to him and kisses the top of my head.

"Let's talk about something besides Tim. How about Tiny Alice? I love her! Her stories are dear, full of history and folksy wisdom. She's lived a kind of life I know nothing about. I think we may become friends. Sometimes I even talk to her a little bit about myself."

"I knew you'd like her. It's okay to get acquainted some, but don't get too attached. It interrupts the objectivity of the interview. Has she talked about her daughter, Charlene?"

"Some. Not in any detail yet. Why?"

"She disappeared when she was in high school and was never heard from again."

"She did mention that." I shake my head. Mothers and daughters apart, I think—distanced physically and mentally. Missing that special companionship. Another argument against becoming a mother. I cuddle my face in the side of his neck. "Poor Alice. We just haven't reached that story yet."

He touches my head, smoothes my bed hair. "It's probably painful for her to talk about."

"Any idea what happened?"

He sits up and reaches for his mug of coffee on the bedside table. "Charlene was a couple of years ahead of me in school. There were rumors that she'd run off with some boy, maybe found herself pregnant and took off with the father. No one could figure out who he was. She never went with any one boy. Just had a few guy friends she hung around with. Like I said, I didn't know her very well, but I always felt kind of sad for her. She was pretty much her own person. Most of us weren't surprised when she left. I don't think she and Alice were close."

Folded at the foot of the bed is the afghan that Chick made for my ninth birthday. I pull it to me, and rub it softly against my lips. The pale-yellow yarn is the softest. "That's very sad. And she never heard another word from her?"

"Not a word."

I snuggle closer against him. "I need to talk to you about Kelly."

"I think I might need more coffee first." He sits up and plumps the pillows at his back, then stuffs two behind me. "Coffee we must. Coffee we must," he chants as he hops from the bed. I laugh as I admire his fine ass as he pulls on his boxers, grabs my coffee cup, and goes off to the kitchen.

I stretch, reaching for the ceiling, tensing the muscles in my legs, pointing and flexing my toes. When he comes back in with steaming mugs and the room fills with the sweet aroma of fresh Italian roast, we do the sit-up-in-bed-hot-coffee-pillow-dance, trying to find our comfortable places without pouring scalding coffee on ourselves. When we both settle, and the coffee is steady in our hands, Grady takes a sip. "All right, I think I'm ready. Kelly?"

"Kelly. I'm concerned about Kelly's emotional problems. The therapy with Dr. Frederick seems to be helping. Her attitude is better and she seems less tense around me. Sometimes she almost likes me. I can tell. I've never thought much of psychologists or psychiatrists. I guess now I believe they can do good work.

"Whenever I ask her how it's going, she just grunts and says, 'it's going' or 'okay.' Then out of nowhere she shares the business about Tim and Kris. That had to take a lot of courage. Kelly. She's been battered by all of this.

I blow on the hot coffee. "I suppose that, as Dr. Frederick says, it's going well and they are 'resolving issues.' She's still angry with me occasionally, even though sometimes I think we've bonded over this or that. She's stopped mentioning her father."

He shifts his position, moving closer to my side. "She doesn't need to know about her father. At least not now, when she's so young." He moves his coffee to his left hand and slides his right arm behind my shoulders. "I think you should tell her that you'll continue as is, and remind her that you care." He presses his hand against my shoulder. "Bert, I think you're an appropriate choice for her guardian, and that her mother had the right idea."

I warm my hands on the coffee mug, and take another hot sip, and shake my head. "I'm still so unsure. The longer we're together, the more I care for her." I grab a handful of my hair and pull. "Ack! I can't make a decision."

Grady places his mug on the bedside table and turns to face me. He takes my cup from my hands and places it beside his. With both my hands in his own, he looks into my eyes.

"Will you let me help? I'm fond of Kelly too. I feel like I'm in this with you. If you decide to keep her with you, I can help. Can't I? If we're together for the long haul?"

I kiss his nose. "I would welcome your help with Kelly."

"Good. Then what if you take this on, with the caveat that I'll be around to do what I can to help. I can be your support. We'd make a good team, don't you think? Plus, you know you'll have your parents' support."

My breathing quickens. I pray this is leading somewhere, somewhere about him and me being together maybe... indefinitely? I mean, he's already said that hasn't he? That he wants to be with me all the time?

His warm smile slows my breathing. Just maybe...I like where this is going.

And then, sitting there in bed with me, my hands in his, his soulful eyes on mine, he says it. "Bert, maybe I'm being presumptuous, but I don't want to lose you. Not to Kelly or to your career or to your stubborn notion that you don't need a man in your life. I don't want to lose you. Period."

I swallow, take a deep breath and hold it.

"Bert, marry me. Would you do that, please? Marry me?"

I release my breath and immediately take in another deep one. I pull a hand free of his and run it through my hair. I open my mouth to speak, then close it. I open it again.

"Are you for real?" I finally blurt.

"Yes, for real! Completely." His jaw is set and he wears his serious face, the one he uses with students who don't turn in their assignments. "What do you think? Have I overstepped? Is it way too soon? I love you."

Now, we're talking about love. I've thought about love. I've dreamed about loving him; hoped that he could love me. Why am I so taken aback?

"I don't know, Grady." I sigh. "It is too soon. Maybe. I don't know. I...oh sweet Jesus, I think I love you too."

He chuckles. "Don't sound so resigned. Love is a good thing between two people."

"How would we make this work?"

"We get married. We can have a wedding if you like. Or not. Then we move in together and begin our lives as a team."

"Move in? Move in where? I don't know if I want a wedding. A party maybe. Move in where?"

He is laughing now. "Here? This is where your life is and Kelly's."

"Here is tiny. No, here won't work, besides your work is in Austin." I'm cracking my knuckles. "Are you suggesting that you'd commute every day?"

"Calm down," he laughs. "We can make the small space work. I'll make the commute. Lots of folks do. We can work out the details later. Right now I really just want you to say yes."

Whoa! As strong as my feelings for him are, a shadow of panic steals up on me. Is this too much being asked of me all at once? New kid. New man. I can't get my breath. Grady keeps talking in that soft low voice of his, a voice so like my father's, that calms and centers me.

"If you need to think about it, take all the time you want. I'm sure." He takes my face in his hands. "I'm sure about this. I've given it a great deal of thought. I want you, and I'll wait for you to decide. And this would be better for Kelly, don't you think? And make things easier if Kelly stays with you. 'It takes a village', isn't that what they say?"

I rest my head on his shoulder and breathe in his scent. He smells clean, and male, and true. I've never even imagined being married. Then, I never expected to be in a relationship like this. I reach out and take his hand in mine, run my fingers softly up his wrist and forearm. I blow in his ear. Hmm, maybe it won't take me all that long to think it over.

When Kelly came along I was alone, concerned only with myself. But now my concern is more for her. And now I have Grady and what we have seems solid and sane. Wouldn't the two of us together, with both our minds and hearts at work for her well being, offer the best option? Better than foster care and far better than risking the chance that she might later be released to her father. I wouldn't feel so awfully inadequate or alone with Grady involved.

He sips his coffee. "I can schedule classes next semester to free up my afternoons. When Kelly gets home from school, I can be there. And, if I ever need to miss a class, one of my TAs can take up the slack."

The more he talks, the clearer I feel.

Sinking back into the pillows, I say, "I guess I can go into the clinic a little later each morning so I can get her breakfast and put her on the school bus. Will you go with me to school events and take turns taking her to her therapy appointments?" He nods and I smile. "It might work."

He gazes at me, a gentle smile on his face. "Kelly is not what you wanted in your life, but it was Kristin's request. She trusted that you would honor that and take good care of her daughter."

"It probably never occurred to her that I would want to weasel out of it." I laugh, embarrassed. Having help with Kelly, having another responsible adult involved takes off some of the pressure. "Chick and Pirate will help, if we want to count them as responsible adults." I chuckle. "And Patti and Tim—no, not Tim! I won't let him close to Kelly. All that help, though, might make this work.

"I think it works." He licks his lips and I watch how they glisten.

"I don't know. You've caught me off guard, Dr. Powell."

He takes my coffee and places it on the table next to his, takes me in his arms and kisses my forehead, and tenderly touches the short hairs curling around my face. He kisses my cheek, my ear, my neck, and then covers my mouth with his own. We slide down into the warm, welcoming sheets again. I wrap a leg over his.

"Of course, you think about this as long as you need," he whispers in my ear. "And at this moment, I'll try to take your mind off the more daunting decisions in your life."

Kelly is home from school, settled in her room playing on an elaborate game console I bought on sale at Best Buy, when Grady and I come in from weeding the rose garden and ask her to join us in the living room. She's plugged in to her earbuds and doesn't wish to be disturbed. I pull out the earplugs. "Time to return to the real world. We want to talk to you."

"Do I have to?" She whines like a five-year-old.

"Yes, please. I need to talk about our, uh, living arrangements. So, can you give us some time?"

"Why? What about my living arrangements?"

"Come into the living room, Kelly," says Grady, "and let's talk."

She gives him one of her disdainful looks. "And what's it got to do with you?"

"Everything," I say, and grab a freckled leg and start to yank her up from the floor.

"All right! All right!" She laughs. *A good sign.*

I bring iced tea for us and we settle into seats, Grady and I in the arm chairs and Kelly on the couch. Kelly crosses her arms over her chest. She refuses to drink the tea I've prepared.

"So. What?" she demands.

I sit forward in my chair. "After a great deal of thought and learning a little more about the foster care system and group homes and—well, my thoughts about you staying with me have been changing. After the little time we've spent together, I'm not at all sure I want to let you go."

"Let me go? Like I'm a captive?"

"No. I mean I'd like for us to be together and try to make it work long term."

"And if you'll let me, I'd like to be part of that." Grady says. "I respect what you and Bert have built together so far. I think it can only get better."

I clear my throat and take a drink of tea. "Grady and I are talking about getting married, and about living here in our home, because this is your home now, Kelly. We want you to live with us and let us act as your parents."

She looks at each of us, wide eyed. I think I might see a tear welling in one eye, but then she says, "So I still have nothing to say about any of this?"

"No, no." I reassure her. "It's not that you have nothing to say. Of course I want to know what you think, feel about all this. That's why we're talking now. That being said, for now, I'm the decision maker."

"What Bert means to say," puts in Grady, "is that you do have a say, but ultimately Bert will decide. And I want to support her in what she decides."

Kelly looks at Grady, like a cobra about to strike, and I think, oh, boy he's in for it now. The minute you show any vulnerability to this kid, you're dead.

"Look," she says to him. "You are nobody in my life. You're just Bert's guy. You guys haven't even been doing each other long enough to move in together. You're just a good-looking guy Bert brought home to play with."

"Don't talk to him that way," I say sharply. "Grady and I are making a commitment to live together and to raise you together. We're ready to commit to you and your future. So, what will it be? Foster care or me and my playmate?"

She reaches for her glass of tea. That's a beginning, I think. At least she's uncrossed her arms and opened up a little. She takes a sip, makes a face and says, "Not enough sugar," then stretches her long legs and looks at me. "So, why the change of heart, Bert? Guilt? Do you suddenly like me now?"

"Kelly, haven't you begun to feel more comfortable with me and the idea of staying here? It seems that you have; that we've had some moments. Obviously, my feelings toward you are changing. I'd like to think you're feeling the same."

"I don't know. I guess there have been some good times. Especially at *Cielo*. I love it at *Cielo*. As for you and me, Bert, it could be better." She laughs. I do too.

"Be kind in what you say, young lady," I tell her.

"Jumpin' Jesus, don't start with the 'young lady'! You just said emphatically that I am a child."

Grady begins again, "Kelly, your attitude is lousy. This is what Bert believes is best for you and it's your welfare she's thinking of."

She spits out, "She sure wasn't thinking of my welfare when she was ready to toss me into the county home. Now, all of a sudden, she's thinking of what's best for me. Jeez, I can't keep up."

I decide to bludgeon my way past her anger and attitude. "Look. When this all first happened, neither of us was thinking clearly for the first couple of weeks. You lost your mother and I lost my closest friend."

"Yeah, never mind what it did to me."

"I'm aware of what it's done, to some extent, though you keep your feelings to yourself. When the news came that she wanted you to live with me...well, you have to admit that you and I have never done well together."

She blows her bangs off her forehead and rolls her eyes. I continue. "You know what I do at work. I know infants. I know newborns. I don't know anything about older children, like inoculations, school physicals. Shit, a thirteen-year-old kid who relies on me completely?"

She shrugs her shoulders, a move that makes me want to launch her into next week.

"But the more I learn about the alternatives, the more I want you with me. I've begun to care for you, Kelly."

"Yeah, right," she says.

"So now Grady and I want to support each other in creating a place for you. I want you to think about that."

Minutes pass before she speaks again. She stands up and walks over to stand in front of a window fan. She bends down, puts her mouth in front of the fan and says, "Ahhhh" to hear her voice quaver with the turning of the blade, and then she turns around and looks at me.

"I never liked you, Bert." She grabs a pillow and fiddles with the fringe. "Maybe I still don't. My mom spent way too much time with you. That pissed me off. It was like you got a part of her that I couldn't have. You seemed irritated by me most of the time. Mom hounded me about what a great person you were and how much you meant to her. Ack, *ad nauseum*. So, I just decided that I didn't like you.

"Since Mom died, you've been different. I usually don't like the way you are with me. I especially don't like it when you crab at me for something like getting a belly button ring, which is totally my business and none of yours. But you were cool about the thing at school and about getting me in to see Dr. Frederick, and I like her. You've been cool about some things."

She sits back down again, this time on the arm of Grady's chair and looks down at him. "You, I don't even know. You just haven't been around enough, but I see you like Bert and, if you like her, then that makes me kinda want to like you. I don't know." She moves to the couch and plops down with an *oomph*. "I hate these kinds of talks. They're exhausting."

I laugh. She reminds me of myself at that age. I was

a precocious little snot, too, but Chick loved me anyway. Loved me extravagantly, though I did sometimes feel like her personal little experiment. I got little structure from my folks, but lots of love and pot smoke, affection, wine with dinner, and rhetoric. And they did give me a great education.

"Let me ask you this, Kelly. Do you think that you and I can leave behind the thing about not liking each other? Actually, you're kind of growing on me," I joke. "I may even like you a little now. Maybe." I wink and she grimaces at me. "If we're going to keep living together, I'm going to have to parent you as we go. So perhaps you can cut me some slack when I screw up? I think I can offer you the same."

She holds my glance for a moment, and then turns to Grady. "And he gets a say in everything, too? I'm not sure about that. But Chick and Pirate become my grandparents, right? That part is awesome!"

I grimace. "Lucky you. I've never known my grandparents, but my folks already adore you and they've been after me from the git-go to take you on. All things considered, do you think we can do this?"

"Yeah. Maybe. I mean, I guess so. Yeah."

"Excellent! I think we've made a good decision."

"Have we? Then can I get a bike and some new clothes?

"Maybe. One thing at a time."

"Can we go out to *Cielo* and tell Pirate and Chick? They'll be so excited! Man, I can learn to ride a horse and perfect my dive in the stock pond." I nod. "And maybe," she drops her voice, "you could teach me about the roses. My mom loved them and I'd like to love them, too."

The roses? She wants to learn about the roses? I cross to the couch and sit next to her. "I'd love to teach you about the roses. Hey, can I give you a hug?"

"Now, you're getting ahead of yourself, Bert."

"Then, go get your jeans on," I tell her, "and something besides flip flops for your feet, and we'll head for *Cielo*. I'll give you your first riding lesson on Belly Up. Yee-haw!"

When she's gone, I let out a deep breath and sit in Grady's lap. He nods his head to my unasked question: How did I do? I mouth the words, "I love you," and he nods to that, too. I relax into his embrace.

Chapter Thirty

CHICK

PIRATE WAS READY FOR A change. He'd researched different areas that he thought would present good opportunities for his jewelry business. Berkeley, with its constant swirl of bristling indignation and anger, seemed an undesirable place to raise our child. He looked at Portland, Santa Fe, and Taos, but decided on Austin, where he believed we could buy a little place in the country and live outside the main hustle-bustle of the city.

We'd thought for some time of leaving Berkeley. We could find people of like mind in Austin, who might also home school their kids the way we were teaching Miso, hoping to arm her against and protect her from the narrower minds of many Texans. I suppose we could have created such safety and protection for her in Berkeley as well, but the decision was made. We were moving to Texas!

I'd be leaving behind my closest friend and sounding board, my dear Ava and her daughter, Miso's little friend Felicity. We promised to stay in touch via phone and mail. Still, we were sad. We'd been together for several years now and had come into each other's lives at such an important time. We'd had our babies a year apart and watched them grow the last three years into baby friends.

I would treasure fond memories of the troupe I'd traveled to California with—Willie, Sunshine, and Glory. I hoped I could get Jana Hughes down from Dallas for a visit when Pirate and I got our place in the sun. I'd love a chance to catch up.

Like a Southwest version of San Francisco, Austin relaxed into the arms of music and poetry, of concerts in the parks, impromptu theater in any available space, free spirited oratory, and the sweet smoke of marijuana.

Pirate studied pieces of land with different realtors, walked over acres and tested ground, scrutinized water tables and planting cycles. He found our special place just south of Bomar. Bomar was still a typical small town. Austin didn't reach it until the late 80s, so there was still a considerable conservative base for us to eschew, and we did so happily on our fifteen acres.

Bomar consisted of six churches and two bars, and was filled with women with big hair, and men with big belt buckles. Lots of pick-up trucks and occasional combines and backhoes on the farm roads. Sitting at the northwest corner of Travis County, over the last few years our fair town has become a bedroom community to Austin. It still is its own municipality, though, and maintains most of its small-town charm, or lack thereof. There are two distinct classes—the churched and the unchurched. (So, if you want to drink your Miller Lite, you do so only on weekends at home. Your booze is delivered quietly by Waxman Mueller, who does it for all of his Baptist friends, and then you go to church on Sundays and then Wednesdays for Prayer Meeting.) The soiled "unchurched" hang at Boniface's Stop-Spot and park on a bar stool. We enjoyed being fifteen miles from the town proper.

We called our place *Cielo*, Spanish for heaven. Our land had several acres of flat pasture that had to be cleared of rocks and deadwood by Pirate's hired illegals (he called them his foreign exchange students). We found a perfect site for our geodesic dome perched atop a small hill covered with juniper, mesquite, and live oak trees. The soil was a mix of sandy loam and dark rich loamy earth from down by the creek.

We hired a backhoe to dredge the pond a little deeper and lined the bottom with gravel to avoid the slimy mud. The workers built a cedar dock with a bench and a ladder for climbing into and out of the pond. We drew up our own plans for the dome. Pirate orchestrated the architecture and construction. Our bedroom and bath would be downstairs with a large, open great room/dining room, small kitchen, and the loft split in two with my stained glass studio on one side and Miso's little room on the other. Half for her and half for a studio for my artwork. Lots of windows throughout to allow plenty of light to pierce stained glass pieces I was making to hang in the windows. We put a triangular window in Miso's room, overlooking the slope down to the pond.

The dome was built of California Redwood and with eco-friendly construction techniques. A cistern collected rainwater, a septic tank for waste, and solar panels for gathering power from the glorious, yet invasive, sun.

Miso was four and a half when we moved. Over the phone, Ava and I worked on a home curriculum for both our girls that included lessons in art, music, and dance. I taught Miso art history and encouraged her to explore different media to find her own unique mode of expression, and I instructed her in beginning ballet and modern dance, both disciplines I'd dabbled in before we moved. She was particularly enthralled by the freedom of movement and expression in modern dance. Pirate taught her science and mathematics, music history including jazz, blues, and rock, of course. He played guitar in a band in the early sixties (hadn't everybody?). He bought a small guitar just right for Miso's sweet little hands and began teaching her to chord.

She was such a serious thinker even then. One day in her music lesson, she said to her father, "Music is like magic, isn't it, Daddy?" to which Pirate replied, "Ah, my little one, it is much more like mathematics. You'll learn."

She was full of questions. Once she asked me, "Mama, what happens when we die?"

"I believe in two possibilities, because, darling, no one knows for sure. Neither of my offerings allows for the conventional religious insistence that there is a physical or spiritual heaven and hell. Preposterous! I believe that we may become celestial beings, like stars perhaps, that wink down upon the earth from the night sky, or—and this is my favorite—that we become a will o' the wisp, a tiny breath that will communicate with you by gently blowing on the back of your neck or lifting your hair on a soft spring day."

"Are you going to die, Chick?" Her little brows drew together.

"Why, no, I don't plan to any time soon. Now, why don't you help me knead some dough."

I explored my new home, driving and shopping around Bomar, occasionally venturing into Austin, trying to meet people and get a sense of the place. Besides its bars and houses of worship, Bomar also had a gas station or two, a brand new elementary school, an old grange hall, four different churches—Baptist, Assembly of God, Methodist, and Catholic—a small HEB grocery store, the beginnings of a public library, a new brick and glass City Hall, a small department store for clothing and sporting goods, a drug store, and a few other mom-and-pop businesses, cafes and cleaners and such. There wasn't much in the way of social life for us, because we assuredly didn't fit in with the majority of the Bomar citizenry . Pirate didn't like wearing clothes, for instance. My hair was too wild, my ideas too big, and my faith only in love. I soon found out that most of the women's groups were an outgrowth of the churches, which automatically precluded me finding any sense of place within them. I missed Ava.

Pirate purchased a small storefront on old South Congress Avenue in Austin, and set up shop as a jeweler. We turned one area of our great room into an office and managed the business from home. I placed some of my stained-glass pieces in the shop, along with commissioned works and we made our living doing what we loved.

There was not much art in Bomar, especially nothing *avant garde*. This was definitely a Baptist town, though there were other denominations represented here. Pirate and I gladly, and rather conspicuously, kept to ourselves, to avoid any discriminatory scrutiny— rules, rules, rules. Don't curse. Don't drink. Don't dance. Don't have sex until you marry. Don't live in sin. Don't take drugs. Don't question. These injunctions represented the overall world view of the town—a world of *don'ts.*

Our little *familia* had a bonny, happy time. Pirate and I watched our Miso grow up, swimming in the pond, and training and loving the horses we bought. Pirate bought himself a big sorrel quarter horse and a Welsh pony for Miso. The pony had a nasty temperament, but Miso soon learned to control him. We built a small shed for the horses to take refuge from the sun. Pirate named his "Jimmy" and Miso called her little guy "Belly-Up." I'm not sure of the etiology of that name. I asked Miso about it and she answered, "That's a character in a book I'm writing." She was six.

During spring and fall and even in winter, father and daughter would spend hours riding around the paddock and then the pastures, talking, and drinking in the big sky.

One crisp December afternoon, sun winking through colored windows, Pirate sat at his desk shuffling papers as I tried to knit a cap for Miso. I wasn't a good knitter—dropped too many stitches and lost track of counting the patterns. I preferred to work simple patterns that didn't require counting or marking rows or anything beyond straight knitting and purling, but I never gave up trying.

"Pirate, darling, I need to tell you of Miso's latest difficulty at Free Child."

I'd stopped home schooling Miso when she turned six, thinking the socialization in a charter school would benefit her. The Free Child Learning Center was an alternative K-9 with a relaxed philosophy and an unstructured curriculum. They designed an individual child's program around the child's interests. Overall, Miso flourished there. Occasionally, she butted heads with the faculty whenever the curriculum became too structured.

Pirate stopped sorting papers, pushed his spectacles up his nose and turned to me. "Okay, hit me with it, Mama. I love our Miso's derring-do."

"Miso corrected her teacher in front of the class. You recall Annabeth Clarins, that tall exceedingly thin and mustached woman? Miso told Ms. Clarins that she had misused the word 'proud' and offered the correct words in the context of a sentence."

Pirate chuckled. He was charmed by Miso's precociousness and even more so when such precocity was expressed inappropriately or under improper circumstances. He liked to see her stir things up. I argued that, even in an alternative learning environment, correcting one's teacher was never a good idea.

"Did the woman try to discipline her?" asked Pirate, and I could see he was prepared to be appropriately outraged, if this was the case.

"No. She handled it well, darling. She sat with Miso during luncheon and quietly explained that correcting her in front of the class was a poor choice of behavior, to which our seven-year-old daughter responded that she found it a poor choice on Ms. Clarins' part to model improper speech for her students."

"What was it the teacher said that Miso took exception to?"

"Oh, pother!" I dropped a stitch and began the wretched task of backing out stitches to pick it up. "She said she was 'so proud to see everyone' that morning; she used 'proud' where she should have used glad or happy or delighted."

"If I'm not mistaken," he replied, "that is a Texas expression. Right?"

He straightened a stack of shop receipts, moved a coffee cup from on top of a folder, now stained with a coffee ring, and slipped the papers into the folder, then slapped the top of his little desk with his hands. "Let's bring her in here and get Miso's take on all this."

I went to the stairs and called up to her. "Miso, my darling, can you please come and talk with Pirate and me?"

Her little head appeared above the railing at the top of the stairs.

"Talk about what?"

"About the situation with Ms. Clarins at school today."

She came down a couple of steps, and then paused. "We had a disagreement." She stepped down one step. "I thought she was wrong." Stepping down two steps. "But..." Hopping down the remaining stairs. "We worked it out, I guess."

I cleared my throat. "Well, come. Come and sit with us and let's discuss it."

Miso came into the living room and went to Pirate, climbed into his lap, put her arm around his neck and said, "I guess the school called. What can I tell you that you don't already know?"

"Ms. Clarins said 'proud' instead of glad?" asked Pirate, stifling a smile.

"I don't think that was the right word." She was serious, our little girl. "Proud is *to take pride in*. She should've said *pleased*. Don't you think? All we did was show up—nothing to be proud of, you see."

Pirate raised his eyebrows at me and then said, "Isn't that

usage of proud what we call Texana? Isn't that a common colloquialism?"

"Maybe. But it still wasn't right. Just like *y'all* is not a real word or *ain't.* And Ms. Clarins should use good English so we learn the right words."

I wanted so much for Miso to have a comfortable, enjoyable school experience in a milieu that recognized and accepted her mature intellect and advanced sensibilities. I wanted her to feel a sense of belonging at Free Child. I'd hoped she would be surrounded by peers rather than children not as advanced as she. That was not to be the case, evidently. This event was a clear suggestion that such an experience was not happening at the Free Child Learning Center. I had researched the area thoroughly to find this school, but perhaps we needed to return to home-schooling, though the demands of such would take me away from my art work more than I'd like.

"Would you prefer to go back to having school here with me, darling?"

She smiled. "I just think Ms. Clarins should have agreed with me. We're supposed to take part in class, aren't we?"

Now her father was laughing. "Perhaps, Miso, you could soften how you correct and say something like 'Ms. Clarins, do you think a better expression might be . . . '"

"I just told her it was wrong." She took Pirate's face in her two little hands. "If I hadn't spoken up, one of the other kids would have."

"To some people," I ventured, "stating the obvious is considered rude. They prefer at least some obfuscation."

"I don't know that word." She pulled back her long hair.

Pirate began to fill his pipe and the sweet smell of rum soaked tobacco filled the room. Miso helped him tamp down the tobacco and then she jumped off his lap. "Are we done here? Can I go play?"

"What will you play?" asked her father.

"Jane, the ape woman. My mate Tarzan and I can swing

on those heavy grapevines in the woods. They're as big around as my arm!"

She bounced out the door with all the manic enthusiasm of a seven-year-old, followed by her father calling, "Can I be Cheetah?"

Chapter Thirty-One

BERT

PATTI'S BABY BOY IS BORN in the night. In a private room of soft grays and blues, she holds her son, gently cooing soft mother sounds. She looks up at me. "His name is Robert. After you, Roberta."

"After me?" I clear my throat, amazed.

I like Patti. We've grown closer through the debacle of Tim's betrayal. And now she names this new being after me? Jeez, I instantly care about the little guy, a feeling akin to how I'm beginning to care for Kelly. Not as strong, but similar.

I sniff and brush at my eyes with my shirt sleeve. "Thanks, Patti. Can I hold him?"

I take the baby. A brand new baby. A tiny human, all set to take on the world. I'm reminded of Kelly when she was new and innocent, before life threw her such a curve ball. I smile and coo, "Oh, I mustn't drop you! Precious one."

I have the baby-dropping dream less frequently now, though it still comes round. Usually when I've had a rough day. I know how to hold a baby. I know to cradle his head, supporting his rump with my open hand. I shift his tiny body and press him easily against my chest, burying my nose in his chubby neck. I breathe in. My eyes close. His scent is like no other. I am lost in wonder. I kiss his sweet forehead and hand him back to his mother.

She grimaces slightly from the pain of stretching to reach for him. “Tim is in the waiting room. He’s been here all night. He spent some time in here with Robert and me, but now...would you ask him to leave?” Her eyes plead with me. “Please?”

“You bet I will. You’ve got a perfect baby boy here, Patti. I think I’m in love.”

In the waiting room, I find Tim. “Patti would like you to leave. She’ll contact you tomorrow about bringing the kids to see their new brother.”

He puts on a pouty face. “He’s my son, too.” His tone is resentful.

I lock eyes with him and nod toward the door.

“I guess I have no rights anymore.” Now he is angry and glares at me.

“Rights or no, she wants you to leave.”

I’m glad to see him go, and return to Patti and Robert. She puts Robert to breast for the first time, instructed by the lactation consultant, and I ponder our friendship. Could Patti possibly fill some of the void Kris’ death has created? Could she be my closest friend? Not like Kris—never. But I really like her, now that I’ve gotten to know her.

Patti’s doing great with the breast feeding. The consultant leaves.

“Tim and I have separated,” she says. “He’s moved across town to a small apartment. He thinks all of my upset is temporary and that I’ll want him back. He’s so wrong.”

“I’m proud of you for standing up to him. I know that isn’t easy for you.”

“And since you didn’t want to, Bert, I called—anonymously, of course—the Vestry chairman and told him about Tim’s affair. The powers that be are investigating, and it remains to be seen how Tim will pay for his sins."

"He needs to take responsibility, Patti. It'll be hard on him, but...Robert's a beautiful little boy. Thanks for giving him such a terrific name." I grin and kiss her cheek and sneak a smooch from the baby. "I've got to get going. I have another interview today. I wish you could meet this woman, Alice Slezak. Tiny Alice. She's a gentle soul like you, and strong as tempered steel. She's nothing like the hard farm wife I imagine she once was. She's world-smart, self-educated and I know you would enjoy each other. I've got to go now, so I'll call you this evening, hmm?"

"Bert, thank you for everything. Your support makes me feel so much better about everything. I feel stronger. Not so alone."

I give her a peck on the cheek and a quick kiss to the top of Robert's head, and make my way to the door. "No problemo. Talk to you later." I close the door softly.

BERT AND ALICE

Tiny Alice and I have grown close over the intimate details of her long life. It's hard to share so much personal information with someone and not become either attached or appalled. I admire Alice. She is smart, but uncomplicated. Uncomplicated, but complex. I look forward to our meetings. Alice calls it *vistin',*a more apt term.

Today we'd planned to eat down by the creek, but the drizzling sky keeps us inside at the kitchen table. Alice has fried chicken and I've brought potato salad (Chick's recipe), healthy with yogurt instead of mayonnaise. Cornbread and butter sit on the table next to a plate of pickles and the ever-present tape recorder. Alice has Dr. Peppers on ice and I help myself to a drum stick.

"Alice, I'm really hear to listen to your stories and learn about you. But I feel we've grown to be friends, and I'd like to share with you a little about me. Would that be all right?"

"Of course, darlin'. Tell me a story!"

I color and my mouth grows dry. "I want to tell you something."

She nods and smiles. "Yes?"

"You know Dr. Powell?"

"Uhm hmm."

"He's not just my professor."

"No?"

I clear my throat. "We're dating. That is, we've grown to care for each other and...he's asked me to marry him." I blush. "We're going to move in together first and sort of see how it goes. Does that sound okay?"

She places a trembling blue-veined hand over mine. "I think it's fine. Back in my day there was a lot of folks never got around to getting' married. And maybe it's smart to sort of try things out before we jump in with both feet, you know? That's wonderful news. I think the world of Grady. He's a fine man and sure deserves a good woman."

I study my plate. "I've never known a man like him—so empathetic and sensitive, masculine, though not *macho.* I've really lost my head over him."

"I think that's just fine." I love how she says that word "fine," drawled with the Texas flat "ah" sound. "I wish the two of you the best. You bring him on out here sometime and we can have a visit together."

"That'll probably happen," I nod. "Alice, will you tell me about your son having polio? The disease had already been wiped out by the time I was a kid. What was it like, during that epidemic?"

She sits back and folds her hands in front of her on the table. "That polio hit Texas like a hot cyclone. It whirled around in the heat and dust devils, just looking for some poor child to sweep away. We had three cases right here in

Fallon Springs. The Lometa boy came down with it and had to be put into a iron lung, and Sadie Barnes lost her little girl, Trixie, after only a few weeks.

"We didn't know much about it then. We knew it could cripple and cause deformities. Even kill. I heard that the doctors thought it might be carried on our unwashed hands, and I worried I was to blame for Benji gettin' sick, because maybe my house wasn't clean enough or I hadn't made him wash enough. Hadn't I fed him right? Oh, I sure didn't want it to be my fault!

"Thank God, Benji didn't have to go on the iron lung, but his little legs grew skinny and wasted. I had to work his legs ever day to make 'em stronger and eventually we were able to take him to the Scottish Rite hospital in Austin, where he was fitted with braces. Even so he never grew strong again." She sipped her Dr. Pepper.

"Benji fell sick in the clutch of a vicious August." She tucks a stray length of hair behind her ears and shakes her head. "All I could think of at first was how my brother Frankie had come down with the flu so long ago and we lost him in no time, and it wasn't until Benji got to complaining about the ache in his stomach and started having pains in his legs that I grew truly afraid.

"What sorrowful work it was to sit beside his bed and watch him sweat in the furnace of that hard summer, and then see the fever take hold of him. He started to shiverin'. In spite of ninety-degree heat, I would cover him with blankets and afghans to warm him. My hands shook something fierce as I'd wring out a clean rag in tepid water and wipe his face over 'n over.

"With the heat like it was, there was no cool water to be had, so Lute went into town and bought us a block of ice like we would buy for the icebox. He chipped off little pieces to put in the water that I dabbed on Benji's face and, sometimes, I'd slip a small piece of ice between his dry lips to cool him further. Lute set the ice block up on a kitchen chair and put the electric fan behind it. It blew a little cool breeze over the bed. But his shivers did battle with the heat in the suffocating room and neither won out."

I trace the ice sweat that runs down my glass. "How awful for all of you."

"I tell you, Lute and I fought that sickness like we'd fight a locust swarm coming down on the farm, with all our strength and what little we knew, and eventually the sickness of it faded and we were left with the damage to our boy's legs and him looking at life as a cripple."

'Mama,' he asked me one day, 'I won't never be well, will I?'

"Now, sweet boy," I told him. "This'll change things for you, but you're lucky to have parents who love you and we'll do anything we can to make things better. You can still help me with your baby sister, read to her, show her how to play with your toy soldiers. Do you think so?' He nodded weakly. 'Tell you what. Now that we know you can't give the polio to anyone else, why don't we see if Mike Ramsey might could come over. Would you like that?'"

Reaching for some bread 'n butter pickles, I ask her about this Mike Ramsey.

"Mike was a couple of years older than Benji and they were friends from St. Ignatius." She takes a bite of chicken and chews thoughtfully. "He used to come over to the house a few times after church to play, and I thought it might lift Benji's spirits to be with his friend and get out of that stifling bedroom where there was so much memory of illness and pain. They could play with their cars out in the driveway, I thought, and it would get Benji outdoors.

"Benji said, 'What's Mike gonna do with me? I'm stuck in this bed.'

"No, you are not! I told him. That's what those braces are for. You need to get out of that bed and let me put them braces on you and we'll drive over to Ramsey's and see if Mike'll come over. Playin' outside with Mike'll help you learn to move better and grow stronger. You know he'll want to help."

"My heart broke for 'im, bless his heart, because I knew it'd take a long time and a lot of work for him to be active again. Still, I was so grateful, knowing it could have been so much worse. He couldn't see that, being a youngster.

"Benji's sister, Deborah Charlene was around two that next spring, a glorious spring with the grasses singing their greens, the trees buddin' out, iris blossomin'. I hadn't been confined to bed with her like I was with Benji, but the morning sickness lasted the whole nine months with Charlene. I had a hard time bringin' her into this world, but she come healthy and screaming. She was a pretty little girl, fair skinned like me but with pale freckles, with deep red hair, and her face was shaped like her father's. She had his strong jaw, and she had a temper from the very beginning. Sometimes, no matter what I tried, I couldn't soothe her.

"Cora Lea came for my lying in, of course, and held and rocked the baby and sang to her and told me jokes and, in general, jollied me back to myself. Gradually, by forcing myself to get up each day and dress and do some little chore around the house, I regained my strength, so I was up and around when Benji fell sick. As always, I was sad for Cora to leave. I loved havin' her with me. She brought a fresh feelin' of energy that I sorely needed."

Alice falls quiet, and reaches for a pickle. She makes a face at the sour taste. I serve myself more potato salad, and think of my sweet moments with Patti and Robert.

"Tell me more about your kids."

She nods at the plate of fried chicken. "Is there a wing in there?"

I pass her the plate and she takes what she wants, then wipes her hands on her gingham napkin.

"Charlene was a bright child and kept me on my toes. That one wanted everthing right now. She took to biting her playmates and that made everbody mad at us. She adored her brother, but took it as a personal irritation that he spent so much time in bed. She'd climb up beside him with his cars and soldiers and play right there on top of 'im. He taught her about his cars, teaching her that this was a Chevy and that one was a Pontiac, and they raced 'em acrost the quilt together.

"It took a lot of time helping Benji, workin' his legs and all, and running after Charlene all day. Took every bit of my strength. In the evenings, once I had Benji all settled in, I would carry Charlene to the rocker and we'd look at a book together. She loved one called, *To Think That I Saw It on Mulberry Street*...would ask for that one special, and she couldn't git enough of *Little Black Sambo*. When she got tired, I'd press her sweet head to my chest and rock and sing her to sleep. *Sweetest Little Feller*, that was her favorite. Then if Benji needed me, Lute would take over and rock her and put her to bed. He was a fine father."

I smile. "Pirate—that's what we call my dad—is like that, gentle and sweet. Do you need to take a break? Get another cold one?"

"Wet my whistle?" She chuckles. "That's what my papa always said. Papa called his beer a cold one, but seein' as I don't drink alcohol, I'll use it for my soda pop. I am a mite dry."

"Let me get them." I jump up and grab two old style bottles (she likes bottles, not cans) from the fridge.

"I get them bottles at the HEB. They're like the ones we had back when. I like 'em better than those plastic ones. There's a 'church key' stuck to the fridge. Use that."

I pop the metal caps off, and think how much I enjoy this process, listening like a friend rather than a researcher with a subject.

"When Charlene was a little older, I had to spank her for sassing her teacher at church, but I hit her with my hand, not with a switch like Siobhan did me. And then, when she was around seven, she stole coins from a Coke machine at

Stoney's Grocery. Lute thought all of this was funny and he almost encouraged her to be as wild as a boy. Maybe because of Benji being sickly. Lute would say to me, 'Tiny Alice, just leave it alone. She'll outgrow all this.' But she never did."

"I think I was a handful too." I take a bite of potato salad.

"Are you closer with your mama or your daddy?"

"My dad." I take a deep draw on my soda. "Mom and I are...we're close in some ways, but we've always seemed to rub each other the wrong way. I never know what's going on in that unruly mind of hers. Only my father really knows her, and sometimes plays referee between us. Mostly, I don't care for her imposing her way of thinking on me, or telling me what to do, you know? It's that...I want to be me and not a replica of her. Sometimes that makes me sad."

"Yessiree, our mothers can surely make us sad."

She looks at me and her bright green eyes are moist. "That daughter o' mine sure made me mad, too! I had trouble with Charlene always. We were so different. I tried not to be harsh with her." She holds up her drink bottle and stares through the glass. "I always felt like I wasn't as smart as she was."

"Do you want some more of this?" I pass her the salad and she helps herself.

"Bert, do me a favor, will you? Go into my bedroom closet. Up top on the right-hand side there is a boot box full of pictures. Will you bring those in here, please? I'll clear the table and wipe it down so we don't get grease all over 'em."

When I return, Alice is sponging off the table and drying it with her flowered apron.

She tosses the sponge into the sink. "Now, you wanna see some pictures of my kids? And Lute? I got a few. It'll give you a way to see 'em in your mind while we talk."

"I'd love that."

"You pull your chair over here next to me so we can look together."

I join her as she takes a deep breath, like she's about to dive deep into a pond, and pulls the lid off the box, setting it to one side.

"I haven't looked at these in so long. I don't know why I don't more often. Always brings happiness when I do." She pulls out a handful of old Brownie shots, and begins to sift through them. "Oh, lookie here—here's Benji graduatin' from high school. He was a good lookin' boy, don't you think?"

I lean in to take a look. "Took after his father. Had that same square jaw."

"They both did, and his sharp blue eyes. Benji never thought of himself as handsome 'cause of his legs and the funny way he walked, but he was a good lookin' young man. Lord, how I miss him."

She passes the photo to me and looks at the next one on the top of the pile. I gaze at Benji's face and imagine I can see there the pain of a boy whose life was altered by an unforgiving illness.

"Here's Lute and Charlene with their horses. They did love their rides together."

She shows me the picture. Charlene sits tall on her horse, grinning ear to ear for the camera. She looks a little like Chick must have at the same age. Her daddy stands nearby with pride in his eyes. "Pretty girl," I comment.

"She was." Alice nods her head. "She had green eyes like me, but hers held something brighter in them; the color was different from mine. More green, somehow."

"How old is she in this picture?"

"Oh, I think she was around fourteen. She was already gettin' in trouble and Lute often took her out on her horse to talk to her about things. They'd work things out that way."

Tears sit at the edge of her voice. I reach for a tissue to pass to her. "Thank you." She wipes her nose, blows it. "I shouldn't let these affect me so. I get a happy-sad feelin'. Guess that's why I don't look at 'em more often. And looky here..." She hands me another photo, this one of Lute, leaning against a fence, rolling a cigarette. "That's Lutheran. A good, good man."

We see another picture of Charlene, mugging for the camera. In a model's stance, she wears tight bell bottom jeans and a halter top, gazing smokily into the camera. All attitude. Reminds me of my mother. Then there is an 8x10 of the whole family, curled at the edges from being stuffed in the narrow cardboard box.

"We had that done at Olan Mills over in Austin. They always offered this special where, if you bought the big one of the family, then you could get all the testers for free. Price was kinda steep, but we got it and I'm sure thankful that we did. That there's my family, Bert. Guess I should put that one in a frame, huh?"

A fine-looking group, I think, and they look happy in the picture. No indication of the sorrows and failures, or the lack of communication that Alice has occasionally described. She finds another one of Benji and Charlene together. Charlene looks hip and a little dangerous, Benji serious and uncomfortable with the camera.

"That Charlene." Alice's head moves back and forth. "I never could keep up with her. She grew fast and she was sure a typical fiery redhead. As she grew, so did her temper and her energy, and the strength of her opinions. She was the exact opposite of me.

"I griped to Lute that her behavior was unladylike and embarrassing to me and that she needed to be taught the proper way for girls to behave, but he insisted she'd be who she'd be, no matter how I tried to shape her, and that I shouldn't expect her to be like me, since she clearly had a different disposition.

"One day she come runnin' into the house, lettin' the screen door slam shut, and stomped into the kitchen with Fern Albert's daughter, Doris, close behind. Benji clumped in on his braces behind them. 'Mama! Mama!' Charlene cried. Doris was crying and Benji and Charlene were both yelling at me. 'The Goodman boys were down by the creek and…'

"Then I saw that Doris was bleeding. A trickle of blood oozed down her forehead over her left eye. 'My goodness, Doris, you're bleeding! What on earth?'

'It was Filly and Curtis Goodman, Mama!' Charlene went to the fridge and got a piece of ice and took it drippin' to her little friend. 'We were wading in the shallows and they were hollerin' that there were cottonmouths in the creek and we'd oughta get outta there.'

"Well, they're right about that," I said. Benji chimed in over Doris's wails, "We got out of that water fast. You shoulda seen how fast Charlene moved,' he laughed. 'But she waited for me. She didn't run off and leave me."

'And then for no reason at all,' Charlene picked up the story. 'Filly starts throwing rocks at us and then Curtis is throwing them wild and one hits Doris in the head and so we ran home and brought her for you to doctor.' Charlene paused for air. 'Will you send Papa to Mr. Goodman to tell him about his boys? That Pettus is nothing but a worthless cornpone.'

"I took the ice from Doris and wrapped it in a clean cup towel, cupped her face in my hands and began to wipe away the blood. "Hush now. Let me see this cut."

"I parted her thick wiry hair and sure enough found a deep cut on the crown of her head that was bleedin' slowly. It was so strange to look in that cut on her black scalp, seeing the pink underneath and the bright red blood.

"My, my, that is nasty. But I think some ice will shrink it down and stop the bleeding. Hold this on your head, darlin', and I'll get y'all something cool to drink."

'And Mama, guess what. Guess what!' Charlene was still full of talk. 'They called Doris a nigger. Called her a nigger right to her face. Can you believe it?'

"I turned to Doris and asked if that was true. She turned

woeful eyes on me and said, 'Dirty nigger. That's what they said, Miz Slezak. Called me a dirty nigger.'

"Charlene said, 'And Filly said I was a lowdown nigger lover! That snake!'

"I was plain shocked to hear this, yet I didn't know quite what to say. Charlene had grown up at St. Ignatius around Doris and her brothers and sisters. We didn't think much about the Alberts being Negroes. Some gossips didn't like it, but the Alberts had been around as long as we had.

"I told 'em, You children go on out on the porch and sit quietly and let Doris rest. I'm gonna fix you some fresh lemonade and I'll bring it out to you in a few minutes. Won't that be nice?"

When Alice falls quiet, I ask her, "Are you holding up? I don't want to tire you."

"Some of these memories are hard. You know that."

I place a hand on her arm. "We could continue at another time. I could come tomorrow after work. Would the evening be all right with you?"

"Will you let me make supper for you?"

"I suppose so," I laugh. "If you feel up to it."

"Oh, I might could turn in a little later than usual to share a meal with you." She smiles.

Chapter Thirty-Two

BERT AND ALICE

THE NEXT DAY, I ONCE again work with Alice in her kitchen, breading and frying pork chops, heating up frozen green peas. Alice makes cream gravy, smooth and white, and I chop squash and tomatoes for *calabicitas,* and set the table. She chatters as we work.

"One time, when Charlene was a little older, the school called to see if she'd stayed home sick. Well, she hadn't. I thought she'd gone to school that morning. I swear that child was growing up too fast and too hard. She was only thirteen and already cutting classes. I thought kids didn't do that until high school."

I shake my head as I place the silverware on the table, which Alice has draped with a white damask tablecloth.

"I started to upset my teachers early on." I smooth the spotless white cloth. "When I was older, I didn't play hooky, but I'm sure they wished I had."

Alice chuckles. I carry a bowl of green beans and a jar of apricot jam to the table while Alice spoons gravy into a gravy boat. "To tell you the truth, I was so damn much smarter than most of them that I'd correct them and make snide remarks when they said something wrong. I think my parents got several phone calls about that." At last we sit down to eat. Alice says grace. "This looks wonderful, Tiny Alice."

"You worked as much as I did." She spears a fat pork chop with her fork. "Dig in. Sounds like you were a rowdy one, too. I was worked up over Charlene missing school so I called Lute at work and told him, and he just chuckled and said, 'I'll handle it, Tiny Alice. Don't you worry none.'"

She takes a sip of her tea and gazes out the kitchen window. I let her have whatever time she needs, thinking these talks must exhaust her.

She turns back to me and shakes her head. "I was somewhat relieved Lute said that, because I never seemed to say or do the right things for Charlene. It's wrong, and probably not Christian to say, but sometimes I don't think my daughter even liked me. No, that's too harsh. I guess she loved me, because it's just natural that she would. But she didn't seem to wanna spend time with me. Do you know what I mean?"

My thoughts turn again to Chick and the tension that often sits between us, even when we're having fun together. I hate that it does, but I can't put my finger on why we are so tentative with each other at times. I return my attention to our meal.

"After a while," Alice continues, "Charlene spent all of her time with her father. She was a tomboy for sure. She wore those blue jeans and boy's t-shirts with white saddle oxfords. She wore them fluffy scarves on her ponytail. She never played with dolls, but was usually runnin' through the woods or down at the creek. She had that pretty red hair, long and thick—real pretty. I think you look cute with your short haircut, Bert. I can't picture you with long hair."

I shrug. "I like it this way. It's easy."

"Lute didn't do anything to punish her for skipping school.

He took her out riding and I guess they talked, which was good because she surely never talked to me about anything.

"I know Lute listened better than me. I tried to when she'd talk, but I'd just git irritated and impatient. I wanted to warn her of all the dangers out there and how a girl can get into terrible troubles. Maybe I shoulda listened better."

I help myself to some jam for my meat and biscuits. Alice places green beans on her plate, letting the pot liquor flow over the meat and potatoes.

"When they got back from their ride, Charlene flew into the kitchen, straight to the refrigerator, poured herself a drink of water, and said that her daddy wanted us to have a discussion, an *intelligent exchange*, she said. She had a high falutin' way of talking.

"I asked what she wanted to talk about and she said about why she was truant from school today. See what I mean? She said 'truant' when I would've just said 'missed school.' I know now what truant means, but back then I sure didn't."

Alice takes what's left of her dinner roll and sops up gravy from her plate. "I wasn't at all sure what we were supposed to say to each other. I thought Lutheran had handled it. He said he would. Now here she was wanting a talk with me, and I had no idea what he thought that would do for either one of us."

"I made some lemonade and we sat on the porch. We sat on the glider and rocked together for a while. Then she said, So what do you want to tell me?

"Why, I'm sure I don't know, Charlene. Aren't you the one who wants to do the talking?

She acted flustered, but told me she'd skipped school to go with some girls—not very nice girls—to the Tastee Freeze in Marble Falls."

'Clemmie Hardwicke had her daddy's car, since he was sick at home. She snuck it out of the driveway.'

"And then Charlene giggled, as she said they'd had to

push it into the road so he wouldn't hear. So, one of 'em drove to Marble Falls and they'd had a grand old time. Much better than school, she said, which was boring her to death.

"I was mad. Lord, I was mad. Clementine Hardwicke and Connie Dinsmore had the worst reputations, and they were both two years older. How on earth did she ever end up with them? I was close to losing my temper."

I think briefly how lucky I am that Chick never dictated to me which children I could be friends with. Alice went on.

"I don't know what to say to you, Charlene," I told her. "I just don't know what all of this means."

"I could see she was gettin' mad. Then she said, 'That I am me and that I won't let girls who mess around and smoke and all influence me.'

"I didn't know the term 'mess around' either, but Charlene soon told me. She was straight forward and so sure of herself. Maybe Lute was right. Maybe she could be with those girls without getting herself into trouble, but I wasn't as sure as her father.

"I calmed myself and told her that I respected whatever Lute had said. 'But I'll not have you smoking cigarettes and chasing after boys, or staying out of school. That's where I draw the line.'

"She was just too young for all that. She argued that Father Mike's talks were 'asinine' and had nothing to do with her, and that she would no longer allow me to treat her like my baby.

"I felt like such a dummy. I didn't know that word 'asinine' or where she was learning such talk, and I would never have spoke of Father Socha like that. She had no idea how she was cutting my heart. I wouldn't argue with her, and she said that was just what she meant. We were not arguing.

'Don't you see? We're just havin' a talk. We just disagree. You're not right and I'm not wrong—just different, see? This is what Daddy wanted us to do. Don't you feel better? I do.'

"With that she stood up and bounced out to the corral

and hopped on her horse again. I didn't see the good in our talk, and I didn't feel any darn better. I felt my daughter was smarter than me and I was sad that this is how I felt after talking to her. I wished she could be more like her brother, nicer somehow."

"Thanks for speaking straight forward about your struggles with Charlene." I savor the last bite of my squash. "I'm lucky, I guess. I don't have any siblings to be compared to. Chick and Pirate just put up with me the way I am. May I have another roll, please?"

"I knew she was different." She went on. "In the third grade, her teachers complained because she sat at the back of the class, knew all the answers and read books she hid in her notebook. They called her a daydreamer and said I needed to be stricter with her. Then the next year they told me they had run some tests and that she was bright and ahead of the other fourth graders. Well, I could've told 'em that. I guessed she was bored with school and needed to work harder to fit in and take her studies seriously.

'Mother, she told me. I get the lesson the first time the teacher gives it. Then she goes over and over and over the same thing until I could throw up! I finish my homework in class because I don't need to listen to her repeat the lesson five times for the other kids.'

Alice sighs. "Then when she got to high school the teachers all kinda knew what to expect and so they tried to come up with extra projects that might hold her attention. She kept on actin' up that year and she drifted farther away from me, though she stayed close to Lute and he sort of saw her through that time of tryin' to find where she belonged in school. She always said she was a loner.

Alice sets down her fork and takes a drink of Dr. Pepper. "Lute got the cancer in his throat when she was just fifteen. I think she and me were both frightened that we'd lose 'im and be left with no bridge to draw us together. She suffered over his illness as much as I did, and we feared so from the start that he wouldn't live. No one would say, but I knew it deep inside me. But I never said a word to him or to her. The knowin' that I'd lose him sat inside me like a hot stone."

She reaches across the table and takes my hand. "When we love deep and true, we're afraid that somethin' might happen to the one we love, that some accident might snatch 'em from us. I don't believe, though, that we're ever prepared for the hard ways of a deadly sickness. It breaks the heart, wounds the family, takes your money, even tests your faith in God. This was all true for us when Lute got sick. I tried to gather in my kids and hold 'em close so's we could be strong at the end. I don't think I succeeded. Benji grew quieter and Charlene got angrier. Lute's leaving just busted us up and we were never right again."

Alice paused and took a deep breath. We sat quietly until, thinking we might need to lighten the mood, I said, "I'm about stuffed with this good food."

She laughed and said she had pineapple upside down cake for dessert. As she cut the pretty golden cake topped with maraschino cherries, I pulled clear glass dessert plates from the cabinet and we sat back down with coffee and dessert.

"Kris is the only loved one I've lost." I dab at my mouth with my napkin. "It's definitely knocked the stuffing out of me. I can't imagine what it's like for Kelly, her daughter. She keeps her feelings pretty much hidden. I hate to stop us at such a tender place, Alice." I push my plate away. But I've got to head back to the clinic. I have a brief meeting."

"I'd like sometime to hear about your work, Bert."

"Oh, sure. I'd love to tell you. You get some rest and I'll call to set a time for us to get together again." I give her a hug and we say our goodbyes.

On the long drive home, I find myself swimming in new

information. While barb wire and golden grasses sweep past, my mind fills with images. Most of the time I love hearing about Alice's trials and her family. Today I'm upset. I don't know why and I don't like the feeling.

I keep seeing her crooked hands chopping meat, the way she shakes her head and fusses with the hair that's fallen loose against her face. Why do I feel off, irritable? It's as if I'm moving through a dream that I don't understand, as if I'm missing something important. She does go on, once she starts talking; makes a point over and over. Is that what's making me cross?

And yet I'm learning so much from her, learning the foundations of her life—family, forgiveness, sacrifice—virtues that last through time.

I wonder about Alice's daughter. I'm fond of Alice and see only good in her. Sad that they couldn't find that in each other. I suppose Charlene simply wanted to be her own person, and not what her mother thought she should be.

Did Alice call her "darlin'" and "sweet girl" like she does me? Still on the country road, I look to the west where orange and gold arc across the horizon. Did Charlene hear affection in her voice? Alice wasn't close to her mother either. Does the friction perpetuate? Does it insinuate itself down through generations?

I think of Chick, the secrecy about her family. There certainly are similarities between her and Charlene. She has an attitude like Charlene's, though she cloaks it in peace and love. She's like Alice in some ways, too, the arthritis in the hands, the wavy red hair, and Chick has always called me "darlin"...

Then I realize what I am actually thinking. Chick and Charlene. It hits me in the gut. Chick hides her past, won't tell me anything about her family. Charlene ran away, disenchanted with her mother. Chick arrived in San Francisco a naïve teenager in 1967, I think, a year before I was born. Could that be the year Charlene left home?

I swerve right onto the narrow shoulder, throwing gravel, and slam the gear shift into Park. There is no one out here but me on this long flat road except for a large jackrabbit with magnificent ears, squatting on the caliche. I catch my breath and stare ahead at mesquite trees, at a collapsed barn in the field to the south, at a tall arched stone ranch entrance on the other side of the highway.

I try to focus. My mind goes back to the heavy way Alice rises from the chair, the terms of endearment that she uses. Have I created a possibility in my mind to salve my resentments of a mother who refuses to tell me what I want to hear? I certainly can't pursue the idea unless I get more details. And there is Charlene's demanding temperament, her deep green eyes. God, could this be true?

I grab my cell phone from my back pack and dial Alice's number. I won't tell her my suspicions yet. I'll say I just have a couple of follow-up questions from today. Five rings before she answers. I know it takes her a while to get to the phone in the kitchen.

"Hello?"

"Alice? It's Bert."

"Did something happen, darlin'?"

"No, I'm fine. I just have a quick question for you. When did Charlene leave home?"

"Why, it was—let's see—she was seventeen, so it must've been 1967, in early summer. Why do you ask?"

"I don't know. I was just wondering. I've got to go now. Thank you. We'll get together again soon, okay?" She agrees.

And then I hang up. I sit in the car in the godawful heat, the sun bearing down from behind, wishing that the roadrunner perched in the gravel would tell me what to do. Thoughts try to form, mental pictures scroll, remembered conversations. I can hear them milling around in there, but nothing seems to congeal. I need to ferret out the truth. I need to talk to Grady. I need more information. And maybe . . . I need to talk with Chick.

My eyes burn. If she did this... if she wounded this wonderful woman...if Chick kept me from her for so many years... Why? Now I'm crying. And in the midst of my anger, I am suddenly awash in my love for my mother. In spite of my resentment, I love her so. And that is why this hurts. I feel I am secure in her love, even though she really does drive me crazy sometime. Like right now. And this time, if what I'm thinking is true, she's gone way over the top.

At last my head clears. I call Grady and tell him we've got to talk. Then, my heart pounding, I call Alice back and ask if I can return right now. Of course, she says. I move the RAV back onto the highway, pull a 180, and head back toward Fallon Springs.

As I near her place, my stomach tenses again. I might have a grandmother after all. Before I know it, I pull into her drive and park, then bound up the porch steps. As she

opens the door, Alice looks befuddled at my quick return, but waves me toward the kitchen, saying, "The coffee's still hot."

"Coffee's good. Thank you, ma'am."

We sit again at her kitchen table and she pours coffee. My underarms are sticky with sweat. My forearms stick to the Formica tabletop. I feel the heat from the old coffee cup through the saucer. We sip for a few minutes while I worry a cuticle.

She reaches over and pats my hand. "What is it, Bert? Whatever has put such a bee in your bonnet? I can see you're upset."

I look her straight in the eye and say, "Is it possible that my mother is your Charlene?"

She shudders a little, a shocked expression on her face. Shaking her head in wonder, she says, "What would make you think such a thing?"

"Just listen to me. Charlene was tall, big-boned you say?" She nods her head. "She had that long vivid red hair, and fair and freckled complexion." She nods again and takes a tiny sip of her coffee. "And you say she left here in 1967? Was it the spring or summer when she left?"

"It was late spring." Looking into her coffee cup, she shakes her head slowly. "They may have their looks in common, but that don't prove anythin'."

I take her hand across the table. I take out my cell phone and pull up a picture of Chick, one taken decades earlier when I was a toddler. "Look at this picture. This is my mother. Alice, I was born in San Francisco in 1968 and I know that Chick arrived there the summer before. Your description of Charlene's appearance and temperament reminds me so much of Chick. And the pictures we looked at? I don't know why I haven't picked up on it until now. I also don't know why Chick would have hidden you from me all these years. But I think it's odd that we moved to Bomar, just a little more than an hour away from you. Am I crazy for thinking this?"

Alice blows across her coffee cup to cool the scalding liquid. She shakes her head again and looks at me, clears her throat. There is a depth in her eyes that speaks of regret, fear, even hope. "Bert, they may sound the same, but surely she'd have contacted me or come to visit after all these years?" She sounds on the verge of tears.

"Tiny Alice, if she is your Charlene, then you're the grandmother I've always longed for."

"That would be a blessing for sure." She smiles.

I go to the sink and pour out my coffee, and then fill the cup with water. Drinking, I savor the cool well water as it slides down my throat. It rinses out the oily residue of the coffee which is starting to burn up my esophagus. I turn to Alice and lean against the counter.

"I have to confront her. I have to talk with her at length, see if she will admit to any of this. If what I'm thinking is true, I'll insist she come to see you."

"Don't insist, darlin'. It's always much better to suggest.

If she has a hot temper like Charlene did, she'll not take kindly to any insistin'."

I agree. I draw another cup of water and then return to the table. Alice again pats my hand. "You don't want your coffee, hon?"

I shake my head. "This has got me all fired up."

"No reason to be riled. If it's true, well, then it's just short of miraculous and the Lord will bring about the best from it. If you're wrong about Chick, then the whole uproar will quiet down and we'll go on. Is there anything I can do?"

"You pray, don't you? Yes, ma'am. You can pray."

Chapter Thirty-Three

CHICK

I RAN INTO THE BEDROOM. PIRATE lounged in bed, nude as usual, with his tea and *New York Times*.

"Pirate, you'll never guess! Grady has proposed! So soon! Oh, but I'm just thrilled. He wants to help with Kelly, so Miso's made the decision to raise Kelly!"

He roused himself and set aside the paper. "That's excellent news, my love. Excellent. I thought all along that she would change her mind. And though we don't know the man well, he seems a steady sort, don't you think?"

"I do indeed. They want to come out for dinner tonight. We had no time to get acquainted with Grady when he was here before. Miso threw that conniption over Kelly's belly ring.

"Of course, I said yes. We would welcome them. I guess she's willing to have us examine him."

We got dressed, and after a short breakfast I sorted through the goodies I'd assembled. I'd driven to the farmer's market north of Leander and had loaded up on fresh veggies and fruit—broccoli and carrots, strawberries, bananas and melon. I got a good price on organic chocolate to melt to dip bananas and strawberries. I even found a *jicama.* I selected two cans of chick peas from the pantry to make hummus. I had a nice Havarti and a box-o-wine. Meanwhile, Pirate ran into Austin to *Maria's* for *pan dulce.*

When I returned, dear Pirate had donned clothes (a sure sign that he was taking this seriously), swept the front deck, oiled the spool table and dragged from against the fence under the crepe myrtle two of our most comfortable chairs. He re-staked the parachute for optimum shade and swept leaves from the dock at the stock pond. Such a dear is my Pirate!

He set the Havarti on a cheese plate. "Chick, my treasure, we actually know anything about Grady?"

I washed the *jicama* and broccoli. "I only met him the other day at the Buttered Biscuit and then saw him briefly, as you did, when they picked up Kelly after their Austin idyll." I began to cut veggies. "They were breaking their fast at that dreadful eatery in town and I must say he has horrid dietary habits—bacon and butter and cream gravy—and Miso acted embarrassed by my very presence. I only stopped in when I saw her little RAV 4 in the parking lot. I wanted to give her that attorney's phone number. She won't need his services now, though.

"When I first saw that boy, there was something vaguely familiar about him. All the way home, I tried to remember where I'd seen him before, but couldn't come up with any memories. I know that he's is much older than Miso. I suppose some parents would frown on that, but I don't think that matters, do you? As long as they are *simpatico.* There is something about him... but I want to be fair." I cleared my throat. "I think he's handsome, don't you? He's tall and has a bright smile and a bit of a twinkle in his eye. Still, one can tell that they're still rather awkward with each other. Of course, that will change. I just wish I could think where I've seen him before. Perhaps in Austin somewhere."

Then it hit me. The truth careened into me. I took a

few deep breaths and exhaled slowly. I'd been dodging the inevitable. I know Grady Powell. I knew him long ago in Fallon Springs. I bit back tears. Why didn't I recognize him before? But now I realize...it's been too long and he was a couple of years behind me in school. And, if he recognizes me, then he knows my past, some of it at least, and could tell Miso what he knows. May already have done so! I bit my bottom lip to stave off crying. My past does not need to be part of our present. My lord, Grady Powell. Surely, he's recognized me by now.

"What the hell is wrong, *mon cher.*" Pirate stood up. "You suddenly look sick."

I left the kitchen quickly, calling over my shoulder. "Oh...I am. I am quite sick, sick at heart I must tell you. The thing that has been dancing in the back of my mind? I've pinpointed it. And it is not good. It's crapola of the purest kind." I placed a hand over my mouth, suddenly fearful I would be sick.

Pirate moved out of the kitchen, placed one hand on my back, and gently moved me toward the living area.

"Come and sit," he said. "Lovey, tell me what has you stirred up." He pulled me down beside him on the futon.

I cleared my throat. "Grady—I know him. I don't know if he knows who I am, but we were at school together. In Fallon Springs."

"Fallon Springs out toward Burnet? That's where you lived?"

I nodded. "My home town. And he may know a lot about me, darling, about me leaving home and the rumored reasons why. What if he's said something to Miso? He knows my mother! He can tell Miso..."

He began to rub between my shoulders. "And why are you so afraid of that, my dear? I've avoided the subject all these years out of respect for your wishes, but I've always counted myself lucky to know all about the young lady you were before I found you in the park. Pre-Pirate and pre-Miso. Perhaps it's time for you to be honest with our daughter."

I rubbed my palms together and bit my bottom lip. "Oh, I don't know. I don't know what's right anymore. It's been so long."

He placed a calming hand over my restless ones. "I've never understood why you're so ashamed of the decision you made, to leave and forge ahead into your future. One, you were a child and did the best you could. Two, it turned out to be the right decision for you. Miso deals with pregnant girls at work all the time. Don't you think she would be sympathetic?"

I shook my head. "Oh, no! I'm not ready. A lot of people here still have the same beliefs and feelings as my mother. They don't care much about women's reproductive rights. I struggle so with ambivalent feelings about the abortion, as well as knowing for all these years that my mother is just a few miles away, and never reaching out to her or telling Miso. I've thought so many times of contacting her, or even driving out there without alerting her first, to look through the windows of that old house. Just to see what she looks like now. But all the thinking hasn't lead to any action. I just can't find a place in my soul where I can be with her."

"And why is that?" He took my shoes off and began to rub my feet. "What do you fear will happen?"

"I carry such guilt. I know you think that guilt is nowhere in my make-up. I pretend that's so. But I carry much regret about my youth—before I met you, of course. I don't see how she can ever forgive me."

"For what, sugar?"

"For leaving her and Benji, and never looking back. For traveling alone to Mexico for an abortion. I left home that spring of '67 and hitched a ride with some kids. Then I met you and I just went on with my new life and tried to put the old behind me. All this time, I've kept myself from her, knowing she must have worried and cried. I thought she was better off without me. I've thought about her so often, but I could never face her."

"I'm sorry you're so upset about this."

We talked for a long time.We came to a decision. I would take a Valium and we'd set the subject aside. We decided that, if Grady recognized me, we would deal with it then. There was little else to do at this juncture.

I took a quick shower and a short nap. I only wanted Miso to be proud of us, as we grew better acquainted with her beau. Pirate helped me in the kitchen and we washed and finished the vegetables and fruit tray. Pirate got the box-o-wine out of the fridge and put it on ice in the old Coca Cola cooler on the patio. I prepared the chocolate fondue and Pirate set out the cheese. Our little feast was ready.

Not too long after, a car crunched up the gravel drive. Miso's 4x4 pulled up and parked next to our van. Miso was alone.

"Miso," I cried. "Where is your friend? Where is that adorable Kelly?"

Climbing out of the car, she advanced on me with a pensive look on her face. "They're coming a little later. I need to talk to you and Pirate first, privately."

My stomach flip-flopped. "Okay. Let's talk inside where it's cool."

I threw a piece of tulle over the food to keep the bugs off and we went inside. When we were settled in the living room, Pirate lit a pipe and I sat with Miso on the futon, nervous about what she would have to say. Had Grady told her what he knows? How much does he know? "So, Miso, dear, what can we do for you?"

She ran her fingers through her hair, causing it to stand up stiffly on the crown. She took a while to begin, so Pirate and I waited, somewhat impatiently, for her to begin.

"You know that I've been interviewing someone for Grady's Elder Project?"

I placed a hand to my throat, swallowed hard. I instantly knew where this was going.

"The woman I've been interviewing is Alice Slezak of Fallon Springs, known as Tiny Alice."

"Oh, Miso, darling..."

"Don't interrupt, Chick. Let me have my say, and then I'll want to hear from you. Alice had a daughter named Charlene..."

"Oh, Gaia defend me!"

She turned a steady gaze on me. "She was a feisty girl with long red hair, tall and willowy, exceedingly precocious and independent. She disappeared in 1967 at seventeen, and Alice never heard from her again. I may be stretching the boundaries of reason here, but the years work out as far as I can see. I wonder, Mother, if you could be Charlene." She looked pointedly at me and pressed her lips together. "Is Tiny Alice my grandmother. Is this she?"

I couldn't speak. Silence pressed in on us. Bert's stare burned into me. I began to cry. Pirate gestured to Miso, and indicated she should come sit on his lap as she often does when we have difficult family conversations. She buried her head in his shoulder. Was she crying, too? She so seldom cries. Then she turned dry eyes on me, eyes that demanded a response.

"Miso, I can't expect you to understand my motivation for being secretive about my family. It was a decision I made when I was very young and confused." I stared at my feet, crossed and uncrossed my ankles. "As I grew older, persistent negative feelings about my mother moved me to continue to say nothing. Then, before I knew it, all these years had passed. Ever since we moved back to Texas my conscience has urged me to take steps to reconcile, but honestly I could never bring myself to act on those feelings."

Miso interrupted me, her voice pitched low. She shook her head slowly. "I don't understand. What did Alice do to you, Chick? What do you hold against her that you could punish her so harshly?"

"It is more what she didn't do, darling. She didn't acknowledge me. She didn't value me. I could never reach her. We couldn't bridge the gap between us. What would I say to her, if we saw one another now? I cannot imagine that she could even want to see me."

Miso shook her head. "Not true. She's kind and tender hearted. She still misses you and I think she is a person who is quick to forgive."

Pirate handed me a hankie, and I wiped my face. I couldn't stop crying. I tried to calm myself. A hush fell again, threatening to swallow us up. Was this all we could say to one another? Was this as far as we could go?

"I've become her friend," Miso shifted on her father's lap. "She spins her tales and, Chick, they are grand. Can you tell me why you felt there was such distance between you?"

"I can't go into that now, my love, but over time I will tell you everything. I give you my word."

"And would you want to see her? Perhaps make amends?"

I began to push back the cuticles on my nails, gritting my teeth. I thought for a while, still teary eyed, and finally admitted, "I can't say. I need to think and meditate on it."

At that time, we heard another car pull up. Grady and Kelly.

"Miso, does Grady...?"

"Yes, we've talked about it. He thought you looked familiar, but didn't realize that you'd been in high school together until I told him my suspicions. He wanted me to come and talk to you both before he came."

"I appreciate that," I said. I stood, and smoothed my hands down the front of my dress. "Well, then..." I started for the bathroom and stopped to place my hand on Miso's arm. "Please try to see some of this through my eyes. Don't condemn me until you know everything." She squeezed my hand. I sighed and went off to the bathroom to pretty myself.

Chapter Thirty-Four

CHICK

THEY PULLED UP IN AN old Land Cruiser, and Grady parked carefully next to the house, for which I was thankful because our Miso always drives up fast in clouds of *caliche*. Grady and Kelly piled out of the car and greetings were made. Grady took my hand and gave me a knowing look. I averted my eyes.

"Pirate," Miso teased. "Thanks for dressing for the occasion."

Pirate wore a *dashiki* and his flip-flops. I knew Miso was not being glib, but was truly glad he didn't greet them in the nude. Dear Pirate, he so loves to go *au naturel*.

Kelly ran up and flung herself at him. She put her arms around his neck and he lifted her up. "Hey, old man," she said, and Pirate laughed heartily.

"Come, come, come to the table, dears," I urged, and Kelly then ran to me with a big hug. "Hello, my darling! How's your belly? All healed?"

"Pretty much. It still itches a little." She grinned at Bert, fondly. "Boy, was Bert mad!"

"Can I get you a glass of wine?" I asked Grady.

"Yes, thanks." He stood rather awkwardly next to Miso.

"Miso?" I asked, knowing what she would say.

"Is it from a box, because I'd rather have a glass of something that's not so watered down."

That hurt my feelings, but her father spoke up that he had some merlot stashed away.

"How you can drink red wine in this warm weather is beyond me, Miso." I turned to Grady. "Which would you prefer?"

"The white sounds refreshing to me, Mrs. Lando."

"Now, you must call me Chick. We must all be on a first name basis here."

Miso piped up. "Chick, or Charl. . .?"

"Watch yourself, young lady." I gasped quietly, which stopped her.

Pirate rubbed the bald top of his head. "Grady, so you're with the Anthropology Department at UT?"

Kelly turned and started off toward the corral, calling back over her shoulder. "Oh man, if you're going to talk about work, then I'm going out to see Belly Up."

"Kelly," called Miso. "Come back and eat your dinner. Then you can mess with the horses."

Kelly made a face and groaned, but walked, dragging her feet, back to the table.

"Yes. My focus," Grady was saying, "is on family systems and I've currently got some fascinating field work going. Miso has probably told you. Students travel to small towns around the state and interview the elders in those communities to record their stories and memories of life in Texas throughout the twentieth century. My teams are made up of students and teaching assistants. I'm hoping to get a book out of it."

"I'll bet you've heard some doozies," Pirate placed a generous dollop of hummus on his plate.

"I think most of them are true," Grady nodded, letting Miso fill a plate for him. "Maybe exaggerated, but basically true. Our memories come through internal filters into at least an approximation of the truth. They may represent the most important part of oral history. At least I think so. Some of the people I talk to are quite accomplished now, but remember the simpler times when they grew up. And some are knowledgeable about government and current events of their times. Some aren't. That's what makes the work so fascinating. I did similar work for my dissertation."

I handed him the fondue fork. "Try the chocolate on the strawberries. It's such a treat."

Miso left to fetch wine for Grady, and then returned to stand behind him. She placed a hand on his shoulder. He glanced at her and smiled, and that is when I saw the true depth of their feelings for each other. I felt extraordinarily happy for them.

After dinner, Miso suggested we all go down to the pond for a swim. She and Grady had brought their swimwear with them, so I changed into my bathing costume and Pirate, of course, once down at the pond, kicked off his flip flops. Kelly wore a little yellow bikini under her shorts and t-shirt.

"I do hope you warned your young man," I said to Miso, "about your father's proclivity for nudity? Perhaps he can be persuaded to slip on his Speedo since we have company."

Grady laughed and said nudity was no big deal to him. "Just as long as we're not required to do the same."

Pirate cracked up. "In your honor and to protect Kelly's sensitivities, I've worn a swim suit." He swept off his *dashiki* to reveal his bright orange Speedo, and dove in.

"Last one in is a horse's..." shouted Kelly as she ran and jumped. Breaking the water as she bounced back up to the surface, she cried. "Whew! The water feels great!"

Miso and Grady slipped into the dome to change. They came back down the path hand-in-hand, and dove in to join Pirate. I eased myself in from the dock edge. We had a nice float and then three of us left Pirate and Kelly in the water and stretched out on the dock.

Pirate treaded water, and addressed Grady. "So, this

work you're doing, does it matter if the stories you gather are not historically accurate?"

"Ack!" said Kelly. "Is work all you can frigging talk about?"

"Young lady," said Miso, "keep those kind of thoughts to yourself."

"The evidence I'm collecting," Grady went on, "is anecdotal in nature. Absolute truth isn't the goal; rather the storyteller's perspective on experiences unique to them, to their families. They reminisce about major events from their times, and how those events impacted their lives."

Pirate ducked under the water, reemerged, and squirted a fountain of water from his mouth. "I'll bet some of your subjects are real eccentrics."

"Like you, Dad?" Miso asked.

"Ha! I think we grow more into our true selves as we age. Would you agree, Grady?"

"I would." He winked at me. "I guess Miso talked to you about Alice Slezak, and our, uh, suspicions about her. She was a good friend to me once, a woman who liked to spend time with a skinny teenage nerd who couldn't find his place with his peers. My parents were both professionals who worked a lot, so she came to my football games and cheered for me, and later sat with my folks at my graduation." He glanced pointedly at me. "From her I learned about kindness and tolerance and the value of quiet listening."

I sighed. He made Alice sound like a saint. "All that?" I chewed on a thumbnail.

Grady continued. "She was born a few years after the turn of the century, and has watched Texas develop from the early 1900s to the present. Her memories are rich, her stories gripping. She lost a brother in the 1918 flu pandemic, saw her father make moonshine during Prohibition to put food on the table, lived through the Great Depression, buried a couple of children. She's got a fascinating history, in some ways a very Texas history."

"But you know all this, don't you, Chick?" Miso interrupted. "She's your mother, and she's my grandmother."

I guessed we were going to have that talk right here and now.

"Tiny Alice Slezak is my grandmother." She shook her head and spoke sorrowfully. "Why have you kept her from me all these years?"

"Wait!" Kelly practically shouted. "You have a grandmother?" She joined us on the deck. "What's this? Why haven't I ever heard of her? Met her?"

Miso motioned for Kelly to sit on her lap, and wrapped her arms around the child's middle. "You'll have to ask Chick about that." She smoothed Kelly's hair; Kelly allowed her to. "You know, Chick, I wasn't able to complete the first assignment I had in Grady's class."

"What was that?"

"To map our family tree. Mine had two branches only—you and Pirate."

"No, now, you had Pirate's parents and his brother and sister."

"That's right, I did. But now I have Alice and a wider family and a heritage she can tell me about.

Kelly perked up. "Now we can all gather for holidays and birthdays and . . ."

"Don't get too far ahead, darling." I turned to Grady. "And you? Do you come from a large family?"

"Don't you try to change the subject." Miso's jaw tightened.

Grady put a hand on her arm. "No ma'am," he looked at me. "I'm an only child. I knew my grandparents, though, and my maternal grandfather was a strong influence on me."

"Well, isn't that nice. You see, Miso. Grady has a small family, too."

"I often thought that," said Miso, "if I had a grandmother, so many things would be easier. She'd be a cushion of sorts. Between you and me, Mother."

"Grandmother, Miso?" teased Pirate. "What about a grandfather? Equal rights and all."

"I found a grandmother. And now I want to know more about the people I come from."

I rubbed two fingers across my forehead where tiny beads of sweat had gathered. "Miso, you know the question everyone down here asks—Who are your people? Now I can say I come from the Slezaks of Fallon Springs."

I sighed, resigned. "You can say much more. Alice's family, the McGloins, were Texas pioneers. They helped settle the land out around Marble Falls and Burnet County."

Miso looked at me open-mouthed. "You have kept all of this from me! Really Chick?"

"Well, good on y'all." Kelly put her chin in her hands. "I don't have any people. My dad is long gone and no one will tell me anything about him, and my grandma is out in la-la-land at the old folks' home."

"Don't disrespect your grandmother," Miso admonished. "We'll try to make up for all that."

"Miso, you've enjoyed a close relationship with your father and me. That's been lovely, hasn't it?"

Grady nodded his head. "It is valuable to know and understand a shared family history. To know where we came from gives us a sense of belonging."

At last, exasperated, I said, "Look, darlings, we are dancing around the elephant here. Why don't we be honest about this? If I can give up my fear of the subject, then everyone else can speak freely." I reached over and placed my hand over Miso's. "Simply put, I didn't get what I needed from my mother. It's paramount to a healthy upbringing, I think, that a girl and her mother connect on a deep level. You and I do so. I've tried to ensure that there has always been little emotional or mental distance between you and me. There was a great deal of distance between Alice and me."

Miso said softly, "You and I have locked horns on a

regular basis. We're very different in so many ways, but you're right—I've always felt secure in your love. I never doubted that."

I squeezed her hand. My breath grew shallow and I felt a bit light headed. "That closeness is what I craved from Alice. We doubted each other. We simply could not find one another across a sea of differences and expectations. She was almost forty when I was born. There was a huge gap in our realities. Then my father died..."

"Lutheran," Miso stated.

"Yes. My precious Daddy. I loved him too much, I think. But when he died, I felt abandoned. Left alone with Alice."

Kelly crossed the dock and draped her arms around my neck and rocked me back and forth. Sweet girl.

Miso raised sad eyes to mine. "Alice says an expectation is a disappointment waiting to happen."

I chuckled softly. "I remember her saying that to me. I suppose I was so wrapped up in myself, I missed the wise, tender parts of her."

Grady interrupted, "Maybe now you could know her in a different way. You might learn a lot from her."

Pirate launched himself from the water onto the deck, and deftly slipped into his robe. He waved his arms as if shooing gnats. "Okay, okay. Enough with the heavy stuff. Let's move to something else. Can we? We can resume this discussion another time. We've ignored the most exciting news of all. Grady and Miso and Kelly—one happy family."

Kelly dropped to her knees and leaned into Miso, stretching thin arms around her neck. "Thank you," she said earnestly. She lay her head on Miso's shoulder and took Grady's hand.

Pirate rose and, crossing to Kelly, placed his broad hand on her head.

My own tears spilled over. "Oh, Miso, Grady, this makes my heart so glad. I think you'll be remarkable together." I stood up. "I'm going to begin straightening up. Anyone want to help? Kelly, why don't you and Miso go visit the horses? Grady can help me with the clean up, and your father can go down for his nap."

Grady rose from the deck and offered me his arm. At the spool table, he stacked the paper plates, gathered skewers and a tray of fruit rinds. I followed him into the kitchen with the sticky fondue pot.

"I'm a pretty good dishwasher, Chick. Will you let me? That was my chore growing up— one of them anyway. Let me make my mother proud."

I gently shoved his shoulder. "Chores are good for young ones. They build responsibility." I heard Pirate come inside and pad off toward our bedroom. "I never turn down an offer of dishwashing. Though Thich Nhat Hahn speaks of the 'washing dishes meditation' and I have to agree with him that the feel of the warm, soapy water does take one to another level."

"I'm not sure I've ever had that experience," he laughed and turned to the sink, "but I'll see what happens."

I turned our conversation to Alice. "Grady, you said you learned so much as a boy from Alice. How did you come to spend time with her?

"Your mama always took an interest in me. After you left, especially. I had good parents, but my dad worked hard and my mom was often busy with committees and clubs. I found myself at loose ends sometimes. Didn't have too many friends. Too much of a geek. Alice took up the slack, having me over for coffee or Dr. Pepper and talking to me, listening to me. Besides my mama, no one had wanted to know about me until Alice. She became my sounding board."

He talked on about Alice's kindness, her interest in whatever he had to say, her willingness to voice an opinion on how he might confront different adolescent dilemmas. He described a woman I'd never known. My chest felt tight, and I forced down my anger and hurt as he continued.

"She helped me get over the slights of the other kids.

I read too many books, wasn't active in sports, did things like edit the school newspaper and run for student body president. I didn't have many friends, and she was there. We shared something special. She helped me feel better about myself and taught me to believe I could cope with whatever came my way."

He placed one final dish into the wooden drying rack, drained the sink, and picked up a cup towel to dry his hands. "It has meant so much to Miso to get to know Alice. It's a gift to have her grandmother in her life. I hope you'll consider meeting with her."

I wasn't yet ready to commit to anything. "Well, you keep drying these dishes and I'll step outside to check on the others. Come on out when you're done. Do you mind?"

"Not at all," he said.

I stepped out into the October air and took a breath. Autumn wasn't far away. The heat in the air would lessen, in the coming weeks, soften like morning fog burning off of San Francisco Bay. I stood for a moment, watching a corner of our parachute flap in the wind, like a ship's flag, bright colors against a blue-white sky. I was happy to be alone for even a moment. This talk of Alice made me profoundly uncomfortable. Could I meet with her? Did I even want to? What could we be to each other at this stage in our lives? I didn't know what to do.

I know there are people who can set aside their own wants and needs, sometimes their own happiness, in order to resolve a quandary, even one as large as what I faced. I admire those people, I do. It's difficult for me to admit that I've been a self-absorbed person. First in childhood as a comfort mechanism, but carried into adulthood because that is how I built my character as I reinvented myself. I suppose there are those who would blame me for that, but part of that self-orientation has allowed me to remain unmoved by blame or shame from anyone other than myself.

And now, after too many years of careful ignorance about

my mother, now the guilt rises from the darker corners of my soul. Guilt, and I think perhaps a secret longing, a longing for the mother I've missed all my adult life.

Chapter Thirty-Five

BERT

IT'S A SOFT, PASTEL MORNING as Grady and I drive to Alice's house, past the giant black iron gate where I'd had my revelation about Chick, the gate set against massive dark stone, with two decorative iron wagon wheels on each side. The big ranches seem to compete for the most impressive entrance—massive stallions worked in wrought iron, the silhouette of a lone cowboy leaning against the gate, his hat tipped down over his face. We turn onto RR 652, and ride into gently rising hills.

I know that this meeting with Alice will be different. I cling to the hope that this

delightful and knowledgeable woman, this charming and consummate storyteller, this brave and devoted mother is indeed my grandmother. If so, I am privileged. I am blessed.

Maybe I've built up Alice in my mind as a paragon of womanhood. I don't want to do that. I know I shouldn't do that. She wouldn't want me to. She doesn't see herself that way, and her natural humility causes her halo to shine even brighter. I must learn to see her more realistically. Is that what children do? No. I don't think so. Certainly not grandchildren.

Don't most children idolize and romanticize their grandparents? If they're good grandparents, that is. Don't grandparents get to spoil their grandchildren? Don't most grandchildren count on that spoiling? Yes, they do. I won't chastise myself for thinking the world of my very own grandmother. And how fortunate that I've had a chance to get to know her and see her character before knowing that we're related. No longer casual friends, but family. Her tales of colorful ancestors and history shed light on the connections that make us kin. Her stories of joy and sadness are my own.

We turn once again onto Pitcher Road. Grady rolls up the windows to avoid the caliche dust that billows up from the dry road bed. We park and I greet Leroy, the yellow dog, as he limps out to welcome us. Alice has seen us coming and stands on the front porch with her hands cupped over her eyes against the sun. As I mount the porch steps, her arms open.

"Oh, Bert darlin'!"

These are the same words with which Chick greets me. I give her a hug. "Tiny Alice. How are you?"

"Now don't you go callin' me Tiny Alice. If what you said on the telephone is true...Why, I've lived half my life wishing I had someone to call me Grandma."

"Grandma. That's what you'd like to be called?"

"I guess, if I'd found you when you were real little, you might've called me Nana or Mimi or Gammie, or some such nonsense, but, since I've got you now, Grandma seems fitting.

"Then...Grandma." I like the feel of it on my tongue.

She takes my hands into hers and beams, pouring love and wonder into me. My eyes fill with tears as I grin back at her. Grady looks on, leaning against the porch rail, his arms folded across his chest. Alice and I stand with our hands joined and our eyes full of mutual love. Each of us is dumbfounded by our good fortune.

Alice pats my hand with hers. “I thought maybe we can have some early lunch and talk some more.

I’m wound up and I take a few deep breaths. “I hope you’ll still tell me more stories.”

She pulls open the screen door, and Grady and I follow her into the house. “I’m sorta weary of my own stories. I want to hear about you two. What are you doin’ in your nursin’ job? Grady, what’s it like teachin’ up at the big university? Let’s get out this food I’ve made and we can eat out under the weeping willow. Grady, in the top of my hall closet there’s an old quilt and my parasol. Can you please fetch ‘em?”

“Alice, do you need help in the kitchen?”

“I can use some help. All the food’s ready.”

She pulls from the fridge some fried chicken, a bowl of potato salad, and a tub of coleslaw. Biscuits rest on the counter top, beside a loaf of freshly baked bread.

“I made some of my best pickle relish. Just for y’all. I know it’s warm outside, but up there on that old hill there’s always a breeze. And we can spread out under the shade of the willow.”

Grady bends over to smell the fragrance of the fresh bread. “Alice, this is a feast! You shouldn’t have gone to so much trouble.”

“Oh, balderdash! What else have I got to do with my time?”

We slice the bread, and I get out two jars of jam. I’m smug and happy that I know where she keeps the jam. She already has sodas in the cooler. Grady helps us tote the food outside, and I make my slow way to the willow tree, with Alice on my arm.

Once there, we spread the quilt on the ground. I set out paper plates and cloth napkins, sewn by Alice I’m sure. Grady takes abundant helpings of everything, filling his plate until it bows from the weight. Alice smooths a napkin across her lap. We dig in, and after a time of contented eating, I address one of her questions.

"I work at a clinic that only sees women for *female issues*, if you know what I mean. We offer many different services for women. It's located right in the center of Bomar. Have you ever been there?"

Alice laughs, and swipes her mouth with the napkin. "I'm not much of a traveler. I been to Burnet, Marble Falls, to Austin a couple of times, and once to San Antonio a long time ago to see a doctor. Oh! Lute took me up to Dallas back in the thirties to the State Fair Park. It was the one hunnerdth birthday of Texas! We had a fine time."

I slide my fork into the potato salad. She makes it with mustard the way I like it. "Parts of Bomar are pretty and our clinic is in one of those older areas where there are big oak trees and lawns around all the buildings. In fact, it's on the lawns and under the trees where the protesters gather."

Her eyebrows come together. "Protesting what?"

"They think we do abortions, but we don't. Grandma, we don't."

She nods her head. "I'm glad to hear it."

I help myself to a thick slice of bread and nibble on it. "It's not a service we offer. However, when a woman's health is threatened, it is sometimes necessary to take measures to save the mother."

Alice shakes her head. "I don't think it's ever necessary to take a little baby's life."

I sigh. "Grandma, can we agree to disagree on that so I can tell you what's going on?"

After a brief, uncomfortable moment, she agrees. "Okay, git on with your story. I'll shut up. For now."

Grady clears his throat, and explains. "The protesters are members of a conservative church led by a man named Tim Axtell. He and his wife are divorced, and Bert is friends with Patti but not with him, for reasons I'm sure she'll share some other time."

"True," I go on. "The church members have been coming to the clinic for weeks now—they bring their kids, and it's almost like a social thing for them, a picnic. Not for us. They harass our patients on their way into the clinic, and have scared or shamed some of them away. Chick is the counter balance. She shames the shamers and convinces some of them to go home."

Alice takes a long drink of her iced tea. "Well, if y'all don't do abortions, what are they all riled up about?"

I tell her about Irene Salazar's death. She seems shocked and nods her head. "She didn't die from how y'all treated her?"

"No, she died from neglect," Grady says, "because her family wouldn't bring her back in for follow up treatment."

"But they blame us," I say.

She nods again. "And you say, um, Chick goes there to try to talk them out of what they're doing?"

I chuckle. "Chick has developed the perfect strategy. Some of the people get angry and shout at the patients, trying to shock them. Chick listens quietly and then, with her maddening logic, *persuades* the protesters that they're mistaken and talks them into leaving. It's pretty amazing to watch her work."

Alice swallows, and folds her napkin over, and then folds it again. "She sounds real nice, this daughter of mine."

"She's nice, but also fierce. Fierce in everything—reason, conviction, and love, especially love. Are you excited to see her and try to bridge all the years apart?"

A long silence falls as Alice sits unmoving, her gaze fixed in the distance toward the creek. She reaches for a boiled egg, cracks it on the corner of the wicker picnic basket, begins to peel off the pieces of shell, letting them drop into the plate.

To leave her to her thoughts, I start to pick up our napkins, put lids back on the plastic bins.

"I don't know about that, Bert." Entranced now by peeling the egg, she continues softly. "Grady, I think there is salt in the basket. Could you hand it to me?"

He does so. I wonder if she's going to expand on her comment or just leave it at that.

"Grandma?"

She lifts her eyes to meet mine. "I'm not sure. I don't know how it'd be seeing Charlene again. I just don't know if that's what I want. You know, to stir that all up again. Why should now be any different from then?"

The last of the egg shell falls away except a small portion that sticks to her hand. She shakes it free and picks up the salt shaker.

"Does she want to see me?" Her voice sounds shy, childlike.

I put the uneaten pieces of chicken in the tub they came in and tuck them into the basket. Then I take out an egg and peel it for myself. "She's uncertain like you are. Could it be that you each have expectations that you don't want to disappoint?"

She takes another bite of her egg. "I love boiled eggs, don't you? Especially when the eggs are fresh. I git these down the road at Thigby's. They're fresh everday."

"They're delicious," says Grady. "Alice, we'd like for the two of you to meet. To see if you could possibly rebuild your relationship."

Alice raises her eyes to me. They glisten with tears. Or is the sun just catching them at a bright angle?

"I don't know, child. Can you let me think on it? I'd like to think on it some."

I nod and the three of us, in silence, begin to pick up the picnic items to return to the house.

Chapter Thirty-Six

BERT

PATTI CALLS AT SEVEN THIRTY as I'm almost out my front door. I've just put Kelly on the smelly, old school bus with the same bus driver who drove when I was in school—a giant woman with thin hair and bad teeth and a worse disposition. Kelly walks to the rear seat, and then waves at me through the back window, and I say to Patti, "What's up?"

"Bert, I need to see you." She gulps, and stutters. "T-Tim keeps b-bugging me about the children. He wants to see them more often. I don't want them around him. I don't know what's fair." She is crying now. "What's best for the kids? When he cries on the phone, it's so damn pitiful. I feel guilty. Then I get angry about feeling guilty. I don't think I should feel guilty. Darn it! And I don't know about a divorce, but I'm so angry now that I can't think clearly."

"You don't have to decide about divorce any time soon. You've taken the first step. You stood up for yourself. I'm proud of you."

She sighs. "I don't know if I'm proud of me or not. But, I'm glad he's gone for now."

"That's okay, Patti. It's okay to feel relieved."

"Yes." She sighs again. "Well, I also called because Operation Ransom is doing a big sit-in at the clinic today."

I shrug. "They've been there all week. How's today supposed to be different?"

"Just bigger, I think. More of us."

"What's all this nonsense about Irene Salazar?"

"Bert, you know that girl shouldn't have died."

"I also know about her medically necessary D&C due to placenta retention, which had nothing to do with her death. And which was *not* an abortion, Patti. If her family had allowed her to return for after-care, she wouldn't have developed toxic shock and none of this would have happened."

"I don't want to argue, Bert. I don't want you to be mad at me."

Why not? *I* want to argue. Patti and I disagree on so many issues, political and spiritual, but it's important that we not allow that to threaten our newfound closeness as friends. I'll be interested to see if we can overcome our differences at some point.

"I'll be there with the demonstrators today," she says. "I just wanted you to know."

"Will Tim be there?"

"I doubt it. The church has put him on leave, so he'd only be there to make an appearance, or maybe just to rattle me. Of course, the kids would want to see him and love on him. I have a sitter for them."

I gnaw on my lower lip. "I hope he doesn't show. For your sake. I'm on my way in. What time do you barbarians plan to descend upon us this time?"

She chuckles. "A little after noon."

"Okay, come in to say hi when you can..."

Four hours, two pelvic exams, and a false alarm later, I am in the back room at the clinic, replacing supplies in my workbag. Looking out the supply room window, I see all the usual suspects, including Chick, who is talking to a young person with a notebook, no doubt a reporter. Chick is surely shaming the girl as much as she shames the protesters. She's an equal opportunity shamer. I shift my attention back to supplies. Next, I'll assist Teri with one of our older mothers who, at forty-two, is about to deliver twins and needs close monitoring.

"Hi!" Patti's pretty head peeks around the corner. "You told me to come in. Can we have a quick cup of coffee?"

"Sure." I give her a squeeze, glad to see her delicate face. "It has to be quick, though. I've still got patients to see. You fix the coffee." I nod toward the machine. "I'll finish organizing these supplies.

As I rummage through the large metal cabinet in the storeroom, a huge pressure suddenly slams down onto the room. A pounding concussion follows. Am I'm having a heart attack?

"Patti..."

A great force pushes on us. A quick, vicious tremor. The roar of what can only be an explosion. I'm thrown across the room. A large, heavy cabinet falls across my body. What on earth has happened?

"Patti!" No answer. I concentrate on my body, the weight of the cabinet. I can wriggle my toes and fingers. No broken bones, but searing pain radiates down my left arm. I've got to get the weight off me, so I begin to heave and barely manage to scoot out from under the cabinet. I lie still. Confused. Ceiling pebbles sift down on me. Smoke curls into the room from the direction of the waiting area.

Am I hurt? Can I breathe? Am I bleeding? What the hell? My ears ring. I can't hear a thing. What just happened? I call again to Patti. Inside my head, my voice sounds vacant and far away.

Gradually, my thoughts clear. There's been an explosion. In the clinic. That doesn't make sense to me. How bad is it?

I stand and check myself again. My arm throbs where the cabinet caught it, but there's no open wound. Still can't hear. A cut above my right eye oozes. It feels wet and blood oozes down my cheek. I grab a gauze pad off a shelf and press on the wound. Black smoke billows from the hall. I lumber over and close the door. In the next second, the sprinkler system kicks in and water begins to pour from the ceiling.

The cabinet is between me and Patti. I make my way around it. Again, I call Patti's name. Then I think—Teri, Sharon, the patients! I pick my way through strewn supplies—sterile packs, gauzes, sponges, dressings. Then I see Patti. She's down, her head bleeding profusely. The cabinet over the coffee maker has fallen from the wall and knocked her down. I limp over to her, my left knee threatening to buckle. Using all my strength I push away the remnants of the cabinet to examine her head. She opens her eyes and moves her mouth, but I can't hear her words.

"Patti, show me where you're hurt besides your head. Do you know?" She shakes her head and then winces.

I grab more gauze dressing and press it against the laceration on her head. "Put pressure on that. Now, listen to me. I've got to check on others. I'll close this door and you rest here. Just stay here on the floor till I come back to get you. I've got to see what our situation is. Okay?"

She nods. I feel the door for heat first, and then cautiously open it. I stagger into smoke so thick that I can't see down the hall to the lobby area. The heat and smoke seem to come from that direction.

"Teri! Sharon!" My voice throbs inside my head. "Anyone?" I can't hear an answer.

At last my emergency training kicks in, and I drop to my hands and knees. There is better air along the floor. I crawl down the hallway, calling out again to my colleagues.

"Teri! Sharon! Who's there?"

Vague shouts and a muffled clamor of voices seem to come from far away. Sirens howl in the distance. Feeling my way toward Sharon's front counter, I peer into the waiting area. Through a haze of thick gray smoke, I see that the wide plate glass window at the front of the room is smashed. Flames lick the draperies and blacken the couch and chairs. I go for the fire extinguisher behind the counter and there I see Sharon. She is down. Not moving. I kneel and take her wrist, find a pulse. I shoot the extinguisher toward the flames, but its force isn't strong enough. I throw the extinguisher away and go back to Sharon. Her arm looks broken. I gently move the arm across her chest and take her by the ankles. Using all of my strength, I drag her toward the back exit. By the time I push open the back door to pull her into the outside air, I'm gasping and coughing, tears running down my face. Sharon still has not moved, and I pray she has no head trauma. I run back in, bent low to the floor. I have to find Teri.

"Teri! Dammit, where are you?"

Another staffer, Bobbie, crawls in from the Medical Records office, then stands at the front door, and screams through splintered glass. "Goddammit, why can't you people leave us alone!"

An EMT runs in through the back door. I point him down the hall towards Patti.

Air from outside feeds the flames. I pick up the extinguisher again. At least I'm doing something, though it's small. Bobbie takes over the fire fight. Demonstrators stare in through grey smoke, looking as horrified as I feel. Then I realize there are people down out front, too. I remember Chick. Chick! Shit! I can see the shapes of the fallen on the lawn. Children are crying, people shouting. An ambulance screams around the corner. Red lights from a police black-and-white pierce the smoke and barrel toward the building.

Bobbie takes my arm, and walks me out the door. "Get some air. The EMTs are here. They'll take over."

I stumble through the back door, and make my way around to the front, grabbing a medical guy as I go. "My mom!" I grip his arm. "I don't know what's happened to her. She's out here. And I couldn't find Teri. Someone find Teri. Inside."

The tech heads inside with his medical kit. I see a fireman and call out. "My mother is out here somewhere. Find my mom! I can't find my mom!" I scream at anyone who'll listen.

The fireman grabs my shoulders, fixes me with a level gaze. "We'll get the fire. You need to get that arm looked at." My arm hangs limply at my side. "Then look for your mom."

I ignore him. "She's out here somewhere. Oh, Jesus God, where is she?"

I force my way through the chaos like I'm wading through a peat bog, eyes blinded by smoke and tears. I move in slow motion. Sheriff's deputies are cordoning off the building with yellow tape. The entire front area is crawling with people standing with dumb faces or tears streaming. Babies cry. Children call out for Mama. EMTs fall to their knees beside fallen bodies.

I notice a TV news van on the side street, and here comes Mayor Jenkins to do a sound bite. I see my cop friend Rick Loughlin and start toward him. He meets me halfway up the sidewalk.

"Rick, what's happened? I have to find Chick. Oh, God, she was right in front out here." I cough. My lungs hurt, but my hearing is better. "Help me find Chick, please!"

"Slow down, Bert. Remember to breathe. Are you hurt?"

"My arm. I don't know. Maybe. My head. Rotten headache." I cradle my left arm. It may be broken after all. It's screaming with pain. I push him away with my good arm, shaking my head, trying to clear my mind, trying to hear Chick's voice in the circus around me. "My arm hurts, and my head. My knee hurts, but I think I'm all right. I can't hear worth a damn. And I'm angry as hell! It was a bomb. Right?"

He nods. "Someone threw it through the front window. We don't know who yet. I doubt they stuck around. It looks to have been a small device, probably a pipe bomb, but it threw shrapnel quite a distance. We've sealed off the surrounding area so no one else can get in or out. Now, let's get you looked at."

Patti appears in the front doorway, led by a rescue worker. He guides her towards me then turns to run back inside. Her head is wrapped in white gauze. Her hair is smushed down, which is a first, and she has soot on one cheek. She still looks charming. And here comes Tim across the lawn, looking as shiny as the silver cross on his tie.

"Patti! Are you all right?" He tries to take her in his arms, but she shrugs him off. "Where are the children?" His voice is pleading.

She pushes Tim away. "They're home. Safe. No. I don't want you near me. I have to go to the hospital... my head..."

I hear them. They seem to be mumbling, but I can hear them.

Tim turns to me. "Bert, tell the police, please—your friend—tell them none of our people could have done this."

"Not now. I have to find Chick. Have you seen her?"

And then—there she is! Seated on the curb, a fireman giving her oxygen. I start over, moving too fast. My wounded arm stops me. I pause and gasp through the pain, then move to her. I'm shocked to see her face is deep red, almost purple. God, is she having a heart attack? There is an ugly wound on one arm, the skin is split and full of who knows what.

"Mom!" I drop to her side and carefully put my good arm around her shoulders. She looks at me with the face of a frightened child, seeking some kind of explanation that I don't have.

"Mom, I couldn't find you. I was so worried." I ask the EMT, "Is she all right? Are you all right, Chick?" She moans. I can barely hear her. She leans against me and tries to catch her breath to talk. Again I turn to the medic. "How bad is it?"

"She'll be all right," says the fireman. "She was having

trouble breathing, but she's getting oxygen now, and she has a wound to her arm. Caught some shrapnel. She should go to the hospital. I don't think she's injured anywhere else, but we'll have to see."

I take her hand and kiss it, pat it, touch her cheek. "Chick. Mom. We're going to get you to the hospital. They'll check you out."

At last she speaks in a dark, tired voice, "How are you, my darling?"

I tell her I'm fine and don't mention my arm. She can see the head wound, though.

"But—blood on your face. What...?"

"It's okay. Don't worry. I bumped my head. Might require a few stitches. Let's just sit quietly until the ambulance comes." I hug her to me. "Chick, I'm so glad I found you. I love you."

She looks at me over the oxygen mask. "And I love you, my Miso."

Rick walks up and lays a hand on my arm. "You should have your arm looked at, too. Have them look at that cut on your forehead. You could have a concussion."

"No, I can move the arm. It's not broken." I run my trembling hands through my hair. "God, the bomb must have detonated only a few feet from Sharon's desk. How is she?"

"She's still unconscious." He shakes his head sadly. "Teri's more seriously injured. Closed head injury, I think, and what looks like a broken clavicle. They'll take them both to the hospital. Chick's all right?"

I hug him and lay my head on his shoulder. I'm surprised by the intensity of my fear when I couldn't find Chick. My heart ached. "I think she will be. Rick, when I couldn't find her I was so scared...I hope she's okay."

Tim, who is standing behind Rick, pipes up. "What about you, Roberta? How are you?"

Rick moves off and I turn to Tim. "I was almost crushed

by a supply cabinet, but I think I'm all right. Bruised, I guess." I cough again. "I breathed a lot of smoke. Tell me something, Tim. If this wasn't done by your people then who the hell was it? Huh? Who is out here except *your people*? My mother is injured! How do you like that? Her arm's torn open and she may be in shock." I turn my attention back to Chick.

I look up at the building. The fire is out now, and the entire façade is a burned-out box. It looks like pictures I've seen of Sarajevo during the war.

"But none of us saw who did it," Tim says. "We were gathered around the big oak, talking with the Salazars. A reporter's talking to them now. Lucky that we were over there, too, or more people would have been hurt."

I stare at the damaged building, at the people being triaged by the emergency team. How could this happen here? In Bomar? These were peaceful protesters. Weren't they? They had been until now. How could it turn so ugly?

I gingerly let go of my mother. "Chick, I'll be back. You wait here for the ambulance. I say to the EMT, "Can you sit with her?" He nods. I push my mother's long red hair back off her shoulders. "I'm going to check on Teri. Don't move. Don't move from this spot until they come for you. Okay?"

She nods. I hobble back around to the back where EMTs are loading Sharon into an emergency vehicle. And then I see Teri's still form on a stretcher. I race to her and lift her hand to check her pulse.

"She's unconscious," a paramedic says. "She was evidently closest to the concussion. We're taking her in." With that, he waves at a second ambulance, which pulls up as Sharon's pulls away, and I watch as Teri is loaded and driven away.

Back in front, I see that Chick is gone. I am suddenly so exhausted I can barely stand. I find Rick Loughlin climbing into his police cruiser, and beg, "Please. Can you drive me to the hospital? To Chick?" I shake my head in an attempt to clear it. "I've got to call Pirate. Pirate needs to know. And Kelly. And Grady. I'll have Grady get them and bring them in to us."

I collapse into Rick's police cruiser, too tired and hurting to say another word.

Chapter Thirty-Seven

BERT

RICK GETS OUT OF THE cruiser, walks around to the passenger side and leans in toward me. “You okay? Really?”

I close my eyes and lay my head against the seat back. “No. I’m not okay at all. I hurt like a hell, and I want to see my mom.”

He gently buckles me in, closes my door, and returns to the driver’s seat. He starts the car and turns on lights and siren. I never open my eyes until we reach Mayfield Hospital. In the front lobby, my head throbbing with concern for Chick, I stumble to a phone and call Pirate. He doesn’t watch TV or listen to the radio, so I know he is blissfully ignorant of this whole scary situation. I pray he will answer the phone, which he always leaves inside the dome specifically so he won’t have to answer it.

“Come on. Come on, Dad. Pick up.” I shake my good knee nervously, urging him to answer.

Thankfully, he does.

“Who’s this?”

"Now, Pirate, don't freak out. We have a situation with Chick. There's been—well, a bomb. At the clinic."

"A bomb?" he cries. "Holy shit! Wait—where are you?"

"I'm at the hospital. Chick and I were both at the clinic when it happened."

"But wait—" His voice takes on a gravelly tone. I hear him swallow. "Shit! Your mother..."

"Yes, she's hurt, Dad. Uh, so am I. We need you."

"I'm on my way, Miso."

Next, I call Grady, who has seen the coverage on TV. "God, Bert, I've been waiting for your call. Are you all right? I tried your cell, but..."

"My arm is banged up, but not seriously, I don't think. We're at Mayfield Hospital here in Bomar. Chick is hurt—her injuries are more serious. Can you bring Kelly?"

"I'm leaving now." His voice is deep, smooth, and calming. "I'll get Kelly from school and we'll be there as soon as possible."

Rick touches my good elbow. "I asked at the desk. Chick is back in the triage area. That nurse over there said she'll take you back."

I follow the nurse, feeling more nauseous and shaky than when I arrived. She leads me to where Chick is being examined by a young doctor. Rick leaves to get an update on Sharon and Teri.

Chick looks very fragile, lying on an exam table. When I come in she turns her head to me and manages a weak smile. The doctor, who has kind eyes and a thin beard, looks at me and, without stopping a moment in his examination, says, "Are you the daughter? She's been asking for you. I'm Dr. Feldman. Ah, you look like you could use my services too. Take a seat. I'll look at you when I'm done here."

With my good arm, I drag a plastic chair nearer to the side of Chick's bed. I take her hand and kiss it, then hold it in my lap. "Mom, I was so afraid. Are you in much pain?"

Though her voice is weak and breathy, she speaks in her

inimitable style. "How lovely that you're so concerned, darling. Yes, there is pain, but they've given me some spectacular pharmaceuticals. Better living through chemistry, you know."

Feldman chuckles. "Good thing to keep a sense of humor. It will take me a while longer to pick all the gravel and shrapnel from the wound." He nods toward my arm. "Are you in pain? Should I get a colleague in here to check that arm? Pretty sure they'll want an x-ray. And that head wound is going to need stitches. They might want to do an MRI of your head."

"Whoa! Just concentrate on my mother for now." Just then, our family doctor, Jim Bullock, pushes aside the curtain. He nods to me, and moves to Dr. Feldman's side. "Hello, Chick. I ran right up here when I heard the news. I see you're in fine hands here." He turns to Feldman. "Ben, we're definitely going to keep Ms. Lando overnight. We need to run tests to rule out any internal damage."

"Fine. I'm done here. Bandage is secure. We'll get her started on some IV antibiotics in her room."

Dr. Bullock nods, and tells a passing tech to get orderlies. The orderlies come and take the head of Chick's bed to push.

"Come with me, Ms. Lando," grins Bullock. "We'll get you admitted."

I kiss my mom, with tears in my eyes. I'm grateful that her condition isn't worse. I could have lost her! I'm not a praying person, but I hope with all my heart that the tests will find nothing more than the arm wound. I think for a second how much worse this could be. To lose my mother after we've been at loggerheads over Alice. Secretly, I wish Alice was here. I think of calling her, but am not certain it's the right move to make.

On my way down the hall, I see Sharon's two boys. I stop and say a couple of words to them. Patti is still waiting to be triaged. Blood seeps through her head bandage. Her eyes are round. She looks like she doesn't have much of a grip on what has happened. Rick brings in another patient and asks about Chick. Just then Pirate races through the ER doors.

"Where is she? Where's our Chickie?"

I tell him she's been admitted, give him the room number. He hugs me gingerly, eyeing my bloody head. "How is she? Is it serious?" His voice quavers.

"She's going to be okay, I think. She just has some healing to do."

"Right-o. And you?" He races off to find Chick.

Dragged out and emotionally spent, I make my slow way to the intake counter and sign my name. I'm well down the list of people to see. I see that Patti has been taken back to the exam area. My head wound hurts and still oozes blood, and my arm throbs.

Grady comes through the automatic front doors, Kelly close behind him. Both are visibly shaken and make a big fuss over me. Grady pulls me gently to him and kisses the top of my head just above the wound there. "So glad you're safe," he murmurs, and the caring in his voice warms me. Some of the chaos around us grows quietens.

Then Kelly is next to us, and spreads her arms wide. "Can I hug you, Bert? Or will it hurt too much?"

"That would feel so good." She puts her arms around both Grady and me, trying to avoid my wounds.

She raises her eyes to mine. "Is Chick gonna be all right?"

"I think she will, yeah. But it will take some time."

At last I'm seen by a triage doctor. My arm is badly sprained and bruised. I'm given a sling. My head takes six stitches, and I have in my pocket a prescription for Norco. I don't want to take any right away, because I want my head clear to watch over Chick.

We make our way to Chick's room and sit with her—Pirate, Grady, Kelly, and I—in a tight circle of emotion, touching each other, warm glances passing between us. Our little family makes me smile. Every move Mom makes sends Pirate or me jumping to her rescue—adjust the bed position, get her more ice chips, or hand her tissues if she cries, and help her to the bathroom.

Grady offers to go for food, then whispers to me, “Should I call Alice? I could go and get her and bring her here.”

I’m still undecided, so I don’t answer. Before he leaves he asks, “Do you need anything? Should I go for food? Kelly and I could go for burgers...”

I laugh. “I don’t think any of us have much of an appetite. But thank you.”

“In that case. I’ll stay here with you.” He kisses me, long and easy, and that says more to me than words. Chick speaks up, her voice weak.

“Do you think,” she asks with an oxygen cannula up her nose, “this was one of the Salazars? Irene’s family? Who else could it be? But why hurt so many people?”

Pirate and I tell her not to worry. The police will find the bomber. For now, she needs to rest and recoup, concentrate on healing.

We fall silent. Chick drowses, riding high on painkillers. I pace. Kelly goes to the bed and shakes Chick’s shoulder. “Hey, Grandma. Are you still in there?”

Without opening her eyes, Chick says softly, “I’m in way deeper than I ever thought...”

She wakes up, has a moment of lucidity, and says, “My darling, Kelly. You know that I am as tough as old boot leather. And don’t call me Grandma.”

Kelly laughs. “I’ve never seen you wear boots, Chick. Only those ugly Birkenstocks. But I know you’re tough.” Then the ebullient and rarely tender Kelly tears up and puts her head on Chick’s breast. “I’m so frigging glad you’re gonna be okay.”

Pirate chuckles. “Come over here, little one. Let Grandma sleep. Come sit in my lap.”

Chick says, barely audible, “Don’t call me Grandma,” then drifts off.

Kelly climbs into Pirate’s lap, which was once my place.

I'm happy now to yield it to her. We stay until Chick falls into a deep sleep, and the rest of us sit with our thoughts. I wait for the air in the room to calm. In stillness, we are content for a while.

Then someone quietly clears her throat. Tiny Alice stands in the doorway. A colorful scarf covers her head. Her hand rests on a blue metal cane. A white vinyl handbag dangles from her thin, ropey arm. She looks around the room and smiles, "Well, she's got plenty of company now, hasn't she?"

I jump up and throw an arm around my slender grandmother. I hold her close with my good arm.

She takes my arms and pushes me slightly away to hold me at arm's length. "Now stand back, darlin', and let me look at you. Tell me you're not badly hurt. Tell me about this whole ugly thing that's goin' on. And your mother, how is she?"

"She's been injured," I say. "And that's put stress on her heart they think. Right now, she's resting."

Grady stands up and they embrace one another. Kelly slips from Pirate's lap and walks up, examining Alice.

"So, you're Tiny Alice. I'm Kelly. Well, you sure are tiny. You're not much bigger than me. You're Bert's grandma? That's my grandma in the bed there, and you're my Great Grandma, I suppose."

"Why, I'm proud to meet you, Kelly. I understand you are the newest member of our clan."

"I guess so. Are you gonna stay till Chick wakes up?"

Alice looks at Chick asleep in the hospital bed, and then at me. "Do you think she'll mind that I've come? I couldn't stay away."

I place a hand on her shoulder. "I'm glad you're here. It's right for all of us to be together."

Pirate hops up, introduces himself and takes her elbow to guide her to his chair. She stands a while longer, gazing at Chick.

Grady asks, "How'd you get here, Alice?"

She chuckles. "I'm old as sin so I cain't drive, but I have my ways gettin' around. I saw the hubbub on the TV and called Bobby Nash. He drives me here and there when I need it. Bobby'll sit in the cafeteria and nurse his coffee till I'm done here. I had to come and see about everone."

We whisper. We chat. Kelly is full of questions about Chick's wound and also about Alice. After a while, we fall silent. Chick doesn't wake. Grady decides to take Kelly home. I say I'll call them if anything changes.

"I'll join you later." I give them each a kiss. Kelly holds my eye and, smiling, wipes off my kiss with her arm. I scrunch up my nose at her, and turn to Alice. "Aren't you going to sit stay?"

"I will." She takes a seat. She's slightly out of breath. "That is...I hope I've done the right thing comin' here, Bert. I just had to see that you were both all right."

"I should have called you. I apologize."

After a while, Chick says in a soft voice, "Miso, darling. Can you get me another piece of that dream coat? Hmm. Technicolor?" She tries to open her eyes, lids heavy with drugs.

"Sure, Mom. Coming right up."

Pirate and I giggle. Alice sighs. "Guess we'll be a while." She pulls a crochet project out of her purse and begins to work on it. She doesn't get very far, though, before Chick straightens in her bed and opens her eyes. "Who's here? Did Kelly leave? Miso?"

Pirate moves to the bed, but Alice is seated next to Chick and takes her hand. Pirate places a hand on the blanket that covers Chick's feet. "I'm here, my love."

Chick turns her head, eyes drooping, and sees Alice without registering who she is. Alice straightens her back and answers, "I'm here, Charlene. Your mama's here."

Chapter Thirty-Eight

CHICK

BERT DROVE ALICE OUT TO *Cielo* for our first meeting since the hospital. I still wore a bandage on my arm, and was still floating on pain killers. Which was good, since I was extravagantly nervous about talking to Alice. It was one thing to have her sit beside my hospital bed while I drifted in and out. Now, though, we would confront one another face to face. At least we were on my own home turf.

Alice stepped through the front door. She extended wiry arms to me, but I wasn't yet ready to embrace. I took her two hands in mine. Bert hugged us both, kissed each of us goodbye, and then excused herself. I needed to meet Alice on my own.

I motioned for Alice to take a seat in Pirate's chair. She did so, looking regal and serene. The late afternoon sun pierced the colored window glass and broke the light into shards of red, green, and blue across the pine plank flooring. I was not serene. I was perturbed, and trying not to wring my hands. I paced.

"Would you care for a drink? I have iced herbal tea and lemonade. I don't suppose you want wine?"

She smoothed her skirt across her lap. Her strong, almost mannish hands didn't tremble like mine. Her placidity in the face of my skittishness did nothing to soothe my nerves. I was unsettled that she could unsettle me so.

"What is that herbal tea you mentioned? Is that different from good old iced tea?"

Her country way of speaking annoyed me. I tried not to let my discomfort show. "Why, yes, it is. It's not black tea. No caffeine. It's made from different plants. Plants different from tea leaves, that is. It's good. Refreshing. Light." I sounded like the spokesperson for a Lipton's TV ad.

"I'll try some then." She tucked an escaped curl behind her ear.

I moved into the kitchen. Standing at the sink, I breathed in the smell of fresh mown grass and the faint aroma of the horses. I breathed deeply, praying to Gaia that I could remember to breathe for the duration of this meeting. As I pulled down my good Howdy Doody glasses, my hands shook and the glassware clinked together. I wondered what Alice thought of the dome. Of our home. Of my life. Of me.

"You're house is so unusual, Charlene. Uh—Chick. Did your husband build it?" She called from the other room. "Remember how your daddy used to work on our little place?"

I poured hibiscus tea for her, and hit the box-o-wine for me. Placing the filled glasses on a rattan tray, I put some *wasabi* peas in a small dish, and carried the goodies into the living area. I offered the tray to her, and she lifted the tea cup.

"No," I tell her. "We had a contractor and professional builders. He did some of the work, and it's our design."

"Does it have a special name when it's shaped like this?"

I set down the tray on the glass-topped tree stump that served as a side table to the futon. "It's a geodesic dome, a design based on the work of R. Buckminster Fuller. He was an architect and designer—well, really much more than that—who came up with the basic plans. Ours is a variation on that theme."

"My goodness," Alice said. "You leave me in the dust with all you know. Imagine my Charlene being so educated and fine."

I sat. I cleared my throat. "Alice. I don't think I'm your Charlene anymore. I'm Chick Lando now and, believe me, there's no going back."

"Oh." She stared at the ice in her tumbler.

My words sounded harder than I'd planned. I didn't mean to shut her down entirely. "I'm sorry, Alice. That came out all wrong. I am so different now. And you don't know me. We don't know each other."

Pirate appeared at the front door, thankfully in a modest *kaftan*. "Greetings, ladies! I'm just here for some refreshment and then I'll be on my way and out of your hair."

I grabbed the chance to escape our conversation, or was it a confrontation? I called over my shoulder as I followed Pirate into the kitchen, "Alice, do excuse me while I help out my dear one."

"You go ahead, darlin'," she answered. "Do what you need to."

In the kitchen, Pirate wrapped me in his arms and nibbled my right ear lobe. I brushed him off. He stuck out his lower lip, faking a pout. "How's it going?"

"We've hardly begun," I whispered. "I don't know how to proceed, darling. It's so uncomfortable. I'm a shamble of nerves."

He took a jelly jar from the cabinet and filled it with wine. "You'll do fine, lovey. Just be yourself, and for Pete's sake try to relax. Being uptight won't help anyone or anything. Chill out."

He was right, and I knew I had to do this alone. I still didn't want to talk to her, to rake over painful memories. I knew the grievances I held against her. I didn't want to learn how I'd injured her.

He placed a hand on my shoulder. I could feel his heat through my dress. His hands were always so warm, his touch such a comfort. I kissed his hand.

"There's my girl," he grinned. "I'll be right outside reading my *New York Times.* I'll soak up some sun and some afternoon vino. If you need me, just yodel!"

He moved out to Alice, and from the kitchen I heard his voice. "Your Majesty. Great Mother of us all. I salute your venerable sagacity." Alice chuckled as he called in my direction, "You two girls behave yourselves." Alice giggled and Pirate made his exit.

I returned to the great room. She sat where I had left her, as poised and seemingly unconcerned as before. I had to get a hold on myself. My thoughts raced. My stomach clenched. My breathing was labored.

She took a sip, weighing what she was going to say next, and then shook the ice. The ice tinkled in the glass. "You're right that we don't know each other. Why, if we passed on the street I'm not sure I would have recognized you. Sad to say." She runs a hand back and forth across her brow. "Still, I reckon that's why we're here. Isn't it? To see if we can come to know each other. Again. As the people we are now."

I willed my hands to stop trembling before I took a sip of wine. "Yes. It is," I conceded. I realized I could not sit still and *chat.* This was momentous for me. Maybe transformative. I put down my glass and stood, looking at Alice. "I can't sit still. Hope you don't mind if I pace." I didn't wait for her answer.

She chuckled. "Okay. You pace, darlin', and I'll talk."

My heart skipped a beat when she called me *darlin'.*

She let out a long, slow breath. Lifting a hand to the back of her hair, she patted her hair, and then took another sip of tea. "Chick. I say we leave the past...well, in the past. It's all water under the bridge. Whatever mistakes we made, whatever we may've done wrong to each other... cain't we just start over? Forgive each other, and start again? That's what I want to do."

I stopped pacing at the window and picked dead leaves off a hanging Boston fern. I was still not calm enough to talk. I resumed pacing, and sipped some more wine. I was beginning to mellow.

She went on. "You seem like a real interestin' person. Bert says good things about how you are as a mother. From what I can tell, your husband sure adores you. I'd like to get to know a woman like you. You're my girl. You cain't change that, no matter what."

She was right. I *am* her girl. I ceased pacing. Perhaps I was safe. Perhaps I could move toward her, and not away. My chest relaxed enough for me to take a deep breath. I blew it out and then set down my wine glass, and shook my hands out. I stopped trembling, and sat beside her on the arm of Pirate's chair. I reached for her hand. She shifted her drink to her other hand and clasped mine. Hers was icy cold, but her eyes were warm as she said, "It feels good to touch you."

I felt myself blush. "Look, Alice. I can't call you Mama yet. Maybe I will. Forgiveness is a tall order for me. Over the years, I have nursed my wounds into a solid grudge. I've blamed you for things that were probably not your fault."

She shook her head. "That don't matter. Not now. That's the past."

"I know it is." I nodded and took another gulp of wine. "And I think it's a fine idea to leave it behind. I do. It's just that—I think the forgiveness part may take me a while. Maybe you can teach me about forgiveness?" She smiled at the prospect. "For now I'm willing," I continue, "to be willing to begin anew, to grow acquainted as women." I heaved a great sigh. "Is that good enough?"

A drawn out silence ensued. My stomach knotted up again, and my throat grew tight, wondering what she was thinking.

"Why, that is surely..." Tears glistened at the corner of one eye. "...surely fine with me. If we can get together with the whole family—maybe it'll be easier on us. If the others are there. But I think, over time you'll see, Charlene. I'm a pretty good old woman. I think you'll be proud to know me. And I'm already proud of you, daughter."

Tears gathered in my own eyes. I squeezed her hand, turned away, and went to sit on the futon, leaned my head back. I took a deep draw on the wine, and smiled. "Well then, Alice. Let me tell you about a young girl's trip to San Francisco."

Chapter Thirty-Nine

BERT

WE SIT IN THE EARTHY elegance of *Cielo's* great room, taking necessary shelter from the heat of late October. Sunbeams spread a soft fan of color across the floor. We reflect on all that's occurred.

I've left Kelly with Connie Barrientos, Kris' neighbor who has been my go-to person to watch Kelly since Kris' death. Grady will bring Alice later. It will be her second meeting with Chick. Chick and I sip herbal tea. I read an AARP magazine as my parents share a little weed. Pirate smokes, exhaling softly, *The New York Times* across his lap. Chick gazes out the window at forlorn hydrangeas and tired pansies. Occasionally we break the quiet with questions, memories. Then the hush covers us again.

This is how the Landos approach discussions. Tea, weed, and musing. Chick needs time to reflect, to weigh consequences, and to let Pirate and I be her sounding board.

"Conundrums," she muses. "Puzzles, riddles. Long nurtured hurts. Old wounds, fresh decisions. I feel as if I'm being borne along on a river of regrets. Toward an unknown end."

You're so damn dramatic, Mother!

She looks at me as if she's read my thoughts. "You were five, Miso, when you first asked about grandmothers. A schoolmate's grandmother had visited your learning circle and you came home asking if you could have one."

I smile.

"Have I really done you such a great disservice, my darling?"

"Alice says that, too. *Darlin'.*" I sip my tea. "I've found my grandmother now. Can I keep her, Mom?"

We laugh, and she continues." Of the two of us, Benji and me, I was the child who was healthy and strong. Alice seemed to think Benji needed her and I didn't. She lost Michael and my sister Minnie in their infancy, and she could never let go of her grief. She expected Benji and I to grieve for them, too. Every grace at every meal we prayed for their souls.

"One Christmas, Mother and I were putting the finishing touches on our holiday dinner. She would fly into a cooking frenzy on the holidays. I was expected to set the table, including places for Michael and Minerva. I would argue that they were dead and she would say that they weren't dead to her, never would be, and that we must honor them in this way. I felt there was something lacking in me that I couldn't grieve for them, too."

"You're so self-sufficient," I say. "Maybe Alice thought you were good on your own. Please stop blaming her. It won't accomplish anything. She doesn't blame you. I don't blame you, Chick."

"I know you're right, darling. I'm so grateful my daddy understood that I felt alone. Bless his dear sweet heart, he attempted to help me as best he could. He made time for me in spite of working two jobs. He was a sheriff's deputy, you know, and eventually became sheriff. But he'd been a wrangler, and always kept up his work with horses." She tokes on the little pipe, inhales deeply, and speaks while she holds her breath. "We've decided to forget the past. Alice and

I." The fragrant smoke rushes out as she opens her mouth and exhales. "And I truly hope that I can do that. I realize forgiveness is called for. And maybe atonement on my part."

"Love. Love is the answer. Let it be, Chickie," Pirate weighs in. "She'll be here soon, my jewel."

"I do want to share something important with you, Miso. Yet I fear it will change the way you see me. I pray it won't. It certainly altered the way I see myself."

I sit forward. "What is it?"

She sets down the pipe, takes a deep breath and exhales slowly. Then she rolls her head around to unkink her neck and shoulders.

"You need to know the reason I left home. Why I had to fly away and never look back. I... there was...when I was seventeen. I was date-raped and left pregnant. There, I've said it out loud. Now you know."

After a quick intake of breath, I try not to rush to judgment. I think back on my first sexual experience. It wasn't rape and didn't end in pregnancy, but it wasn't pleasurable by any stretch of the imagination. And I think of my young patients who face this same predicament. "Go on, Mom. Please."

She looks at me and I see in her deep green eyes, so like Alice's, a plea for understanding. She looks at Pirate and he smiles softly and nods.

"I was seventeen and already considered one of the *bad girls* in town. Fallon Springs was maximally provincial, my darling. Not the sort of place where opinions were easily changed. Mainly, though, I couldn't face my mother. I couldn't break her heart or betray all of her beliefs. I loved her. I did." She reaches for the pipe, then pulls her hand away. "And so, with the help of an older friend—long story short—I flew to Mexico City for an abortion, the tale of which I will save for another time. And after that...I ran away."

"You didn't share this with Alice, did you?"

"Certainly not. I don't want to upset her sensibilities. Definitely not now."

We sit, saying nothing. I'm at a loss. I want her to know that I don't judge her. I know my dad doesn't either.

"It's all right, Mom," I begin.

"Oh, it wasn't all right, *ma cherie.* It was expedient, but it was so wrong in so many ways, worst of all leaving Mom and Benji without a word. I can only imagine what that did to Alice. But honestly, I couldn't face the humiliation that I had failed her so completely. I couldn't stand strong and bite the bullet. I couldn't *buck up.* I had to run.

"I hitched a ride to San Francisco. That's when I met my dear friend Ava. And then I met Pirate and began a new life. I needed not to look back—not to consider any further the decisions I'd made."

Pirate's voice is gentle. "But at any time in the following years, you could have contacted Alice to ease her mind. To let her know about your happy life, about Miso."

"I couldn't." Tears fall. "I thought about going out there to see her so many times. I never did. It would have demanded a type of courage I did not possess."

My father draws her into his arms and she buries her face in his neck. I tear up and swipe my eyes with my hand. My dear, sweet mother. So full of life and color, facing a memory that reduces her usual strength and knocks the legs out from under her. I've never seen her so vulnerable.

In a while, she sits up straight and shakes out her shoulders and arms. Breathing deeply, she rises from her seat, stretches, and slips on her sandals. Her voice trembles.

"Do I need to make some iced tea? Will you get me a tissue, my dearest?"

Pirate hops up. Chick fixes loving eyes on me. Suddenly she is strong again and, in my eyes, valiant and admirable. She did what she thought best for herself and her mother. She chose not to be a seventeen-year-old unwed mother. She put herself in danger to spare her mother. I hope she'll come to see it that way.

"Did you get the Dr. Peppers for Alice?" she asks.

This brings a smile to my face. "I did."

She turns toward her bedroom, and flips her long hair to one side. "And I believe I'll take a Valium."

"Maybe I'll make the tea," I say on my way to the kitchen.

Not long after, I hear Grady's car crunching on the gravel, bringing Alice to us. We've all agreed that Pirate and Grady will hang at the pond for a swim and I'll stay with the mothers for their second meeting—the child at their feet, a fly on the wall, an observer, and, if needed, a referee.

Pirate and I greet Alice at the door, and I walk her to the futon.

"Can I take your sweater?" I ask.

"Oh, no. I think I'd rather keep it with me, if you don't mind. I'm cold most of the time." She looks up and around, an expression of wonder on her face. "Oh my! I surely am impressed by these stained-glass windows. And all these beautiful plants."

"Chick made the stained glass. It's her art."

I bring her a glass of tea, when Chick calls from her bedroom. "I'll be right there."

Alice looks at me, biting her bottom lip. "I'm thankful to see her again. Our first meeting was real uncomfortable. But it ended okay. Maybe this time we'll both feel a little easier."

Just then, Chick sweeps in. I pray she only took one valium. Her red hair, only lightly salted with gray, trails down the back of her golden kimono which she wears with a flowing purple skirt. She looks stunning, imposing, completely ready for this meeting. I'm aware of the crackling energy in the room.

She reaches for Alice's hand. "It's good to see you, Alice. Welcome."

Alice squeezes Chick's hand. "You sure look like your father, Charlene. It takes my breath away. You have his... you're tall like him. Have his high cheekbones."

Chick takes a seat in her chair, a wicker confection with

a fan shaped back. "Yes, I remember people saying that when I was a child."

Their conversation skims the surface of what they truly need to express. But they have to progress at their own speed. After a while they turn to more serious subjects—Charlene's rebellion, her withdrawal from Alice's attempts to show her affection, her deep attachment to her father.

I say nothing, content to watch and listen.

"Mother," says Chick. "I suppose I can call you that. Maybe. I don't know what I would have done without Daddy. He held my broken little girl self together."

"I know that," Alice replies. "You are one lucky young lady to've been blessed with such a good daddy. Whenever I felt I couldn't get through to you, I was thankful to have Lute there. You were his brightest star."

"His death killed something soft inside me," Chick whispered.

Alice nodded her head. "Me too. I didn't think I could go on. But he sure had a way with you. Remember how you'd get all het up about somethin', and he'd get you out on your horse, and the two of you would ride and ride..."

Chick nods with a smile. They talk for a while about Lute, their love for him, their reliance on him in the hard times, and the vast emptiness when he was gone.

Chick shakes her hand at me. "Miso, could you fetch me a glass of *vino, por favor*?"

Filling a goblet with white wine from the box in the refrigerator, I hear Chick say, "So you understood I clung to Daddy because I couldn't reach you? You knew that?"

"I knew we weren't close as I thought mothers and daughters oughta be. But there was a lot I didn't get."

I continue to listen from the kitchen. They'd had so little in common, and all of that misunderstanding lay like a rough canyon between them. And here was perhaps the one thing in life that they shared – their mutual mother-daughter disappointment. After a painful quiet, Alice changes the subject.

I return with Chick's drink as Alice pats the cushion next to her. "Come over here, daughter, and sit beside me."

Chick does so. Alice takes her hand.

"Mother."

I smile each time Chick says that.

"What has happened to Benji?"

"Benji left me a few years after you did. He caught a virus that turned into the pneumonia and his lungs were weak. He couldn't fight it off, poor boy. Well, I say boy but he was a young man. He's buried next to your father if you would like to visit his grave."

"I'm sorry he's gone. I don't have the same beliefs you do about life after death and heaven and hell. And Benji and I were never close.

"Before I left, I'd hoped sometimes that you and I might connect the way most girls do with their mothers. That we might sit on my bed, and talk about my crushes, and how I was in love with Fabian, and you'd tell me who you liked in the old movies. I thought you might sew me cute outfits for school, like your friend Fern Albert made for Doris, instead of taking me to J. C. Penny in Marble Falls."

"Charlene, I did the best I knew how with you and Benji. I lost two children before you. I treasured you and your brother."

"I don't want to list grievances. Let's let them lie, and move on."

"Hurts can be forgiven." Alice's voice is calm and soothing. "And I agree. They're best left behind us now."

Chick takes a drink of wine. Alice looks her in the eye. Chick takes a moment before she speaks.

"Mother, Pirate and I, when raising Miso, pretty much flew by the seat of our pants as far as parenting went. And we were both just kids. I was eighteen and he wasn't much older."

"And how do you think you did, now that she's all grown up?"

Chick clears her throat. "I'm ever so proud of her. We have our differences. We're often frustrated with each other. She primarily questions my philosophies of life and Self and society."

Alice chuckles. "What children don't? That's pretty common."

Chick snorts. "I guess so. She's closer to her father, as was I, but we also spend time together, and she comes to our place for dinner and a swim. She has brought Kelly to us and her nice young man, Grady. Over all we're close. There are only one or two issues on which we clash."

"That sounds good, darlin'"

Chick laughs. "Yes. Despite our differences, we actually get along rather well. Don't we, Miso?"

I grin. "We do now. Pretty much. For a long time I resisted being close to you. But now, I feel differently. Now I feel like we get along quite well."

Chick goes on. "I like to think I have given her the freedom to be herself and have not insisted she be just like me."

"I certainly didn't ask you to be like me," Alice says. "Now I will say this and you listen." She puts an arm around Chick's shoulder. "I loved you before I held you for the first time. I loved you all these long years that you've been gone from me. I think there's nothin' finer than having you back in my life. And Bert, and Kelly."

Chick's face shines. "I'm glad."

Alice releases her and winks. "I think I'm a darned good person and you might just like me if you try."

Chick looks over to me, then back at Alice, and then says with genuine affection. "I can try, Mother. I want to. I can certainly try."

Alice becomes more animated, and reaches for her large purse. "Now, I brought something to show you." She pulls out a stack of photos. "I thought we might go through these together. What do you think?"

They sit close together and look at the photos one at a time. Chick shakes her head in wonder.

"There's Daddy." She takes the picture and presses it to her chest.

"There's not that many of him 'cause he always took the pictures. There's more of you and Benji. Look at this one."

Chick takes the photo and considers it. "That's Benji. What—about twelve years old? Kelly's age." She glances at me. "And he's just about as skinny as she is, too."

Alice shows her another. "This was that party at the Dairy Queen for your friend, Doris."

Chick glanced at me. "Bert, darling, Doris was black. In high school, people made such a big deal of it."

"Yes, everyone sure made a lot about you havin' a Negro friend. I never had a problem with it. Her mother had been a girlfriend of mine when I was a child."

"Oh, let me see that one." Chick reaches for the next photo in the stack. "Who's this?"

"That's your brother, darlin'. Just before he died. See how thin and weak he looks? Sad, sad, sad."

I interrupt. "I'm hoping that now that we've reconnected, maybe we can see each other on holidays and for special occasions? That would mean a lot to me."

They look at each other and nod. Then they sit in silence for several peaceful moments. Chick shuffles through the photos again.

I run my hand through my hair, and start for the front door. "Um, I'm going to go check on Grady, if you'll excuse me."

I slip out ... smiling.

Chapter Forty

BERT

SEVERAL WEEKS LATER, IT'S LATE November, Chick and I work together in her kitchen, cutting pineapple, kiwi, star fruit, mandarin oranges, and Asian pears. Mom's old friend Ava has flown in from California. Chick puts her to work slicing a baguette, while I mix a lemonade punch.

Chick fusses. "Be cautious, darling. Don't let that knife slip. Your father just sharpened those on Tuesday." She reaches and pats my abdomen.

I cradle my belly in both hands. "Don't worry, Mom. I won't do anything that might hurt this treasure."

Grady and I are pregnant. That's not the *reason* we're getting married, but it's an added blessing. Everyone is excited. Even Kelly is happy, especially about the baby. When we told her the news, she gushed, "Oh, man! I'm going to be a big sister. I will be a *phat* big sister." And my parents are thrilled. Pirate is beside himself.

At first, I fretted about Alice, but she doesn't care that we're not yet legally married. It's been a several weeks since she and Chick began reclaiming all they'd lost, and I'm happy to have them together today.

Autumn sunlight flows through the small octagonal kitchen window, dappling the counter tops, caressing us in warmth. The temperature at last has cooled softly. A mockingbird sings through his playlist. The kitchen smells like fresh fruit and a hint of Chick's patchouli perfume.

Chick cuts the top from a pineapple. "Have you thought of names for the babe? I've come up with several, if you'd like to hear them."

Ava speaks up. "I'm not sure you want Chick to weigh in on that subject. She has a strange way with names."

"Don't I know! Charlene to Chick to all the pet names that Pirate calls her? And she saddled me with Mystic Soul. Yeah, Mom. I'd like to hear your suggestions as long as you don't get ruffled if I don't choose one." I kiss her on the cheek.

Our baby is a girl and we've talked about the name Alicia, in honor of Alice. I'll wait for a while to share that with Chick. For now, I change the subject.

"Alice should be here soon. Grady left to fetch her about an hour and a half ago."

Ava gives me a wide grin. "I can't wait to meet this woman. The matriarch. What a joy that you've found each other. And for you too, Chick?"

Chick has worked up a sweat and her moist face is flushed from the work and probably some frustration with me. "Yes, Ava, darling. It is a good thing for me. For my soul. Healing has commenced and I am on a new path."

Chick's proficiency as a hostess humbles me. Entertaining is not something I do with ease, so I'm thankful to have her in charge of this production, directing those of us who want to help. As she slices the ripe pineapple, her hand shakes and her swollen knuckles are red. I'm aware that her arthritis causes her pain, but she'll never comment on it or seek sympathy.

"Chick," Ava says, raking baguette slices off the cutting

board into a tightly woven twig basket. "You don't object to Alice being here today, do you?"

Chick shakes her head. "I get nervous just before I see her," she says. "I know she should be with us today. She's family, after all."

I spread almond butter onto celery sticks. "Have you fully forgiven her yet? Has she forgiven you?"

Ava laughs a low throaty laugh. "What's to forgive? Mothers screw up as much as daughters. Why would you expect otherwise?"

My mother pushes back a stray curl with the heel of her hand. "That's true, I'll concede. We do occasionally screw up—royally!"

I stop what I'm doing, take the knife from her, and set it down on the counter. I squeeze her hand, make eye contact. "When the clinic was bombed, I realized what you mean to me. How I adore your charm and endearing quirks and eccentricities. I need you. I need you in my life, close to me."

Ava laughs again. Chick slides pineapple pieces into a plastic bag, and places it in the fridge. "Pooh! Charming? Endearing? I doubt my quirks are either! I'm afraid I'm a rather high maintenance eccentric."

I hug her. "I'm hoping that today you and Alice will grow even closer as the matriarchs at this family gathering."

"Don't you call your mama a matriarch, child." Ava shakes a finger at me. "Uh-uh. That word implies age, and your mama's not going to have anything to do with that."

Chick and I both laugh. "Yes," says Chick, ruffling my spiky hair. "We'll let your grandmother wear that crown."

She wipes sweat from her freckled forehead with the dish cloth tucked in her apron pocket, then places her hands on her hips, a familiar stance that is so "Chick" that a lump forms in my throat.

"I am looking forward to having Alice with us today," she says. "It seems only fitting. I confess that I've not yet forgiven her completely. Not yet. But I'm close. And I will, darling. I know that I will. But I don't know how I shall ever atone for my abandonment of her." She turns to Ava. "I did enjoy perusing those old pictures with her." She wipes her hands on the dish cloth. "Ava, darling, Alice has hundreds of old photos of my family—my father, my brother, through different chapters of life. Of course the pictures of me ended in 1967. Still it's marvelous to see a photographic record of who we were."

She squeezes my hand. "I'd like to show them to you one day. I must confess I don't believe I've forgiven Alice completely." She is thoughtful for a few moments. "I might have exaggerated my own feelings of being emotionally on my own. I was an imaginative child. I read too many books. In Victorian times, novels were thought to have a detrimental effect on the moral pulchitrude of young ladies." She giggles like a girl. "Maybe all those Gothic romances gave me the idea of the good girl locked in the cellar by the evil step-mother, an archetype that I translated into my own life. Who knows?"

"You read Gothic romances?" I'm stunned.

Ava snorts and shakes her head, smiling. Chick shushes us both.

"Now, hush about that. It was when I was in grade school."

"Chick and Gothic romances," I tease. "Geez. The two seem mutually exclusive. What was your favorite, Mom?"

"I loved Victoria Holt. I'd read anything she wrote. My favorite? Maybe *Bride of Pendorric* or *The Hunter's Moon.* Now, you cease and desist. And don't you dare share my adolescent reading habits with anyone."

I take a covered bowl of sweetened strawberries and a jar of Marshmallow Fluff from the fridge as she continues. "Ava's the only one I've ever shared that with, except for your father, of course. And they're both sworn to secrecy."

"I'll keep your secret." I put my arms around her and whisper "I love you" in her ear. Her eyes lighten and a broad grin slips across her face. Her apron bears the image of

Michelangelo's David. I shake my head at the audacity of it, and then I push aside a tray of *rumaki* to make room for mixing up Chick's ambrosia.

When I hear tires on the gravel outside, I quickly rinse my hands, and dry them. I hurry out in time to see Grady pull up with Kelly and Alice. As he steps out of his 4x4 and races around to open the door for Alice, I open the back door for Kelly. She piles out into the fresh air, and hugs me tight. I'm pleasantly surprised by her show of affection. Every new day is a wonder.

"Are you excited, Bert?" Kelly squeals. "You look nice." Then she runs to Pirate who reclines on his chaise, clothed for the occasion in his uniform—*kaftan* and flip flops. "Hey, Pirate! Is that what you're wearing? Do you even own a suit?"

He sits up and takes her on his lap. "I do not, young one. Nor do I consider that to be a deficit of any kind on my part."

"You guys all talk funny, you know that?" She plants a big kiss on his cheek. "Where's Chick? In the kitchen, I'll bet." And off she goes into the dome.

At the car, I greet Alice with a gentle kiss. She looks a little unsure, but walks with her back straight and her head held high. Her chin juts forward a fraction. She is ready for anything. We chat as we walk toward Pirate. I feel so easy with her, quiet and calm. I wonder how Chick will feel.

"Grandma," I tell her. "It means the world to me that you can be here today."

"I'm just tickled pink." She pats my arm. "Why, I wouldn't be anywhere else in the world."

Pirate steps up to greet her. He bows. "Welcome to *Cielo*, Great Mother."

Alice is accepting of my parents. *Does that come with age?* She knows about differences, and human nature. She has the confidence to avoid wielding knowledge like a cudgel. I admire her ability to wait softly until subjects present themselves and fall naturally into conversation. Though, if asked, she is always ready to share her opinion. I hope that one day I will possess that kind of wisdom and reserve.

Chick steps out from the dome, a tray of fruit in her arms. She and Alice exchange a look across us all. A look just for the two of them. My chest feels tight. I smile broadly, and feel such joy. Ava follows Chick, bringing two baskets of bread.

Kelly bounces up to Chick, chattering. Her cheeks are flushed around her wide grin. She has dressed for the occasion in slashed jeans and a sleeveless Madonna t-shirt. Her pierced nose sports the new diamond stud I bought for her.

Dust rises on the drive. Our guests are arriving.

Chick sets down the tray and takes Alice's hand in hers. "Welcome, Tiny Alice. I'm so glad you are here today."

"Thank you, my dear. I'm proud to be here."

Chick putters, placing the fruit trays on the table. Ava brushes crumbs from the vintage lace table cloth that dresses our old phone cable spool table.

Kelly tells Alice, "Chick makes this bread from scratch. Every Saturday. Sometimes I help. It's the best."

"That's lovely," responds Alice. "Is Chick a good cook?"

"She's super! A lot better than Bert."

"Hey, watch it, wise guy," I counter.

"Wise woman," she tosses back with a confident grin.

I turn to receive our guests. I see Teri Slade's Mercedes, her partner June Freeman, driving. June is a nurse who took care of Teri in rehab. They fell in love and have been together since. Teri will never fully recover from the closed head injury she sustained in the clinic bombing. Still, she is running the clinic with June's help. Her work ethic hasn't changed.

They are followed by Sharon Hilgers, our intrepid clinic receptionist, and her boys. Sharon's broken bones have healed. Chick's wounds have left some scary scars, and the movement in my arm is almost back to normal. We'll be slowly recovering for a long time.

Rick Loughlin follows Sharon in his black-and-white cruiser. He has told us the police have arrested Juan Salazar for the bombing. He is the cousin of Irene Salazar, the patient of mine who died unnecessarily because her family wouldn't bring her in for follow-up care. The family's civil suit against us has been dropped.

Grady's colleague, Bill Patterson, who teaches linguistics at the university, arrives with his wife in his overly large pick up truck. She is a stately woman with honey colored hair. The three of them stand to the side, quietly visiting.

Patti Axtell brings up the rear. While we're all greeting each other, I see Patti climbing out of her SUV. She reaches into the back seat to lift baby Robert from his infant car seat, while her other three--Rachel, Ruth, and Moses pour out the opposite door. No Reverend Tim. And that is a good thing. I race to take Robert in my arms, showing off my namesake to Alice.

Welcomes and introductions are made. I've not met Bill Patterson before, and I'm happy for Grady that he could act as best man. When everyone has arrived, Pirate begins to round us up and place us in position for the ceremony.

Grady and I stand side by side at the foot of the steps leading up to the dome's front door, holding hands beneath the muted colors of the patio parachute. Bright gold, yellow, and brown chrysanthemums in brass pots march up the steps before us. Bill Patterson stands beside Grady and Patti stands to my right, the baby snoozing in a cloth carrier on his mama's chest. Patti's hand rests lightly on my shoulder. She believes in the laying on of hands and I believe her hands are certainly holy. I've come to love this girl.

Alice sits regally in a place of honor—Chick's fancy wicker chair, in the front of the guests.

She watches over us, a diminutive empress, gazing over her beloved subjects.

Pirate, fully clothed now in jeans and an old Nehru jacket, is licensed by mail as a minister of the Universal Church of Sunshine and Light, is flanked by two florid hibiscus plants. Chick, with a very solemn look on her beautiful face, takes Alice's hand and leads her to the seat of honor, Chick's regal wicker chair.

"Thank you, Daughter," says Alice.

"You are welcome . . . Mother," says Chick very quietly.

Chick takes up her position behind me, fussing with my hair that is so short it doesn't ever require fussing. She smooths the white linen tunic I'm wearing over my jeans. Kelly stands to my left, and I slip one arm around her tiny waist. Teri takes a seat next to Sharon in the beat-up metal folding chairs we reclaimed from the barn.

Grady is dressed, as usual, in pressed jeans and a starched white shirt, and has added a malachite and silver bolo tie. Pirate fumbles with his notes and clears his throat several times. Tiny Alice looks over us all, a diminutive deity shedding silent blessings. She emanates deep love and powerful pride. I am deeply moved by her presence.

"Beloved family and friends," Pirate begins. "Welcome to the nuptials of Mystic Soul Roberta Lando and Grady Mervin Powell."

"Mervin?" says Kelly in a loud whisper. Everyone chuckles.

"We are here to celebrate and formalize their commitment to a union of mutual trust and passion."

Kelly says, "Eew." I shush her.

"We are here," he continues, "to witness their public declaration of their intention to build a home and family together, for Kelly and our little stardust niblet nestled in Miso's lovely womb."

"Double eew," Kelly says with more fervor.

Pirate clears his throat again. He addresses me. "Miso, my lass, make your promises to this man."

Holding Grady's hands in mine, I say in a shaky voice, "I promise to love you extravagantly. I want us to laugh and dance together for as long as we can, to read poetry and pay bills together, to parent together and turn to one another for perspective and guidance. I promise to love you exquisitely and excessively for as long as we both shall live."

Pirate nods to Grady. His voice is so low and intimate that I can barely hear him.

"Bert, I promise to be everything you and I believe a husband can be. To love you exclusively and to always cherish you. Let's make decisions together. Let's raise these girls together. Let's be happy together. I love you."

Grady slips a plain silver band on my finger and I do the same to him. I think of the horseshoe nail rings my grandfather fashioned for himself and Alice. Their love for each other, and that of my parents inspires me.

Pirate looks up at the gathering. "So we have heard their vows, a testament to their love for each other and their plans together. Miss Patti will say a brief prayer to (as Chick says) bring down the blessings of the patriarchal god, at which point Chick will intone Gaia's blessings. We're covering all bases." Our guests laugh.

After the prayers, Pirate gathers our two hands in his own and intones, "In the name of all that is holy and groovy, I now pronounce you unionized! You may kiss my daughter, man."

Grady kisses me, deep and full of promise. I turn around and wrap my arms around Chick. Tears glisten on her lashes. "Thank you," I say. She fusses and waves her hands. Alice comes toward us, offering Chick a thin embroidered hankie.

I look at Kelly, our little opinionated rebel. She eyes me suspiciously, then she takes a step back and puts her hands on her boney hips. "I suppose now you expect a mushy hug from me. Well, you got it!" We throw our arms around each other.

Then I am beside Alice, basking in her smile. "Finding you is a big part of what we celebrate today."

"Oh, no, sweet girl," she demurs. "This is your day, yours

and Grady's, and I wish for you the same overwhelmin' and everlastin' love that your grandpapa and I knew." She touches my belly with tender hands.

Tiny Alice is a part of our lives now. On warm Indian Summer days, she is fond of sitting in our rose garden with her Dr. Pepper on ice. Since learning that I'm pregnant, we've all gone nervy and deliriously happy with the prospect. The pregnancy is a bit of a surprise. We weren't really trying, but then we weren't being all that careful either. Either way, we are joyous and full of anticipation.

I think that we all eventually let go of our embedded expectations of mother-love. After years of self-doubt, we embrace our own unique style of loving. I vow to myself silently that I'll do my very best as a mother. I'm sure I'll disappoint Kelly in ways neither of us can see now. And I know the same is true of our new baby. I'll hurt them in ways I may never know about, but I'll do my best by them and that is the best we can hope for. And I have Grady—calm, steady, smart Grady.

I refused for so long to cling to some outdated notion that love with a capital "L" would find me someday. I didn't want it to. I was afraid. Now it's fallen into my lap. I am, of all women, most fortunate.

There are some things over which we have little or no control—who our parents are, what ridiculous name they stick us with, how many times throughout our lifetime they will horribly embarrass us, anger us, disappoint us, and whether or not they will approve of the adults we each become. After all of the drama and feuds and secrets, love is a huge, hearty, rambunctious, affectionate, glorious, silly, life-changing, rollicking circus. We'd be fools not to dance the dance.

I haven't had the awful baby-dropping dream for some time now. Baby Lando-Powell will join us in seven months, in the heat of June, and she will have a father, a mother, a sister, a grandfather, a grandmother, and a great grandmother. And, who knows? Maybe we'll name her. . . Peace Blossom.

About The Author

Rebecca Ballard is a novelist and playwright who has been writing since childhood, and is a voracious reader. She studied acting at the University of Texas, Austin, and graduated with a B.A. in Acting from George Mason University. Her writing is informed by a thirty-five-year career in live theatre, television, radio, and film. Her psychological thriller, *Wild Game,* is available on Amazon, and she has written three dramas for the stage, as well as feature articles and book reviews for print media, and a blog on spirituality. She lives in the historic small town of Lockhart, Texas.

Made in the USA
Middletown, DE
15 September 2019